FREDERIC RAPHAEL

Oxbridge Blues

PENGUIN BOOKS

Penguin Books Ltd, Harmondsworth, Middlesex, England
Penguin Books, 40 West 23rd Street, New York, New York 10010, U.S.A.
Penguin Books Australia Ltd, Ringwood, Victoria, Australia
Penguin Books Canada Ltd, 2801 John Street, Markham, Ontario, Canada L3R 1B4
Penguin Books (N.Z.) Ltd, 182–190 Wairau Road, Auckland 10, New Zealand

The stories were originally published in two separate volumes:
Sleeps Six and other stories first published by Jonathan Cape Ltd 1979
Copyright © Volatic Ltd, 1979

Oxbridge Blues and other stories first published by Jonathan Cape Ltd 1980
Copyright © Volatic Ltd, 1980

First published in one volume by Penguin Books 1984

Made and printed in Great Britain by
Richard Clay (The Chaucer Press) Ltd,
Bungay, Suffolk
Filmset in Monophoto Photina by
Northumberland Press Ltd, Gateshead

Alister Ross

PENGUIN BOOKS

Oxbridge Blues

Frederic Raphael was born in 1931. He was educated at Charterhouse and St John's College, Cambridge. His first novel, *Obbligato* was published in 1956 and this was followed by *The Earlsdon Way* (1958), *The Limits of Love* (1960), *A Wild Surmise* (1961), *The Graduate Wife* (1962), *The Trouble with England* (1962), *Lindmann* (1963), *Orchestra and Beginners* (1967), *Like Men Betrayed* (1970), *Who Were You With Last Night?* (1971), *April, June and November* (1972), *Richard's Things* (1973), *California Time* (1975) and *The Glittering Prizes* (Penguin 1976). His latest novel is *Heaven and Earth*.

He has also written two biographies, *Somerset Maugham and his World* (1976) and *Byron* (1982), translations (with Kenneth McLeish) of *The Poems of Catullus* (1976) and of *The Oresteia* (1978, televised as *The Serpent's Son*), and plays for radio and television. His screen plays include *Nothing But the Best* (1964), *Darling* (1965), *Far From the Madding Crowd* (1967), *Two for the Road* (1968), *Daisy Miller* (1974), *The Best of Friends* (1979) and *Richard's Things* (1981). For his highly acclaimed sequence of television plays, *The Glittering Prizes* (1976), Frederic Raphael won the Royal Television Society's Writer of the Year Award. He is married and has three children.

Contents

Special English

When they first met, leaning on the saline rail of a winter steamer, she had no English. He took her, his prize, to a remote island, where they rented a cottage from a peasant who had never before seen a typewriter. Each evening they listened, on a transistor radio, to broadcasts in special English from the American airbase on a larger island across the wine-dark sea. These broadcasts were slanted towards those who did not understand English very well. They were delivered in slow tempo and the vocabulary was instructively simple. They were, however, news broadcasts and the main news of the moment was a series of atrocities and counter-atrocities being committed in the course of a colonial war. Every night brought distinct variations on the gruesome theme. The lovers listened in the warming lamplight to unhurried stories of murder and mutilation. As day succeeded day, evening evening, the remote girl understood more and more. He watched her, smiling in the golden light of the paraffin, as her eyes kindled with closer comprehension. There was pride in her glance, for soon she would be able to follow his work and her chances of holding his love would, no doubt, be enhanced. Thus she would sometimes laugh, with newly educated vanity, as the tales of ambush and fratricide, of massacre and reprisal, grew more and more clear to her. Slowly then, and in pace with that unhurried, educating voice on the radio, the vocabulary of their understanding was stained with the world's blood and slowly, as she smiled across at him each night with dawning confidence, he read eyes eloquent with bright knowledge of special English; he learned, at funeral speed, to hate her.

Acute Triangle

He knew that she had long had a lover and she knew that it had long made him unhappy. One evening she came into the drawing room, special dress rustling, and told him that she had at last broken with her lover. She came and sat on the carpet near his chair, her bare shoulder convenient to the hand which held the whisky. He did not touch her with his fingers, but slid the cold, chiming glass down the slope of her shoulder and rested it, at an angle, against the blue margin of her dress. A bead of iced moisture detached itself from the base of the glass, impersonal tear, and rolled beneath the edge of the dress and down her white breast. She turned suddenly and looked up at him with promising eyes. 'It was always you really,' she said.

He raised the whisky to his lips, while she found an old ticket in the turn-up of his trousers, a sixpenny one, for God's sake, and held it up to him, smiling, like some silly proof. That night, she pressed the bell off early in the bedroom. She bathed and prepared herself, amused in the steamy mirror as she perfumed herself out of sight of herself. Her neat and fleecy apron was prematurely grey with pretty powder. In the morning she bathed appreciative bruises and was happy.

That evening she arranged the room for her husband's return; she composed chosen flowers and lit low lamps to give him pleasure. She looked at herself in the angelic mirror and saw that she was as delectable with virtue as she had always been with vice. Already she could imagine – and it made her walk with a particular slow stride – the urgency with which he might again make love to her. Would he propose again the cruel pleasures of the previous, startling night? He did, and more: she gasped and grasped at the tender violence of his renewed desire. She knew now for certain that she had done the right thing and she rejoiced all next day that virtue had such mounting rewards.

A few evenings later, returning after a longer day, it is his abrupt pleasure, so it seems, to question her at some length about the breach with her lover. Delicately – with some sense that his desire is piqued by judicious revelations – she discloses some of the short-comings of the man about whom for so long she would suffer no ill word to be spoken. She repeats, under repeated questioning, that her lover wept when she told him of her decision and that he even promised to marry her if she would recant. She comes and kisses her husband and reassures him by encouraging his hand to her soft breast. She draws in her breath for him to hear at the sudden nip of thumb and forefinger. Yet that night he is more reluctant between the sheets which have had recently to be replaced daily. Two nights later, he misses dinner (though her cooking has again become deliciously saucy) and does not even telephone to warn her. When he comes in, whisky makes no apology. 'What is the matter?' she asks, after his coat has come off and his jacket almost with it. 'I saw him.' 'Him?' 'Him. In the street. With a woman.' 'Well?' 'I saw him with the same one a couple of nights back.' 'What about it?' 'He had his arm round her. And tonight she kissed him. I saw them in a taxi.' 'Why do you still spy on him? It's over. I never lied to you.' 'She loves him,' the husband says. 'But what has that to do with us?' She looks at him and sees the old cataract of suspicion in those icy eyes. 'He left you,' he says. 'No,' she says, 'no!' When she goes up to the bedroom, he is putti·~ things into his case.

Upstairs, Downstairs

They had, by chance, had rooms on the same staircase during their last year at the university; the intellectual downstairs, the economist above him. The intellectual was the unmistakable pride of his generation; even his caricature was flattering. While still an undergraduate, he had an article in the haughtiest literary publication of the day; an overrated poet never recovered. He himself became an editor of such ruthlessly high standards that during his editorship the smartest student magazine once failed to appear at all. He believed fervently in the unique revelation of D. H. Lawrence; his dearest wish was to die of tuberculosis while his devoted wife held his ankle. He was so convinced by the Lawrencian doctrine that marriage was the only mature relationship, in which passion and integrity could survive together, that he was soon engaged, to a handsome, ambitious girl who had read the books he recommended, and no others.

His upstairs neighbour was never invited to the intellectual's Cyprus sherry parties. He accepted his ostracism bravely and shared the lugubrious drinking company of a bicycle-clipped Mancunian who lived opposite him and was reading Geography. In general, however, the economist preferred female companions. He was rarely short of them. Members of the intellectual élite, meeting in editorial conclave to scrutinize jejune poems and embarrassingly sincere short stories, would hear his footsteps (and her lighter ones) as they clattered up the wooden steps. Within what seemed a very few minutes, they would then be treated to the rhythmic creaking of an accelerating bed. If the ladies did not talk much of Michelangelo, they certainly did come, and go. The economist had a foreign-sounding name which began with an unfashionable letter of the alphabet and his Latin eyebrows met above a noticeable nose. The intellectual's shrewd fiancée suggested that he probably had money, or a particularly effective collection of etchings.

After their prompt and popular marriage, the smart couple took their First Class Honours to live in Islington. Other intellectuals who could stand the competition soon came and lived in the same square. All was, for a while, well: pregnant silences were followed by infantile noises. And then a terrible thing happened: D. H. Lawrence went out of style; marriage was abruptly less smart than it had been. The intellectual had been dispensing accurate taste to the readers of the back end of a forward-looking weekly, but many of them now deserted dated severity in favour of the new facetiousness. The weekly began to founder; the intellectual went, reluctantly, to television, but found television reluctant. His rejection confirmed his worst fears for modern culture. He became very sullen and was often the last to be chosen when he went to play in pick-up soccer games in the park. To avoid people of shallow judgement, he formed a side of his own, composed of ex-Lawrencians and other men of reliable fibre, and they went and administered Fabian kicks to other Sunday sides on selected suburban grounds. The intellectual remained faithful to his wife, but he felt increasingly guilty about it.

One Saturday, he was startled to see, at centre-forward on the other side, the economist who had lived above him all those years ago. Casanova had lost his figure (and his hair) but he had somehow kept his speed off the mark. He scored three times, without any particular sign of effort. He gave no indication of wishing to revive past acquaintance and was walking off the field, after no more than a routine handshake, when the intellectual chased after him and asked him to come and have a beer, for God's sake. The centre-forward looked at his watch: he'd love to normally, but he'd promised the wife and kids ... 'I'll bet,' the intellectual said. He persuaded the other at least to come for a quick one. The economist was uneasy in the face of so renowned an intelligence (he had spotted the other's name in a subsidized review his dentist happened to take) and disclosed that he was still rather a boring character. He had five children, a house in Pinner and owned six supermarkets in North London. 'Hey, that's not your bloody Rolls by any chance, is it?' said the intellectual. The suburbanite hung his head and admitted that it was. 'I wish I'd worked harder at university,' he mumbled, 'so I could have done something worthwhile. I never read enough. I still don't, I'm afraid. I really wish you'd tell me, is there anyone to compare with D. H. Lawrence these days?' 'Never mind that rubbish,' said the intellectual, 'how the hell did you manage to get them up there? What's the secret, you bastard?'

Still Life

They worked for the same newspaper. She helped to edit the fashion pages; he was an erstwhile lawyer who specialized in economic news. Both were married, happily they promised each other when they first stood beside the broad bed, with its lemon-coloured sheets, which the dramatic critic kept for first nights. If the affair had begun out of a feeling that, at their ages, it was absurd to be faithful to marriages which had been going on so long, it soon became a kind of controlled obsession. Each, after all, had the children to think about and the present situation suited them both. She was fond enough of her husband, whose main fault was that he collaborated on comedy scripts with a man called Ronald. Ronald was always at their place and he called her 'lovey'. He valued his wife for the patience she showed to their middle child, who was fat and garrulous on account of some congenital defect neither money nor drugs could correct.

It pleased them to conduct their affair entirely in the West End. They never spent a whole night together. The secrecy, even the haste, with which they were obliged to make love spiced their desire. They ate in restaurants where he had entertained financiers for lunch. (He specialized in collecting spilled beans in return for quite a decent house claret and a duck thing they do rather well here.) It gratified him to be with a fashionable woman; his wife was much too sensible to wear those sorts of things, and in any case they hadn't really got the money, had they? The affair had begun with good humour. 'If this doesn't work,' they promised each other, 'we won't let it worry us.' Even when they had become regular lovers, there was something provisional in their passion.

One summer, when it had been going on for over a year, she told him that she was taking a holiday with her husband (thank God no Ronald!) and the two girls, in a farmhouse they had been lent by some friends in the Gorges du Tarn. 'That's really amazing,' he said, when he heard the address, 'because we've taken a cottage that can't be more than a dozen miles from where you're going to be!' 'Fate's at work,' she said, in that voice which seemed to mimic some unknown butt. He loved the slight jogging of her foot as she sat, one glistening leg crossed over the other. The slim slipper dangled from her nylon heel and inside he could just see the maker's gilded name, scarcely yet trodden upon. 'We must on no account meet,' she said. Yet the possibility that they might glimpse each other while engaged on some summer errand could not fail to enchant them. If only, by the way, they were going together. Imagine!

The holidays came. He could not help watching out for her when he went on the Saturday to the local town, efficient with his wife's neat shopping list. She was doing a chicken *à l'estragon* for lunch and hoped he didn't mind marketing alone. The kids were sick of the car and had gone up to see a new-born calf at the farm. He walked around the stalls, pretending to be as French as possible to keep the prices down, ears eager for English voices. Could that be her behind those dangling ducks, in the headscarf and the Woking accent? Of course not. On the way back to the cottage, he drove slightly out of his way and saw the signpost leading to the village featured in her address, but refrained from turning off.

Then, in the week, he took the family to the swimming pool near a mill where they had had some particularly good salmon trout the previous evening. He left them, on some cultural excuse, and drove away. It was not far to the village he had seen indicated. Though it contained only a few houses (two deserted), he had to ask an old woman, who was topping and tailing a colander of beans, which of the various tracks led to 'Les Pechs'. 'Le monsieur est sorti,' she said, in her harsh local accent. He started the car again hurriedly. If it was true that only the Monsieur had gone out, she might be there alone. The old lady would not have said if the children had gone with their father.

The farmhouse was an ancient building, opportunistically renovated with patches of beige concrete, its thick walls pierced with ready-made french windows. He knocked, but there was no answer. He tapped again on the locked kitchen door with a pebble, to sharpen the sound. Might she be upstairs? He cupped his hands and peered between them into the sun-splashed room. Used plates, badged with unfinished egg, were still on the table. He looked at his watch. It was four-fifteen. He looked again; a plastic bowl of overboiled potatoes already turning black; next to it, a ripped packet of chocolate biscuits and by them broken bread, a knob of butter stuck in its strawberry wound. Curled ham and a segment of cold pizza, scabby with tomato, were exposed, in creased wrapping paper, to the flies. One of the kitchen chairs was on its back, as if it had passed out. In the corner of the room was a gaping suitcase; toys, anoraks and packets of cereal had been dug out and lay in a spoiled heap beside it.

He went back to the car and turned it in the awkward lane. He went too fast down the ruts back to the village and nodded at the old lady, who had finished her beans, before going on, more placidly, towards the main road. He had scarcely got there when a Volvo station wagon, unmistakably G.B., came towards him, slowing down. He looked and, sure enough, there she was, commonplace with her humorist husband and the growing girls. The latter, seeing another English number plate, pressed their faces against the badges and cross-Channel stickers on the side window. 'Ullo, ullo,' they mouthed, lips moistening the dusty glass. He gave a little wave, and mouthed back, 'Good-bye, good-bye!'

Aperitif

'Yes,' she said, 'this is the place. I knew it was.'

'You came here with him, did you?'

'Twice,' she said. 'We came here twice. I recognize the lettering. It's more faded now, of course, but I remember it distinctly. We came here first on our honeymoon. The bed was hell.'

'It wasn't the first time you slept together, though, surely?'

'Oh good heavens no,' she said. 'I was pregnant with Nicholas. But not very. We had room number 7. The key was very stiff in the lock.'

'Suitably symbolic!' he said.

'Of what? Oh I see. We never had any trouble in that department as a matter of fact.'

'Pregnant with Nicholas,' he said. 'That certainly makes it quite a long time ago. Why, that must be –'

'Let's not bother to be precise, shall we?' she said.

'I hope Nicholas and I are going to be able to work out a modus vivendi,' he said. 'Of course I appreciate it isn't going to be easy.'

'In the final analysis,' she said, 'what is?'

'Personally,' he said, 'I always hope it won't *get* to the final analysis. It's almost certain to be too far. What's the food like?'

'If it's the same people, excellent. The *écrevisses* are sensational. I don't remember having better food anywhere. Although the first time I hardly ate anything. It is the same people! Bonjour, Madame Rigaud!'

'Madame. Monsieur.'

'Nous voudrions une chambre, s'il vous plaît –'

'Je regrette: nous ne faisons plus de chambres.'

'They don't do rooms any more? But it says hotel!'

'Je suppose que nous pouvons dîner, quand même, madame?'

'Mais oui. Vous n'êtes que deux?'

'Que deux,' he said.

'J'enlève le troisième couvert.'

'Do you think she recognized me? I thought she looked at me as if she had some idea –'

'When was the last time you were here?'

'About eight years ago,' she said. 'We left Nicholas and Hannah with the grandparents and had a trip on our own. It was rather a disaster. It was meant to repair things and it turned out to be rather a disaster. That's why I remember the place so well. We had an awful quarrel.'

'After you'd eaten, I presume.'

'Why?'

'Because the first time you hardly ate anything, you said, and yet you say the food's so good. So presumably you ate well the second time and had the row afterwards.'

'Aren't you logical?' she said.

'Why do you think there's no one else in the dining room?' he said. 'I hope it doesn't mean they've lost their chef.'

'As it's the same lady, and she's married to the chef, I don't think it's very likely.'

'You're the same lady,' he said, 'but you're not still married to the chef.'

'Michael was a good critic of cooking,' she said, 'but he didn't do any.'

'I was merely suggesting –'

'She looks older, she looks older and rather sadder.'

'That's what looking older is.'

'Oh do you think so?' she said. 'I rather hoped one got rather more – what? – characterful as one got older.'

'What did you quarrel about?' he said.

'It was rather funny, actually.'

'You'd rather not talk about it.'

'Oh I don't mind,' she said. 'I don't propose to have any secrets from you.'

'That makes it sound as if there are lots you could have.'

'What was funny was that we quarrelled about something that happened the first time. And it must have been – oh – almost ten years between the two visits.'

'Would you rather not talk about him?'

'Would you rather I didn't?'

'You don't find it morbid?'

'I don't mind a little morbidity,' she said, 'from time to time. Why do you suppose they don't do rooms any more?'

'Staff, I presume,' he said.

'It's rather like a ghost story,' she said. 'As if someone died, or was murdered or something. The first time we came we'd been driving all day. It was a bit foggy and we'd picked this place out, because it had a star for the restaurant, earlier in the day, before the weather turned foul. I said we should stop somewhere else, but you know how obstinate he could be. He wanted to come here and he said he could get us here and we drove and we drove. It was obviously going to be hellishly late when we got here, but he was determined.'

'I can imagine.'

'Yes, and by the time we did get here, I had absolutely no appetite at all. I was past it, I suppose. I felt sick. He made me drink some champagne, but it only made me feel worse, and then he was annoyed because he was stuck with the bottle and I didn't want any more.'

'Quite natural in the circumstances.'

'Oh perfectly. Don't imagine I'm criticizing. Anyway, I said he should eat before it was too late, even though I didn't want to, so we both came into the dining room, even though I really couldn't face the thought of food, let alone the sight of it –'

'I say, I wish they'd bring us the menu.'

'They probably don't start till half past – and there was another couple sitting in here, just one, finishing their raspberries. Over there. Michael took one look at them and blushed like a schoolboy. A middle-aged man and his rather dowdy wife. They didn't mean a thing to me. Well, it turned out that he was a don from Michael's old college.'

'Extraordinary coincidence!'

'Yes. He didn't seem particularly pleased to see Michael. They hadn't had anything in common at Cambridge – the man was an archaeologist or a geologist or something – and I don't suppose he was particularly glad to hear English spoken at all, let alone be accosted and introduced to some ex-undergraduate's wife. He said hullo and they finished their raspberries and said they'd take their coffee later, when they'd had a bit of a stroll. Michael bobbed up again from his chair as they went out and said perhaps we could all have a brandy together afterwards. The archaeologist or whatever he was didn't give that idea more than about three out of ten, but he said perhaps and out they went. Michael went on eating and then he said, "I suppose I should have said cognac. Not brandy." And I said I didn't really think he should have said anything at all.'

'You were a bitch even then.'

'I didn't say it bitchily. You've got me completely wrong if you think that. I smiled. Don't think I didn't love Michael at that point. I loved him very much.'

'I know that.'

'Anyway, I was feeling a bit better. I had some of Michael's chicken and I rather wanted to get him upstairs to bed, as a matter of fact. Well, after dinner he ordered coffee and generally rather dawdled about and I realized he was hoping that this don of his was going to come back and have this famous brandy. Eventually I said I was going up, if he didn't mind, and he decided he might as well come too. They must have slipped up to bed themselves or something. So up we went.'

'And how did it go?'

'What? Oh, the sex. Very well. Probably the belated effect of the champagne. Though Michael and I rarely had problems in that department.'

'Then what was the row about?'

'The row was ten years later.'

'But presumably something happened?'

'Ten years later. After dinner.'

'Of course. I say I do wish she'd at least bring us a menu.'

'Madame insisted on showing us her *Livre d'Or*. You know, her distinguished visitors' book. I suppose Michael looked sufficiently haggard to deserve an entry or something.'

'Why did Michael get to look like that?'

'Being married to me,' she said. 'Why don't you ask me a difficult one?'

'You're beautiful,' he said. 'That's not always easy to handle, is it, in wives?'

'Anyway, there in the book – when we looked back, you know how one does – was the signature of this don of Michael's. And

21

he'd written this elaborately effusive nonsense about the hotel and about how it had been recommended to him by a wiser and a better man, some professor or other he obviously wanted to oil up, and so on and so on. Well, I just burst out laughing. It was absolutely ludicrous. And that was it. Michael was furious. I couldn't believe it. He was livid. He said I'd been absurdly jealous and bad-mannered and it was no wonder that they'd never come and had their brandy with us –'

'Their cognac –'

'Their cognac, whatever it was – because I'd been so graceless it was embarrassing. I said I'd had a headache and I'd done the best I could and – well, you can imagine –'

'Easily,' he said. 'Ten years later, this was?'

'Yes,' she said, 'and he went on about how I'd always resented his Cambridge friends. It all developed from that. I said he was hopelessly fixated or why did he care so much about the drinking company of some stupid, overweight don who obviously didn't want to be bothered with him anyway?'

'I can imagine how it ended.'

'I can't remember which one of us it was,' she said, 'but of course eventually one of us had to say that it was a pity we'd had to wait ten years and two children and God knows what before we discovered that in the final analysis we absolutely despised each other.'

'You see?' he said. 'The final analysis. That's why I profoundly hope we never have one. Ah, here she comes. You're sure you don't mind eating here in the circumstances?'

'No,' she said, 'as a matter of fact it's given me quite an appetite. Telling you all that.'

'Me too,' he said, 'me too. Poor old Michael. Pity they don't still have rooms.'

All We Want Is Your Happiness, Bryan

1959. They were staying at Juan-les-Pins, two weeks, the whole family, at the best hotel (of course), right on the beach behind the Casino, a soft walk from the sea. The parents and Estelle had flown to Nice and he had driven the Austin Princess down, ahead of time, to meet them off the plane. He was twenty, with some weight on him. At the moment he was hardly more than the office boy, but his shadow was larger than he was. One day he would be Jackson Gowns (Mayfair) and everyone knew it, including himself.

He was a good son. He carried his mother's bag and her best-sellers to the reserved mattress every morning and he went golfing with his father in the afternoon. He took his sister to her tennis lesson at five and the whole family to the Casino in the evening, after a good dinner considering, when they ate most things on the menu but didn't take the shellfish. Some good friends of theirs, the Lessers, were due to arrive on the second Monday. Joyce Lesser was a nice girl, wasn't she? He liked Joyce, didn't he? Gerry Lesser was a nice boy, and clever, but Estelle was only fifteen. Still, it would be nice for her to have someone to play tennis with, apart from the professional. Why didn't Bryan play tennis?

Bryan was a good son. He watched the girls on the beach, as any young man was entitled to do, except for those who turned round and stared when Estelle was pulling down the elasticated bottom of her one-piece. When Joyce Lesser arrived, Bryan's mother reminded him, he'd have someone to go out with. They could go dancing. Bryan did not say that he did not like Joyce Lesser, or that he did not like dancing either. He was a good son, Bryan.

He took his sister to her tennis lesson on the Friday and sat and waited for her. The courts were an awkward distance from the hotel; he scarcely had time to get back and sit down before he had to leave again. Why couldn't she walk home from her lesson? Estelle was tired and Bryan didn't mind waiting, did he? That was how he came to meet Julie.

She was taking photographs of four ranking players, warming up for the tournament on a nearby court. She wore an all-white linen suit. She was blonde, lots of curls and a face, Bryan had to admit, of remarkable stupidity. Frowning, he watched her as she giggled and postured, skipped and crouched around the four bronzed men. When she had finished, it took her an age to fit her equipment back into its shaped leather cases. Bryan did not find her ineptitude entirely charmless. As she bent, she presented a flawless rump; and as she squatted, her breasts were squeezed against her knees or fell forward with elastic resilience. What began with contempt ended in the pounding hope that, as she passed, he might find words to detain her. He did. He too had photographic equipment, from his *bar mitzvah*, and it had been supplemented at successive birthdays. When he asked what shutter speed she'd been using, she stopped and soon sat down beside him and turned her blue eyes on him with sufficient warmth for their smallness to matter less than it had.

By the time Estelle had finished nodding to the wizened Italian coach's repeated warnings about her grip on the backhand, Bryan had made a date for that night. He had forgotten that it was Friday and his parents were not pleased. He pointed out that they were not at home, that there were no candles to light and that they had only intended to go to the Casino as usual. And if they wanted to go for a drive? Bryan said he would leave them the Princess. Julie had a white sports car of her own. A girl with her own car sounded independent, and independence was dangerous, and sometimes infectious. Bryan was apologetic, but he was stubborn. He met Julie as arranged.

Her company was not an immediate delight. He had to make all the conversation over the lobster. 'Yes' and 'no' might have been tongue twisters, so difficult was it for her to pronounce them, but soon there was more yes than no. And by the time they had been to a club or two, conversation was at once easier and less important. Dancing now seemed to Bryan a most enjoyable affair. She drove the little Austin-Healey Sprite barefoot from one place to the next, dumping her high-heeled gold sandals in Bryan's lap, for safe keeping. She wore a woollen pompom cap, with a bobble on it. She had been on the Coast three weeks, she told him, and this was the first night she had had a good time, honestly. He was absolutely certain, as she said that, that he was in love with her. Her parents were divorced; her father an alcoholic ex-Commander R.N. who sold insurance, her mother a successful film editor, hence her equipment, and the little studio on the Croisette.

It did not seem to Bryan much less than a miracle that Julie not only looked good in her clothes, but was also willing, after a yummy evening, to prove that she looked even better without them. She did not even turn out the light; she concealed herself from him in no way at all. She ran ahead of his dreams, allowing them all to come true, one after the other, without seeming to make the smallest favour of it. He reeled down the stairs from the studio drunk with ecstasy. Her monosyllables were eloquence now, elegance replaced her awkwardness. He would have asked her to marry him, had not marriage sounded too flat a reward for all the pleasure she had given him.

The next morning he lay in a glazed torpor on the mattress next to his mother. At last he made an excuse and went back to the room to telephone. He dreaded that he had drained his ration of paradise and that she would not answer his ring. Had she minded that they had done all of those things, first time? She answered the phone slightly out of breath, and her panting reminded him of the previous night. Had she someone else there or had she just run up the stairs? She had just run up the stairs, she said, and couldn't find her key when she heard the telephone. Imagine how she felt, thinking it must be him. 'When do I see you?' she wanted to know. Five perfect monosyllables!

They made a date for six-thirty, the first moment he could be sure to be free. It was a freedom not too happily conceded by his mother, and hence by his father. They had been hoping to go into Monte maybe that night – their last chance of being just the four of them before the Lessers arrived, Monday. Bryan was sorry, but he was also determined. Dad could drive the Princess, they didn't need him, but he was twenty years old, and he had a date. 'Who is this girl?' He said it was someone he had met at the tennis club. 'Nice?' 'Very.' The predictable questions were predictably answered. The last of them was, of course, 'Do we get to meet her?' 'I only met her yesterday. We're not –' A little gesture indicated what

they were not. 'Nice-looking?' 'She's blonde,' Bryan said, 'and very
nice-looking.' 'Blonde,' his mother said. 'I see.'

The girl's bare toes looked so delectable on the pedals of the
little Sprite that Bryan would gladly have gone on his knees and
licked the dust from between them. She smiled across at him and
took his wrist and turned it over for the time. 'Can't eat yet,' she
said. 'What shall we do?' He looked at her in the roll-neck sweater,
its loose stitches enchantingly distended by the thrust of her breast,
and he hardly dared to say. She did. 'Bed first, then eat?' She tasted
of salt and sun-oil between those pretty toes.

'I like Jews,' she said, when they were lying on the white rug
under the french windows after they'd done what they liked. He
almost cried. Instead he said, 'I love you.' He said it several times,
until she said, 'I love you too.' It thrilled him all right, her declaration, but he could not help noticing how little it cost her. Love
was natural to her, or commonplace. It was certainly not all-
consuming, as he found when he proposed that they meet the next
day. She was very sorry, but she was going to St-Paul-de-Vence.
He wanted to go too, but she shook her head. She was climbing
into her pants at the time. Her denial aroused his desire. She was
not in the least inconvenienced, but she didn't change her plans.

He wanted to ask if she was going with a man, but he was wise
enough to keep the question to himself. Perhaps he was wise,
perhaps he was not, for now he did not know whether his jealousy
was well-founded or not. The uncertainty revived in him, if only
as a precaution, his memory of her original cheapness. At dinner
it was he who was now monosyllabic. She assumed he was sleepy
after all the sex and teased him that she would have to be less
demanding. The joke did not amuse. He felt now that she was
threatening to limit what until now she had given without measure.
She caught his sulky expression and said, 'Now I can imagine what
your mum goes through!'

Afterwards she drove, very fast, towards Nice, where she was
supposed to collect some processed film. He was silenced by the
speed and his thoughts ran wild. He imagined introducing her to
his mother. He could just hear Julie announcing, by way of
encouragement, that she liked Jews. The phrase made him shudder
and, as he thought of her saying it again, it provoked a sudden
violent desire. She smiled across at him, and the tyres shrieked as

she looked up at the coming corner rather late. He gestured to her to slow down and pull in at one of the lay-bys where they could look over the wall at the midnight sea. His eyes told her, as they leaned on the wall, what he wanted to do. She shrugged, O.K., but there was something in his urgency that made her say, without stopping him, 'Can't get enough suddenly, can we?' He caught her roughly and she said, 'O.K., O.K.,' and made it easy for him to do what he wanted, which was not exactly now what he wanted.

They arranged to meet on the Monday, after she had returned from St-Paul-de-Vence. His mother was at the end of her patience. What was she going to tell Joyce! That he would see her on Tuesday. And what would her parents say? 'Plenty, I should think, without even noticing that I'm not there.' 'Bryan, must you tonight?' 'It's the last time,' he said, 'promise.' He went into town on the Monday morning and bought two chunky gold bracelets.

She did not offer to take him to the flat before they had dinner. Over the coffee he gave her the jeweller's box and explained that the Lessers were coming ... 'Your fiancée?' Julie said. He shrugged. 'Sort of.'

She sniffed. 'It was good while it lasted,' she said.

They went to a bad film, during which she clapped her hands when the villain fell over a cliff, and then she drove back to the hotel, fast. 'See you,' she said, and then her tyres were shrill in the roadway. 'See you,' he said, and sniffed the pines.

He took Joyce Lesser to the dinner dance at the Casino on Tuesday night. She had new glasses and she looked better than he had remembered. Well, she looked all right. They joined the parents at the *boule* wheel for a while and then they went to a night club where the compère said, 'Ooh la la,' and blew raspberries which needed no translation. Bryan did not attempt to kiss Joyce good night, although her dancing had certainly improved, and he went upstairs, unexcited, to bed. It occurred to him as he lay listening to the sea that Julie might be pregnant. You never knew, and there was that time on the Corniche. Imagine if she turned up one day in Highgate and said it was his.

The next day he took Estelle to her tennis, but the adjacent court was empty. There was a wind. He decided to dash back to Juan to the English Tea Room where his parents were sure to be having toast and strawberry jam. He was driving down the steep road towards the town when he had to pull up. The traffic had come to a stop and people were leaning out of their cars. He jumped out and walked on down towards the corner. He asked an Englishman in an R.A.F. blazer what had happened. 'Accident. Some stupid girl in a white sports car.' He ran on down, past the *gendarme*, to the ambulance. There was a blanket over the body as they lifted it, but the bare feet were sticking out, dust between the toes.

That night, after they had dined and danced and returned to the hotel, he took the Princess and drove into Cannes. He found a girl on the Croisette and paid her well to do what he said. When he had finished and was walking down the steps from her room, he said to himself, 'Well, at least my mother can't disapprove of that.'

The Siege of
Mrs Smith-Paris

The siege of Mrs Smith-Paris began, although she did not know it, on the day when Timothy Landon discovered that she owned a Ruysdael. It was only a small Ruysdael, but it had taken Landon no little ingenuity to track it down. It figured, just before etcetera, etcetera, in a scribbled list of paintings acquired from aristocratic fugitives by a certain Friedrich Kapelmann in Brussels during the height of Robespierre's Terror. From the moment of purchase it disappeared from recorded knowledge. Landon, however, discovered to his delight that Kapelmann had subsequently made two journeys to London where his diary disclosed that he sold some pictures, one designated merely with an R., to Lord Perceval Rankin. It required some intelligence but no great wit to follow the trail to Fareham Wick, where Mrs Smith-Paris, Lord Perceval's direct descendant, was still living.

Mrs Smith-Paris was a widow of a certain age and weight, suspicious at first but soon mollified, and eventually charmed, by Landon's knowledgeable admiration for the family and the house. He listened understandingly when she told him how every penny she had had gone in the upkeep of the place. She had not had a holiday in years and she did not know how she was going to be able to go on. Timothy did not at once disclose his commercial purposes; he preferred to establish first how deep was his attachment to the history of the cadet branches of lapsed earldoms, and especially of the Rankins. His knowledge of Mrs Smith-Paris's family tree extended to the remotest windfalls. How could she fail to warm to a man who pulled her forgotten relations from the long grass of obscurity and burnished them to colourful life before her eyes?

No one, for years, had so sympathized with the problems of maintaining the Wick. And he knew so much about it! He not only recognized the death-watch beetle in the library roof, but he was able to tell her that it had been constructed by out-of-work ship-wrights during a recession caused by the Dutch blockade, under Admiral Tromp, of the Thames Estuary in the late seventeenth century. The beams, now he pointed it out, were constructed like an upturned keel. To judge by the frequency of his visits, Fareham Wick was evidently a source of as much pleasure to Timothy Landon as it was of worry to Mrs Smith-Paris. His earnest enthusiasm at first added to her anxiety, for he was forever noticing new signs of decay and suggesting new, essential repairs and restorations. Only when she was almost in despair at the demands of his loving diagnosis did he break the news that the single blackened landscape in the morning room was valuable enough to take care of all the repairs and still leave her enough change to restore the grounds and pay for their upkeep. And only then did he reveal that he sometimes acted as a consultant to Paget's, the auctioneers in St James's Street. There was nowhere in the world where she would get a higher price. Oh couldn't they sell the picture and make Fareham Wick the shining monument to the Rankins it cried out to be?

Mrs Smith-Paris held Timothy in a long and searching glance. It was a search and a glance for which he was prepared. He was careful to leave on show nothing but honest devotion. After all, he was indeed everything he said he was, even if he was also a few things that he did not. He had always loved art, though next to art, alas, came money. Nowadays one needed so much of it. Why else should he put his rare nose for hidden treasures to such catch-penny purposes as scouting for an auctioneer? The trouble was, he had expensive tastes, and he also had Rupert, which was much the same thing, but on two legs. Once or twice, when Rupert was going through a fidgety phase and required ostentatious reassurance, Timothy had even been driven to indicate to some rather louche companions the existence of certain ill-guarded heir-looms in country houses whose stuffy owners had not taken kindly to the suggestion that they send their valuables to auction in St James's. He would never have dealt so callously with Mrs Smith-Paris, for there had sprung up between them one of those touching friendships between late spring and early winter which lent warmth to both, but Timothy did not fail to mention the increasing number of country house thefts and when he heard for how much (or rather how little) the Ruysdael was insured, simply as a genre landscape, he almost insisted that Mrs Smith-Paris allow him to put it straight in the car, for her safety's sake.

Timothy devoted much subtlety to the siege of Mrs Smith-Paris. He wooed her with pressing patience, and having won her, he played upon her affection with delicious cruelty. He would sometimes break a promise to visit her for the sheer pleasure, it seemed, of making it up to her with fresh freesias or a transparent box of pot-pourri from Jermyn Street. He bought the fragrant, desiccated petals from a scented place near his shirtmakers, where his tissue-thin silhouette hung on a named hanger, under a brown-paper overall. Timothy loved his clothes, and so did Rupert, who had the same neck.

Mrs Smith-Paris was no easy mark. Timothy teased her and she, in her turn and fashion, teased him. Of course she was thrilled to think of Fareham Wick being once again the ornament of the county, but she was a widow and the place was very big and lonely. Timothy assured her that she would never lack for his company. What about the hateful industrial estate they were threatening to sanction not five miles away and this talk of a thousand new brick homes to service it? All the more reason, Timothy insisted, for teaching them a lesson. Besides, she had enough acres to keep them at a distance. *Noblesse oblige.* Mrs Smith-Paris sighed. 'You know,' she said, 'I rather like that little landscape. I'm not sure I really want to sell it anyway.' Only when Timothy had been unable to come and see her for over a fortnight, during which a strange motor car twice came up the drive and then went away again, at speed, did Mrs Smith-Paris telephone her surrender. Timothy was down by the next train. But he entered the castellated courtyard less like a conqueror than a missionary king who celebrates his victory by welcoming his worthy adversary into the true faith. Together he and Mrs Smith-Paris would make Fareham Wick a shining example of what a cadet branch of a lapsed earldom could still do, with the right advice.

When, ten minutes before cheap hours began, he telephoned her to give her the thrilling price the Ruysdael had actually commanded, he could not refrain from saying how excited he was that 'we' could now do everything 'we' had always dreamed of doing. He could not wait to get down to the house and set men to work.

That night he and Rupert took their new shirts out to a wildly expensive meal. His share of the commission on the Ruysdael was sufficient, he commented complacently over the sweetbreads *aux marrons*, to enable them to eat there every day for a month. ('Then why don't we?' Rupert said.)

The next morning he was actually packing for Norfolk when the telephone rang. It was Mrs Smith-Paris's solicitor. He had been deputed to tell Timothy that Mrs Smith-Paris had decided to sell Fareham Wick and all its ancient acres to the property company which was developing the district and to take all the proceeds with her to Monte Carlo, a destination for which she had already departed. What, after all, was the point of pouring good money after bad when Timothy had proved to her that she could live in carefree comfort for the rest of her days? 'She can't do that,' Timothy said, 'she can't do that. 'She's done it, I'm afraid.' Landon crashed the telephone into its cradle like an unwanted baby. 'The mercenary old bitch,' he shouted. 'The damned mercenary old bitch!'

Similar Triangles

It was not a cosy, modern adultery. There was much anguish in it. They spoke sometimes, lying in afternoon shadows in borrowed or hired beds, of the long cost of the thing, in pain and deception. They were confident that their spouses knew nothing of the passion which, with irregular regularity, hurried them, hot, across town to hastily scribbled, then crumpled, rendezvous. Their affair had its own narrow and precise language; after each meeting, his mistress would clip a single curl of hair, in the Italian fashion, from *that* part of herself. Byron to her Teresa Guiccioli, he kept those black and glistening hairs, softly crepitant, in a self-addressed envelope in his bottom drawer at the office. They never wrote to each other. Their ordinary lives were happy with homes and cheerful with children; the durable shoe of marriage pinched but slightly and they scarcely noticed their wedded blisters. He had respect for her husband, a coeval at university, whose boring business luckily took him abroad every now and again; she was flattered by the beauty of his wife, whose vanity kept her unsuspicious, but whose looks, it was evident, did not entirely satisfy him.

The lovers would sometimes talk, as they wondered, naked, where their temporary host kept his tea these days, of their own one-day-perhaps marriage. They held the prospect enticingly ahead of themselves, donkeys who dangled their own carrot, but they were sensitive people and why should they hurt Tom or, for that matter, Rachel? They settled, with stimulating resignation, for the *status quo*, though privately she could not but think that her condition was more painful than his. Her sentimental education had been founded on French models, though more on Beauvoir, she liked to think, than on Bovary. While she agreed to clip the triangular hedge of her sex to suit his topiaristic taste, she took sour pleasure in the belief that her love was more profound than his. He, for his part, salted his sweet wounds with the fear that she and Tom were really closer than he and she. His Narcissism saw itself in triple mirrors.

He was a rising civil servant, discreet to a fault, wise to a virtue. One day, just as he was about to go in to see his Master, whose latest Bill was being mauled in Committee, his secretary buzzed. His mistress seldom called him at the office and he raised the receiver with fond vexation. She was sorry to do this, but her husband had been at a conference at an out-of-season resort on the Bay of Naples and had been knocked down by a lorry full of soldiers. He begged leave from his understanding, displeased Minister, who hated all private life, and dashed into Whitehall for a cab. As he was driven across town, the unwanted comedy of his rival having been killed by, of all unlikely forces, the Italian army twisted his lips into a grin he had positively to manipulate into condolence.

But if he had sometimes wondered whether he truly loved his mistress, her tears soon washed away all doubts. In the unusual surroundings of her mournful house, he talked to her for the first time with a tenderness unspiked by desire. His wife was as generous as he had expected – the couples were amiable strangers – and, hearing that he had been the first on the scene, insisted that he stay and do anything he could. For the first time, he spent a whole night under the same roof as his mistress. Of course it was unthinkable that they make love. In the succeeding, painful days, tact continued to tailor modest skirts to a love whose shamelessness had always been its badge.

She had no idea that he could be so practical and so considerate. The children adored him. No one questioned his compassionate presence; neither her friends nor his, even when they were identical, passed the smallest sly observation. They hid their love in the open, and none remarked it.

Their desire had always before been a matter of urgent opportunism; its fervour was a function of its haste. Now decision was required to revive it. Neither doubted that it would come promptly when wanted, but they hesitated before pressing the bell. A week after the funeral, they sat one evening in the orange basement kitchen, among the blue-hooped dishes, while her daughter practised the clarinet upstairs and the au pair girl called out 'Good night then' as she set off to meet her Italian waiter, on his night off from the *trattoria* where he told show biz people how nice it was to see them again. They discussed the future and the past; they toyed, as with a new diet, with the idea of telling Rachel. When they did indeed come to make love again – the children at their grandmother's for a day or two – there was between them a certain gentle constraint; they told themselves it was because it now meant so much more than it had before. Yet he was kinder than was quite congenial to him; she was more touched, she found, than roused. And afterwards, she omitted, as if by mutual, mature consent, the ceremonial snip.

She understood, of course, of course she did, when he felt obliged to revert, at least for a while, to his familiar style of living. Rachel had been so terribly nice, I mean, hadn't she? His mistress was surprised, however, at how abruptly rare his calls became. How could he confess to her his unwanted and inexpressible dismay at the suddenly enlarged emptiness in his mistress's life or his unwillingness, his inability to fill it? She started to complain of his neglect and never heard the ugly tune she sang in her lover's ear.

In brief, though at length, he became inexorably, remorsefully, estranged from the woman with whom he had for so long dreamed of sharing his life, if only she were free. Resentment did not exorcize her love; truth to tell, his display of decent maturity had been rather unexciting. His new indifference promised that the old beastliness was not, after all, gone in him. She smiled, as she wept, at his cruelty. Friends saw that she was missing Tom badly and were kind in his stead: her evenings, if not her afternoons, were quickly filled. She dined out and soon she met a very nice man. Within a year she had married him. Her lover read the announcement and swore to himself that he would never see her again. But one evening, sullen with his sullen wife, he did see her, and the new husband, at a concert. During the Albinoni, he observed, in the calm possessive glance her husband slyly gave her, how much he resembled the dead Tom. A few days later, he called her during his Minister's question time. She told him, of course, how very happy she was with her new husband and he, of course, told her how happy he was that she was happy. Ned was a lawyer, she said, involved with the Common Market; he was quite often away for a day or so in Brussels or Strasbourg. Love and desire rose in grateful resurrection. When he proposed that they have lunch one day, she was reliably on cue: 'I say, can you get the flat, do you think?' Guilt returned to his life like spring. In very little time, the pattern was restored, as in a play which falters when a key actor has to be replaced, but which soon, when the casting is right, resumes its unfaltering rhythm.

Once again he did not have to say good night to the au pair off to her Italian or to smile at Clara's clarinet. Once again, in those brief brackets of infinity in which their passion had to be compressed, the deep and constricted flood of desire turned love's secret mill. Once again, with that old lost smile, she came to the borrowed bed with a pair of glinting nail scissors which, bending naked, she put on the bedside table, next to the telephone they always left unanswered if it rang, for the eventual climactic snip. Once again, his wife came to believe what she had sullenly begun to doubt, that he did indeed still find her beautiful.

This Susan Person

'It's really funny,' one of her letters said, 'we've never met.' They had become friends on the long-distance line and, above all, through the mail. He was a Professor of English in a small, rather rich College in a large, rather poor state in the South. He taught Twentieth Century Criticism, and practised it in the prestigious *University Journal*. She was the Critics Editor of the *Weekend American*, which had offices on Sixth Avenue in New York, and a readership of half a million. She admired an article he wrote on 'Sex and Sociology in John O'Hara' and, as a result, offered him for review the latest books of sexual and sociological boldness. He did her a longish piece on 'The Rise of Masturbation and the Decline of Dialogue', and followed it with another on the New Feminists, those who wrote, as he put it, with their fingers crossed but never their legs. The readers of the *Weekend American* liked to keep up with the outrageous without themselves being outraged. The Professor took prudent care to spell all his four-letter words with seven or more letters. His relationship with the *Weekend American*, and with its Critics Editor, pleased both his pocket and his vanity.

Though the Professor was happy to live a mountainous five hours' drive from the sophistications of Kansas City, he was not without larger ambitions. He had already published a volume of short stories replete with fantasies of sex and violence which rather surprised those who knew the exemplary fidelity of the Professor and the restraint of his quotidian exasperation.

His wife was a jealous woman. She watched him with a loving vigilance at once onerous and endearing. That he, almost alone of his colleagues, had no extra-curricular curriculum seemed to afford her little reassurance. She could still resent his sitting in the Campus deli discussing the Black Mountain poets with a teaching assistant who was having an affair with the Afro-headed seven-foot captain of the basketball team.

37

But she was jealous above all of his long correspondence with the Critics Editor of the *Weekend American*: 'this Susan person'. The Professor protested in vain that their letters were on purely literary topics. Gloria was welcome to read them whenever she wanted to. She never wanted to, though she often did. Their tone of growing intellectual camaraderie pressed bruisingly on her dark apprehensions of scholastic inferiority. When this Susan person took to calling station-to-station from New York, she took the messages, if the Professor was out, and relayed them with the dutiful dignity of a wife who had learned to wear humiliation as snappily as a uniform. He grew wary and weary of Gloria's resentment and diverted the calls to his office on Campus; he typed his pieces for *Weekend American* before he came home and posted them, covertly, with the Faculty mail. His routine and prosaic articles, obedient to the house style of the *Weekend American*, were accompanied by longer and longer covering notes of a more self-revealing nature, in which he presented himself as a wry wit, sardonic and world-weary, at once uxorious and impatient.

One day he had a call from his literary agent in New York. One of the short stories in his collection had excited the interest of a movie producer. Could he fly up to New York all expenses paid, to take a meeting with Mr Lazlo Konradi? He told Gloria that it looked like they might be able to build that new rumpus room for the kids and maybe have enough change to go to Europe in the summer. She drove him to the little local airport with grim grace; he had suggested she come too, but she had her sculpture class. Anyway, he'd be happier on his own, wouldn't he? No, he wouldn't he said. Yes, he would, she said. He'd have a chance to go see this Susan person at last. He said he wouldn't have time for that. He said he loved his wife and he'd see her soon, but he was glad when they called the flight.

And of course there was plenty of time. Mr Lazlo Konradi was delayed on the coast. The bookish Professor went to Brentano's and to Doubleday's and he processed, with other worshippers, past the latest expendable and expensive acquisitions at the Museum of Modern Art. The sensual Professor wandered down to Times Square and, in the interests of research, he visited a blue movie full of unwrinkled pink flesh and was reminded of the brevity of life's candle. What the hell, he called the *Weekend American* and was put through to the Critics Editor. Susan uttered a shrill coo of delight: 'You're in New *York*? Can I *see* you?' 'I am visible to the naked eye,' he said. 'I love it,' she said. The conquest was as good as made; it remained but to see what had been conquered, for the Professor had, of course, no notion of what this Susan person looked like, though his recent imagination had not failed to bless her with the black hair and unbelievably white skin, the unfallen breasts and elastic lips of one of the girls on the great mid-morning screen of the movie house where he had been doing his research.

He took a taxi to Sixth Avenue and went through the mill of revolving doors and down the lobby to the express elevators. As he entered the first available car going to even floors, he noticed that an empty elevator on the other side of the lobby was leaking. Water poured from the lintel and splashed down the crack in the threshold. He pressed the button for the thirty-sixth floor and the smooth doors closed out the lacrimose sight. He thought briefly of his wife and then, with greater enthusiasm, of the woman he was about to meet.

The Professor was a tall man – blue eyes, brown hair, straight nose, firm mouth, a regular paradigm of handsomeness – and he found himself looking at a woman scarcely shorter than himself who, when she rose from behind her book-barricaded desk, appeared to be of an admirable and amiable outdoorsiness he had certainly not expected. She was more like his sister, though he had no sister, than the dark and sensual lady to whom, provisionally, he had imagined himself playing sonneteer.

When the coffee had come and the sweetener had been administered, she said: 'You're not really like I imagined.' 'Nobody is,' he smiled. 'You smile a lot,' she said. 'I can see from the lines around your eyes. I never thought of you as a smiling person.' 'You're not like I imagined either,' he said. 'How did you think I'd be?' 'Dark, as a matter of fact, and smaller. More New York.' 'I come from Iowa,' she said, 'my name was Svensen before I was married.' 'I didn't know you were married,' he said, 'nobody ever tells anybody these things any more. I just put Mzz on the envelope and hope for the best.' 'And what is the best?' she said. She looked at him again and had to apologize: 'I'm sorry, but you just don't look the way you write, I mean not a bit. You write so savagely, that irony, that wit – I can't get over it, you seem such an easy person in the flesh, and I've been waiting here for you practically *shaking*. I wish I'd known.'

They smiled at each other and she made an awkward little gasp and put both hands flat on the blotter in front of her and let her hair fall forward over her face. She shook her head, as if she were emerging from the shower, and was just saying, 'Well, listen, how about taking a couple of books to review while you're here?', when a loud bell started to ring in the main office.

'What is that?' Susan asked over the intercom. 'Seems like we have a fire, Susan.' 'I'll bet we don't,' Susan said to the Professor. 'I'll bet it's a false alarm. Karen, will you check? Because I bet it's a false alarm.' The Professor and the Critics Editor sat looking at each other, with something new and public to smile about. 'Do you live in New York City,' he asked, 'you and your husband?' 'It seems like it's the real thing,' Karen said over the intercom, 'they say we're to proceed to fire stations.' 'We seem to have a fire,' Susan said, with a spread of white hands. 'Here's your chance to save my life,' the Professor said.

He looked with amused dismay at the faces of the staff of the *Weekend American* as they converged in the narrow corridor and trooped past a bronze bust of George Bernard Shaw ensconced by the teak door on to the main landing, where members of Deakin, Hayes and Gerhardi, Attorneys, were also assembling and whither, in due course, the fraternity of Manchester Brothers, Public Relations, came grumbling, interrupted in mid-campaign. They stood close by the flashing red light of the Fire Assembly Point and the Professor, boyish man of the world, took the opportunity to steady Susan's elbow when the Public Relations men jostled her. A nasal and disembodied voice instructed them to stay where they were and not to move. 'Not the kind of orders you need a lot of nerve to obey,' he said, 'at least until your ankles start to sizzle.' The Professor sniffed the air and craned his neck for the Fire Exit. 'Maybe we should make a separate peace,' he said. 'How do you say we sneak away and look for the stairs while there's still an "r" in the month?' She rewarded him with a show of white teeth. 'It's a false alarm,' she said, 'I bet you.' 'I could still take you for an early dinner,' he said. 'I can't,' she said.

After a few minutes, the people on the thirty-sixth floor were informed by the same nasal and disembodied voice that the alarm

was terminated. 'What did I tell you?' Susan said. 'Let's go back
to the office and get those books, shall we?' He sat down again
opposite her, but their conversation had, as he might have said
in a short story, lost its erection. He did ask if she was really doing
anything that night, because an out-of-town hick could do with
an intelligent theatre and restaurant guide, but she was really and
truly not free, even though she wished she was. He shook hands,
took his books and they each said how really, really glad they were
to have met at long last, really. He went out past George Bernard
Shaw, blunting the chaste old philanderer's nose with the flat of
his hand. In the lobby, men were trying to staunch the unceasing
Niobe of an elevator. It seemed that the sprinkler had been set off
by mistake and as a result the alarm system for the entire building
had gone into spasm.

The next morning the Professor took the meeting, in the Oak
Room of the Plaza, with Lazlo Konradi. They ate a lot of English
marmalade and Mr Konradi explained that his wife was in the
hospital undergoing surgery, so he couldn't make any firm plans
right now, though he still absolutely intended to make a meaningful
offer for the Professor's story as soon as some key people on the
Coast got back from Europe. Meanwhile, could he persuade the
Professor to make the girl not an epileptic, because that was one
area where he wasn't too happy? The Professor said he saw no
problem there, once they were really in business, and Mr Konradi
said there was no problem about being in business, just so long
as the girl – 'Sandra?' – 'Francesca' – 'Francesca' – didn't have
to be an epileptic.

The Professor read the proof copies of the books the Critics Editor
had given him on the plane on the way home. One of the books
dismayed him with its catchpenny erotica; the other with its bullet-
ridden opportunism. He wrote a scathing and unsmiling review
and mailed it, with a briefly congenial covering note, to the Critics
Editor of the *Weekend American*. A few nights later, the telephone
rang at his home. Gloria answered. 'It's this Susan person,' she
said, holding out the receiver.

The Professor took the phone and smiled into it, 'Hi, Susan, how
are you?' 'Hi,' she said. 'Did you get the piece?' 'Yes, I did! That's
the thing,' she said. 'What is? I think it's one of the best I've done,
don't you?' 'Listen,' she said, 'forgive me. I really enjoyed meeting

you, and maybe if I hadn't I wouldn't have been able to say this, but I feel like you wouldn't want me to say I liked something if I didn't.' 'Try me,' he said. 'I think it needs work, I really do.' 'Needs work?' he said. 'I think you have one hell of a nerve calling me like I was some first-year student.' The Professor became more and more angry the calmer and more dignified he tried to be.

As his wife watched and listened, his language ripened into a show of scatological imagery profuse with obscene fruit and florid with colourful contumely. He raged at the Critics Editor, smiling across the room at Gloria at the same time, so that the very words which shocked and insulted the girl in New York rang like amorous charms in the ears of his wife. By the time he had exhausted his rage and vocabulary, she had been drawn across to him and slipped her arms low around his waist. When he finished by flinging the receiver into its plastic holster, she had her lips to his ear. 'What in tarnation happened in New York?' He looked at her with spent eyes. 'Nothing,' he said. 'We had a false alarm and that was it.' As he kissed her, she had a feeling that he had been glad to say all those terrible things to a woman and that he would never have said them if she had not been there to hear them. When they made love that night she had the satisfaction of knowing that he took her, in the brutal dark, for that Susan person.

Bridal Suite

'Strange things honeymoons,' he said to her in the limousine on the way to the airport.

'Stranger still,' she said, 'when you've been together as long as we have.'

'I sure hope we did the right thing,' he said, when Central American Airways called the flight.

'Getting married?' she said. 'Not much we can do about it now. We already ate the cake.'

'Maybe we did,' he said, 'but do we have to fly to the dysentery belt to blow out the candles?'

'You seem different,' she said, with a smile to prove she wasn't.

'Maybe I am,' he said, 'I was never married before.'

'I was,' she said. 'And please don't be. Different. I like you the way you were.'

'That was yesterday,' he said, and seemed to resent the way she helped him fasten his safety belt.

He had known her three, going on four years. He had always thought her face unique for its wide blue eyes and its white, incisive teeth above that neat, narrow jaw. It was rather a shock to observe, at the wedding breakfast, that she had three sisters and, almost more disconcerting, two brothers (Alvin and MacMichael, for God's sakes), all of whom had the eyes and the teeth and the neat, narrow jaw.

They were going only two and a bit hours from Dallas, but the faces in the jet were mainly swarthy; the Spanish announcements were more clearly understood than the English. He just hoped that the hotel was going to be all right. It was American-owned, but he still thought maybe the whole thing was a mistake. 'The honeymoon,' he meant, 'not the wedding.'

They drove at last into the modern section of the city, concretely rebuilt since the recent earthquake, along a fancy avenue named after the American president whose vice-president had had to dodge the stones of the mob on his way to the *casa del presidente* where the prevailing general had taken receipt of the funds for the construction of the highway. The general now lived in some luxury in Lucerne; the highway was not as long as the purse allotted to it.

There was nothing obviously wrong with the hotel. It had a coffee shop and a gourmet restaurant and a heated pool and two hire car desks and there were tours available to the unspoiled hinterland. The bridal suite was on the seventh floor and it was already embarrassingly effusive with flowers and good wishes from the folks they hoped they had left behind. The management had been thoughtful with fruit. She watched, dismayed at his dismay, as he winced at the florists' cellophane. She wished that they were back at the twelve bucks a night motel where their affair began, in a place called Alexandria, Louisiana. It had been a hundred and fifteen in the shade when they checked in and the shower wasn't working and who cared? Now she took a shower, but he didn't seem to want to come in and get anything. She came out and he was standing at the window looking down, without enthusiasm, on the crowded evening buses taking workers back to their shanties. The sides of the buses were badged with the portraits of the new generation of contending generals who hoped one day, if elected, to live in Lucerne.

The hotel promised American service, but it was staffed mainly by local Indians. There was trouble getting a drink; there was more trouble obtaining a sandwich. As darkness fell, the sky was luminous with flashes. They heard distant explosions. 'Sounds like they have a fiesta going on,' she said. 'I hate fiestas,' he said, and made it sound as though he also hated her. She wriggled silken toes and smoothed her stockings up her gleaming thighs. He stared out of the window. 'We're going to have folksongs next,' he said, 'you wait and see.' He sighed as a crackle of festive fire made him flinch. He opened the terrace window and stepped into the flashing night. She followed him, accepting an invitation which had not been offered. The sky was splenetic with low and temporary constellations. The evening air prickled in her nostrils like a summer cold. She stood by her husband and willed him to admire the gaudy dazzle of the city.

Suddenly a mass of people, shouting and waving things, came running out of a side street opposite the hotel and spilled into the avenue. They were followed by a squad of masked and shielded police who seemed rather comically slow on cue as they began, with no evident order or purpose, to fire into the crowd. People screamed and ran in various directions. From the high terrace they could look directly down to where two men were being thumped with rifle butts as they slid down the railings of the hotel compound, access to which was blocked by a limousine carrying a diplomatic quartet.

She looked down then with appalled condescension at the bloody scene below them. In the distance, as she glanced away, she could see the trickling raw redness of a volcano, like a picked scab against the far sky. Her throat was sour with the tear-gas which, even at the height of the seventh floor, rasped her lungs. 'You're right,' she said, 'we have to get out of here; it's horrible.' Fear and revulsion made uneasy stilts of the high heels she had decided to put on. She leaned her head on his shoulder, for help. His arms promptly bracketed her, his hands were hard where she was soft. She wanted to go in, out of the vicious dark, but he held her there on the terrace, while the violence from the street rose like a savage drug. She shook her head – no, not now – but he was smiling. 'It *is* our honeymoon,' he said.

Benchmark

His father had been a barrister and it seemed only natural that he should read for the Bar. He was clever; he might have been anything and so all decision seemed to him at once temporary and arbitrary. Versatility made him docile. As he counted up to forty the quota of dutiful dinners at his father's Inn, it amused him to think of himself as a dangerous monster, blessed (or was it cursed?) with three eyes. Unless he concealed his extraordinary gift, the crowd might become aware of it, and turn on him. He developed a habit of putting his hand over his forehead when talking or arguing. It is said to be in the middle of his forehead that man once carried that third and terrible eye. You can still feel the dip of the socket.

He was, in all observable respects, a normal and intelligent young man of his time. At the university he was known for his sometimes savage mimicry of personalities of the day, but by the time he had finished his dinners and, thus fortified, was approaching his Bar Finals, he had ceased to imitate anyone but the striped-trousered, stiff-collared young devilling junior he proposed to become.

One day, at a party overlooking the river by Turner's Reach, he met a girl. The flat was very grand; it belonged to a rich business man whom his father had extricated from some taxing trouble. It was so big that it contained a fountain. He was floating a frilly garter from a cold lamb chop in the throbbing water when he met the woman whom he would marry, and who would marry him. She was dark, with a long face, beautiful enough to be painted and distinct enough to be caricatured. She wore a black silk dress, no jewellery. Her hair was in a bun, swollen, yet firmly contained; it was lustrous, the dark hair, and seemed to pulse with life, as if it were flesh, as if it had nerves and, when touched, would flinch or flower. She was recently down from Oxford; she had read English. Her father was the business man. She disdained the law, as beauty may, and was not impressed by the brilliance of his results so far.

And so, as if to disclose his third and magic eye, he told her that he sometimes wrote poetry. Her eyes lost their cataracts of contempt. Did he have any of his poems with him? He did not, and was glad, for now it was easy to find a reason to meet again.

They did so in the Criterion restaurant, where crustless triangular sandwiches and a choice of tea cakes were once wheeled on trolleys under a gilded mosaic ceiling. Now the ceiling alone remained, a golden heaven above a mundane modernized earth: the place had been converted to self-service. Fish and chips and individual fruit pies had ousted cucumber sandwiches and creamily tumescent éclairs. She wore a tweed skirt this time and a sweater that was both green and blue. She put on a pair of glasses and swallowed and began to read his verses.

'Well, what do you think?' She looked from the pages in her hand to his face, and back again, as if seeking a likeness. She rested the poems in her herringboned lap and leaned forward over a steeple of white-knuckled fingers. 'I think I love you,' she said. 'About the poems,' he said. 'I like them,' she said, 'a lot.' 'But are they any good?' 'I think they're very good,' she said, 'do you?' 'I write poems,' he said, 'but whether or not I'm a poet . . .' She smiled – oh that red unreddened mouth! – and the steeple came suddenly down. 'That's a critical question, isn't it?' she said, and laid a long hand on his.

She was a virgin, but she was promptly moist for him, as if she had already known men. He wanted to marry her; she intended to marry him. By day he worked for his Finals, behaved as correctly as ever and aped, with the skill he had always contrived, the ways of the pedestrian world. He knew she was rich and he was fired with ambition to give her everything she had already. He was ready to give his life for that. Their desire was so strong and, to them, so reckless that it seemed as necessary as it was delicious to hide its pulse under commonplace clothing. They married and they were lovers. He became an advocate of mordant effectiveness: his bite rewardingly worse than his bark. He relished the polite mercilessness of legal debate; it particularly pleased him to be known as an expert on matters of which, until the eve of a case, he knew virtually nothing.

His marriage was at first his passion, then his delight, later his pleasure and always his comfort. His wife continued to excite both his desire and his admiration, even when they had been married for more than twenty years and their children had lovers of their own. (His son did not want to go to the Bar; he was a garage mechanic and wore a dog collar and a gold earring in his left ear.) His wife was as publicly assured as she could still be privately demanding. She dressed as the wife of a fashionable Q.C. should, and her cocktail parties were unostentatiously showy: nothing was too much trouble and nothing appeared to have been any trouble at all. The ham and the smoked salmon – where did she get them? – came from a famous, known-to-few smokery near their cottage on the east coast. Soon after their silver wedding anniversary, he was made a judge. He was knighted, in happy consequence, and his wife enjoyed the embarrassment of being her ladyship. They celebrated in bed; public position lending piquancy to private.

As a result of his elevation, he had to vacate his chambers, which had belonged to his father and were crammed with ancient, jaundiced papers. He was already installed on the Chancery bench before he had completed the job. He was somewhat dismayed to find that he did not in the least like being a judge: it was tedious and it was lonely. He sat for long periods, properly attentive, with his hand over his forehead. He felt himself to be concealing that third eye in the centre of his brow which already saw, and too clearly, where the whole thing was leading.

He had quite forgotten about his adolescent poetry and was astonished to come across a batch of it at the bottom of a cupboard. He smiled – golly! – at the sight of it and took it out and started to read, for a laugh. He expected clinching evidence of the folly of youthful pretensions. His whole happy life had been founded on the assumption that he had been right to abdicate before his wife's gentle, unmistakable judgement. He sat on the floor of his chambers, boyishly grey, and prepared to be embarrassed by those unburnt embers. Instead, the poems passed sentence on his life. At last, he closed his eyes to escape their indictment, but the unblinking eye in the centre of his forehead gazed and blazed with unique and undeniable vision. He cowered on the floor of the dusty cave and saw that the years of his life had escaped, like Odysseus' men under the panicky sheep of the blind, deluded Polyphemus. 'Who are you, who are you?' he cried. And the voice of the man who had blinded himself replied, 'No one. No one.'

Cheap Day

Every three or four weeks there came a moment when, as she would say to her husband at breakfast, she simply had to go up to town. She had been born in London; her mother lived there; she had friends, the dentist, and things to do. She had come to love the estuary, the open skies, the smell of the mud-stained sea, but every three or four weeks she simply had to go up to town. 'Why do it if you don't want to?' her husband would ask. 'You go sometimes,' she answered. 'But I want to,' he said.

There was a new car park at the station, into which commuters' cars could pass only one at a time. Seasoned travellers had taken all the spaces near the booking office and she was constrained, in her camel-hair suit, with its rather narrow skirt, to hurry on foot from the back of the old coal yard, where late traffic was driven to park, along the cold rows of early cars, uneasy on her higher-than-usual heels. The London train was already chattering into the station as she stood panting at the booking office. A cheap day ticket was placed on the little bisected turntable and rotated to her. She ran down the stairs, through mottled puddles and along the long platform from which, thank God, belted bundles of old Sunday supplements were being loaded on to the train. There was plenty of time and she would not really mind, she promised herself, if she didn't go to London anyway, and yet she ran.

She grabbed open the door of an apparently empty non-smoker. A man in a brown corduroy jacket and fawn trousers was crouched down collecting a jumble of papers from the floor and posting them in the mouth of his rigid briefcase. 'Sorry,' he said breathlessly, 'but I've been an absolute idiot and opened my briefcase the wrong way up.' 'I shouldn't worry,' she gasped. 'Oh,' he said, 'you've been running too.' 'Isn't it too silly,' she said, 'when we still haven't even left the station?' 'You didn't stop to buy a ticket, did you?' He had noticed the tab of cheap paper in her gloved fingers. 'I'm always afraid of being accused of doing something wrong,' she said.

The train was soon moving through flat fields and then alongside the by-pass where they could measure their pace against shirt-sleeved salesmen who were proving that their company cars had effective heaters, and how far they had come in them. Frost still made mountainous birthday cakes out of molehills in the meadows. 'I hate to run for things, don't you?' he said, as he felt for his pencil. 'And yet one does it,' she said. 'One does so many things one doesn't want to, and so few one does,' he said, 'why is that, do you suppose?' 'Perhaps one isn't sure which is which,' she said. She had neither a book nor a paper. He looked up at her from the things in his lap. 'For instance, I should dearly like to tell you what remarkable eyes you have, but the habit of reticence is, of course, much too strong to admit of such impertinence.' 'Do you often talk to women like that in trains?' As she recovered her breath, youth came back into her face, defeating time. 'I'll tell you the truth,' he said, 'never. But to act out of character is to escape, if only for a moment, from the human condition. Don't you agree?' 'I think you talk to women in trains quite a bit,' she said.

He made a mark on the print in front of him. 'I've been visiting my ex-wife,' he said, 'and the children. Perhaps that's what's responsible. She left me for another man – not that I was blameless – and then he was killed in one of those holiday air crashes. Forty-fourth out of a list of forty-six victims; he was on business, the rest of them weren't. Much it mattered; Ginny was left with virtually nothing.' 'And you help her?' 'Of course.' 'But you never got back together?' 'It's as if there were a sort of membrane between us,' he said, 'thin and invisible but terribly durable – a man-made fibre, no doubt – and we can never quite breach it; *hymen hymenaeo*, the moment is never quite propitious.' 'Are you a don, by any chance, or a lecturer?' 'I used to be a schoolmaster,' he said, pencil against page, 'but now I compile reference books and things. What makes you ask?' 'Propitious,' she said, and crossed blue-stockinged legs.

As they careered through a station, their view was hedged with the blurred faces of local passengers, waiting for the next train. 'We travel at different speeds from each other,' he said, 'and so are prevented from joining those with whom we should dearly like to travel.' 'Isn't that the reason we imagine we'd like to travel with them?' she said. 'Look here,' he said, 'may I ask you something: what are you doing this morning, when we get to town, and are you free for lunch by any chance?' 'I've got my mother,' she said. 'Well, what about before?' 'And rather a full morning,' she said, 'I'm afraid. I go up to town only once or so a month and –' 'Why are you afraid?' 'It's only a manner of speaking,' she said, 'I'm not actually all that afraid –' 'I never supposed you were. What about coffee? It's only eleven.' 'I've got to go and see a cousin of mine who's in hospital. The Royal Free. You don't happen to know where it is exactly by any chance, do you?' 'The Royal Free,' he said, 'that sounds very expensive, but I'm sure we can find it. We'll share a cab.' 'But there's no evidence it's the way you want to go.' 'There's every evidence,' he said, 'as far as I'm concerned.'

She observed, having nothing of her own to look at, that the papers on his knee comprised the table of contents for some literary conspectus. 'One of the books you've written?' she asked. 'One of the ones I'm going to write,' he said. 'How come it already has an index and page numbers, if it isn't written yet?' 'We start with those,' he said, 'these days. Publishing is now a branch of futurology. I project, therefore I am. Descartes before the horse, you might say.' 'Forgive me looking,' she said, 'but I'm not used to being without something to read, it's like being naked.' 'Allow me to lend you something to cover your nakedness, though I must say you wear it with a good deal of style.' 'Tell me,' she said, 'how often do you travel up to see your wife and children?' 'Ex-wife and children. When I can. Once or twice a month.' 'I wonder if I've ever seen you before,' she said. 'Yes,' he said, 'I wonder.'

They stood side by side in the queue for taxis, decorously impatient. The cabs had to come down a narrow ramp and execute a hairpin turn at the bottom. People shouted 'oy!' as burdened travellers, or foreigners unfamiliar with local proprieties, sought to board prematurely. 'There's really no need,' she said, 'for you to take me to the hospital. The driver'll know where it is.' 'Why deny me the pleasure? I've nothing else to do before midday. I shan't assault you, I promise.' 'Oh, I'm not worried about that,' she said. As he opened the door of the ticking taxi, she put the return half of her ticket in the inside tuck of her purse and straightened her gloves.

While the cab was moving up the ramp to the street, he said:

'Listen, I swear to you I've never said anything like this to a stranger before, and I probably only could say it to a stranger, but I very much want to make love to you. Love.' 'Look,' she said, 'I honestly think it'd be better if I got out –' 'No, please. I mean it. You have extraordinary eyes: you must have Mediterranean blood some-where – Egyptian possibly or Persian – and I find you enormously attractive. Something happened in that train, you know it did.' 'We were both out of breath at the same time,' she said, 'coming from different places, and going to different places.' 'Can't you see your cousin later in the day? I want to take you somewhere and undress you and caress you, very gently, very slowly, and really make it last. How can I persuade you that I'm really sincere?' 'I believe you're really sincere,' she said, 'but you can't persuade me.' 'Deny that it appeals to you, the idea. Deny that you're tempted. Not with those eyes, you can't. You've got too much pride to tell yourself a lie.' 'But not too little to tell you one,' she said. 'Two transient creatures on a transient earth,' he said. 'I'm a transient creature with a home and a husband and children and a sick, frightened cousin who's waiting for me,' she said. 'Two hours in a hotel,' he said, 'and we both have something to bank against oblivion. What on earth makes you say no?' 'Perhaps you making the decision mine,' she said, and then put up a gloved hand against his kiss. 'You said you wouldn't.' 'Promise me something, promise me that if we ever meet again like that, if it ever happens again, we won't talk, we won't say a word, but when we get to London, you'll come with me to a hotel and make love. It'll almost certainly not happen, but promise me that if it does ...' 'Certainly not,' she said. 'That's a bargain then,' he said, and opened the door for her to get out. 'Where are we going now then, guv?' the driver said. He gave the address of a members-only library, his eye on the little red figure punched up on the clock, denoting extras. His late companion sat there with him still and he frowned to see the date against her name in the unwritten chapter of his future contents.

She did everything she had scheduled and even had time for a new hair-do, a present for her husband. She told him she never wanted to go to London again and embraced him breathlessly. But some three or four weeks later, she told him that it was maddening, but she simply had to go up to town. There were several things she wanted to do and someone she had to see.

We Won't Talk About Jonathan

'The first really decent night's sleep I've had,' she said, 'in months.'
'I said it would do you good,' he said, 'being just the two of us.'
'I didn't even have a single nightmare,' she said. 'Personally,' he
said, 'I always dream that it hasn't happened.' 'So do I,' she said,
'that's what makes it a nightmare.' 'We mustn't give up hope,'
he said. 'Oh I think we must,' she said, 'I think it's the only hope.'

He paid the bill and waited for her, with the overnight bag, in
the brown lobby of the little hotel, under a poster advertising the
Château of Biron. Some Germans were speaking French to the
patron from whose right hand dangled a blanched duck, his excuse
for not shaking hands. She came down at last, careful around the
mean slices of the tight staircase. 'Here I am,' she said. 'Is everything
all right?' 'It seems to be,' he said.

They saw the cathedral high up ahead of them across the plain,
the fortress shrine of a faith once imposed by force and now
maintained through courtesy. The road found curves and gradients
in the apparently easy terrain. Heavy weather cast the landscape
in pewter and verdigris. He had resolved not to drive at all fast.
Even a sudden magpie made him glance at her: 'All right?' 'Fine,'
she said.

The cathedral put on rusty height and swelled until it dominated
the city. They were not a dozen kilometres from the place when
the silly motorcyclist began to buzz them. He wore an orange
helmet, with chin piece, and a green anorak which the wind puffed
into quilted supermanly muscles. His machine was not powerful
and even the slow car provided race enough. He seemed to be
teasing them, surging noisily past and then easing the throttle so
that they were bound to catch up again, the old game. 'Let him
go,' she said. 'If only he'd make up his mind,' he said. 'We could
just pull in,' she said. 'There'll only be another one,' he said. A
measly rain began to fall, sticky hint of the storm piling up around

the town. The orange helmet drifted alongside them and hung there as they went into a bend. Then it shot on ahead, the motorcyclist easing himself up on the saddle, parading his youth.

There was a complex roundabout below the town; they had to stop and saw the orange helmet flashing away to their right. 'That's the end of him, thank God,' he said. The route to the cathedral was belatedly marked and their tyres slipped on the ungracious gradient when they took the steep corner. The cathedral was invisible now, they were so close under it. They eased round and saw the boy lying in the black wetness, his motorbike slewed so that it appeared that he was coming back down towards them. The green anorak was puny round his narrow chest. 'Oh God, I shall have to do something.' 'Is it him?' she said. 'You stay here,' he said, 'and I'll . . .'

The boy's arms and trunk were frantically energetic; his legs were still. There was nothing to be done except make him comfortable. He eased the helmet from the childish head and folded his coat under it to keep the fair hair from the wet. A window opened high above the scene and a women leant out. 'Go and call an ambulance,' he shouted up to her. 'I've already called one, Monsieur,' she replied. 'They'll be here in a minute,' he said, and stroked the brow of the frantic boy. 'Monsieur, will you please phone my parents, *please?*' 'Of course,' he said, 'in a minute as soon as someone gets here –' 'My parents,' the boy said, 'please. My father –' 'You just relax.' 'My leg hurts.' 'I know,' he said, 'but help's on the way. They'll be here in a few minutes.' 'I want my parents,' the boy said. Already the ululating sound of the ambulance was audible. 'I'll do it right away,' he said. 'I'll give you the number,' the boy said.

A police motorcyclist led the ambulance efficiently to the spot, supervised by the woman in the high window, whose neighbours had joined the spectators. The ambulance men approached with professional briskness and he honoured the boy's anguish by running to the transparent telephone booth by the cathedral parking. He dialled the number he had been given, but the number was engaged. He signalled to his wife in the parked Rover, but its windscreen was now veiled with the falling and fallen rain. He waited a few seconds and then tried the number again. Again it was engaged. By now they were lifting the fallen boy into the ambulance. He ran back along the road to the Rover. 'Well?' she said. 'I was just trying to get his parents,' he said. 'He's alive,' she said, 'isn't he?' 'I'm sorry,' he said, 'this happening. One of those things, I'm afraid. I ought to give it one more try, the parents.' 'They'll find out sooner or later,' she said, 'it'll either be good news or it won't.' 'Yes,' he said, 'I expect you're right. Look, do you want to go into the cathedral or not?' 'Let's go on,' she said, 'I think it's probably better if we just go on.'

Sleeps Six

They always took a villa on the Mediterranean during the month of August. 'Mugs' month it may be,' Geoff said, 'but this mug can afford it. The kids're at home; Sherry and I keep it free and I can look forward to it all the year round.' Of course he did not lack sane advisers to tell him that he should invest in a decent little property. 'You could let it eleven months in the year, and the twelfth's on the firm.' Geoff preferred to hire his paradise than to be landed with it. Too many dream villas (look what happened to Jilly and Sambo) turned into nightmares from which their owners did not wake until local builders, and local vandals, had parted them from their last property dollar. 'I do not propose,' Geoff said, 'to become Madame la Marquise, and nor does Madame la Marquise!'

'Suit yourself, Geoffrey,' Philip Witham said, small feet, big desk.

'I do,' Geoff said, 'down to the ground.'

'Well, in your case it isn't far.'

'Christ, isn't it marvellous, honestly, Philip? How things've turned out? And a lot of it is thanks to you.'

'Skip the thanks, ten per cent'll be quite sufficient,' Philip Witham said.

'This year I'm bloody well standing you that holiday. This place we've taken sleeps six. The extra bedroom's off on its own, windows on the sea. I can show you the transparencies. They want a thousand quid deposit and they won't take it off just anybody. Six references! Stanley had it last year, he says it's a dream.'

'I'll take it,' Philip said. 'Only I'm never going to make it for more than ten days or so. I have got other clients, you know, even if I do keep them quiet.'

'We'll be there the whole month. It's yours when you want it,' Geoff said.

He and Sherry lived in a Georgian house in Chiswick ('I know,'

56

Philip said, 'it originally belonged to a man called George.') with
an alert staff from whose alertness, come August, they were not
wholly sorry to escape. Big Annie was sent on a paid package with
her mother ('Anything in the brochure short of the Seychelles,
Annie dear') and Pontecorvo was free, in Geoff's words, to buzz
back to Italy and flog all the petrol he had siphoned out of the
Rolls during the year. Geoff drove the family down to the Riviera
or the Costa Mucho. They stopped at all the places they had liked
before they had money and liked even better now that they had.

Geoff had left school at fifteen to enter, as the year-books put
it, 'the industry'. 'What did I do?' he would say to interviewing
journalists who promised not to take much of his time, 'I made
tea for the teaboy.' He had been industrious ever since. Before he
was a producer, he was the best production manager in the business. Everything he had was paid for out of taxed income. If people
thought it an immoral extravagance to live as he did, they were
welcome to their opinions, but not to his drinks while they told
him so. He had come from next door to nowhere (it was on the
Central Line, if anyone was interested) and today he could pick
up the phone and make a five million dollar deal before the pips
had gone. He thought the tax structure in the U.K. 'frankly
diabolical' (he was the director of a Second Division football club
only three points south of the leaders and a mile east of where
he grew up), but he liked it here. He accepted the bloody fool decisions
of the majority until such time as he could get them changed. Sure,
he worked for the Tory party ('Someone has to') and, yes, he did
have an addict's taste for social occasions. He was at Ascot every
year ('with a wife who can wear clothes like Sherry, wouldn't you
be?') and they went to see Rodney at Eton on the Fourth, with
a case of Mumm in the back of the Rolls and a quantity of Fortnum's
canapés to attract the quality. Geoff was a generous host and an
eager guest. He had had plenty of time in his boyhood to discover
how the other half lived; he preferred the half to which he had
now graduated. It amused him to have Philip Witham as his agent,
but would he have stayed with his lordship if he had not been the
best in London, as well as a peer of the realm?

Philip had been born into easy circumstances and made them
difficult. He was sacked from his Public School for introducing a
girl into the celebrations of the first eleven's victory over its

traditional enemy (he scored the winning goal), despite his protest that they had been licensed to bring their own refreshments. He had subsequently been obliged to resign from the army after some trouble with, as he put it, 'the Jews'. He was a man of the eighteenth century born into one which, in the flat fifties at least, suited neither his morals nor his purse. After the army, he drifted around London and earned a fresh set of debts, which his father declined, this time, to settle. He turned for help to Gerry Pereira who happened to be in the process of setting up a talent agency.

'What's that, some kind of a knocking shop?'

'You have it precisely,' Gerry said, 'and you can play the piano in it, if you're good. It's about time you did something for your living apart from signing promises you can't keep.'

'I'll do more or less anything to get your Kosher cousins off my back, Lieutenant Pereira. Buy me a nice lunch and make me a proposition.'

'I'm not sure I wouldn't sooner watch you sweat, you fat *goyish* pig, but I'll take you to Wheeler's first. You've got just one asset, Philip, and that's your charm, what's left of it. It's something I might just be able to get to market for you before it goes off. I'll pay your debts, God help me, and then I'm going to ram your upturned nose against the grindstone until I see sparks. That's my proposition. Take it and you damned well won't leave it.'

'I hope they've got gulls' eggs,' Philip said.

They had been brother cadet officers at Mons when the foundation of the state of Israel was proclaimed. Some ass had made a jeering remark about its prospects. Pereira ordered a bottle of cheap champagne and, with proper and sudden ceremony, uncorked it in his unsubtle neighbour's eye. 'What I admired instantly,' Philip said, 'was your not giving the chap the ghost of a chance to defend himself.'

For all his profligate history, Philip had one undeclared vice: he was, in the right circumstances, extremely diligent. The scholarship he had devoted to racing form was now dedicated to the hurdles and handicaps of show biz. He became an assiduous and, when he had learned the silken ropes, a winning member of Mayfair Management. He was at once ornamental and effective. He did not give himself airs, but he dressed like the lord it flattered the clients not to call him. Americans were enchanted by his shameless vocabulary and his noble willingness to enunciate the unspeakable. (He told one producer that his client could not possibly come to Rome for the money suggested: 'I will not have him endanger his health by having to choose his women from the syphilitic side of the street.') He treated the business as a joke, which was why, being very business-like, he often had the last laugh.

Gerry Pereira introduced him to Geoff in the early days, when neither was anything much and Geoff was slightly less: he was coming up to thirty, married to Lesley-with-the-accent, and making a sorry living in television commercials. His unglamorous status did not prevent him from having half a dozen jejune projects: he had optioned a bad thriller and was waiting for a writer to do a worse script. He dealt from a deck of sweat-darkened visiting cards with 'producer' in dated italics after his name. He frequented pubs in Wardour Street and had coffee where others had lunch. He was trying all the old tricks, but he lacked the right rabbits and he had far too many hats. Philip found his naive ambition endearing; he found Philip an education.

One evening, after Philip had wangled an associate producership for him and they had been out for a claret lesson to celebrate, they were walking through Shepherd Market when a particularly dishy tart got out of a taxi just ahead of them. Philip conducted the negotiations. She led them – cantilevered tits, tightly waisted light blue skirt, flared over naked legs and high heels – up uncarpeted stairs to a well-lit room with a small electric fire. 'How do we go about it?' Geoff said.

'We toss for ends,' Philip said, 'don't we?'

Afterwards, they walked to where Geoff had left the Rapier. They made no spoken allusion to Polly either then or later, but if Geoff threatened to become pompous (success would put a bust of Napoleon on his trophy shelf), a reminding humour would flash in Philip's eyes. And if his lordship was too lordly (the new offices had a waiting-room where some clients waited), Geoff's look could recall to him that night when Philip, finished, sat on the floor looking at Polly's printed recipes for resurrection while he himself went on to the final. ('*Well*, dear,' the girl said.)

In the street, as Geoff was unlocking the Sunbeam, Philip said: 'You really want to get rid of that wife of yours, don't you?'

'You haven't even met her,' Geoff said.

'That's what I mean,' Philip said.

He had nothing against Lesley-with-the-accent, but it needed no Pythian powers to divine that sentimental lust had propelled Geoff into an adolescent marriage he was now too squeamish to quit. Philip introduced him to Sherry Holland.

Sherry had been working in Mayfair Management, but she wanted a more responsible job. Geoff needed a girl Friday, didn't he? ('I need her Thursday,' he said.) She was tall and slim and had just come back from a year in the States (a cousin was a travel agent in St Louis). She was wearing a narrow black skirt and a white blouse, one button undone at the throat (coral pendant), when Geoff first saw her. There was a sort of intense modesty about her. She was very pretty but she was without vanity. 'She's actually much too good for you,' Philip said, 'but then so are most of the things you're likely to need.' In fact, not only did Geoff fall in love with Sherry Holland but – the long joy of his life – she also fell in love with him. 'I greatly distrust happy endings,' Philip said, when Geoff asked that he 'stand beside him' at the wedding, 'but what can a poor pander do? All I ask is that you allow me to choose your tailor before the ceremony.' (Lesley-with-the-accent had been primed to be properly indignant and sued for a prompt divorce.)

Geoff wondered, nudged by that realism which neither vanity nor sentiment could banish, what made Sherry prefer him to Philip. Why had she turned her back on a title and money in order to take up with a not yet established producer with a charmless background? 'I love you,' she said.

'I love *you*,' he said, as if there was a contradiction somewhere. 'I love you so much I can only say that I can promise you one thing –'

'Only one? Perhaps I'd better be going!'

'There'll never be anyone else. Not for a night. Not for ten minutes. Never. No matter where I go and you don't. No one.'

Philip was best man; the reception was at the Festival Hall (smart, but not pretentious) and they went on their honeymoon in the new Jag: 'touring', as the social columns used to say when Geoff read them in the Public Library out where Lesley-with-the-accent was holding the baby. They made their first contact with the Med during that trip; they had been going ever since. Their Augusts were celebrations of a marriage which showed not a scratch after nearly twenty years. Sherry was the foundation of Geoff's private happiness and his public reputation. 'If it weren't for her, I might well be the biggest shit unhung. But I can't swindle people during the day and go to bed with that lady at night. She'd know. I don't make dirty movies and I don't make violent movies; I'm a family man and incidentally it's the best investment I ever made.' He drove a Rolls and a hard bargain, but though he would always give you a lift in the one and keep his word in the other, he was perhaps too much the victim of envy (mother of I-must-be-honest criticism) to be entirely popular. People sneered at his social climbing and at the commercialism of his taste. When he put a Henry Moore in the garden, people said it was because he wanted to watch it grow.

Philip was as successful, financially, as his clients. He bought out Gerry Pereira in the mid-sixties (Gerry went to California to make custom-built cars) and under his firmly lackadaisical control Mayfair Management looked after the best stable of writers, directors and producers in the business. 'I'm not exclusive,' he said, 'merely greedy. I won't play nanny to clients still in their prams.' He seemed always to have time for those he did have: each had the impression that he was the favourite. When Geoff went to South Street, the telephone never rang in Philip's office; not a single file or letter suggested that he had any other clients at all. He was never in a hurry and he was always there before you were. What kept him so nimble? 'There's no exercise like a four-figure phone bill, it keeps you right on your toes, and other people's.'

His pleasures were as costly as his business, and less fortunate. He pursued his ladies with flowers, hire cars (he had never learned to drive, 'except a tank, briefly') and tickets to theatres and winter sunshine. He chose frequently and he chose badly. 'I have,' he said, 'a propensity for beauty at any price, and you know what the price usually is.' He craved fidelity from the faithless, steadiness from the flighty. He was on top of the world one week and ready to jump off it the next. The spare room (later suite) at Chiswick saw a succession of 'fiancées' whom Geoff and Sherry would cherish with optimistic attention. At first they regarded Lady Jane as no more likely to endure than Davina or Stephanie, though they were pleased that she appeared to have some genuine affection for Philip and she did actually volunteer to take something out to the kitchen, to which neither Vanessa nor Wendy, Nuala nor Miranda ever found the way. (Big Annie had Sundays.) Lady Jane was not the most beautiful of Philip's ladies, but she had a slow and humorous drawl and her blue eyes seemed to see something in dear old P.W. apart from the main chance. She was the daughter of an earl ('That's why I thought I'd bring her straight to you, squire,' Philip said) and she treated the expanding Philip with casual and correcting confidence. Her father had been in the cabinet, though not for very long, during the early sixties, and he was still counted in the Conservative party. Geoff was pleased when Philip asked him, over billiards in the refurbished garden room (the builders, like all builders, had almost finished), whether he was willing to be his best man if and when Lady Jane said yes.

She did so the night before they all had dinner at Cunningham's on the eve of Sherry and Geoff's departure for the continent. Geoff ordered a bottle of Dom Pérignon; Philip ordered more. When he rose to announce to the restaurant that he was the luckiest man in the world ('He can't be,' Geoff whispered to Sherry, 'because I am'), Lady Jane said, 'Philip, sit *down*, there's a good dog.'

Philip hung penitent paws in front of him and winked.

'You know,' Sherry said, 'it's going to be very difficult to know who to introduce my girl friends to, now Philip's going to be out of the running.'

'Introduce them to me,' Lady Jane said.

On the pavement, by the shining Rolls (Pontecorvo's parting gloss), they all looked forward to the tenth, when Philip and Jane were flying to Nice. Geoff kissed Lady Jane, Sherry kissed Philip and then his fiancée; Philip and Geoff shook hands, smiling. The entrance to Shepherd Market was just across the road. 'Many, many congratulations,' Geoff said, 'both of you.'

The first ten days of the holiday went so fast, Geoff said, that he thought there must be a hole in the month. The villa was merely sensational; it had its own pool ('Alison,' Sherry said, 'if you dive in much more often you'll wear a hole in it') and access, between exaggerated pink and purple bougainvillaea, to a tiny private beach, where they could laze and swim without any clothes on, impervious to binoculars. Geoff put the Ambre Solaire on a bundle of scripts ('essential in case the Chancellor shows up') and admired his wife's unfallen breasts. 'Nearly twenty years,' he said, 'and look at me: ready and willing.'

'Nearly twenty years,' she said, 'I suppose it's about time you were.'

'I'm looking forward to Philip and Jane, aren't you, darling?'

'Don't worry,' she said, 'it'll be fine.'

Alison and Rodney were playing tennis with some residents of Jersey they had met at a party on Bernie Pinto's yacht, so Sherry and Geoff drove into the airport alone. They had gin fizzes at the bar, while they waited for the flight and waved to a Peruvian princess they had met at Bernie and Bunty's. Sherry's eyes were shining, her shades on top of the springy hair, slim fingers enjoying the cool of the chilled glass. When the London flight was announced, Geoff said, 'Lots of time for one more. They're bound to be loaded with luggage they'll have to wait for. When a woman's going to take her clothes off on the beach, she generally brings plenty of them.'

Eventually they ambled towards the gate as passengers with hand luggage began to come through, going on tiptoe to look over and see if anyone had got the message to meet them. 'Christ,' Geoff said, 'here comes Phil.'

Philip was wearing a heavy blue pinstripe suit, a pink shirt and almost matching tie. He was unshaven and stumbled under the weight of a small attaché case. 'Oh God,' Sherry said.

'Fucking bitch,' Philip said.

'What the hell have you done now?' Sherry said.

'Not enough,' Philip said. 'Whatever it was, it evidently wasn't enough. Sherry, my darling, I want to sit down and cry and I want you to hold my hand. Where does one go?'

They had had Philip on bad days, and nights, but nothing compared to his present desolation. He smelt awful. He refused to be jollied or bullied from his slumped misery. He followed them about, in his pinstripe suit, sweaty and disconsolate. He almost telephoned his lady a dozen times and then flung the phone inaccurately into its cradle. They tried patience, they tried impatience. Nothing worked. Philip's capacity for self-mockery had been left in London. The children, who had always looked forward to seeing him, were prudently evasive. The weather turned grey. They had three days of lacrimose hell. Philip's socks became so smelly that he discarded them and wore his Jermyn Street shoes without any socks at all. Geoff finally had to order him to have a bath or leave the house. 'You're right,' he said, 'you're right, and don't think I'm going to forgive you for it. While we're at it, I may as well tell you something, I'm going to sell out. Mayfair Management, I'm selling out. They've been after me for it, they can have it. I'm sick to death of the bloody place. You've had fifteen years of my bloody life. I'm damned if you're getting any more. Nanny is hanging up her boots.'

'Oh for God's sake, Philip, pull yourself together. You're behaving like a silly old woman throwing crockery at the wall.'

'If I'm a silly old woman then I'm a silly old woman.'

'You're a silly old woman who's ruining my bloody holiday. I don't mind for myself, I mind for Sherry. I mind for the kids. Pull yourself together.'

'I've had my fill of that. I now propose to pull myself apart.'

'What the hell went wrong?'

'Did you ever tell the lovely Sherry about that night in Shepherd Market?'

'Suppose I call Jane and ask her to come on down here. Will you get a hold on yourself? You know she's fond of you –'

'Fond of,' Philip said. 'We're all fond of each other, aren't we? You're fond of me. What good does it do us? Did you? Tell her?'

'I really can't remember,' Geoff said, 'and I certainly don't want to talk about it now.'

'No, you certainly don't, do you? I should never have let you have her, you know that, don't you? Sherry. Shall I tell you why I did?'

'I think that would almost certainly be a mistake,' Geoff said. 'And probably a lie as well.'

'Shall I?'

'What happened, Philip old lad? Between you and Jane.'

'I let you have her because I thought you two suburbanites would set each other off to perfection.'

'Well, you were absolutely right, my son: we did, to perfection. Now, shall we have a drink?'

'Let's have a couple,' Philip said. 'And how did I know she was a suburbanite?'

'How did you know who was, Philip?' Sherry said, up from the beach.

'You know who, my pretty, you know very well. Because she was such a bloody prude, weren't you, in those days? Are you still?'

'I can't remember them,' Sherry said. 'But I expect you're right. You usually are. Do I get a drink? You sound terribly savage about it though, why is that?'

'Because I love you, of course,' Philip said. 'Oh don't look so bloody patient and amused, you bitch, will you?'

'I thought I was looking touched and sympathetic. You can see why I quit Drama School, can't you?'

'I remember looking at you at the Festival Hall at that ludicrous bloody wedding reception and thinking, Christ I've been a bloody fool. Why can't you have a row or something, Geoffrey? Why can't you get kidnapped or something and I could comfort Sherry as she deserves? I am your oldest friend, aren't I?'

'You were. Philip's thinking of selling the agency,' Geoff said. 'So we don't really have to go on being nice to him if we don't want to. Shall we kick him out?'

'Kick me and I kick back, and probably bite and scratch as well. I had my colours for biting and scratching, in case you didn't know. Sherry, *are* you still a prude? You'd give me a kiss now if I asked you for one, wouldn't you?'

'Possibly,' Sherry said. 'If you went and had a shave and brushed your teeth.'

'Done,' Philip said, 'I'm prepared to close that deal right away. *Un seul baiser*. In my room in five – no, seven – minutes, all right?'

'It seems cheap at the price, don't you think so darling?'

'Doesn't concern me,' Geoff said. 'It's a matter between consenting adults.'

'I'll go and have a shave,' Philip said, 'and clean my teeth. And you'll be down, right?'

'Seven minutes,' Sherry said.

Geoff smiled at his wife, glanced at his watch and went into the villa. The children had decided to stay on the Pintos' yacht for a couple of nights. They were going down the coast to San Remo if the captain approved of the weather. Geoff took a script from the stack and sat in a loosely buttoned chair, Gucci feet on the matching beige stool, and took out his new glasses. Outside, cicadas were winding their watches for the night.

He turned a dozen pages and then put the black folder face down on his lap. Sherry came in through the now dark windows from the terrace. 'I hope you only gave him one,' he said. She bent down and kissed him on the mouth. Her lips were warm, her tongue promising between his teeth. 'And I sincerely trust it wasn't that one.'

Philip arrived, looking pink. He was shaved and he had combed his hair. 'I've been an absolute cunt,' he said. 'I'm sorry.'

'Well!' Geoff said. 'Sleeping beauty! Cured by a single kiss!'

'*Un seul baiser*,' Philip said. 'You'd better go and change, my pretty.'

'Better call them first,' Sherry said.

'Call who? What's going on around here?' Geoff said.

'I've decided it's time to turn over a new leaf,' Philip said, 'and we're going to make it a gold one. We're calling the Oasis to see if a peer of the realm can persuade them to let us have a table for three. Never underestimate the importance of things people no longer consider important.'

It was difficult to get a table, but it was not, for his lordship, impossible. They drove into La Napoule, inspecting the unsteady parade of yachts tethered in the wobbly water. 'You know,' Geoff said, 'I'm not a carping man by nature, but it seems a bit weird old Bernie getting a life peerage when it's an open secret he's been avoiding tax on overseas earnings for the last God knows how many years. It's not illegal and I don't grudge it him, but it seems a funny carry on.'

'It's all a funny carry on, Geoffrey. Bernie's bilked the Chancellor with one hand and lashed out a hundred and fifty thou on his kiddies' ophthalmic unit with the other. Good luck to him. How else could he do it? And how do you think Jane's great-great-grandfather got to be an earl? Virtue? It was all on account of what happened when the Prince of Wales didn't have his armour on. You think there's justice? There's love and there's money and that's about it. In my case, the latter without the former, but what can one do? We're going to have a sumptuous evening and tomorrow I shall telephone London and get the invaluable Fiona to send me some clothes. She can put them on the next plane.'

'Tomorrow we'll go into Cannes and *buy* you some bloody clothes, you old Jew,' Geoff said.

'You ought to call Jane,' Sherry said, 'and tell her she's a fool and she's to come down here at once. I'll bet you she's only waiting for the chance.'

'Sherry my pretty, you may be right, but I'd sooner not discuss it. Let her wait. We'll have a sumptuous evening and we shall not look back for any reluctant Eurydice. Onward and upward, my friends.'

Philip was as gracious as he had been surly. Yet Geoff's gratitude was, for all the petalled excellence of the *millefeuilles de saumon*, more effortful than spontaneous. His appetite was curdled: something in the script had disagreed with him. Sherry smiled and laughed and leaned to touch his hand as she proved to Philip how much she was enjoying herself. Philip smoked a cigar and promised that he was completely cured. 'Don't ever put your kisses on the National Health, my darling. They're strictly London Clinic.'

They drove home in silence. Geoff thanked Philip for the evening, with an effusiveness that proved how glad he was to have something for which to thank him, and then went into the big drawing room and resumed his script while Sherry got ready for bed. She came in at last, in her nightie, and asked whether he was coming or not. He looked at her through his new glasses and said he would be there in a minute.

There was a note from Philip on the coffee grinder when they went into the kitchen in the morning. He had woken early and had decided to take the bicycle (there were a couple in the garage) and ride into Cannes. 'We shall have the whole morning to ourselves,' Sherry said.

'Yes,' Geoff said.

Philip telephoned at lunch time to say that he would not be back till later, if that suited them. And later he telephoned to say that, if they didn't mind, he might not return till after dinner. Sherry came out and stood by the lounger where Geoff was still working his way through the stack of scripts. 'We've got the whole day to ourselves,' she said.

'What's left of it,' Geoff said. 'I wish he wouldn't bugger about.'

'Well, if he's going to, surely it's better if he does it on his own. What do you want to do for supper?'

'I don't mind,' Geoff said. 'Do you want to go out?'

'Do you?'

'Last night was as much going out as I can take for a day or two, quite honestly. I wish we hadn't gone with him now. We could've gone on our own.'

'I'll make an omelette and we can finish the Brie.'

'I don't really want anything,' Geoff said.

Sherry said: 'Darling, what's the matter? Migraine?'

'All these bloody scripts,' he said, 'trying so hard to please. Shit with sugar, all of them.'

'Is it me kissing Philip? I wouldn't have done it if you'd said you didn't approve.'

'I didn't approve. I didn't disapprove. Christ, when you think of the business we're in, the way people behave. It's probably not that at all. It's probably the thought of Alison with the pimply Pinto boy. I don't know what it is.'

'Philip was being so bloody I thought it was cheap at the price,' she said. 'He said it'd cheer him up and, after all, at least it did.'

'At least or at most,' Geoff said. 'I expect you were absolutely right. Perhaps it'd cheer me up.'

'Come to bed then,' she said.

'We haven't eaten.'

'It might give you an appetite.'

'Sherry, there's no need to play Nurse Edith Cavell for my benefit.'

'Ah! Sorry.' The smile remained on her lips; the flesh stiffened around it. 'I'll leave you to your scripts.'

He read on for a while, lowering the script to his lap from time to time, but lacking the will to go in search of her. Silence filled the house like a Trappist's eloquence. After a while, he heard her come on to the terrace again. He put his espadrilles back on his feet and went outside. She returned his kiss but avoided his lips. 'Finished?'

'What did he mean about you being a prude?' he said.

'Oh! Beginning! I *see*. What did he mean when?'

'What did he want you to do?'

'What do people ever want young girls to do? Open wide, I presume.'

'Was there something specific?' he said. 'It sounded as if there was something specific.'

'Oh darling,' she said, 'please don't.'

'Why the hell did I have to ask him down here?' Geoff said. 'Everything was perfect till he arrived. He doesn't seem like the same person at all.'

'He is,' Sherry said.

They were in bed when the taxi drove up. Doors slammed and there must have been some mishap unloading the bicycle from the boot: they heard curses and a yelp and then giggles. 'He's got somebody with him,' Sherry said.

'He's got the driver,' Geoff said.

'Good night, Geoffrey,' Sherry said.

The girl was on the beach when they went down for an early swim, bright with determination to start the day afresh. She was wearing a pair of boxer shorts and plastic cups over her eyes. She was blonde and about twenty-three years old. 'Oh hullo,' she said, 'I hope you don't mind, only Phil's still snoring away and I thought I might as well. Chrissie Hollins. I hope it's O.K. if I'm here. You're Geoff and Sherry, aren't you? Phil told me all about you.'

'That was quick,' Geoff said.

'Sorry?'

'You're very welcome, Chrissie. Did you sleep all right?'

'I never have any trouble there,' she said. 'Lovely place. I hope you don't object to me not wearing me top, only I might turn a decent colour if I get some early sun.'

'Not at all. We rarely wear anything down here,' Geoff said.

'I've burnt the tops of my legs, that's why I put these on. My bum's bright red. If I showed it in the street, I'd stop the traffic. All I need now is to burn me boobs. I've never met a film producer before. I don't suppose you'd give me a part the way I look at the moment.'

'It would depend on the part,' Geoff said.

'Look, please don't mind me. If you want to go in swimming or anything. If I'm in the way, say.'

They swam out into the deep water where it was bruised purple by the reef that closed the bracket of the little bay. 'Nice figure,' Sherry said.

'And a nose you could open letters with,' Geoff said. 'What the hell does he think he's up to?'

When they went into the kitchen after their swim, Philip was grinding coffee. He had on a pair of pale blue shorts and a T-shirt MADE IN THE U.S.A. 'You've been shopping,' Geoff said.

'Did you see Chrissie? What do you think of her? Isn't she divine? She's the straightest thing I've ever met in my life. You're a silly bloody snob, Geoff, you know that, don't you? Lady Jane! This girl's the real thing. She makes me feel like a bloody schoolboy again. Three times in one night, no trouble! She's a fucking marvel, literally.' He put his arms round Sherry's neck and kissed her. 'His lordship's back in the race, my darling.'

Geoff said: 'What does she want for breakfast?'

'Same as she had for tea. These kids, Chrissie's generation, they're amazing. They've got a lesson for all of us. There's only one kind of sincerity that means a damn and that's the sincerity of the flesh. What do you want? What do I want? Simple as that.'

'That certainly sounds very simple,' Geoff said.

'Look, be honest, would you sooner I took her to a hotel? I'm perfectly willing. Only she was dying to meet you. Films, you know what they think of films, her generation. She's completely unspoilt. I'm going to change all that, of course, but for the moment, that's what she is. She does everything, Geoff, everything.'

'I'm very happy for you,' Geoff said.

'But naturally. Everything Polly did, in spades. For the sheer devil of it.'

'Who was Polly?' Sherry said.

'It none of it matters, old boy, that's what she's taught me. Liberation. It none of it matters. I'd better go and find her. She's very shy, you know, socially. She thinks you're bloody royalty. I'll go and give her a shout.'

'I wish to Christ,' Geoffrey said, 'that we could find a way of getting out of here for a few days.'

'Tell them to, if that's how you feel about it.'

'Be honest. How can we? We can't. Can he really not see what a grisly little tart she is?'

'Of course he can,' Sherry said. 'Why do you think he's so happy?'

The girl wore her boxer shorts and a pair of tennis shoes and nothing else, all day. She was, they had to admit, eager to please. She washed up, she brought them drinks and she certainly made conversation. If she was shy, she was not reticent. 'I hear you and

Phil used to knock about together quite a bit,' she said to Geoff,
while Sherry was doing something about lunch.

'Once upon a time,' he said.

'Your wife's lovely.'

'Thank you.'

'Considering her age. You must treat her right.'

'I try,' Geoff said.

'Do you mind if I take these trunk things off? Only I think I could
afford a little sun again. I don't see much in my job.'

'By all means. What do you do, Chrissie?'

'I'm a telephonist, aren't I? Solicitor's office. You have to take
what you can get. Phil says he's going to find me something better.
I'd like to be a receptionist really.'

'Would you really?' Geoff said.

'I'm into pop a lot. He says he might be able to get me into
something in music publishing. He says I've got the credentials.'
She turned and grinned at him. 'You weren't always a stuffy bugger
from what I hear.'

'Who's stuffy?' he said. 'And I'm certainly no bugger.'

'Give us a kiss, Geoffrey.'

'I don't seem to have one on me,' Geoff said.

'Trying to give them up?' she said. 'I was only being friendly.
Is Sherry jealous?'

'No,' he said, 'I am.'

'I don't think I get,' she said. 'You've come a long way, haven't
you, since you started?'

'Judging from the miles on the clock,' Geoff said. 'Not to mention
the hours, and don't you!'

'She's beautiful, Sherry. Should I go and help her?'

'She said she was all right. Philip's with her.'

'He's been potty about her for years, only you're his friend, so
he's not done nothing about it.'

'I don't think he'd necessarily have got all that far,' Geoff said.

'He told me about what she did the other night. I thought that
was the nicest thing I ever heard, honestly. Oh look at that, my
skirt's turning colour too! How about that? Me homespun! It's
usually much darker.'

'I never heard it called that before,' Geoff said. 'That's nice! When
do you have to be back at work?'

71

'I don't really,' she said, 'do I? Not now.'

'The great thing about her,' Philip said, when he and Geoff were watching the girls swim that afternoon, 'is that she's so independent. You might not believe it, but she's very competent. She was running her mother's shop when she was fourteen. Did the accounts, the whole thing. Her dad died when she was eleven. She's really had a rough time.'

'What kind of shop?' Geoff said.

'How should I know what kind of shop?'

There was a telephone call during the evening of Chrissie's second day. 'Alison,' Sherry said. 'The Pintos are taking the yacht to Corsica for a couple of days and they've got two spare berths. Do we want to come?'

'After protracted thought,' Geoff said, 'yes, please.'

They hoped that Chrissie and Philip wouldn't mind, but the children so wanted them to go on the trip and they saw so little of them these days. 'You and Chrissie're welcome to the place, obviously, and we'll see you when we get back.'

Bernie and Bunty were, of course, conspicuous with generosity. Bernie wore a cap with an anchor on it and was for ever going up to have a word with the skipper. He took the wheel when the automatic pilot had been set and he consulted the chart when the cliffs of Corsica were clearly in view. Bunty wore diamanté wedge heels and a trouser suit so badged with glitter that Sherry had to keep her shades on. They sat in chintz chairs on the scrubbed deck and were served with incessant meals. The Pinto children complained that there was something wrong with the cassette-T.V. 'The sweet smell of excess,' Geoff said, 'and I never needed it more.'

'You ought to get yourself one of these,' Bernie said.

'I lack your touch, Horatio,' Geoff said.

'From what I hear from Sidney, you've got the half-Nelson touch all right,' Bunty said.

'Sidney!' Geoff said. 'He should talk. And obviously does. I've got to go out to L.A. soon as I get back to London and all because of S.G.M. Bernie, tell me something about this Ophthalmic Unit of yours. I'm not in your league, obviously, but I do feel I ought to do something in the charity line. What do you think really deserves looking at?'

'Depends what you're after,' Bernie Pinto said. 'The big one, or just a knighthood.'

'I don't care about those things, for heaven's sake. What about Spastics?'

'More money than they know what to do with. I'll tell you what, if you're serious, Geoffrey, there's a man in London, ex-Colonel Coldstream Guards, you ought to go and see.'

'Lieutenant-Colonel,' Bunty said.

'He's got the whole thing at his fingertips. The Honourable Terence somebody. Lieutenant-Colonel. I've got his name downstairs. He's the fellow to get in touch with. Calls himself Colonel, doesn't he?'

They had quiet hopes, Geoff and Sherry, that when they returned to the villa three nights later, Philip and Chrissie might be gone. They were packed, but they had not left. Philip insisted on a last dinner in town. Alison and Rodney had been warned; they were tactful, but nothing could quite prepare them for Chrissie. When Norman and Dixie came by the table (Norman was scouting locations for a war picture from a command post in the *Hôtel du Cap*), Philip introduced her as 'my fiancée'. Chrissie's independence had apparently been overcome. 'And you know my best man, of course,' Philip said.

'How are you, Geoff?' Norman said. 'Congratulations.'

'What on?'

'Enjoy your dinner,' Norman said.

As they drove to the airport in the morning, Philip said: 'It's not going to be anything flashy. Just a few friends. You know how she hates ceremony. Only if you'd just do the routine honours, I'd be – you know – and so'd Chrissie, wouldn't you?' Philip turned and smiled at the girls in the back.

'Just tell me the time and place,' Geoff said.

'I love her Geoffrey,' Philip said, head down. 'She's not Debrett, I know that. My mother'd have a fit. I don't give a bugger. She's what I want. She hasn't got a mean bone in her body. She's alive, Geoff, that's what it comes to. There's nothing you can't say to her. For once in my life, I'm not jealous even of you and Sherry. Don't think badly of me, will you?'

'Not unless you sell the agency,' Geoff said.

'Chrissie'd kill me. She's a businesswoman, Geoff. She's got a brain. She's clever. She was reading one of those scripts in bed the other night – during the intermission – and she made some very shrewd comments. Very shrewd indeed.'

'I'd like to hear them,' Geoff said.

'You and Sherry are my dearest friends. Always were. And now I have additional reason to be grateful. It's thanks to you I ran into Chrissie. If you hadn't asked me down here – made us feel welcome –'

'Oh shut up,' Geoff said.

'You can trust her, you know. She's open and honest, but she won't say anything she shouldn't. You don't have to worry. She may know, but she won't say.'

'Won't say what?' Geoff said.

'Those things just aren't important to her,' Philip said. 'If I tell her to keep her mouth shut, she won't dream of opening it.'

Chrissie kissed Geoff on the mouth when their flight was called. 'She probably didn't know you can kiss people anywhere else,' Geoff said, when they had finished waving.

'Bet she did,' Sherry said.

They had another nine days in the villa and they made the best of them, which meant that they were not quite as good as they had hoped. True, Alison and Rodney were with them again, content to return to the domestication which had earlier made them so restless. ('Nice to be back to Norman,' Rodney said.) Geoff and Sherry found themselves wondering, when they were alone (in bed or washing up), whether Philip had changed or whether he had always been like that. Geoff was uneasy at Sherry's indifference to Philip's fall from graciousness.

'I thought you liked him.'

'I do like him, but he's always been a shifty bugger, everyone knows that.'

'You're awfully nice to him, if that's what you think about him.'

'I like him. I said. But he's an opportunist.'

'In other words, you don't trust him.'

'I trust him to be an opportunist. Be your age, Geoffrey.'

'Not if I can help it,' Geoff said.

The telephone rang. It was (of course) Philip; there was good news, if you could call lots of money good news. Geoff had a pencil, put on the new glasses and jotted down some figures. 'I told them you might not be happy cross-lateralizing it with the other picture,' Philip said, 'but otherwise it seems quite a decent arrangement.'

'It's very decent, Philip my dear, as well you know. Except that I'm never very keen on cross-lateral deals. They only come into operation when one of your horses takes a toss. Tell you what, tell them I'll agree if they'll raise our percentage by, say, five per cent, when both pictures are in profit. Try that one on them.'

'They won't agree.'

'In that case, fight to the death until you surrender. O.K.? How's Chrissie?'

'Something I wanted to ask you on that.'

'You already did, and I agreed. When's the ceremony?'

'Something else,' Philip said. 'Cross-lateral with that. She wants a job.'

'I thought she was going to work on you.'

'Do you think she could come and see you when you get back? She's no fool, you know, and she really took a liking to you. Father figure.'

'Thanks a lot, brother figure,' Geoff said. 'Well, of course, she can come and see me. What does she want to do?'

'Anything you want her to, roughly. How's the weather?'

'I think it'll last till the end of the week,' Geoff said, 'if we don't use it all at once. Anything else?'

'I think that's about it,' Philip said, 'unless you have.'

They drove home without haste, looking forward to Big Annie's welcome and the sight of Pontecorvo, mahogany with native sunshine, ready to resume custody of the Rolls ('Rather a nasty squeak in the cocktail cabinet door, Ponters'). They saw plenty of English cars but no English papers until they were back at the house. Sherry went straight for the gossip, Geoff for the Trades. Her news was hotter than his. She brought him the *Mail*, folded back to display Philip in grey topper and all the trimmings. On his arm was Lady Jane. 'St Peter's Eaton Square,' Sherry said.

'I don't believe it,' Geoff said.

'Yes, you do,' Sherry said.

'He never said a word.'

'He may not have, but he's certainly signed on the bottom line.'

'He never said a bloody word. When did I speak to him?

Wednesday. When he asked me to find Chrissie a job. He never said a bloody word. You know what it is, don't you? I'm not good enough for the bloody Earl of Stratford. I'll bet you anything you like that's what's behind it.'

'Not much of an arras,' Sherry said, 'if that's all there is behind it.'

'Who the hell do you think he got? As best man?'

'Gerry Pereira,' Sherry said, 'it says in the *Express*.'

'I wonder what the Earl thought of him.'

'I expect they enjoyed a joke together,' Sherry said.

'At my expense,' Geoff said. 'I'm not standing for it, you know. I shan't stay with him.'

'Oh darling, you know Philip –'

'I do now. I'm sorry, Sherry, but this is sheer malicious treachery, it really is. He could've told me. If he was in that much of a hurry, we could've flown home and sent Ponters out for the Roller.'

'He probably had to strike while the iron was tepid,' Sherry said.

'No, I'm sorry, it's a deliberate slap in the face. It's sheer bloody snobbery.'

'Oh darling,' Sherry said, 'you're much posher than Gerry Pereira.'

'I wasn't an officer,' Geoff said, 'and that sort of thing is more important to Philip bloody Witham than anything else, when it comes to it. And it's come to it. I shan't stay with him, I mean it.'

'I enjoyed our dawdle home, much better than going to some silly bloody wedding.'

'I enjoyed it too, but that's not the point.'

'It's my point.'

'What makes you so willing to forgive Philip suddenly?'

'He got lucky with Lady Jane and he thought he'd better tie the knot while he had his finger on it. I don't say he won't regret it, but you don't have to take it personally. He couldn't believe his luck; he grabbed it before it changed. I should call him up and give him a big kiss.'

'Like the one you gave him,' Geoff said.

'You wanted him to cheer up, didn't you?'

'It's a deliberate humiliation. God, when I think of that awful little tart and how nice we were to her! I spend God knows how many hours of my precious holiday pretending to be pleased that he's wished an illiterate little scrubber on to us, making her welcome, listening to her nonsense, commiserating with her red bum and finally agreeing to be best man at their wedding and then I come home and find that I've been – been –'

'Let off the hook,' Sherry said, 'just like Philip. If you're his friend you ought to be glad. You wouldn't want him married to her, would you?'

'And I've got to see her, I've got to give her a job. I'm fucked if I will.'

'Probably,' Sherry said.

'He knew then, when he asked me, he knew then it was all off. He's dead sly, you know, he really is. He takes a malicious pleasure in deceiving people.'

'Usually on your behalf,' Sherry said.

'He got you to do something, didn't he?'

'Who was Polly?' Sherry said.

'He even told you about that, did he?'

'He indicated.'

'They're shit, those people, aren't they, finally? The so-called aristocracy. Give me Bernie Pinto, frankly.'

'Birthday or Christmas?' Sherry said.

'He's a poisoner, Philip, and he always was. What did he get you to do?'

'You're a fool to go on about this, Geoff, you know.'

'If he fucked you, I'll kill him.'

'I lent him a hand,' Sherry said. 'Do you want a divorce?'

'Very modern of you,' Geoff said. '*Très* show biz.'

'I thought it was the least I could do.'

'I can think of less,' Geoff said.

'I didn't want the holiday buggered,' she said. 'Now do what you like about it.'

'That's what you wouldn't do for him twenty years ago, is it?'

'I suppose so,' she said, 'roughly. If I hadn't been so prim and proper, I suppose *I* might've been her ladyship. It's a thought, isn't it?'

'You still will be,' Geoff said, 'I promise you. You still will be. And we won't ask either of them to the party.'

'Just the Earl,' Sherry said.

He'll See You Now

She had been in analysis for seven years. When she first came to New York, there were weeks at a time when she feared she would not be able to afford him any more. She preferred to wait table (*and* not eat) rather than to break her appointment. He was, she told him, the only thing that kept her going: if she was successful now, it was because he had gotten so expensive. ('I'm not expensive, Miss Carlsen,' he told her, 'but I do have an office to run.') Recently everything had started to come up roses: she was writing and performing in her own T.V. show; she had cabaret; she was busy busy. Yet she never failed to show up at 93 Central Park West, on the button, even when she did a month in Vegas and had to take the Red Eye Special, there and back in ten hours.

The elevator opened into a little private lobby (tropical plant in capillary-action tub, long-snouted orange watering-can on stand-by) and sometimes she would meet Mrs Stein, anxious with keys, glasses on a steel-ball necklace, propping a lap full of packages against the hall stand. 'Hullo, Mrs Stein,' she would say, and press the patients' bell, though the same entrance was common to office and home. She waited at the open door till the nurse came. The doctor favoured formality (his nurse never varied: 'He'll see you now,') and he wore a dark suit and British-looking tie. It took four years of weekly meetings (except August, when an emergency number was handed to the suicide class) before she dared to suggest that maybe he could call her Nattie. By then he had learned of her eight lovers (seven male) so far and of her fear that one breast was bigger than the other ('It is, Miss Carlsen, often, but no one's going to criticize you for that.'); he had encouraged her to tell him about her father ('Is that love or hate, Dr Stein?') and she had confessed her uncertainty about whether or not she should depilate totally. She wanted to be more naked than was humanly possible. Why was that, Dr Stein? She told him she wasn't sure whether she really wanted to be fucked by two black men in masks ('A Jewish girl from Philadelphia!') or whether she just wanted to tell him she did. It was after that session that he came to call her Nattie.

In those seven years the world was changing and she felt the tide of those changes. The moon had cursed women for centuries; now it was C.B.S. news that made her bleed. Throughout the sixties (a decade that counted much of the seventies), she tormented herself with hourly bulletins: others were on drugs, she was on Eric Severeid. ('Dr Stein, the world!') She marched and she cursed; she petitioned and she yelled. The simple ambition which first brought her to New York embarrassed her with its Narcissism, sent her diving, from higher and higher, into bigger and bigger pools. When she made scathing fun of ambition, the candour of her monologues procured more of the very success she derided. Her bleeps became famous on the network which gave her provisional carte blanche. ('Put it this way: they let me say anything they like.') She plaited her contradictions into a career. Things went so well that had it not been for Dr Stein, she might have hanged herself. In a world brutal with uncertainty, he provided the still centre. ('You never napalmed anybody, did you, Dr Stein?') Of course, even at 93 C.P.W., there were changes. After what happened, twice, to Mrs Greta P. Fineberg in the elevator, they had to install closed circuit T.V., but in Dr Stein's office only the drapes changed, once, and she liked the new colour.

'You're going to laugh at this one, doctor,' she said one day.

'I think you can depend on me by now not to do that, Nattie.'

'Remember last month I was saying I couldn't fall in love ever again? Guess what's happened now. Not just one, *two*. You can smile. Oh yes you can, if you try. I know you must want to.'

'These things happen. They happen more often than you think.'

'Everything does,' she said, 'but it still hurts. I mean this is a really painful situation for me.'

'Do you want to tell me about it, or them?'

'I'm not sure about one of them, whether I really love him. But *which* one? That's the problem. Deep breath, start at the beginning. O.K. You see a lot of naked guys around the theatre and places, right? Everyone knows that. It means strictly nothing. I guess they like to show themselves. "Come in – whoops, I'm sorry," all that stuff. Means strictly nothing, right? So there's this dancer, I never paid any attention to him and then I see him showering. This was maybe a month, six weeks ago. I didn't tell you about it because I figured it was kind of immature. So I see a guy taking a shower. I seen a million, right? Not that there wasn't a time, when I was a girl – and that's going back a coupla months now – when I was really and truly disturbed seeing naked men. I had to go to museums to fully accustom myself to the idea of a dick. I told you about that. I come of a generation – God help me, but I do – wasn't acculturated to seeing dicks all over the place. I thought you had to love a man very much before you could look at him down there and not feel a little sick to your stomach. I used to try and imagine this plaster cast of Michelangelo's David with a hard-on, just to accustom myself. Dr Stein, frankly, I was not a terrifically hip little girl, right? O.K., so I've been through a lot of changes since then. I had problems with giving head; you saw me through that. I don't have that particular problem any more. Giving love, that's something else, or was. So anyway, I see Rick in the shower – it has to be Rick, doesn't it? – and he has this beautiful body. I don't just mean he's hung, although he surely is, I mean everything. He has the full ready-to-drive-away metallic finish and what happens then hasn't happened to me too often. I'm suddenly totally turned on by the sheer physical beauty of the guy. A hoofer, I figured maybe he was a fag. So he sees me looking at him and, I couldn't believe it, he pays me the big compliment, right there, in the shower – looks at me and, yo-ho and up she rises!'

'She,' Dr Stein said, 'do you want to talk about that?'

'The drunken sailor,' she said, 'an English folksong. Dr Stein, you're dear, truly, but *suspicious*. Jesus! So that's how it starts, O.K.?'

'He's black, this Rick?'

'*Rick?* Dr Stein, maybe we should talk about *you* for a change.'

'One day,' he said, 'but not on your tab, Nattie. Go on.'

'He is most certainly not black. Pure Caucasian, hairless, white Caucasian – hairless, chestwise anyway. A true blue-eyed *goy*, and gorgeous. Uncircumcised and I can even manage to dig that. So it starts. But here's the capper. I thought it was going to be purely epidermis versus epidermis, right? Twelve-inch dick, two-inch brain. Instead of which, guess what. Turns out he's a poet. This crazy stud is a poet. Beautiful. I have some critical faculties where poetry is concerned and I tell you this guy's a poet. I start reading, I wind up thinking he's a goddam genius. Lyrical! Result? We fall in love and then guess what. He can't bring himself to fuck me any more. He wants to talk about ictus.'

'I'm sorry?'

'A mistake anyone could make, doctor. Ictus? Stress? Metre? I tell him, could we possibly forget literature at least long enough to fuck once in a while? Dr Stein, he can't; or he won't. He said he always finally despises a woman he puts his dick into. "Don't put it in," I tell him, "let me handle that end of it." Not a smile. He loves me. I'm thrilled. I'm a wreck. Enter Sidney. Re-enter Sidney. Because Sidney's been around a while already.'

'He's the director of the theatre in New Jersey, am I right?'

'Dr Stein, you are some terrific note-taker. I salute you. He is indeed a theatre director, and a heck of a good one. I've always admired hell out of his productions. *Hedda Gabler?* You have to see it for yourself. A-O.K. is faint praise. Ace! He's been after me to do this play his ex-wife's written. Sidney is a terrific talent but he's no gatefold. He looks like a bald cocker spaniel with a one-way ticket to the pound. Respect him? Sure. Love him? Never. And wouldn't you know it, this is a guy's been trying to get me in the sack for the last like year and a half when all I want from him is to improve my timing and broaden my range. O.K., so you've guessed. I come from reading poetry with Rick and Sidney is explaining dramaturgy as usual, with his hand on my fly, and I think, what the hell. And what do I find? You've guessed it again. Sidney Petropoulos can fuck. And more than that. He is tender. Once I have my clothes off, is he imaginative? He's a lover, Dr Stein. I realize that he was right. Timing begins in bed. Here's a man I can fully learn from now. But I sure wish he had Rick's body. I mean that's a Cartesian dichotomy I wish didn't operate with me, but it does. I love them both, I swear to God. I guess I've told it like it was a routine, but it's not a routine; unless my whole life's a routine, which maybe it is. What am I going to do?'

'What do you ever do, Nattie?'

'I live it through, right? I find myself. But what am I, Dr Stein? A tunnel that can't get enough traffic? A whore? A soul-mate? A literary critic? An earth-mother? I have to get cast pretty soon, Dr

Stein, or I'm going to have to take on additional help. This is getting way beyond a one-woman show. Seriously, I need to know. Tell me.'

'You tell me, Nattie.'

'Shit, Dr Stein, I love you but you are sometimes so goddam *passive*! Any minute you're going to tell me that it's perfectly normal and acceptable to love two guys, to give love to one and head to the other, that I have to hang loose and not let it get to me? Well, it's got to me. What do I have to do to prove it to you? I'm in distress, Dr Stein. I have to decide. Rick wants me to marry him, right? So what if I marry him and he still won't do anything with his dick except write iambic pentameters with it? Big letters, right? Don't laugh. I love him. Sidney – Sidney has a great talent and a great need. ı can help with the need and in return ... fine, I can handle that, but is that love? I can't swallow him, does that indicate something?'

'Does it?'

'Fuck you, Dr Stein, you know that? Sometimes just fuck you. Because I have been coming here for seven years, forty-something times a year, right, come rain, come shine, and you've taught me a whole lot of things. No one denies that. But there comes a time when I have to say fuck you. Here's a situation I need to make a decision.'

'And I'm here to help you make that decision, Nattie, but it has to be yours. You know yourself better than anyone in the world.'

'Shit I do. If I know myself so well, why all those notes you've been taking about me all these years? You know me better than I know me. I don't have that material. Help me.'

'Nattie, you know as well as I do the conditions of analysis, the code under which a reputable analyst has to operate –'

'Well, stop being so goddam reputable for five minutes, will you? Be disreputable for a change. Lay your dick on the line, if you have one. You listen to me, because this is match point here. Either you tell me whether it's Rick or Sidney – and I tell you it has to be one or the other – or I'm terminating our relationship right here and now. Either you come out of your coma or I'm pulling the plug. I'm serious, Dr Stein.'

'Nattie ...'

'Sidney or Rick, Dr Stein? Harold. Harold, is it Sidney or is it Rick? You have ten seconds starting now.'

'You're putting me in an impossible position.'

'Do you keep your pants on in bed, Harold?'

'You're making this an excuse for something, aren't you, Nattie? Is it my fees? Do you have problems there? Because ...'

'You want it in cash, doctor? You can have it in five different currencies, you ass-hole. I'm an international star, you bastard. I can open big in Toronto, any time I like. It's not your fees, it's you. You bore me. Harold, and you hold out on me. When I get out of here you'd better check your pulse, because I have a feeling you may be clinically dead. If you are, don't panic, just pull the shades and call the mortician. You have the number?'

'You think I don't want to help you?'

'I think just precisely that. I think you're the kind of guy likes to watch people agonize. You're a wimp, Dr Stein. I'll bet you haven't fucked in ten years. Harold, please. To you this is maybe kind of a comic interlude; to me it's important, very very important. I guess Sidney's just a substitute for the real thing, right, which is Rick, right? On the other hand, Rick makes Narcissus look like a real master of the meumtuum sense. He's a guy doesn't want anyone to have access to his dick in case it gets dirty. Is that a recipe for a relationship? Is there something wrong with my cunt, Dr Stein?'

'Why do you ask that?'

'Sidney isn't too clean as a person ... Why do I ask that? Do you remember I was talking about a guy called Rick? Why do I *ask* that? I know what you're doing, Harold, you're trying to take the heat out of this. You're trying to keep your diary straight. You have me pencilled in for next week and you don't want to have to alter anything. You're compulsive, Harold. You had problems with toilet training. If you were a Christian, you know what you'd keep in a little box in your inner sanctum? A fragment of the True Shit. You're full of it, Harold. You've wasted seven years of my life – or a goodly percentage thereof – and when the big moment comes, you don't have anything to give. Three, two, one, zero: that's it. I won't be here next week. You're fired, Harold, I won't ever come back here again, not ever.'

83

'Nattie ...'

'That's enough. Call me Miss Carlsen. Say good-bye to Mrs Stein for me. I'm the one helps hold her packages when she's lost the key to the third lock. Boy, I don't know which of you is more compulsive. Good-bye, Harold, has it been good knowing you? *You* answer for once.'

When she got down to the street, two police cars were whooping. A long line of hack-drivers' sleeveless elbows jutted from stalled traffic. She looked up at the heavy building and started to cry. She was torn between the desire to howl and the fear that some of the cabs' passengers, glaring at the sidewalk because it was going faster than they were, might recognize Natalie Carlsen in trouble and go sell their shares. She put on her shades and waded into the stream of traffic until she saw an empty taxi. ('We ain't going anywhere in this, lady,' Alfredo Sanchez told her. 'That's exactly the destination I had in mind,' she said, and found her Kleenex.)

That night she had some kind of vaginismus when she was in bed with Sidney Petropoulos. He was dear about it, but he felt rejected, obviously. When Rick came round in the morning with his new elegy ('Natalie, have I really and truly licked the irony in the third stanza?'), she told him to try it between her legs and he got insulted. At that point, the telephone rang: 'Miss Carlsen, this is Harold Stein.'

'You just missed me, Dr Stein. I just this second jumped out the window.'

'Can I see you?'

'I terminated our relationship yesterday afternoon, Dr Stein. I mean to stick to that. You let me down; I'm not a girl forgives a man does that. In fact I'm not even sure I'm a girl at all. I think I may be turning into a crone, Dr Stein, and anthropophobe, Dr Stein, and it's all your fault.'

'I'm serious, Nattie.'

'You sure are. Is it haemorrhoids?'

'I want to see you on a personal basis. I accept our professional relationship is over. I want to see you person-to-person.'

'Won't that require two of us? I'm a person; do you have any evidence you are?'

'Please. I have a patient due in a few minutes. Could we have lunch?'

'You *eat*? I thought you just got plugged in like the juice extractor.'

'One o'clock in the Oak Room at the Plaza?'

'That's one hip rendezvous, Dr Stein. O.K., I guess. If I don't show, it's because I already made the choice and got married or threw myself into the East River. Or both, of course, or both.'

'One o'clock.'

'He'll see you now,' Nattie said.

He was sitting at a window table reading the *Wall Street Journal*.

'Hi, Dr Stein,' she said. 'Are you buying or selling?'

'I'm so glad you came,' he said.

'Were you worried? I was held up in the street by a guy wanted to interview me about my choice of toiletries. I washed my hands of him, of course, but it took time. This is really nice of you –'

'No, no,' he said.

'Oh, it *isn't* nice of you? In that case I'll order something expensive. You're going to pay for this, Dr Stein, literally. A new experience, right? A reversal of the flow. Stand right back, this could change your life! I know, you wouldn't like that too well, would you, Dr Stein?'

'Do you think I could be Harold from now on?'

'If you think you can get used to it, why not? I'll take the *potage du jour* – no *croûtons* – and the – what's that when it's not in French?'

'The English is underneath, Nattie.'

'I'll take it in French.'

'I'll have the same, waiter,' Dr Stein said, and took off his glasses. 'Nattie, what I have to say to you isn't easy.'

'Well, at least it's free.'

'Could we possibly be serious for a moment?'

'Excuse me laughing, Dr Stein ... Harold, but we've been serious for seven years and where did it get me?'

'You asked me to make a decision for you yesterday. You knew very well I couldn't do that, professionally –'

'Oh fuck it, Harold, did you get me here to take me through all that again?'

'That's preliminary to what I want to say. What I have to say to you is predicated on the strict assumption that you meant what you said and our professional relationship is definitively terminated. Unless that's understood, I can't say anything else.'

'Roll on, thou great and mighty river, roll. I meant it.'

'How could I possibly help you choose between those two men? I had no way I could do that, and you know why?'

'Yes, yes, yes. You couldn't drive your patients out of their minds if you actually did anything for them, and then you'd lose them and who'd pay Mrs Stein's charge accounts?'

'I love you, Nattie.'

'Oh fuck.'

'I've loved you for seven years. I've loved you ever since your second appointment.'

'When I told you about my father in the shower without his glasses on?'

'I don't recall exactly.'

'Check your records, Harold. That was the turn-on. I bet you.'

'I love you and for seven years I've been unable to declare myself.'

'That's some constipation you've had in there.'

'So you see, when you terminated our professional relationship yesterday, I wasn't as upset as maybe you thought.'

'I was. I cried. Call Alfredo Sanchez if you don't believe me. Call him anyway, he gave me his card. Night and day, he's the one.'

'And now, you see, I'm free. I may be absurd in your eyes, but I'm free.'

'I said some shitty things to you, didn't I, in the course of those sessions? Not only yesterday. I had you down for a guy'd sold all his blood and ran strictly on diet seltzer.'

'I'm a man, Nattie, like any other.'

'Don't show me, not in the Oak Room. They'd be glad to throw us out. They need the table.'

'I'm serious about this. You think it's some kind of sudden thing. It's not. I've dreamed of this day, of being able to say this to you.'

'Do you make passes at all your ex-patients? Is this a revenge syndrome, Dr Stein – ?'

'Harold. This is not a pass. I love you. I know you – I know you – better than you know yourself, Nattie, and it doesn't help me a bit. Isn't that a comedy situation you could make something of?'

'If you know me so well, how am I taking this? Am I full of bitterness and contempt? Am I thinking, here's a guy I relied on for dispassionate advice all these years and all these years he was wishing he could join me on the couch – it's kind of narrow, that couch, I guess that's why – or am I thinking, Dr Stein, all this time I was playing the field and it was you right along? Tell me, Harold.'

'Nattie, will you marry me?'

'You're married already. Or are you only living with her?'

'My wife knows nothing about this.'

'Harold, I have this powerful urge, which I'm sure you empathize with, to laugh right in your face. But that wouldn't be a true response, because truly I'm touched and – well – a little over-whelmed. I mean this is, forgive me, Like Nixon going to China. A twist. I'd like to hear Eric Severeid on this before I finally make up my mind.'

'I love you. I believe I can give you the stability you need.'

'But what about your wife? Your boy?'

'He's through Law School this summer. Ira can handle this. He has a stable relationship in his life. A girl called Taxi! I don't believe one should indefinitely live a lie just in order to shore up a mature child's soon-to-be-shucked identity structure.'

'Put that way, I guess you're right, Dr Stein.'

'I have no marriage, Nattie. I have had no marriage over a period of years. There comes a moment when a man has to take cognizance.'

'I guess. I guess. You look tired, Harold. You know what you should do? You should cancel your afternoon appointments.'

'I don't think I could possibly do that.'

'Yes, you could too. You should cancel your afternoon appointments and come up to my apartment and tell me your troubles. When you run out of troubles, we can watch the soaps together. What do you say?'

'You're laughing at me.'

'Harold, do you want to get laid or don't you?'

'I love you, Nattie.'

'You're not going to tell me that doesn't come into it? Not after seven years of analysis, seven years of trying to get it together, you're not going to tell me sex is *irrelevant*, are you?'

'Of course not. But I'm talking about love. This is a critical experience for me, Nattie. I never slept with another woman apart from my wife since the day I was married.'

'You did it on the day you were *married*? I'm not easily shocked, Harold, but that's ripe.'

'Nattie, you're a serious girl. You've made a living out of laughing at what is most precious to you. I take comfort from that. I take hope from it, I truly do. But this isn't a joking matter. I know you're a lonely, frightened woman and I want to help you to realize your full potential. When I say I want to marry you, that's because I'm willing to go that far to prove to you how committed I am, but –'

'But you're coming round to the idea that maybe an afternoon in the hay would be better than nothing at all, right?'

'I don't even know that I can function in the hay, as you put it, Nattie. Sex isn't something casual with me, it isn't a form of recreation. It means something.'

'It means three precious hours out of the middle of the day, for instance, but that's a loss we have to take. I wonder if this dish tastes any better in English.'

'Is there something wrong with it?'

'Don't shoot the chef; maybe it's just that if we're going to bed I'm afraid my tummy will rumble. I told you about that one time, didn't I? Men hate signs of humanity in the sack. Remember Vic, loved my ass until I farted?'

'I'm prepared to leave my wife and live with you, Nattie, if you want me to do that. You thought you were hurting me when you walked out; you did me the biggest favour I could have possibly wished for. I broke down and cried.'

'I wondered why you had that fancy blotter always with clean paper in it.'

'Are you serious about cancelling my appointments?'

'You'll even do that? Harold, this is true love.'

They went to her apartment and she made some coffee. Alone with him, she was dry of jokes. He stood in the window and looked out at the Puerto Ricans in a lot just down the street. 'You're in danger here,' he said.

'They see me on T.V. I'm O.K. They call me "Bleep".'

'You expose yourself to danger all the time, Nattie. Times I've been so anxious for you I nearly followed you out of the building.'

'Harold, this is terrible. I feel so – so *constrained* – I mean this is ridiculous, isn't it? We've talked about everything there is to talk about. I've stripped myself verbally naked in front of you a thousand times and now suddenly I feel like maybe it was all truly leading up to this and it makes me shaky. Stage-fright? Life-fright! Could you possibly bring yourself to kiss me or something? And we'll see how it goes? What do you say?'

'I love you. I love you.'

'Oh God, Harold. I see we're both going to have to be very patient. Oh, that's better. That's a lot better. I think. Isn't it?'

'What's the matter, Nattie? There's nothing to worry about. I love you.'

'Maybe that's what I'm worried about.'

'We don't have to make love. That was your idea. We can sit and watch the soaps. I'm with you, that's what I care about. I don't care what we do.'

'We have to fuck, Harold, or we're not grown up.'

'That's ridiculous.'

'You can't love me, you can't know you love me until you've seen me as I really am.'

'All in good time.'

'This is a good time. I want you to enjoy me, Harold. I'm all I have to offer. I'm proud that you say you love me. And a little embarrassed, I guess.'

'I've waited seven years,' he said. 'I can wait a whiles longer.'

'One of my breasts is larger than the other one, Harold.'

'Nattie, I love you.'

'I've always wanted one person to know me through and through and I realize now it was you. I want to be completely naked with you and that scares me.'

'What is there to fear?'

'All these years I've wanted to show myself to you, and now ... Harold, will you go into the bedroom and get into my bed, will you do that for me, alone?'

'If that's really what you want.'

'That's really what I want. I want you to go and get into my bed and then when you're ready, I want you to do something for me, will you? I want you to call out something to me and I'll come in to you. Will you do that?'

'Sure I will. What?'

' "He'll see you now." On a green light, are you ready?'

That Was Tory

'Oh God,' Clive said, 'what did she want?'

'Not what she's got,' Gigi said, 'that much is evident. Dunk's done a bunk.'

'I don't think I'm with you,' Clive said.

'Duncan, your old and trusted friend, has walked out.'

'*Duncan* has? I can't believe it. When?'

'Last week-end apparently. After Fiona's Parents' Day. The poor lady sounds as though she's been in tears ever since. Not that I blame her. I'm sure I shall be in precisely the same condition the day you decide that the children are now quite old enough –'

'The children are quite old enough now,' Clive said, 'but I'm not. If anyone's liable to walk out, it certainly isn't me. As past events have proved, though we won't bother about that one now. Anyway, I hate walking. Funny, I always thought if either of them went, it'd be her. You still haven't said what she wanted.'

'Just a fresh shoulder to cry on, I think, poor girl.'

'She's hardly a girl at this point, is she? She must be a good forty.'

'There's no such thing,' Gigi said, 'as a good forty.'

'You look better than ever,' Clive said, 'and what's more you know it. You could have a perfectly good life without me. What about that Arab last week? He was practically offering you gold bathroom taps for openers. Incidentally, this quiche is absolutely ace. You've got the pastry bang right this time. And the Meursault goes very well with it. Pretty impressive, don't you agree, we can still do a bottle of this quality at under three-fifty? How the hell's Duncan going to manage without her?'

'With a little help from his friend, one assumes.'

'Oh, he's got one of those, has he?'

'It's always the woman who gets whacked in the end, isn't it?'

'She wasn't very clever with him, was she, when you come to think about it?'

'Just because you never liked her.'

'I never showed I didn't.'

'No,' she said, 'and it showed.'

'Apart from that very first time when I lashed out and she burst into tears on me. I never saw a grown woman crying until that moment. I'd assumed she was rock-hard Knightsbridge through and through. Must be fifteen years ago now. More. Silly argument about nothing, but even you had to admit I was right.'

'Everybody did,' Gigi said. 'What she really wants is a job.'

'Only she can't do anything, I know. What about getting her to answer the phone to your sheiks and people?'

'We have precisely one sheik; the office is two by two; and what would Crispin say?'

'I daresay he wouldn't find that noble bosom much of a turn-on, dear Crispin.'

'Is it that noble?'

'She wasn't a bad-looking girl à l'époque. Quite attractive, if only she hadn't had a touch of the debs about her.'

'I always thought that was the attraction. She can type a bit, she said, and she's got some French. She was finished in Switzerland, you may remember.'

'Positively château-bottled, I know, but what am I supposed to do with her?'

'She doesn't mind what she does.'

'People always say they'll do anything, but they always mean anything except what you want them to do. She can't exactly hump crates of Xmas booze about the place, can she? It's really up to Duncan to find her something. God knows, the Ministry of Transport's big enough for two these days. Frankly, it's the least he can do.'

'But more than he's prepared to.'

'She would do him such a bloody great favour all the time.'

'For which he had more than good reason to be grateful. At least at the beginning. You may remember his feet.'

'She did cope with his feet.'

'She also worked her way up. She even got him to wear shirts that weren't a size too small. *And* she eliminated the heavy breathing.'

'Suffocation does that,' Clive said. 'Unfortunately it eliminates breathing of all kinds, which is presumably why he done what he done finally.'

'He's a shit, after all those years she propped him up. They always seemed happy enough.'

'We rather guessed there was something wrong, didn't we, that last time we went there? It was in the depths of winter and they gave us prawn salad, followed by tinned rhubarb which did absolutely horrible things to a rather nice bottle I'd brought.'

'I still think it was the wrong night,' Gigi said. 'No one else turned up, which was rather ominous, and Duncan had a suspiciously blank look on his face when he opened the front door. Not that he wasn't capable of looking blank on the right night too, of course, when he was in one of his moods. When one thinks about it, could anyone have been more patient than she was?'

'Which makes it all the more surprising he didn't check out years ago. Imagine what all that Knightsbridge patience must have been like in bed.'

'One never knows what people get up to in bed. I don't honestly think you can draw any inferences.'

'Then that's because you don't think honestly.'

'Would you like the rest of the quiche, my darling? And if so, in which eye?'

'She did him a lot of good on the surface and underneath she humiliated him. Like you with me.'

'Oh sure.'

'She'll find someone. Whom do we know that's lonely?'

'There's always Cecil.'

'Apart from Cecil.'

'What about Tony Lovecraft up in Norwich?'

'He's up in Norwich, though, isn't he? I expect she's got bags of friends. If I hear of anything in the job department, I'll obviously give her a ring, but she has rather left it a bit, and I'm up to my bloody eyes, what with the spring catalogues *and* Christmas.'

'You might be able to do with some help in that case.'

'The trouble is, my darling, some help never helps.'

'I'll ask Crispin,' Gigi said, 'but I can't see him being keen.'

Gigi and her partner, Crispin Trenchard, ran their interior decorating business with hermetic efficiency. After the first consultations, not even the client was admitted to the premises on which they were working until the place was ready for occupation. Clive was invited the night before, to enjoy a test pilot's brief *droit de seigneur*, after which Gigi and Crispin accepted his compliments, allowed him to insert six of the best bottles shipped by Redman and Slater into the kitchen bin and delivered the key (and the account) to the client.

A few days after the sorry news about Tory Jameson, the telephone rang in Clive's office and the trunk-calling voice of a country solicitor ('Oh, Ivor McCauseland here from Ipswich, Mr Redman') was afraid to say that an old customer of the firm had died and that the executors would be immensely obliged if Clive could dispose of the rather important cellar for them, in the usual way. Since the law required the contents to be sold at auction, it meant cataloguing, didn't it, and transport? Clive said, 'Yes, of course,' and put the telephone down and said, 'Damn.' He then called Tory and asked her to have lunch with him.

'It's probably rather a miserable job and damnably chilly too, if I know anything about country house cellars, but there it is: honour says it needs doing and I don't suppose you'd find it very difficult.'

'I don't mind what I do,' she said, 'and it sounds fascinating.'

'No, it doesn't, Tory, and it certainly won't be, but the executors'll pay you a few bob and it might take your mind off your troubles, or give you a surreptitious chance to drown them, assuming they still exist. Take a corkscrew, whatever you do!'

She was wearing a floppy hat and a pink suit. Her shoes were rather pretty: pale toffee, with a narrow strap round the ankle and over the instep into a diminutive gold buckle. 'You are kind, Clive,' she said.

'Well, there we are then,' he said. 'The best thing is to go down to Ipswich on Monday – they'll put you up in a hotel – and that way you'll have the best part of two days, which should be ample. Old McCauseland swears most of the bins are labelled, but you'll probably end up by having to scrape a certain amount of rat shit away to locate the Taylors'. I'll buzz down Tuesday p.m. and tidy up the odds and ends with you, O.K.?'

'You are kind, Clive, really. How's Gigi?'

'Oh deep in her usual secrets. She and Crispin are tarting up a penthouse for some chic sheik. Have you met Crispin?'

'It's a long time since I saw either of you,' she said.

'Well, we've been through the standard mid-life crises, but things aren't too bad. Gigi's making a terrific success of the business. Crispin's turned out to be a godsend. What's the right term for an affair between a married woman and a homosexual, do you know? *Une affaire blanche*, perhaps.'

'Delicious smoked trout!' she said. 'This is the first time I've felt hungry since it happened. I don't think I'd've minded so much if he hadn't shown me her photograph.'

'Not very tactful of him.'

'She's so plain,' Victoria said. 'That's what hurt.'

'How's Fiona taking it?'

'She's glued to her horse. Yoiks tally-ho and I haven't seen her since, honestly.'

'I always took you to have been rather horsy, were you?'

'I never got further than rabbits.'

'I always thought you had the thighs for the job. Horses, I mean.'

'This is really an awfully nice place.'

'Yes, Michael doesn't run a bad kitchen, does he? His portions aren't getting any bigger, though, I notice. One favourable mention in the glossies and you can kiss the second vegetable good-bye. All he needs is a rosette in the Michelin and he'll stop giving salad either. Oh for God's sake, wear some trousers when you go down to Ipswich or you'll freeze to death. You didn't have an affair with Dickie Bannerman at one point, did you?'

'I never had an affair with anyone, Clive.'

'Sorry; I didn't mean to pry. Well, that's not quite true. It's rather strange this kind of thing, isn't it. Suddenly you aren't the same person; and at the same time it's perfectly evident that you are. Do you remember when I made you cry?'

'You never made me cry. You're thinking of somebody else.'

'Come on, Tory. It was virtually the first time we met. Dunk brought you round to the flat. We were living in that mansion block opposite South Ken. You slept in the sitting room and we all had breakfast the next morning and we were drinking our tea and burning the toast and you and I had this terrific flare up and it ended with you bursting into tears. We went for each other like mad. Surely you remember? It was basically political.'

'I remember the flat,' she said, 'and how nervous I was.'

95

'You looked as cool as Harrods. That's why I was so embarrassed. It's coloured my whole attitude to you ever since.'

'You've always been very sweet.'

'That's what I mean.'

'Will you thank Gigi for me, when you see her?'

'She was really sorry for you the other day. So sorry she gave me quite a *mauvais quart d'heure* about the iniquity of the male sex. How you hate us really, all of you, don't you?'

'I never hated anybody,' she said. 'That was what was so ghastly with old Dunkie: the things he dredged up out of the past. Things I'd begged him to talk about and he never would. Suddenly out they came. How I'd failed to do this or let him do that – and all the time I'd really thought he quite liked me –'

'I know,' Clive said, miming more coffee for the waiter.

'You and Gigi can talk. We never could. It was all – iced over – like a cake. I kept a piece of my wedding cake for years and then one day I opened the little box – a sort of baby silver coffin it was – to show Fiona, because she was at the tea-party stage, and the whole thing was mouldy – green dust, horrible! He seems to have thought I was a monster, Clive. Am I?'

'I used to think you were a bit stuck up. I certainly don't think you're a monster.'

'I really thought everything was fine. Stuck up? I always considered myself very easily satisfied. I never wanted much.'

'Or you wouldn't have married Duncan,' Clive said, 'would you?'

'I had an idea, when I was a little girl, that if you were enough like other people nothing bad ever happened to you. Even death. And now this has. I don't know: perhaps I deserve it.' She stirred her new coffee. 'I'd love to see Gigi some time.'

'I'm sure she'd love to see you,' he said.

The Parsonage was a double-gabled pink farmhouse, in the Suffolk style, with a bell on an iron hoop outside the front door. He arrived towards the end of a yellowish afternoon, the sky stacked with fuming clouds which seemed to carry lurid reflections of some invisible conflagration. The road was wet with a storm he had not experienced.

He jangled the bell, but no one answered, so he pushed open the door and went into the flagged hallway. 'Victoria?' Pictures had already been stripped from the rosy walls. The hall was narrowed by a dressing table and a dismantled bedstead which the men had evidently abandoned until the next day. An elephant's foot full of canes and walking sticks stood under the stairs. 'Victoria?' The house was cold. Through the hall window he could see fresh rain falling into the gravel; it sounded like boiling fat. 'Anyone here?' The deserted house had the unsettling stillness of a corpse.

Clive ambled into the drawing room. Beside the chimney-piece, a collection of German bandsmen stood tall in a glass barrack. In the bookshelves, slumped volumes, their more valuable neighbours already gone to auction, had lost their dignity. An urge to steal something began to beat in Clive like a pulse. He sighed and made loud footsteps across the hall and into the gunroom, in search of the kitchen. 'Victoria?'

There was china in crates on the laundry table in the scullery. Clive edged a blue-hooped saucer to the end of the table and allowed it to crash on to the hard floor. On the mantelpiece, like a last invitation, stood a box of matches. Through a rounded doorway, the kitchen proper displayed a startling modernity. Had some plausible salesman sold the old man all the latest pine and formica or had his cook blackmailed it out of him?

A door was ajar on the far side of the kitchen. A dull light, the shade of marmalade, shone from below. Clive went down the noisy steps. Victoria was sitting on a stack of crates in the middle of the cellar. Her face was veiled with cobwebs. She was wearing a tweed suit. 'Oh Clive,' she said.

'You couldn't manage it,' he said.

'I've been at it for two solid days.'

'Have you?' he said. 'Then what's the problem?'

'I've done all this side,' she said, 'but over here it doesn't make any sort of sense at all. Some of the bottles haven't even got labels. He just bunged things wherever he felt like it.'

'Disobliging fellow,' Clive said. 'What about these? They seem fairly simple to deal with.'

'I've done most of those,' she said. 'It's these.'

'Well, come on, cheer up, let's get on with it. Here I am. Why aren't you wearing trousers?'

'I don't like trousers,' she said.

'I told you to wear trousers. How can you expect to work in that? This isn't a bloody point-to-point, you know?'

'I'm perfectly happy in this, don't worry.'

'No wonder you're all hot and bothered. I'll tell you what we'll do, we'll work through everything that's in half dozens or more and we'll liberate the rest.'

'Liberate? What's liberate?'

'Liberate. What's the matter with you? We'll drink the bloody stuff. Help ourselves. Oh for goodness' sake, Victoria –'

'I'll be all right in a minute. I was just so afraid you'd be angry.'

'I am bloody angry. Now come on, you've got work to do. If you'd worn trousers, you wouldn't have got yourself into such a state. Take that bloody skirt off and we'll get to work.'

'I'm all right now.'

'Take it off when I tell you. Why can't you do as you're told? No wonder Dunk pissed off.'

She took a cobweb from her hair and wiped it on to the unsanded wood of the wine-rack in the recess behind her. The breath sounded in her nostrils as she unzipped her skirt and stepped out of it. She was wearing a pink slip. 'All right?'

'Now let's get this done,' Clive said.

They worked without speaking. When one section was cleared and catalogued, he indicated the next. He might have been training an animal. The bare light was glossy on her pink slip as she bent and straightened. Sweat scalded her eyes.

By the time they had finished, they had been in the cellar for close on five hours. As the last lot was tabulated (eight bottles of Château la Tour du Pin, 1937), she stood panting in front of him. 'I'm so sorry it wasn't all done before you got here,' she said. 'I did mean it to be.'

'I don't mind about that,' he said, 'but I specifically told you to wear trousers. Why didn't you? I'm talking to you. I didn't tell you to put your skirt on again, did I? Why are you?'

'Clive, don't be silly. We've finished.'

'I haven't,' he said. 'Take it off again. Take everything off.'

'Clive, really, it's late.'

'But not too late.'

'Gigi'll be waiting,' she said.

'Gigi!' he said. 'Take your bloody clothes off when I tell you. If you don't do as I say, you'll be sorry.' He picked up a bottle and broke its neck against the brickwork. Victoria started to unbutton her jacket. When she was naked, he looked at her in the light of the dulling bulb and then he sloshed the sharp wine over her breasts and shoulders from the jagged neck of the bottle. It ran down her rumpled stomach and bloodied her groin. She stood at last in wet sandals. 'There,' he said, 'how do you like that?'

'I don't mind,' she said. 'I don't mind if you kill me, if that's what you want.'

He slapped her breast. It was loud with the wine and shook, glistening. 'All I consciously intended,' he said, 'was to do you a good turn, you silly cow.'

'I know,' she said. She reached to touch him. In the stale heat, fumes from the wine came from her body. 'Is there something you want me to do?' she said. 'I will.'

'Why is everything so terrible, Victoria?' he said, at last. 'We have the chance to lead pleasant, civilized lives and everything is absolutely terrible. Why?'

'Oh God,' she said, 'I don't know,' and sighed and reached for her slip and began to wipe her feet.

Someone Else

Even at the university they had been marked for each other. (In the library, one could leave a slip in a book and be sure, in those days, that no one else would take or touch it.) At the white wedding, the families elected, in hired and hatted propriety, to regard them as innocents; their contemporaries conspired not to reveal what was common knowledge: that each had had a previous lover, though it had only been the other.

She did not take her first-class degree to market: she wanted children and a home. He went into industry and was industrious. He lacked her brains (said those who coveted her beauty), but he was vigorous and confident. Her friends announced that she was wasted on him, but she knew what she wanted, and needed. In perfect health, she married the right doctor.

That others thought them ill-assorted confirmed their complicity; their love was its own witness and they took private pride in it, as if in a separate creation. When Charles was born, he came as the customary cuckoo and displaced that earlier, honeymoon nestling, the talisman – aren't we lucky? – who had never woken them in the night (except to pleasure), as the newcomer did. She was not dismayed that the baby brought schism; she was well-read in the perils of the quotidian. When abstinence made him pettish, she was pleased to please him without tasting pleasure for herself. She drew the spurting sullenness out of him and smiled, with undisgusted lips, to see him better. He loved her for that soft succour, but its promptness was disturbing. How could she be at once so tender and so practical? It made her seem, for the first time, a stranger. He saw wit in her kindness and it made the first distance between them.

He was good at his job. Old Cantlie thought well of him and favoured his promotion. (They played golf together.) He handled people well and was soon showing the door, politely, to men who had shown him the ropes. His cheerful energy and undrawling accent belonged to no particular class: he could strip down a

machine as well as he could ask Mrs Cantlie for a waltz at the annual
shindig. ('I think they've done us rather well, don't you, this year?')
His advancement seemed to incur no envy; it was only natural. He
had his rivals (and liked them), but he had reason to believe that,
among the raciest rats, he would win by more than a whisker.
(Denton was the most capable of his age group, but one could not
see him playing golf or chatting up important secretaries.) His
popularity on the shop floor encouraged him to patronize the desiccated Denton (bright lace-up shoes, unfashionably tight tie); there
was no spring in Vivian and the deciduous fair hair already
promised a long and early autumn.

She went on seeing some of the brighter females she had known
at university. Those who had disdained marriage rarely stayed un-
married, though their husbands – lecturers and publishers and
poshish civil servants – seldom obliged them to live in a provincial
town. Most of them continued to work, with fat absences for babies,
after which they longed to get back to the office, frankly; breast-
feeding, even in public places, seldom brought the promised thrill.
Some of them sought to recruit her to their busy, full way of life.
(Oh look, there was always proof-reading and indices to do for some
academic!) She embraced the banality they guessed to be so suf-
focating. She had William and then Sarah. Others passed the age of
thirty with sighs for lost opportunities and waistlines; she celebrated.

He thought that a junior directorship could not be far away. Good
old Cantlie contrived that he should have a car appropriate to the
rank he could expect within the year. (This wretched minor recession meant that a salary rise might have to wait.) It was certainly
no fault of his that the recession deepened. He had helped to make
the rather effective contingency plans (he was number two on the
subcommittee) without which things might have been a lot worse.

When Cantlie was fired, at a week's notice, he had no cause to
feel menaced, though he was shaken. The firm had been taken over
by a larger, more liquid group quick to seize its greedy chance. The
old man's departure was as painful as it was abrupt: the handshake
was golden, but firmly final. Cantlie's name vanished from office,
car park and stationery. One felt positively guilty, a couple of weeks
later, at being seen playing golf with the older chap on a Saturday.
(Not that those four-foot putts were easy at the best of times.)

The people who came down from London – and over from Baltimore – reassured the work force that rationalization would not mean a reduced number of jobs. He was deputed first to convince his union contacts that the new management would keep its word, and then to supervise the reductions. He was also asked, confidentially, which of the second-echelon management he regarded as perishable: would he mark them, for Harry Beach's eyes only, on a scale of, say, ten? He contrived to upgrade – to a reprieving seven query plus – several who had been proscribed by Denton, but he could not, in the nature of the business, save them all. He was wounded when a couple for whom he had actually fought rather hard were easily overheard to call him 'that shit' at the gate one night. He was hardened by their suspicions and frankly rather wished now that he had gone over whole-heartedly to the Harry Beaches and the Cyril Lacks. He proceeded to affect towards them a bluff good fellowship he had earlier reckoned either unnecessary or unworthy. He even clapped Denton on the back as they went into a meeting and said, 'Well, Vivian, m'boy?'

She listened to his stories, over larger whiskies, and winced at the stratagems of executive in-fighting. She had shared his scandalized amazement at the departure of old Cantlie (for whom she had recently cooked another of her bloody marvellous dinners), but she was less comfortable over the sudden zeal with which he elected to join the axemen, as he had earlier called them. She read his callousness as the symptom of a latent disease. Looking back, she saw its germs even in the intimate life she had, until now, considered so healthy. (His desire for her had been as regular as it had been passionate; now she saw in its clockwork heat a statistician's coldness.)

The situation in the executive building grew more anxious. Was there any end to the economies London (and Baltimore) had in mind? Every new concession proved only that not enough had yet been conceded. When several people were given notice whose jobs he had thought (and had said) were safe, he told Harry Beach that he had so much to do generally in the plant that he would be glad if he could resign from the steering committee. ('If it's more than you can handle, of course.') He came home that night thirsty with shame that he had tried so cravenly to ingratiate himself. After all, he knew more about the plant than anyone; even Denton had to admit that. His own position could scarcely be safer, could it? Imagine Denton trying to keep the brothers sweet!

She remained a patient audience, offering neither advice nor criticism. She applied her intelligence to remaining normal in abnormal times. However, she began again, in those chilling weeks, to do some serious reading. (The two boys were at school now and Sarah was no trouble.) When he came home one winter night, flushed with humiliation ('Nobody even *hinted* they weren't happy with me'), she put aside the journal she was flagging and went, almost with relief, to sympathize with what had surprised him but she had to pretend surprised her.

His collapse proved her strength; she could almost welcome it for the vitality it discovered in her. She was partner to his scorn, but not to his dejection; she bloomed. If she despised those whom he despised, the contempt was not new in her; she could simply express openly what she had always felt. No longer did she have to offer bright car-to-car waves to company wives or bend in Tesco's to admire dummy-mouthed kiddies; never again would she have to offer Sunday morning drinks to young execs who sat there and asked if there was anything they could do to help.

At first he was grateful for her resilience, but later it hinted at sarcasm in her that she took his wounds so bravely. The firm was not ungenerous in its severance payments (though he had to give back the car, of course) and they promised excellent references, but the employment market was not happy. There was a period of distant interviews, of stamped addressed envelopes (folded to fit in another of the same stock size) and of returned phone calls for which one waited all bloody day. Her resumed reading qualified her for part-time work in the field where she had gained her degree. He got to know his children. Her unexpected readiness to step into the breach made him feel that perhaps there had always been some weakness in his character about which she had kept a knowing silence. Her ability saved the day, but the nights lost their regular charm.

He was dashed, but not broken. He believed so strongly in his star that he insisted, even at its darkest eclipse, that the future was bright. (He was basically a lucky man who had had a bit of bad luck.) And after nearly three months of blue-suited anguish (always ready for interviews for jobs he did not really want), his old boss introduced him to some people who were hunting for his kind of head. They were manufacturers of kitchen equipment and had a new infra-red operation, poised to break into Europe. It meant London and it also meant travelling. She would be all right, wouldn't she?

Of course, she welcomed London; it was convenient for what she was doing. The night before they left the cottage, when everything had been packed (the children were with the grandparents) and they were finishing drinks under the apple blossom whose fruit they would never eat, he wanted to tell her something. He turned his whisky in his fingers and thanked her for all she had done to see them through. She laughed and tried to cut him short. But they were leaving all this behind and he wanted to be shot of the whole business, to travel up to London clean.

There had been this girl. She was an ex-secretary. 'Do you have to tell me?' she said. 'Probably you guessed,' he said. 'Possibly,' she said, 'but I'd sooner not have the details.' 'There aren't any,' he said, 'I just want you to know that I love you. She didn't mean a thing.' 'Then why tell me?' she said. 'Because it didn't,' he said, 'and because it wasn't anything to do with you.' 'Ah!' she said. 'It was stupid and – I don't know – a bit sadistic, I suppose. I needed to hurt someone. Myself maybe. I love you – I need you – too much to hurt you, so –' 'Is it still going on?' she said. 'Going on? It never went on. It was this one time. I bumped into her in Oxford. Pure chance. She'd changed jobs. She didn't even know I'd been fired, it turned out. I thought she did. I wanted to – I don't know – prove myself, avenge myself. We walked into Lincoln and went into somebody's rooms. Mad! She used to work for Vivian Denton. Apparently he's a secret poof, did you know?' 'No,' she said. 'He is. Anyway, that was it. I wasn't actually sadistic with her, don't worry about that: I'm not Jack the Ripper or anything. I just needed it – it was the job, not you – and suddenly – there it was.' 'Why tell me about it?' 'I thought it might explain something – about how things have been between us. I know you've been worried.' 'And now I feel better, do I?' 'You've been so marvellous. I want to start again from now. Everything's going to be good from now on.' 'Good,' she said.

The new job went well. He was as able a salesman as he had been organizer. His side of the operation was divorced from manufacturing and he had a team of eight, all young and all eager to prove themselves to the parent company; there was none of the pettiness of Jack Horners who know themselves cornered and must fight each other for the plums. He did have to go abroad rather often, as he had feared, but he promised her that there would be no more Margarets. 'You don't have to promise,' she said. He suggested that they have another child (there was room in the new Putney house), but she was researching, for a rather impressive man, on the psychology of arson.

He told himself, and her, that his absences lent zest to their marriage, rather than interrupted it, didn't she agree? 'I think you're enjoying it more than you were until quite recently, aren't you, darling?' 'I think I am,' she said. 'Is there anything – you know that's bothering you,' 'I don't think so, is there?' 'I'm very happy,' he said, 'don't get me wrong. Routine check! I just wondered if you were.' 'Very,' she said. 'Am I getting rather dull for you?' he said. 'Not in the least.' 'I realize this job –' 'What?' 'It's pretty mundane. Selling kitchens.' 'It's pretty mundane researching for Nikolai,' she said.

One day, at London airport, sitting in the crowded lounge listening to indistinct apologies for the delay, he met a man whom he had last seen at his wedding. (They had played college hockey together.) 'Hullo, *Gerry*, where are you off to?' 'I'm off to the bar, which is about as far as we're likely to get this morning by the look of the scoreboard. Strikes! Bloody stupid self-destructive nonsense! Care to join me?' They took limes and lagers to a newly swabbed table, brackish with wiped ash. 'Amazing bumping into you like this, after last week.' 'What happened last week?' 'Didn't she tell you?' 'Didn't who tell me?' 'I bumped into your wife in the White Tower.' 'My wife?' 'Assuming you're still married – she was having lunch at the White Tower.' 'I very much doubt it.' 'But I spoke to her. She was – oh Christ!' 'I think perhaps you've got the wrong wife.' 'Look, I'm terribly sorry.' 'Nothing to be sorry about,' he said. 'I don't keep tabs on where my wife has lunch. And memorable as you are, Gerry, it is conceivable that she met you without feeling obliged to pass on the happy news.' 'Look, I had absolutely no intention –' 'I don't know what you're talking about.' 'Oh well, fine in that case. Anyway, how's things?'

He told himself that he should have known. He aged walking to his delayed flight. The recent past, seen in sudden new light, was badged with luminous clues. He could not blame her. Had he perhaps even incited her to it by telling her about Margaret? She seemed to have taken it so well. Bed had never been better, but nor had it ever been quite so – what? – dispassionate. The blow raised no immediately remarkable bruise. He conducted his business in Munich with conspicuous good humour. The secretaries giggled at his German jokes and the wife of Fritzi Behr stood on one long leg, a deliberate hand on his forearm, while he repaired her heel. It was a salutary surprise to discover that he was more indifferent than he had thought. He found he could smile at her deceit and imagine a slow revenge. He was not vindictive in his fantasies, but there was always the chance that he would meet a fanciable woman. He had never regretted his marriage, but now he had the chance to repair the nagging paucity of his adolescent experience, didn't he? Yet he flinched from Inge Behr in the back of the taxi which – on her instructions? – had taken a long way round to the suburban house of the Herr Direktor. He returned home, after all, primed with a sort of vindictive fidelity.

Everything changed; nothing changed. What had been commonplace was suddenly trapped with duplicity. He did not challenge his wife, nor mention the meeting with Gerry (what the hell was his last name?). He made love to her no less urgently, but the gasp of her orgasm was an amusement to him and his own, later, was a smaller pleasure than the knowledge that she had been deceived. He schooled himself to be his old self and discovered in that detachment how death is the unsmiling tutor of life. He watched with killing admiration the care with which she prepared her excuses. How adroitly she almost made him responsible for her elongated absences! Unfortunately, she sighed, she would have to work a little later in the library, because he was going away the following week and she would be more tied to the house. The observation of her subtlety did not lead him to hate her. Sometimes, not least in bed, he felt so strongly that their love could be restored that cruel questions stirred in his mouth like nestlings. Only his exuberance was muted. He was more patient with the children. His long malice domesticated him.

One day he left his office before noon and went to the library where she worked. He waited in a telephone box until she came out for lunch and then followed her to a vegetarian restaurant, where salads and organic bread symbolized modern virtues: one could be slim and economical. He waited for her lover without any plan for violent confrontation. On the contrary: he quite treasured the prospect of seeing his wife a new woman, because of a new man. She glanced round and then she took a tray and helped herself to eggs and shredded celery and cabbage with sultanas. She looked at her watch and, after closing a torn shred of napkin in her paper-back, began to eat. It was as if he had never seen her eating before (he hid, private detective, behind his *F.T.*); he relished her as entirely alien and he longed to approach her, the fool who cannot think of anything to say. He saw beside her the ghost of her admirer and yet there was no one there. He shared her fancied disappointment, quite upset with the man who had failed her. He kept his eye on the door, hoping for a flushed, overlarge person, ponderous with books and thrusting late taxi change into his pocket. She rose presently (no pudding) and went past him to the door. He thrust the *F.T.* pinkly into his mac pocket and strolled out after her. She walked springily along the pavement. The bunting of cheap clothing at high prices festooned the famous street; cheeky slogans and raunchy symbols were loud for attention. She was wearing low-heeled shoes and he fancied that she had a naturalness none of the other women, thrust up on wedgies and platformed boots, managed to attain. He followed her (she still tossed her hair as she began to cross the street at a zebra, shy thanks to the motorist who fanned her across) as far as the corner before the library where she was researching. He won-dered if he could contrive to dodge round and get ahead of her, so that he might meet her by chance and be pleased. He was about to cross at right angles to her, so as to gain ground on the far side of the street, when she turned left and went down a side street. He frowned and, frowning, smiled, as if at a touching foible. He followed her again, at a slightly greater distance, and was barely in time to see the kiss before the pair of them disappeared into a doorway which, a moment later, he saw to be flagged with the names of tenants. Nikolai Pollak had the third floor. Staring at the names, he remembered Gerry's last name, Cartwright, and hated him.

He went home to one of her best dishes, the chicken with the cream and mushroom sauce. He ate with a good appetite and talked about his day, and hers. He had been promoted to the mini-board, responsible for the kitchen operation, and there was talk of a share option if the accountants could work something out. She listened to him with marvellous earnestness; he was more touched by the sincerity he knew to be false than he had ever been by her undivided devotion.

He came to be a connoisseur of her treacherous tact. She took such credible pains to deceive him painlessly that her cunning seemed positive evidence of love. His resentment was purged by a fatuous exhilaration. He had lost her, he feared, and yet here she was: why should she be so dedicated a caricature of fidelity unless, despite everything, she cared for him? Her deceit made her alive for him in every gesture she made. He was moved almost to tears by the sight of her (through the summer kitchen window) bending to put a dish away. Her shoes, worn by the weight of her heel but gilded with the remains of the maker's name where her instep arched over it, provoked in him a fetishistic throb. He began to tease her with treats, suggesting that they lunch for a change ('The White Tower? Why not?') or that they go down to Glyndebourne (he favoured Mozartian opera, with its shameless swindles), and he tried to guess when her smile was secretly dismayed by the ruin of her plans for Nikolai. She was rarely irritated and never implausible. Somehow she crammed her double life effortlessly into normal time. He never tasted her lover on her body. She was as sweet as a girl. He could almost persuade himself that Nikolai was not really her lover at all, but then he remembered the kiss, and hated Gerry Cartwright again.

He met an early girl-friend who had recently been divorced, had re-married and was already thinking of leaving her musician. Her availability struck him like a rank breeze. He listened to her without enthusiasm and, when the chance came, preferred to be faithful to his own delicious agony. He made no arrangements to see Pamela again and ceased even to chat up the girls at the office. When he went abroad, he refused the standard round of night clubs and the promise of a bit of spare. ('Everybody does it.' 'I don't.') It was obvious that he was very happily married.

Patience became a way of life. Had there been a period, soon after his confession about Margaret, when he had been indifferent to his wife? (She had gone dull on him, fearing herself dull.) His complaisance by no means entailed resignation. It was a phantom game with real prizes (never had their sex life been so beautifully tortuous) and at times he could believe that Nikolai was the dupe, not he. When it became clear that she had not seen her lover for more than a week – and then for a *fortnight* – he became so solicitous of his rival's feelings that he deliberately stayed overnight in St-Étienne to allow her some leeway. He found his life full at last. He had feared himself shallow, but now there were currents plaited into dark depths by the unstaunched confluence of love and hate. He could never be sure which was guiding his sly devotion. When he did something for her – the new kitchen – what was the motive? He accepted her tiptoe kiss with joyous suspicion. Nikolai was in the room for him as he touched her breast and he had, in that common gesture, the greedy thrill of the adulterer. Without having another woman, he enjoyed another man's.

The weeks spread into months. He came to feign love so cleverly that he learned its language better than when it had been natural to him. He read books instead of magazines; he bought records. He became a different man. His counterfeit of love was so carefully nurtured that it began once more to take in him, like a graft, and in a stronger strain. In consequence, jealousy grew green again. He had schooled himself to control his dread when she announced – ah that delicious affectation of regret! – that she was going to have to go to some damned seminar ('Shall I come with you?' 'Oh darling, you'd hate it!'), but suddenly what had been endurable was fresh agony for him. He could not eat. He made no scenes and concealed, as best he could, the bite that tormented him.

One breakfast-time, she said, 'Are you lunching today?' 'I don't think so.' 'Then why don't we?' 'If you're not busy,' he said. 'When am I busy at lunch-time?' she said. He put down the *F.T.* and went to her. She was in her blue dressing gown, without make-up. He kissed her morning lips and the cuff of her ear. 'Where shall we go?' he said. 'The White Tower? Or Veggies?' 'You say,' she said.

He could hardly believe his luck when there she was. As she saw him come in, she raised one hand and tucked a shred of napkin into her paperback and put it on the pine banquette beside her. He kissed her unremarkably. 'I'm having an affair with my own wife,' he said. 'Can't you find anyone better?' she said. 'I don't think so,' he said. 'Perhaps you haven't tried,' she said. 'What do you think of the nut cutlet?' he said. 'Well,' she said, 'it's something you can get into your teeth, isn't it?' The blush told him that her remark was borrowed (foreign change in the lining of her mind). Had she dropped in front of him some deliberate clue, a handkerchief for Othello? Was there malice in it, or a gentle attempt to broach the unspeakable? He watched as she put slaw into her mouth. 'I love you,' he said. She finished her mouthful, eyes on his face, and wiped her West End lips before she spoke. 'Well, I love you,' she said. 'Do you?' She broke wholewheat bread and pressed the crumbs together. 'Something's worrying you. What?' 'Nothing is.' 'You're not eating.' 'Yes, I am, look.' 'Generally,' she said, 'so presumably something's worrying you. It's not the office, is it?' 'I worry the office,' he said. 'I promise you I'm fine. I'm nearly forty, you know. I don't want to put on lard.' 'There's nothing to worry about,' she said, 'I promise you.' 'Then I won't worry,' he said. 'Nothing,' she said, 'unless it's something you're keeping from me.' 'I don't keep anything from you,' he said, 'except my Swiss bank account.' 'Keep it,' she said, 'I'm not bothered about that.' 'I don't keep anything from you,' he said. 'We went through a bit of a time,' she said, 'didn't we?' 'Did we?' he said. 'It's over now,' she said. 'You've been so lovely these last – I don't know – months, I suppose, that I think I love you more than I ever did before.' 'Before what?' 'Before,' she said. 'Will you marry me?' he said. 'I can't,' she said, 'I'm married already.' 'Seriously. If we weren't married, would you?' She took the wadded napkin to treacherous eyes and nodded briskly, three times, and then turned and put her face against his chest and wetted his floral shirt, her favourite. He held her like a prize, while the rest of the room lost focus for a moment. 'I really am a lucky man,' he said, and blinked and looked to the door for a jealous face to spice his victory. 'I don't want anyone but you,' she said, 'not ever.' 'Good,' he said, deprived.

On the Black List

Matt Hyams drove into Torreroja on the afternoon of the summer *corrida*. Cars with red-lettered international plates were parked by the bull-ring. Donkeys and a couple of horses, with red-tasselled trappings and fat stirrups, were tethered under a spear-leaved eucalyptus tree. The bull-ring was the colour of old bread; the doorways and woodwork crusty with burnt sienna. Hyams had the window of the V.W. rolled down, his elbow jutting out, hand latched to the roof to make a breeze for his face. As he came by the barn doors at the side of the ring were open and a furious-faced man was hurrying an old horse through them. It dragged a sidelong carcass. Hyams had a glimpse of crowded faces and caught the brassy vamping of the band. He had never heard of Torreroja, but it looked as good as any place else along the coast, so he pulled off the dusty *carretera* and nosed the bus against the wall of the new, starch-white church.

He climbed out and stretched. The V.W. bus was advertised for the whole family, but he seemed too big for it, even on his own. He had no family, not any more. He was over six feet three inches tall and he weighed two hundred and thirty some pounds. He was not fat; he was big. He wore size thirteen and a half boots (even when you were large, half a size made a difference) and he had on a blue Levi shirt and off-white cotton trousers, baggy and creased from those six hours over the mountains. He squatted and braced his shoulders back: a one and a two and a three. He winced up at the sun and smiled, more grimace than greeting: he was working the stiffness out of his face. He had been wheeling into that sun ever since Granada.

He straightened up and ducked under the strung lights to go into the casino bar. The shutters were closed; two slow fans stirred the atmosphere like tepid soup. Heaped dishes of anchovies, olives and inky *calamare* stood on the long bar. A single customer, a scrawny man in a yellow linen suit, with a string tie, was prising open pistachios. Hyams put hairy hands on the flat of the bar and pushed himself up on to one of the stools. 'Beer,' he said,

'They call it *cervesa* around here,' the man said, though the bartender was already putting Hyams's glass on the bar. 'Did you hear the news? Hemingway is dead.'

'That's damned good,' Hyams said. 'Gimme another one of those, will you, please?'

'Near as dammit blew his head off with a 12-bore shot-gun. Did you know him?'

'No,' Hyams said.

'He came through here a couple of times. He loved to go to the bull-fights.'

'You don't say.'

'I'm Charles Larsen. They call me Chuck. Bull-fights give me a headache. On vacation?'

'Not exactly,' Hyams said. 'I'm a painter.'

'Oh one of those,' the man said. 'We have some painters in town already. Arnie Pallenberg? That's one of them. Wesley Van Groot? They come; they go. Me, I stay. I've been here five, going on six years. I was in Ibiza before that. Know Ibiza? It got to be so damned high, I figured it was time to move on. I'm on a U.S. government pension; ninety per cent disability. This is where the money goes furthest, so this is where I am. Were you in the service?'

'Yes, I was,' Hyams said.

'Ninety per cent disability,' Larsen said, 'and I never left U.S. soil. Climate suits me here; I've only got one lung. I got T.B. in Fort Worth and they shipped me out – ninety per cent disability. I fought for a hundred, but they said, "Heck, you've still got one lung, haven't you?" I had to give 'em that. Thinking of staying a while?'

'I might.'

'Take a tip from an old hand: don't show your money around. They respect a man's not too liberal, if you understand me. You haven't told me your name.'

'Matt Hyams.'

'And I'm Charles Larsen. They call me Chuck.'

'You said,' Hyams said.

'He was tired and one of these villages looked to be much like another. Why not stay here? Chuck Larsen introduced him to a Canadian called Spanier, who ran a fancy, foreigners' bar (the *Quijote*, of course) and a little real-estate agency on the side. Hyams was in luck: despite it being the month of July, there was a big old house available in the *José Antonio*. Folks had been coming, but they'd 'cancelled óot', the Canadian said. The house was in the middle of the village, so Spanier was sorry, it didn't have a view. 'I don't want a view,' Hyams said. 'I'm a painter.'

'He doesn't want a view,' Larsen said, 'he's a painter. I like that. I'll remember that. You hear Hemingway was dead, Spanier?'

'Blew his head off with a 12-bore shot-gun,' Spanier said.

'See what I mean?' Larsen said.

The house had double doors flush on to the dusty street, but there was a vine-shaded patio at the back. Inside, the big, cool rooms had chequer-board floors and there was a long studio under the rafters, with whitewashed walls which would suit his work. He worked big. A woman from the village, Paquita Martin, went with the house; she would wash and cook and make his bed. He rented the place for two months, with an option to keep it on through the winter.

Chuck Larsen helped carry stuff into the house. 'I'm only ten per cent,' he said, 'but here I am. Honest to God, I never saw canvases this big. You always paint pictures this big?'

'No,' Hyams said. 'Tell me, do you know this Paquita by any chance?'

'Paquitas are a dime a dozen in this town. But they're all the same,' Larsen said. 'They all tell you they've got four children and no money and they all rob you blind. She'll feed you well enough for four, and that's exactly how many she'll charge you for, as well. They all carry these canvas bags, you know, so you can never tell what they're bringing in or how much of it they're taking out again. My advice is, get her to do the accounts with you every week – and the first time around make like you aim to see every single used match-stick before you let her buy another box. I'm assuming this is your first visit *aqui en España*.'

'Not quite,' Hyams said.

'Torreroja, the red tower, that's what this village is called, you know. And red is right. See the church just now? Brand new, right? They burned the old one down. And the priest in it. Not that they talk about it. No, sir, they don't call this place red for nothing. Only village along the coast doesn't have a jetty. No jetty for the fishing boats. Know why? Because they're still being punished for that priest and that church. Franco won't give 'em a jetty, even if it is nearly twenty-five years since they barbecued that reverend. No jetty until they've paid good. He's got a memory and a half, that smart old bastard.'

'Thanks for your help,' Hyams said.

'*Tranquillidad* is what he believes in. You know what that is?'

'Sure do,' Hyams said. 'It's what I've come for.'

'No family?' Larsen said.

'No.'

'I have a son lives in Newark, New Jersey; engineer. My last birthday, he sent me two pair of socks. I'm fifty-one years old They wanted fifty pesetas duty. Two pair of socks, fifty pesetas Catch me! I wouldn't take 'em; I said they could send 'em back. Name's Howard. Mother chose it. Howard could have 'em back as far as I was concerned. I haven't seen him in ten years, he sends me two pairs of socks and they want fifty pesetas duty. Forget it, you know what I mean? Let 'em take you once and, brother, they'll come right back and try and take you again.'

'You've been a real help,' Hyams said.

'And don't be tempted to give her anything extra, Paquita. You heard what Spanner said: three hundred pesetas a month, tops. No extras. No matter how you watch her, she'll rob you anyway.'

Paquita was a widow, she said, and she had four children, all daughters. She was short and kind of plump, but she had the coal-black eyes and the red mouth and gleaming dark hair. She sang all the time she was in the house. Hyams began with very little Spanish apart from '*buenos dias*' and '*por favor*', but he soon learned '*dinero*' (she asked for money with a little shrugging laugh) and '*corazón*', because it figured in all of Paquita's heart-felt songs.

He worked from nine till half-past two, when she would call out to him from the bottom of the stairs, '*Señorito, la comida.*' He would come down and learn the Spanish for a new dish: *boquerones* in crisp yellow batter, *paëlla* roofed with *pollo* and *gambas*. She grinned as he protested at the quantities she prepared. The *señorito* was a big man and he had to eat. '*Todo*,' she would say, and stood over him till he had eaten it all, or all he could eat. When he asked her to share a meal with him, she frowned and shook her head, the wrong suggestion. She stood in the doorway as he sat at the table in the patio, her hands on her hips, a tutelary frown on that humorous face. '*Todo*,' she repeated, when at last he pushed his plate away. 'Take it home with you, Paquita,' he told her, but she shook her head.

Her honesty touched him. He asked her to pose for him. She looked alarmed. She was no longer a young girl and she had nothing suitable to wear. 'Wear what you have on,' he said. 'I like you just as you are.'

'Oh *señorito*,' she said. 'Will it take long?'

He might have been the dentist. 'Not long,' he said, 'and don't worry: I'll pay you for the time.'

She came back the next day with a black lace mantilla and a big silver comb and a pair of red high-heeled shoes, which she had concealed in her black canvas bag. When the time came for the sitting, she piled the hair on top of her head, fastened it with the comb and draped the mantilla over the top. She sat in a cane chair and smiled. She did not have good teeth.

Hyams sketched her quickly in charcoal and then in oils. He had always had an extraordinary felicity. Envious fellow-students had said that he could get a stranger's likeness if he ran past his window. He could draw so easily that he had never been tempted to abstraction. His lack of modishness sentenced him to a provincial life, even before he was thrown out of his professorship. Nobody wanted figurative stuff in New York and unless you were wanted in New York, you weren't really wanted at all. He accepted that.

Hyams had enlisted in the Abraham Lincoln Brigade when he was seventeen years old. His father had been a Union organizer who was run down on a picket line by a bunch of strike-breakers in a big car no one ever got the number of. Matt spent three weeks in camp at Gerona and then they shipped him home again. After that, it was art school and then the Marines. He used to say he was the toughest marine in the Pacific; he mowed them down with his bare brush. He never even had to hold a gun.

When the Regents of the University where he was teaching

discovered his unhidden past, he was dismissed despite having tenure and being a veteran. 'I'm afraid you're a veteran once too often, Mr Hyams,' the Dean said. He attempted to bring suit, but he lost. The Junior Senator from Wisconsin had them all on the run, judges included. Karen was great, even though she had the two children. She supported him in front of the Regents and she even went up to Washington and told someone that being an anti-Fascist didn't necessarily mean you were a Communist, because she was an anti-Fascist and she sure as hell wasn't a Communist. The man said he would do what he could, but what he did was nothing. Karen fought until there was no one left to fight, except for Matt. His cheerful virility, the unashamed bulk of him, became an affront to her. He refused to mourn: who was dead, after all? He was; they were. She could not forgive him for forgiving those bastards. He said he was a painter, not a teacher; maybe they had done him a good turn.

'I do nice work,' he said. 'I can always sell my stuff. What's to worry about?'

'Nice work,' she said, in the house where the telephone never rang any more, though they knew everyone in the street, 'nice work! They've killed you, you slob. You slab.'

'I never felt a thing,' he said.

'No,' she said, 'no. But I do. I feel it. You were a professor, I had a life. I had a community. I was alive. Now ...'

'Maybe I'll never be de Kooning,' he said, 'but then he'll never be me. I can always sell my work is what I mean.'

'Oh in Peoria,' she said. 'In Miami maybe, to those drecky millionaires, but ... what gallery's ever going to take your kind of stuff? It's dated, Matty, it's art teacher's stuff. I'm sorry, but you know that really, don't you? Don't grin at me like that. I'm tired of you grinning at me like that. You take it so lightly. Matt, please don't do that, you'll tear something. God dammit, Matt, I told you. Can't you understand? I'm through. I can't handle it any more. I'm sorry, but really, I'm through, I really am.'

He wanted to go to pieces. He tried drinking, but it upset his stomach. He threw up before he was anything like high. He sat in the empty house and read newspapers. He told himself he would never paint again. He went to ball games and found he was sketching the players. He went back to work. His disgrace was not famous enough to hamper his sales. When he had a stack of pictures, he drove down to Miami and had a show. It was a sell-out. Karen's drecky millionaires commissioned portraits of their wives, their children, their lovely homes and even, once or twice, their lovely power boats. They were generous and hospitable and Matt was soon his old cheerful self. He even dated a couple of air hostesses and got spectacularly laid. He gave them charcoal sketches of themselves in the buff and they were so pleased they wanted to start again. Why not?

By the time the Junior Senator from Wisconsin had drunk himself to death, Hyams had got a bunch of money together and one of the millionaires wanted to help him buy a property. But the comfort he could now afford brought out the pain of no Karen and no kids. He saw the boys, of course, from time to time, but there was no going back. Karen had re-married. It was painful to be in the same country. He decided to go on his travels. He was not sure that he ought to go to Spain, because of Franco, but then he wanted to go just to spite the old so-and-so. He wanted to paint goats and olive trees and the faces he remembered, or thought he remembered, from those three weeks in Gerona, the faces of the defeated as they moved towards the border, the scandal of betrayal worked like ink into their skin.

He painted goats and olive trees and the face of Paquita Martin, whose husband had been killed on a merchant ship when their oldest daughter was five years old. Hyams painted Paquita's gappy smile and her hairy legs and her red shoes she could no longer wear in the village. He painted her when she posed and he painted her secretly from sketches he made when she wasn't looking, when she was scrubbing a floor or fanning the charcoal with that clapping, whickering noise the little basketwork fan made in her brisk hand. Paquita stood for all those women whose men had crossed the border beyond Gerona. Her husband had actually been hit on the head by a crane-arm, but there was no insurance and she was too poor and too ignorant to think of suing the ship-owners. Wasn't that Franco too? Matt Hyams liked Paquita's scowl, that covered her embarrassment whenever she sensed his eyes on her, like a sly caress, and looked round abruptly. He laughed once, when she caught him like that, and threw his arms around her. '*Señorito!*' she said.

'Damn right,' Matt Hyams said, and let her go.

The British and American expatriates of Torreroja did not greatly appeal to Hyams, though he accepted their society amiably enough, when he walked up to the casino bar after the light faded in the evening. He drank a glass of beer or sipped an *aguardiente*, stabbing at Ramon's anchovies with a toothpick, but he made no effort to belong to the groups that formed round Arnie and Gita Pallenberg or a seersuckered Californian called Fred Deedes, who had made a killing in Mutual Funds. He didn't even pick up a woman, though one day a dark-suited man in Malaga offered him a girl, very clean. He couldn't bring himself to go along.

He was surprised when Arnie Pallenberg stopped by the house. Pallenberg was on a Guggenheim and had a relationship with a gallery on Madison Avenue. He was short, bow-legged, balding and smoked cigars. He wore a Levi suit and local boots, hand-made by a guy on the *carretera*. When he saw what kind of painting Matt Hyams did, he was fulsomely embarrassed. Trouble was, it wasn't the kind of work he really knew how to relate to any more.

'Don't worry about it,' Matt Hyams said.

'I guess I've moved on from naturalism.'

'Don't worry about it,' Matt Hyams said.

'I guess I'm too design-oriented at this point. I'd like for you to come round some time and see what I'm doing right now. It might give you some pointers. Gita pots, you know; she's very talented too: she makes beautiful things. Stop by whenever you want to.'

Matt Hyams did not stop by. He didn't want any pointers. He went on drawing goats and olive trees and the working figure of Paquita Martin. After a few weeks, his studio contained a number of studies of Paquita, the majority from his secret drawings. He turned them to the wall or draped them when she came up to sweep the floor. He was afraid that she would think he was taking advantage of her. Perhaps he was. She was a small, hidden passion with him, Paquita.

He never made any effort to check her housekeeping. He gave her so much every week and when she asked for a little more ('*Señorito*, the price of *boqueron*!') he never held his hand out for the change. He was working well, thanks to her, and he had never been a careful man. He left money around in the bedroom, partly because he never wanted weight in his pants when he was working, mostly to advertise to Paquita that he trusted her. He told her that she was always to tell him if she needed cash. He despised the conspiracy of foreigners who made it a point of honour to pay wages none of them would have dared to propose at home. At first, Paquita would not allow her daughters into the house; she would shoo them out and talk to them only in the street. But after a while they began to come inside. He'd hear the door bang. Then someone would bring a chicken or a bag of charcoal, her cousin Jaime or one of his friends.

At first Hyams did not consciously miss the missing pesetas. The small coins meant nothing to him; he never knew which was worth what, but it was the custom (Chuck advised him) to tip the postman when he brought a bunch of letters and Matt was surprised one day to find that all the change had gone from his dresser. Paquita was quick with a couple of pesetas for the old *cartero*, saying without a blush that it was the *señorito's* money anyway. He grinned at her easy impudence, but she set her face against any acknowledgement that she had been caught out. He was not annoyed that the coins had been taken, but he was sorry that she could not make it the occasion for humorous intimacy between them.

While she sat for him, he tried to make her tell him the history of the village. She told him about the thieving gypsies and about the carriages of the *ricos* in the old days, but if he so much as hinted at the Civil War, let alone at so specific an event as the burning of the church, she stiffened and put away her formal smile. Once he sought to reassure her by alluding to his own abortive attempt to take up arms for the Republic. She was unable to understand a word of the Spanish on which, the day before, she had been congratulating him.

For a week or two, no further money disappeared. But the house was unusually silent. Paquita no longer sang. The lunches grew smaller. Hyams was more relieved than vexed. It did not occur to him to chide her for the modesty of portions which still gave him more than he could eat. Nor did it occur to him to ask for change from the weekly money. One had to allow, after all, for occasional extras, like soap and polish. He managed to improve her temper by paying her more than usual for her sittings. One afternoon he told her the story of Goya and the Duchess of Alba, how the great painter (of whom, she swore, she had not heard) had painted one respectable picture of his patron's wife and another of her '*desnuda*'. Paquita showed him the gaps in her teeth. The *señorito* would not want her to do anything shameful like that, would he? 'Not unless you want to, Paquita,' he said.

'A duchess did that?' she said.

'Oh, a duchess will do anything,' he said.

'Not here in Spain,' she said.

He did not tell her that experts considered that Goya had never actually had the duchess model naked for him. The form of the body suggested that he had imagined the nakedness beneath the pretty woman's clothes. When Paquita had gone, Hyams removed the black dress and the mantilla and the red shoes and painted the naked woman as if she were sitting before him.

Chuck Larsen came by the house. He was going to get married and he wanted Matt Hyams to come to the wedding.

'Who's the lucky girl?' Hyams said. 'Not Caroline Valenti?'

'A Spanish girl, from Malaga,' Chuck Larsen said. 'Her name is Fatima.'

'A Spanish girl! Wow. I take my *sombrero* off to you. Where are you marrying? In church?'

'It's the only place,' Larsen said.

'Then that's where you'd better do it. I'll see you right after the ceremony. I never go into churches.'

'I saw Paquita's children in the kitchen just now,' Larsen said. 'They're turning out to be the best dressed kids in town.'

'My best congratulations to your bride-to-be,' Hyams said, 'and I'll see you on Saturday. Where are you planning on going for the honeymoon?'

'We're staying right here in town,' Larsen said. 'I have my cheque due, first of the month.'

'Spanish girl eh?' Hyams said. 'They sure as hell better've left you with the right ten per cent is all I can say.'

Arnie Pallenberg told Hyams that Chuck's bride was a hooker from Malaga. She had two children, one very dark, to say the least, and no husband. She had a great chest on her and she was taking

Chuck for every cent he had. She was nineteen years old. If Chuck tried to screw her, he'd probably have a heart attack and Fatima would have a United States pension for the rest of her long life.

Chuck seemed to have no idea that he had been suckered. He wore his linen suit and a big carnation in his buttonhole and he came out of the church with the girl on his arm as if he had just turned twenty-one. The foreigners threw rice and the Spaniards whispered and managed to keep a straight face and to giggle at the same time. They all went into the casino bar and drank enough quick drinks to excuse a lot of laughter and the usual ribaldry.

Arnie Pallenberg drank, but he did not join in the laughter.

'What's the matter?' Matt Hyams said to him. 'If Chuck wants to be happy, whose business is it?'

'You mean you seriously haven't heard?'

'Somebody died?'

'Damned right,' Pallenberg said.

'Matthew, really,' Gita Pallenberg said, 'you seriously haven't heard? Hard-edge is dead. It was in *Time* magazine.'

'Hard-edge is *dead*. How did it happen? Not with a shot-gun?'

'You think it's funny,' Arnie Pallenberg said, 'but I've been hard-edge for three years. I have upwards of a hundred hard-edge canvases all ready for my show when we get back to New York, and now it's dead and so are they.'

'No gallery is going to even *look* at hard-edge.'

'That *Time* magazine,' Hyams said, 'it sure can be a bitch sometimes.'

Hyams gave his small present to Chuck Larsen (a hand-made coffee set from Coín, with a brilliant vari-coloured glaze) and ambled back to his house. The Californian who had done well out of Mutual Funds had asked him to come to dinner in the new *finca* he had just built. He wanted Matt to paint his wife, or was it the girl he lived with. Matt had to buy gas before leaving town, so he went to get the five hundred pesetas he had left in the top drawer of the dresser in the bedroom. Only three hundred were still there. He might not have noticed, but the denomination of the notes was too high for the theft not to be obvious, even to him. He was not so much angry as hurt. He was humiliated by the blatancy of the thing. He was willing to be generous, but he would not be taken for a slob, or a slab. Monday, he would certainly say something.

Paquita listened darkly to his story of the missing cash. 'But who could have taken it, *señorito*?' she said, when he had finished.

The patronizing endearment was too much for him. 'Who do you think took it?' he yelled at her. 'No one has a key except for me and you. I didn't take it. Now guess who took it. You got one guess, Paquita.'

She stood there for a few seconds. 'I'm going to my house,' she said.

'And I'm going to the police, god dammit,' he said. 'I'm going to the *Guardia Civil*, so help me.'

'I'm going to my house,' she said.

He grabbed her arm. He was strong and he held her. She endured his grip. 'You listen to me, you dumb broad,' Matt Hyams said. 'I told you: you need money, you tell me. You don't have to steal anything from me, not a *peseta*. O.K., you do it and I know you do, small amounts, fine, but this is too much, god dammit. If your family needs money, all you have to do is come and tell me. But this ... Paquita, I – I *like* you, *comprende*? I don't want you to do this to me. I want us to be *friends. Amigos, comprende*?'

'I steal nothing,' she said. 'It was probably the gypsies.'

'You know better than that,' he said. 'If it wasn't you, who did you give the key to? Jaime? One of the girls? Come on, Paquita. I'm not just any one of those damned *extranjeros*, I'm an artist, I'm a man, I'm somebody cares for you.'

'You don't go to church,' she said. 'You never go to church.'

'Holy Christ,' Matt Hyams said, 'the last time people were free to do what they wanted in this town, what did they do? They burned the goddam church down to the ground. They burned the *iglesia* down to the ground, right? Now don't tell me you're sorry. Don't tell me you blame them. Paquita, can't you try and understand? I'm on your side.'

'I steal nothing,' she said. 'I'm going to my house.'

'O.K.,' Matt Hyams said, 'Franco took the money. As a contribution to the new jetty. Or maybe you think I took it.'

'You ask me to pose for you *desnuda*,' Paquita said. 'I'm going to my house.'

'Go,' Hyams said. 'You want to go, go. If you want everyone to know you're a thief, why should I try and stop you? Get the hell out of here as a matter of fact.'

She stood in the doorway with her black shopping bag and the shawl over her shoulders. 'Friends?' she said. '*Communist!*'

The Muse

At school he was exceptional, but in an unexceptionable way. He had a commonplace name (Colin Smith!) and he came from a common place: the suburbs of South London were not, in those days, sprigged with smart addresses. He learned early to make the first joke at his own expense; it was less costly in the long run. By calling himself 'four-eyes', he forestalled anyone else doing so. But if he wore glasses, he was not weedy; if he knew a lot of things, one of them was not to be a know-all. He was cautious, but he was careful not to show it. For instance, he did a killing imitation of the Reverend Barry Pratt and could seem to be in full flow even as the chaplain was opening the classroom door. Yet he was back behind his own desk, head in Homer, while the rest of the Remove was being told off for idiotic laughter. Why couldn't they be good like Smith? Perhaps Pratt would not have been all that mortified if he had come in sooner; for along with other pilloried members of staff, he applauded sportingly enough, at the end-of-term 'Merry Evening', when young Smith was persuaded to parade his mimicry in public. His darts flew straight at their targets (¡pobre Señor Guzman!), but they carried no barbs. He aped his betters without making apes of them. The headmaster congratulated him on a performance for which another boy might have been flogged.

You could tell the day he was due home from school, the Smiths' daily used to say, because the sun always came out. He was a young man to go to the cricket with (ah Fishlock, ah Gover!) because when he was at the Oval, rain never stopped play. In the High Street, shopping with his mother, he was prompt with a smile for the dullest neighbours, a hand for the heaviest loads. He suffered fools with a gladness that never failed to gladden; his achievements – 'A Cambridge scholarship, do I hear?' – were somehow shared with Mrs Cramp and three-fingered Major

Hutchinson and even with the postman who brought the telegram. He was welcome to his success, for though he surpassed
them all, he never left anyone behind.

He arrived in Cambridge prepared to be lonely and industrious.
At the station, he saw a tweed-coated girl struggling with a
cumbrous trunk (his own had gone P.L.A.) and, with the un-
premeditated good manners he showed when toting Mrs Cramp's
potatoes up the hill, he went to give her a hand. He would have
raised his cap, if he had still been wearing one. Her name was
Ellen and she was bleak with apprehension. A good fortnight passed
(mostly in her company) before he realized that she was also a
beauty. And then it took the unsubtle envy of someone on his
staircase to make him appreciate that he had made the catch of the
year. ('I'd use her shit for toothpaste,' the ex-squaddy said. 'You'd
better watch it, Watson,' he said, nicely. 'That's just what I'm doing,
old son, up and down the stairs; it's driving me bonkers.')

Ellen was not only beautiful – the blue eyes, the fair hair, the
English rosy flesh – she was also extremely pleasant: she laughed
at his jokes and she nodded at his seriousness.('I *like* owls,' she
said.) She too was a suburbanite; it took no *coup de foudre* to make
them fall in love. They were, they were happy to think, made for
each other. They took their time: they held hands, they kissed. It
was a wonderful year.

Since she was so pretty, Ellen was asked (by the vigilant
Watson) whether she would take part in a College play. And what
about old Colin, come to that? His unannounced talent for mimicry
proved to have travelled well; if Ellen was charming, Colin was a
riot. Very soon he was performing his own monologues at Foot-
lights' smokers. Monologues were generally the preserve of the
egotist, but Colin's earned him a reputation for self-effacement.
Could it truly be a monologue if it contained more than one
character? Ah philosophy! Anyway, Colin never began a modest
proposition, but he was interrupted by himself in the monstrous
form of Bragg. No sooner had he outlined the topic on which he
proposed to offer not so much an opinion as a tentative sketch of
a *possible* opinion, than Bragg would burst in, loud, confident and
dogmatic. Bragg was polyglot, polymath and – it raised a laugh in
those days – polytechnic. He was intolerable and Smith C. was
the first and only one to tolerate him. Oh the pleading patience

with which he would implore the audience to 'hear Bragg *out*'! Bragg combined humourlessness with a jeering laugh, waspishness with a thin skin. When he promised to summarize an argument, Smith C. would beg him to declare it in full, 'to save time'. (Ah the sweet swell of laughter as they got it at the back!) Bragg crushed Colin's attempts to make even the mildest interjection and he did it so unfairly that people actually yelled for Bragg to ease up. There were limits; Colin was much too yielding. 'Well, Bragg's a genius,' Colin said, 'what can I do?'

Colin became well known; Bragg became famous. Colin would play up to his creation's notoriety at parties by glancing nervously at the door when any loud-mouthed person was announcing his own arrival. 'Hullo,' he would say, 'Bragg's here, I think ... oh no, sorry. Nasty moment that. Hullo, *Watters*!' The girls would laugh and say, 'Oh do do him, Colin, for us.' Colin would shake his head. 'What will I do if he comes in in the middle?' He appeared genuinely afraid of the hirsute monster he had conjured up. 'I wouldn't like to see Bragg come into this room,' he warned, 'because what he does to women is *frightening*. He makes them feel sick. No, no ... jealousy, ladies, pure jealousy! He has a way with you, beware!' Colin joked that Bragg was following him around; he felt socially haunted, intellectually intimidated. 'All I want to do is some research, you know, on one – or *possibly* two, two at the *outside* – aspect or aspects (you can see how tentative I am on this) of the relation or relations between a statement and a proposition, if indeed there is a distinction to be made between them, or it, if there isn't. All I ask is, *please* don't breathe a word of this to Bragg, because he thinks it smacks of "reckless neo-fascist speculation" ...' His voice boomed out the last few words and he glanced over his own shoulder, quite as if the Reverend Barry Pratt had come in a moment too soon and caught him in spiteful spate.

One day he confessed to Ellen that his dread of Bragg might be a joke to others, but that it was increasingly real to him. 'I *love* Bragg,' she told him. 'You see?' he said. 'You *see*? Now he's breaking up my engagement!' He feared that he had become celebrated for a degrading comic invention; he did not want to be a funny man, he had serious things to say. Ellen reminded him that once they had gone down, he could be done with Bragg and all his nonsense. He could take that academic job in the provinces, or overseas perhaps. America, why not? 'Bragg's doing that,' Colin said.

Ellen saw that the joke was no joke and Bragg was allowed to lapse. The owl rejoiced. Dear Ellen, she would make a perfect wife; he knew she would. She was even-tempered, she was domesticated ('You're wrong,' she told Watson when he begged her to try the stage, 'I really *like* cooking') and she was ready to want whatever Colin wanted. She had a mind of her own, but she preferred his. Only occasionally, now that they had begun to make love, was he startled by the expression of determination on her face when, on the brink of pleasure, she would race on, furiously and alone, for what they had come to share. When it was over, she blushed and turned her head away; he loved her for it.

He did well in the Tripos (she did quite well too) and his tutor told him that he would be making a mistake if he went off to some backwoods lectureship. He had spent three years trying to persuade himself not to call Humphrey Botting 'sir' and now he could only stammer that he was not particularly ambitious. The backwoods might well be his proper habitat.

'Nonsense,' Humphrey said. 'You ought to be in London. If you want to be a writer, that's where you've got to be.'

'A writer, sir?' (Damn!)

'That's rather what one assumes.'

'I'm not sure that I have the – the – what shall I say? –'

'That'll come,' Botting said, 'that'll come. Think of those monologues of yours. And your *Granta* bloc-notes, of course. As a matter of fact I've already spoken to someone on the *Review*. (I presume you read it.) Do you know Andrew Burgess? He used to be here. Philologist.'

The *Review* had offices in St James's Court; its collegiate affectations – oh that first 'house lunch'! – did not rule out (rather demanded) an intense, acutely polite rivalry among those who toed its pinstripe line. Here Colin could shine, but he could also defer; it was a delectable option for any fledgling (but volatile) Janus. He resolved that both his faces should henceforth be indistinguishably solemn; his maiden assessment, of 'the European dimension', was as shrewd as it was humourless. Andy Burgess congratulated him in a pub favoured – for its sausages – by our leading Catholic novelist, when he was in the country. 'Everyone thinks you're bang right on Brussels and no two people agree which side you've actually plumped for. You're *Review* timber all right, Colin; the article was first-rate and, if I may say so, wise.'

'What was wrong with it?' Colin asked.

'Let me put it this way. We shouldn't object, we should even be quite favourably disposed, if you were to give – how shall I put it? – if you were to give a little more tongue to your cheek.'

'Give . . . ? Ah, I see. You mean – ?'

'Funnies? I do rather. You know what I should like to propose to you?'

'No,' Colin said.

'Why should you? An occasional column: we could call it, say, "On The Margin", say – every six, perhaps seven, weeks, a sideways look at the politico-diplomatic scene, or at least at its *vocabulary*.'

Ellen was pregnant (with the first of the boys) when the *Review* proposed to make his column a regular feature. There would be a modicum of extra money (they didn't want to abbreviate his serious contributions) and, of course, his photograph in a box at the top, slightly to the left, presumably. 'Don't do it, darling, unless you want to,' Ellen said, but she was glad when he decided that he would. She loved to laugh (and he loved her when she did), even when she was afraid of splitting her stitches (Timothy came out weighing over ten pounds, and he had his father's head). 'You know what you ought to do though, don't you? You ought to make them give you three months off in the year to write that novel, do something personal.'

'They'd never wear it.'

'You don't know your own value,' Ellen said. 'Luckily I do.'

He kissed her. God, he was happy.

The column had earned chuckles in the right quarters even before Bragg put in his clinching appearance. Thereafter, it was merely the talk of the town. Bragg, after failing (for manifestly political reasons) to get his lectureship, had gone to be a professor in America. He returned – on a sabbatical – King of the New Frontier, kitted out in the kinks and kudos of the kids. His opinions provoked a sublimely po-faced correspondence, of which

Bragg pre-empted the lion's share ('Being the only lion'), to the point of repeatedly answering his own last letter, terming this 'The democratic right to reply'. All of his letters ended 'to be continued'; he always had more to say; he always said it. He declared popular music the harbinger of a new 'creed without a credo', and he saw in the rock *group* the signs of an end to 'pair-bonding, the binary fetish and the whole tight-ass logic of scientistic truth-functional analysis – and it just could also imply a radical re-orientation of gin rummy. No, to be serious ...' A doodling sketch Colin did of Bragg, freedom riding in Alabama, in a litter carried by blacks, was taken by Andy B. up to Sir Thing and turned into the first line drawing ever to be published in the *Review*. 'Now ask them about the three months,' Ellen said.

When the top Sunday paper made its offer, Colin wanted to refuse. Over more celebrated sausages, Andy said that he would be a fool to turn them down. He had the boys (and would soon have one of the girls) to consider; Ellen deserved a house. He could continue to contribute to the *Review* on European perspectives and perhaps he would like to do something more light-hearted for their Christmas number: 'Bragg drags in the New Year' or something of that order.

'You'd better ask Bragg about that,' Colin said.

In a period of intense, often agonized, social commotion, when many of their friends' marriages ruptured either into divorce or into less irreparable fractions, the Smiths remained the perfect couple. Buying the rectory in Barnes had come just at the right moment. They were insulated, but not isolated, safe but never sorry. They were the first to enjoy their friends' good news (promotions, re-marriages, even a title!) and quick to commiserate when it was bad. They were comfortable, not showy; they were satisfied, not smug. No one knew anybody quite like the Smiths, and the Smiths knew it.

Colin did his column and he contributed to the boom in television satire. He managed, as ever, to be trenchant without being savage. (The producer remarked, 'Colin's so clean-cut, even when he goes right down to the bone, it never goes septic.' Everyone laughed; he *was* the producer.) Before long, of course, Bragg had bullocked his way into the studio. He boasted of his open marriage and his revolutionary ardour – 'Man, I clench my fist round people's *heads*' – and his attitude to L.S.D. ('I take the pounds and I let the pennies look after the kids. No seriously, Col . . .') Bragg's California Yorkshire accent was the more hairy for issuing from Colin's thin suburban lips; the dummy's gargantuan garrulousness made a fool of his master's voice. The top Sunday paper wrote three months annual leave into Colin's new contract without a quibble.

He took Ellen and the boys and Lucy down to Bandol and wrote the novel which was to put a quality burnish on his (he feared) lightweight reputation. He longed for quality company in which he did not have to be a T.V. personality. *The Stephanus Factor* won a major prize. His acceptance speech at the black-tied dinner was modest, even rather earnest. The literati smiled at his literacy, but were disappointed not to laugh. Wasn't he supposed to be a T.V. personality? If only Bragg had won the thing!

The prize-winning novel concerned a man delegated to an arcane diplomatic mission. (It opened with an instantly classic briefing session, which ended with the typical Smithism 'The darkest mystery was why they called it *brief*ing'.) Parachuted at night into a country he will 'recognize when he sees it', the hero finds himself in a strange city, with his sole credential a numerically coded message from a man called Stephanus. He observes the cold-blooded murder of an old man whose library the murder squad proceed to burn. The witness is discovered and pursued by the killers. After a series of chillingly close shaves – the blurb promised – he finds refuge with a woman who, in the course of a tingling *nuit blanche*, tells him her experience of the city and its laws. The bitter and witty picture is one of inescapable narrow-mindedness, 'for the good of the Good'. As light comes up over the Acropolis the man perceives that the woman is living in Plato's Republic. When 'the Helpers' come for the 'mad lady' in the morning, he stands aside and allows them to do their hypodermic stuff. The politics of perfection lead inexorably to terror. Such is the Justice of which Stephanus, the sixteenth-century scholar, was the enumerator. The vicious virtues of the Ideal State, its cleanliness and its freedom from pornography, from licentious music and from the vagaries of public dissent were spelt out with a straight-faced ambiguity which lent itself to flatteringly fulsome précis. 'A minor masterpiece,' threatened Angela Lane, under the headline 'Platonic

Affaire'. When her notice appeared in the quality press, Ellen burst into tears. ('What are you so happy about?' Colin said.)

Bragg was less impressed. He launched a campaign – he even collected *signatures* – against the 'crappy, souped-up little fictions of a tight little island'. Bragg, having straddled the Atlantic for many years, was putting his weight more and more on the American side of the 'grotesquely uneven equation'; the States was where it was all happening. And what was it? That was what was so exciting: no one was too sure. Maybe the whole place was going to go up in smoke. Maybe its *giant* technological clout would see it through. Maybe everything would happen: *something* certainly would. Whereas one thing was for sure: minus zero was going to happen in Britain, with its grey grievances and its unmanned Mandarins. Britain was *through*, man; look at its prissy prose and its pissy pose.

Colin and Ellen now had four children, the house in Barnes, the Citroën estate and the Mini and now there was the cottage (and Humbert the pony) near Newbury. People were amazed: they had everything anyone wanted and they still wanted each other! Colin was able to write whatever he chose for longer periods of each year and his imagination proved promptly prolific. Ellen had become a super cook and she remained as cheerful and affectionate as ever. 'Ellen never changes,' people said. Didn't they have any problems? (Even their children's teeth were straight, for God's sake.) Well, as the roads grew busier, it did take longer and longer to get in and out of town. Colin had to leave the West End not later than half-past five if he wanted to be home for dinner. And he wanted to be home for dinner. Why then go to the West End? Let Bragg jeer at the 'drab acolytes of the quotidian'; did Bragg have a wife like Ellen, or his own kids to play with? (Bragg was into his fourth on-off relationship this year, sharing a Wellesley girl with a Panther.)

Living in suburbia (even in up-and-coming Barnes) was particularly irritating when there was a party in town. Parties were nothing one desperately *liked*, but some invitations were less dislikeable than others. It was nice when people like the Bernsteins asked one – with Boatie's hand-written '*Do* come' in the corner – but then you found that Ellen was in Barnes and you were already at the Beeb or wherever. Ellen had intended to join Colin in town

– he was doing his proofs in Gray's Inn Road – but Lucy had a sore throat and she didn't really go for the Bernsteins.

'Boatie isn't going to be there apparently,' Colin said. 'She's in Viareggio with a Siamese abortionist, or so Felix says.'

'Felix?'

'Felix del Rio. *¡Feliz!* You remember. So she isn't going to be there. I say, I do wish you'd come.'

'No, you go on your own. It'll do you good for a change.'

'Perhaps I'll just come on home,' he said.

'*Viareggio?*'

'That's what Felix says. Well, it *was* Puccini's birthplace.'

The Bernsteins had a house on Primrose Hill. The yellow door was wide open; *le tout Hampstead et ses environs* passed in and out. Colin approached the noise with all the unworthy apprehensions of the suburban boy (despite his forty years). Even in sophisticated circles, he was famous for his humour, but sophistication was, he knew, beyond him. (It was up those stairs and in all that shrill noise.) Many of those present – 'Hullo, *Watters*!' – were familiar: Cambridge chums, jostling, joshing journalists, sated satirists whose savagery had dwindled rewardingly into whimsy, but there were also those – weren't there? – who inhabited a rarer world of intellectual urgency and demanding excellence. He walked up to the freshly painted, he hoped not *sticky*, house (Bernstein's *important* new film had been a commercial and critical *smash*, with its 'accurate, exhilarating, revolutionary optimism', as Angela Lane had put it) and Colin felt that he personally had so far achieved absolutely *nothing*. The gleaming white house flashed its superiority at him. Big, bearded Bragg was sure to be somewhere up there under the dimmed spotlights on the first floor, plastered and masterful as only Bragg could be. Colin went up the steps, past three film directors in jeans and Levi tops who did not budge an inch when he said 'Excuse me.'

Bernstein, it turned out, wasn't at the party either. He had flown to Corfu with Toby Jarrett's wife. Toby had decided to come out of the closet, so there was no immediate hassle there. *He* was with Simon Porter on Fire Island. 'And where's Jay Gatsby?' Colin said to a very dirty girl.

'Jay who?'

'Wrong party,' Colin said.

'Do I know you?' the girl said.

'Colin, *really*,' Mike Watson said, 'what are you doing talking to that?'

'Prick,' the dirty girl said. 'Shit bastard.'

'I love you too, darling,' Watson said.

'You'd *better*. He walks into my house all the time,' the girl said to Colin. 'He comes right into my bathroom. Shit bastard fuck.'

'It's been that kind of a day,' Watson said. 'Where's Ellen?'

'At home. Lucy's got a sore throat. How are things South of the River?'

'Chaos.'

'Improving, eh?'

'You're so together,' Watson said, working one wrist.

'Everyone's American suddenly,' Colin said.

'Bragg's influence,' Watson said. 'You ought to know that.'

'I want to meet the intellectual élite,' Colin said. 'Which floor is that?'

'They're probably in Bernstein's bedroom. He's got porno up there, you know.'

'Poor who?'

'Knock it off, Colin, will you, old son? They're showing his Danish skin flicks; he made them before his accurate, exhilarating, revolutionary optimism made him a fucking fortune.'

'Can you date the first free use of fuck in mixed company in this country? To the nearest year? Just for a little survey I'm running . . .'

'Don't be so bloody suburban,' Watson said. 'I'm sorry Ellen's not here.'

'So am I,' Colin said, 'because then we could both leave.'

'I think I'll go and call her. What's your number again?'

Colin drank something that the drunk Irish barman promised him was a Margarita and began to retreat towards the door. One of the film directors was promising to show the other two the secret of the universe. It involved taking off his trousers.

'Colin Smith?'

'Right first time,' Colin said.

'I'm Angela Lane.'

'Oh good heavens,' Colin said, 'how absolutely marvellous!'

'I've got a feeling you're on your way out.'

'I was until I read your review of *The Stephanus Factor*.'

'Wasn't I sweet? I'd like to talk to you about it.'

'I'd like to talk to you about almost anything.'

The dirty girl came and pulled Colin's arm. 'They tell me you know Bragg,' she said.

'Never heard of him,' Colin said.

'Let me tell you something: I've *fucked* Bragg.'

'No wonder he's dropped out of sight,' Colin said.

'And he's a *wimp*. He's a *wimp*, Mr Smith.'

'Write to the papers,' Colin said.

'I fucked him for three weeks,' the girl said. 'Zero. Zilch.'

'You missed out zebra,' Colin said.

'Get *striped*,' the dirty girl said. 'I never even remotely came. Never remotely.'

'I'm sorry,' Colin said, 'but I really must get out of here.'

'So that's Bragg for you, O.K.?'

'O.K.,' Colin said. 'Wow, yes. Absolutely. I'll spread the word.'

Angela Lane stepped over the film directors and joined him by the car.

'Are you as hungry as I am?' she said.

'Do you terribly mind if I just call my wife?' he said. 'Only Lucy, that's our eldest daughter, she's had this throat and ...'

After Ellen had said that everything was fine and to take his time and enjoy himself, he and Angela Lane went to a floating restaurant on the canal not far away, near the zoo. She was a small woman (older, or older-looking, than he expected) with hennaed hair chopped rather boyishly, in the style of the twenties. She wore a blue linen suit, crumpled, and a whitish shirt with a torero's black string tie. Her voice had a smoker's harshness and she coughed, impatiently thumping her chest, as she spoke. Her eyes were dark and alert, the irises as large, it looked, as sixpences. The hands that fumbled with lighter and cigarettes were very white, as if she had stayed too long in the bath. She had a wrinkled throat and no breasts he could see. He described her thus to himself, as they waited for the sole, and wondered why, if she was that easy to disparage, he was so charged with excitement. Was it simply that she had been with three or four of the smartest men in town? She was, as they were saying, her own person. She had made her name reviewing films, *scorchingly*, and she had, it was widely reported, refused to speak to several members of the Royal Family (who seemed to *mind*). She was unquestionably one of the most charming of the charmed circle. (She reviewed novels here, films *there* and theatre somewhere else. When she put you down, down you stayed.) Her huge eyes snatched at him with flattering urgency. This was the woman who had loved his book and who had hated so many others. He only hoped he would choose the right wine. 'I wonder,' he said, blinking at the list, 'what Bragg would drink on an occasion like this.'

'Balls,' she said.

'I don't think I know that one,' he said. 'Is it Dutch by any chance?'

'Bragg,' she said. 'Balls. Order anything that comes in a bottle. I need it. I was in New York yesterday. With a drink I just might get here in a minute or two.' She leaned forward. 'I'm not interested in Bragg. I'm interested in you. I'm interested to know,' she coughed and coughed, thumped and thumped, 'what's keeping you back, what's behind this furtiveness, all this Bragg baloncy. Why isn't Bragg in your *books*?'

'I thought ...' Colin sniffed his wine. 'I thought Bragg was balls,' he said.

'Bragg's *your* balls,' she said. 'And where did they go, that's what I want to know?'

'They were never all that big.' he said. 'Seriously, Bragg was just a little idea that met a sorcerer's apprentice one dull day and ...'

'Don't give me that, Colin. You're laying yourself off, that's what you're doing. You've been doing it for years. Well, the years are running out. I had an abortion last week, so ... well, I know about these things.'

'I'm sorry,' he said.

'Forget it,' she said. 'I haven't got time for those things. You wish Bragg was dead, don't you?'

'I *am* sick to death of him,' Colin said. 'I'm sick to death of trying to be funny, as a matter of fact.'

'Then why do it?'

'It pays the rent.'

'Then why do it?'

'Oh Christ,' he said. 'We'll have a bottle of no. 63, if . . .'

'I'm serious. You have a real talent, but – forgive the cant – you've copped out. I liked your book –'

'You were incredibly perceptive. You saw –'

'I saw what was there and I said so. I also saw what wasn't there and I didn't say that.'

'Which was?'

'Let's say "The Bragg Factor". You've turned your seriousness, the real thing about you, into a subject for cosy comedy.'

He dipped fish into the tartare sauce, put it in his mouth. 'You're the first person who ever saw that.'

'It only needs one,' she said.

'Possibly my tutor,' he said. 'Botting.'

'Oh Cambridge!' she said. 'Forget it. You're a man pretending to be a boy. Usually they're boys pretending to be men. Are you still hungry?'

'Not really,' he said.

'Then let's get out of here. I'm feeling seasick.'

'It is a little rough tonight.' He raised a hand for the bill ('No sweet tonight, *dottore*? No cheese? No coffee?') and they went ashore; she had the unfinished bottle of no. 63 by the throat. Of course they had to meet Watson (with the dirty girl) on his way in.

'You've made Bragg funny,' she said, 'because you know he's right. *Seriously* right. Everything he says about you proves that . . .'

'He stands for everything I deplore and detest,' Colin said, the evening air restoring his common sense. 'What do you mean right? Bragg's a buffoon.'

'Do you want a snort?' she said.

'I'm sorry?'

'Do you want a snort?'

'Oh no thanks. I'm driving.'

'You're so afraid of being dull,' she said. 'Don't try to amuse me. You think women have to be amused. I don't want that. I don't want any of that shit. I wouldn't mind if you bored the pants off me.'

'What about that character on the steps? The secret of the universe!'

'Let me ask you something. How many women have you had in your life?'

'Oh no,' he said, 'oh no you don't.'

'I thought so,' she said. 'You're a married virgin. I can smell them.'

'Look,' he said, 'I think I'd better take you home.'

'What will your wife say?'

'Oh boy,' he said, 'oh boy, oh boy.'

'Fuck,' she said. 'All right? I'm hard to handle, I'm not like most women. I don't want to be like them. You're beginning to think I'm more trouble than I'm worth. That may well be so. But I'm also worth something. You're worried about your wife, right?'

'Well, she worries about me . . .'

'There you go again. That fake shit: sliding away, being cute.'

'I've got a feeling you're jet-lagged, am I right? You just flew in from New York . . .'

'I'm younger than you, Colin. Does that give you something to think about?'

'No.'

'It should. Because you're treating me like an older woman. It's time you led a completely different life, Colin, that's what I'm trying to tell you. You don't love your wife, you don't want to be with her any more, you can't go on this way.'

'Angela, I very much appreciate the nice things you said about my book in the paper. They were not only nice but also extremely perceptive . . .'

'Rule for creative people: never read reviews and, above all, never review them. You have quality; I like quality; I said so. Finish. Now we're talking about you and your crisis.'

'Me and my crisis are going to take you to where you and yours live and then me and mine're going home to my wife. I and mine.'

'I want Bragg here,' Angela Lane said, coughing into her white hand.

'Screw Bragg. Bragg doesn't exist.'

'Everything that's been invented by an artist exists,' Angela said.

'He's journalism. Nothing a journalist invents *ever* exists. Look, where are we going please? It's getting late. And if you want to know where you can find Bragg, your nearest stockist is situated in the barge where we just had that rather funny fish, because Bragg is really just Mike Watson in stars and stripes. Bragg is all the things I fear and detest. With Thousand Island sauce.'

'It won't wash, Colin.'

'*And* that won't wash, Angela.'

'I'm a damned serious critic, Colin Smith, and I won't be put down by you because you're afraid I'm after your body. I *am* after your body and I still tell you that I know what I'm talking about. I read every line you ever wrote, fuck it, give or take a clipping or two that wasn't in the library, and I know you. This country is a clapped-out, giggling nowhere land; it needs something harsh and true and vicious said to it and you're the man to do it. And all you're doing at the present time is peddle pap. You're giving them sugar to snort, Colin. They need something else.'

'I never wanted to be anything other than what I am.' Colin said. 'I have a very good and happy life. I'm doing what I like.'

'You like mashed potatoes?'

'Wrong: Lyonnaise – and my wife does them just right.'

'Tell me the truth, Colin. I'm the one chance you've got. Why won't you do it?'

'*Look*,' he said.

'What I said to you I don't say to many people. I'm *feared*, Colin; what do you think about that? And here I am offering to be your fucking nanny, for God's sake, and all you can say is "*look*". I need a drink.' She threw the empty wine bottle into a St John's Wood hedge.

'I'm not too sure what's open at this hour,' Colin said.

'I'm living in Lower Eaton Place,' she said. 'Let's go.'

'How does that relate to Eaton Place?'

'It's lower,' she said, smoking a cigarette in long red pulls, angry eyes on the night streets.

'I'm sorry,' he said. 'I'm not very good at this kind of thing.'

'Retreat, retreat, retreat,' she said. 'One more talented coward. They're all bloody talented cowards. I can't fuck because I had this abortion, but I'll blow you if you want to come on up.'

'No thank you very much.'

'O.K., I'll blow you here, if that's what you want.'

'It's awfully nice of you,' he said, 'but ... I'm sure we both have things we want to do.'

'Christ,' she said. '*Christ*.'

'A lot of what you say is perfectly true,' he said, as she turned and fought with the door.

'That's all men want, you know.'

'Is it?'

'They want to hear you say it,' she said. 'That's what they want. God, I'm so goddam exhausted. They want to hear you say things. At least all the ones I ever met want you to say things. I think I'm going to kill myself, Colin.'

'Oh now look here.'

'I think I seriously am.'

'Well,' he said, 'that's your trip, isn't it?'

'You filthy son of a bitch,' she said, losing interest in the door. 'I could kill myself right here, in your silly car. What kind of a car is this anyway?'

'It's –'

'As if I cared. I could kill myself here and now.'

'You have the wherewithal?'

'Who said I was going to kill myself with a wherewithal? What *is* a wherewithal?'

'Now who's doing the funnies?' he said.

'I want to see your cock,' she said.

'That's easily arranged,' he said, 'but I don't think we'll be doing it now. Seriously, Angela, shouldn't you – ?'

'As a matter of sober fact,' she said. 'As a matter of sober fact ...'

'You wouldn't care to rephrase that, I suppose?'

'What I have said to you this evening, tonight, whenever it is, I said out of the goodness of my fast failing heart, if you can believe that.'

'I appreciate it. And there's a lot in what you say,' he said. 'I told you that.'

'How many cunts have you seen in your life?'

'How should I know that? Really ...'

'You *know*. Only you're embarrassed, you're *shaking*. Look at you: you're abject. You could be a totally different person; at a pinch you could even be yourself. You could be Bragg. He's seen *thousands.* And you daren't. You absolutely daren't. You look at that review of mine, when you get home to Tooting. Read *between* the lines this time. *Memento mori.*'

'I remember Morrie all right. Angela –'

'You're going to die, Colin. You're going to die refusing to be what you are. It's coming. Christ knows it's coming. The politics and *mores* of the free world are fucking insane, you know that, don't you? We're all being set up; fight or be fucked, Colin.'

'I think I should warn you that I happen, despite everything, largely to be on the side of the free world.'

'You're spoiled, Colin. And in return for being spoiled, you've agreed to be nice. And that's a lie. You know why? Because no one is nice. No one. *You* certainly aren't. You know what you should do with Bragg? You should kill him and eat him. You heard those animals, didn't you, when we were in the restuarant? I'd like to go and let them out. Just because we've agreed to be locked in a zoo doesn't mean they have to be. I'd like to see them stalking the streets, in the underground ...'

'All those zilchs and zebras and things? That's scary. Imagine them on the escalators.'

'Patronizing Colin, patronizing bloody Colin Smith. You think I'm some drunken, clapped-out lush, you think I'm some ugly, sick, pathetic object – will you *contradict* me, you shit? – but I'm telling you the truth.'

'I know,' Colin said.

'You *know?*'

'Of course I know. But I'm a very lucky man ...'

'You don't have any idea what your wife really wants, so don't start giving me that. She might be thrilled if you went off with someone else. Or just went off. Bang! She may be aching for you to. Try thinking about that, instead of being so goddam condescending, will you please, for once?'

'She isn't,' Colin said, 'aching for me to. You really like New York, don't you?'

'You only have one life,' she said.

'Promise?' Colin said.

'I'm not offering you anything,' Angela said. 'My life ... is my business, my affair, oh shit; it's nothing to do with you. London, New York ... you're right, I'm totally knackered, I really am. Well, that's my bag. But I am right about you, Master Smith, and I advise you to pay attention. No one else knows about your talent except you and me, that's all that keeps us together. Otherwise ... hips that pass in the night. Maybe not even those. No.' She lurched across the pavement, wincing at the tall building in front of her. 'Well, it isn't the north face of the Eiger, is it, getting up to the fifth floor? I shall have to take my chances.'

'Do you want me to help you?'

'I'm a critic, you bastard,' Angela Lane said. 'I don't need anybody's help. I call the shots. Of course I want you to help me, how am I going to get up there otherwise, especially with my present wherewithal?'

Even their silence seemed noisy. The mere progress of their bodies seemed to make splashes in the expensive air, as if they had fallen into a late swimming pool. He expected angry tenants to burst out of their Banham-locked doors. The lift came on its oiled coil and he got her into it and clashed complicated gates behind them. When he looked back, he was almost surprised not to see footprints full of blood; she was walking wounded. 'I hate this place,' she said, 'but it was all I could get.'

The flat was very large and full of manifestly valuable furniture and artefacts. A *Giacometti*? 'The only place you could get?'

'Isn't it cheap?' she said. 'It's disgusting. Do you know the Moncktons? It belongs to the Moncktons. Bankers, I hate the bastards. It was all I could get. Look, my mouth's just here somewhere, why don't you kiss it?'

'Are you going to be all right now?'

'You're a bloody virgin, Smith.'

'You're pretty pissed, Angela.'

'Forget the pissed, concentrate on the pretty. *Am* I pretty?'

'No,' he said. 'You're not, you're ...'

'What am I?' She sat on the thick woollen floor without a bump. There really was very little of her. 'Am I ugly? I am, aren't I? I'm a wreck, Colin. Not fit for salvage.'

'You have very remarkable eyes,' he said, 'and that's my last word, all right?'

'You should write a play. Never write a film, whatever you do, never do that. I'd like to find one person who'd dare to be great just because I said he could be. Then I could die happy.'

'Good is better than great,' he said. 'What's all this about dying?'

'Oh you've heard about it too? I'm thirty-seven years old, Colin, and look at me. All I have left is my eyes. You can't get wrinkles in your eyes, can you? Just candy-stripes. So I have candy-stripes. Great is *much* better. Is it my breath? I do suck things. *Any*thing.'

'You should get to bed, Angela.'

'Fighting talk, Angel. Show me your cock.'

'I don't think this is the time, to tell you the truth.'

'I'll tell you the truth, Smith: you're not a happy man and I'm the only person in the world who knows it, the only person in the world you can tell it to. I am the Pythian priestess, Col m'boy, priestesses don't come pithier than I am, or more pithed, so what do you say?'

'Am I going to see you again?'

'Oh boy. Oh boy oh boy, the fruit is ripening before my eyes. Are *you* going to see me again? Am *I* going to see me again is a slightly more pressing question at this point. What *was* that wine you ordered?'

'It was a Sancerre,' he said. 'I don't think it travels.'

'It travels all right. It's just that I don't. What time is it in East Hampton?'

'All I know is, it's one-fifteen in Hampton Wick –'

'Hampton *Wick*? Hampton *Wick*? Fucking Simon Porter. Fifteen-bedroom shack in East Hampton.'

'– and I'm on my way, if that's all right with you.'

'If you're looking for something to kiss, kiss my fucking foot.'

'I'm looking for the door as a matter of fact. I could have sworn it was here when we came in.'

'Those books behind you – the *Decline and Fall* – they're all phoneys, push volume five and see yourself out, why don't you? It wouldn't *hurt* you to kiss my fucking foot.'

'I don't know which one it is,' Colin said.

'I've done it all,' she said. 'Name something I haven't done. Because I've done that.'

'How about saying good night?'

Lucy was asleep, nostrils caked with green. He picked the clotted muck off with a gentle thumbnail and flicked it into a linoleum corner of the bedroom. Even his daughter seemed alien and vulnerable; she too was suffering from the inevitable affliction of life. What could guarantee that she would not end slumped and coughing like Angela Lane, the queen of the arts, all alone in the only place she could get? His own loneliness, as he moved through the breathing house, careful not to disturb its rhythm, seemed to him like a fledgling germ, caught through foolish contact with someone he should have known could give him only something he did not want. He cleared his throat, raking the vestiges of her cigarette from his tonsils, restless for a cure to the malaise he knew he must not catch, now that he had it. He went downstairs and stood self consciously in front of the old Dutch dresser where they kept the hospitable drink. (They scarcely touched it save when they had guests.) He took out some brandy and poured himself a glass and then poured it warily back again. Some ran down the dusty side of the bottle and he dabbed a finger of it to his lips, chagrined at his clumsiness. He sat down in the dark sitting room and tried to cry, or laugh, but both were inappropriate. He hit his cheeks with the flat of his wrist and went upstairs where Ellen was asleep, or had been.

'Are you all right?'

'Did I wake you?'

'What time is it?'

He laughed at the sweet predictability of it and took his warm wife in his arms and kissed her frown.

'How was the party?'

'I'll tell you in the morning.'

She winced at the clock. 'It *is* the morning.'

'It's only just after two.'

'It must have been a very good one.'

'It was b. awful,' Colin said.

'Who was she in that case?' Ellen said.

'Don't be silly,' Colin said.

Ten days later they saw Angela on television, the only woman with three men on a chat show. 'She's the one who reviewed *Stephanus*,' Ellen said.

'So she is,' he said.

143

'You're very terse tonight,' Ellen said.

'Am I? I don't think I am.'

Angela was articulate and biting. A fattening novelist lost weight before their eyes, sweat coursed off him like snow from thawing pines. A philosopher with logically positive hands withdrew them, chastened, when she alluded to his witless habit of juggling with hot air. The rumpled suit had been replaced by velvet trousers and a Maoist silk jacket. She said clever things without looking smug and witty ones without laughing at them.

'Just the sort of woman you ought to have married,' Ellen said.

'Don't start that,' Colin said.

'Isn't she slim?' Ellen said. 'I don't know how she does it.'

'She doesn't have Ellen Smith cooking for her, does she?'

'Keep her end up like that with those people.'

'You went to Cambridge, didn't you?'

'A long time ago,' Ellen said.

'What the hell are you crying about?' Colin said.

'I don't know,' she said.

'You're not jealous, are you?'

'I haven't got anything to be jealous of. *Have* I?'

'I meant of Angela's sharp tongue, because there's no remote reason for you to be. You can be quite sharp yourself. I shall never forget what you said to Andy-Pandy Burgess that time.'

'My one entry in your dictionary of quotations. It isn't much in twenty years, is it?'

'I love you,' Colin said.

'You know her then, do you?'

'Know her?'

'You called her Angela.'

'Well, I've *met* her,' he said.

'You never told me.'

'It was too late,' he said. 'Ellen, what's the matter, for God's sake? We sit here watching a bunch of trendies doing the routine chatties and somehow ...'

'I could see you wishing you were up there, flattening them with your U-turned phrases and your general air of being quite the nicest intellectual steam-roller on the road.'

'You must have been sleeping with Bragg,' Colin said, 'the line you're taking.'

'I've never slept with anyone except you,' she said.

'That sounds remarkably like an accusation,' he said. 'Why does it?'

'Probably because I'm going to be forty and I don't like it.'

'You don't look it,' he said.

She inspected him with unsmiling eyes. 'I feel it.'

'Well, as long as you don't look it.'

'You really can be a fool,' she said, 'sometimes, can't you?'

'I'd like to bring the panel in on this,' he said. 'Seriously, Ellen, this evening's beginning to take a rather sour course. Have I upset you in some way?'

'Presumably she was at the Bernsteins'.'

'Along with three thousand of their closest friends,' Colin said.

'I'm not happy, Colin,' Ellen said.

'Not happy? Not *happy*? Who's happy?'

'I thought so,' Ellen said.

He went into the den (a little porcelain plaque 'Your Father Is Working' had been affixed to the door, a larky Christmas present) and sat down at his Heal's desk. A rough draft of next week's column was held together by another present, a clothes-peg with WON'T WASH on it. He read through the day's jokes and sighed and began to take dictation from Bragg's loud whispers in his ear. The diatribe did not last long enough. Soon he was sitting there again, comparing the electric clock with his watch. Neither, he suspected, was right. Then he pulled a box of writing paper towards him and started a letter. What postal district, he wondered, was Lower Eaton Place in?

By the time he had gone upstairs, Ellen had turned out her light. He bent and kissed her sheeted ear. Then he went and kissed Lucy. She had gone to sleep in her riding hat.

Angela had a new cigarette holder which jutted at a Roose-veltian angle from her raspberry-red mouth. 'I was so pissed,' she told him when they met at 'San Gimignano', 'I can't remember a word I said, and probably just as well.' Rested, the wrinkles had been ironed out of her face no less than her clothes. She was as spruce and as trenchant as she had been on the television; their lunch – served by mattress-ticking Calabrians – was a proud pleasure, though he could have done without Watson in a pitch-pine booth across the room with a revolutionary actress who quizzed the waiters loudly about their conditions of work.

'It was a very sweet letter you wrote me,' Angela said, when they had at last got their *spaghetti alle vongole*.

'With genuine vongols, I note,' Colin said. 'You were very impressive, you really were, on the box.'

'Say two sensible words on television and you're Socrates.'

'There's an overrated talent!' Colin said. 'I thought of bringing him into *The Stephanus Factor*, as an illegal immigrant in the Ideal State.'

'Forget it,' Angela Lane said. 'We talked about that, didn't we?'

'In a manner of speaking, yes. You may have been jet-lagged –'

'I was stoned,' Angela said, fiddling with a jade earring. 'If it falls among the vongols I shall never find it again. I think you were rather disgusted. I never expected to hear from you again.'

'You *were* faintly disgusting,' he said, 'and I was ineluctably prim and proper, so there we are.'

'Ineluctably? Were you really?'

'Oh listen, I don't even have to try,' he said. 'What do you think of the vongols?'

'What's the next book going to be about?'

'I've got till May or so to think about that. I start my mini-sabbatical in June; we generally go down to the cottage. I'm toying with doing something about security.'

'Aren't you a little old for toys?'

'In a manner of speaking. I have this idea of a business man, a self-made man, sharp, perhaps even slightly shady, who becomes obsessed with the idea that they're after him – the standard paranoia – so he decides to make the world safe for himself. He hires a security firm to do a feasibility study, only to discover as things go forward, that he has encompassed his own total sur-veillance, so that eventually the only way he can survive is by breaking out of the made-to-measure trap he's commissioned for himself. Do you know, I actually think she's persuaded the wine waiter to join the Party? He's certain signing *something*.'

'It's in exchange for her autograph. She always does that. She gives hers; you give yours. Fair's fair. Have you ever asked your-self why you always have recourse to whimsy?'

'Bragg says it's because that's my bag,' he said.

'Have your wife and children got enough to live on?' Angela said.
'If you went off and left them for a year?'

'Yes, but –'

'Yes is sufficient; "but" is irrelevant. Because if so, why do
you insist on slaving away in this servile fashion? I'm not saying
anything against your wife.'

'You'd better not,' he said, pouring the Valpolicella. 'I do what
I want to do.'

'Then why did you write to me?'

'Because you were a stand-out on the box the other night. Didn't
I say? Good heavens ... and also because – department of total
naivety, trendy division – I rather wanted to keep in touch with
you; you're worth knowing. Despite my affectations of diffidence,
I can be quite the eager little star-gazer; hence here I am,
gazing. You may not, to be serious, remember what you said the
other night, *du côté de chez Bernstein*, but I do, and it's been
giving me indigestion ever since. I suppose I've come back for
more.'

She looked at him without speaking, the cigarette holder straight
up, a Dunhill exclamation mark. Watson and the revolutionary
actress were squabbling about who should pay what proportion
of the bill. 'No one takes *me* out to lunch,' she was heard to say.
'You should hear Doris on men who give you lunch.'

'As long as I can have the bill,' Watson said, 'just for admini-
strative purposes –'

'That's tantamount to fraud,' the actress said.

'Robbing a capitalist institution is a proto-revolutionary act,
darling; and please don't crumple it.'

'These waiters should be permitted to form a union,' the actress
called out, waving a clenched fist at the customers. 'Meanwhile
overtip them. Viva Cuba!'

'I have great respect for the Bolsh,' Angela said. 'She has
balls.'

'You have brains,' Colin said. 'If it's not evidence of my suburban
prejudice, I rather prefer those in a woman, among other good
things, of course.'

'Who is this book going to hurt,' Angela said, 'of yours?'

'Me mainly, I suppose. Every morning and most of the afternoon
until it's finished. Do you *enjoy* writing?'

'If it's not going to hurt anybody, why do it? You're drowning, Colin Smith. In a tank of distilled water. You'll be growing gills soon, you're in so far over your domesticated little head.'

'Hence my security book,' Colin said. 'My head's quite big as a matter of fact.'

'But that's to please them, to be *sweet*, to prove that there's nothing to be afraid of. Forget the cheap jokes about the Bolsh; she is at least *aware*.'

'There isn't any hope, Angela,' Colin said, fingers pressing down on the foot of the glass with San Pellegrino seething in it. 'Nothing is going to do any good. You know that and I know it. No system works and men can't work without a system.'

She put the cigarette holder into her leather briefcase and pushed uneaten *scaloppine* towards the waiter. 'Why do you have to be so honest?' she said. 'Do you think perhaps that's your trouble? You're so *fair*. Why can't you be a bastard for a bit?'

They walked up towards Eaton Place.

'Where are we going?' she said.

'I rather assumed you'd be going back to –'

'They came home,' she said.

'The Moncktons?'

'Bloody bankers. They didn't like Antigua.'

'I thought you'd rented the place, I didn't realize.'

'Rented it? They get a thousand a week for it. He's putting money in some magazine that wants me to do their travel column for them, so they said while they were away, I could . . .'

'– dust the Giacometti? What was wrong with Antigua?'

'Christ knows.'

'Where are you staying now?'

'The Bernsteins.'

'Oh, are they back?'

'Of course not.'

'Are you going there now? I mean, do you want me to drive you? I shall have to take the car off the meter; it's no problem.'

'Why don't we go to a hotel?' she said.

'A hotel,' he said. 'Ah!'

'Unless you don't feel like it.'

'I shall have to move the car in any case,' he said.

He was surprised at how easy it was. One really could walk into a London hotel at two-fifteen in the afternoon, with no more luggage than Angela's briefcase, and be given a room, quite as if one were a grown person. He probably overtipped, to stop the Spanish bellboy proving to them that bedside switches controlled the drapes, but otherwise he handled it all very suavely. 'I shall probably stay the night,' Angela said, kicking off her shoes and becoming shorter. 'The Bernsteins' bed has one leg shorter than the others. You can always go to Barnes on business, if you want to. Or we could stage a terrific quarrel. I'll throw shoes. I'm quite accurate.'

He was home for dinner. There was not, so far as he could check, and he checked as far as he could, a mark on him. He might have been to the dentist; he was aware of a certain numbness, that was all. Ellen was trying to cope with Lucy's homework (she was back at school) and called him in on the French. '*Pas de problème*,' he said. He was patient and helpful, insisting that Lucy make the first guess and only then, with a smile, putting her right, unless she was right already.

The great thing, he thought, about having an affair with Angela Lane was that she could be relied on to be discreet. She was a sophisticated woman. It was not like some reckless involvement with a sentimental secretary who insisted on being loved and who would demand that he prove his affection by dismantling his home. It was true, in part (like most things, only partly true), that he needed a new subject, that he could not for ever cocoon himself in the carapace of domesticity which had served him for so long as a *point d'appui* (the phrase came in Lucy's *dictée préparée*). What surprised him was how easily he could support the idea of sustained duplicity. He elected to ignore the appetite for scandal, even for buffoonery, of which Angela had shown some dangerous signs. (She *did* throw her shoes, *in*-accurately.) It remained hard for him not to read her as a basically sensible person; his whole posture – not least in the weekly column in which he punctured pretentious poseurs – assumed that we were all really more or less agreed on the best way to live, and that the best way was within the chaffing but East-West-home's-best confines of married life. Belatedly, as he watched Ellen serving a very good veal stew, with *nouilles au beurre* (*damn* Lucy's French), he recognized that all his assumptions were called in question by the attitude towards her which was growing upon him, that perhaps his private life was a parody of his public statements, rather than the reverse. He had told himself, as he enjoyed Angela's rather original ideas of room service, that nothing need change between him and Ellen. But now he was aware that either he must hope that she would be a fool and guess nothing or, if she did guess, that he would have to treat her with an explicit savagery which would ruin their long felicity. He had done nothing of which, on a liberal view, he need be very ashamed; he had at least yielded to a normal desire rather than, for instance, starting to stone babies in their prams. He had been seduced by an admirer of a certain *poids* (oh *pas encore!*) and by one that reflected no discredit on him (*tout au contraire*), since she was well known to offer her favours only to the first eleven, or possibly fifteen.

It occurred to him, as she glanced away at Lucy, to wonder whether anyone had ever called Ellen, on his day at the paper perhaps, and proposed a hotel room, or anything of the kind. As she proceeded to help him to a little more stew, (*'pas de nouilles'*), he was tempted to despise her for the qualities which had until now made her a paragon: she was too boringly honest to deceive him and too cloyingly decent to know how. He had no illusions about Angela loving him (his illusion was that there was no danger of it), but one dirty afternoon – the ironies did not escape him – was sufficient to reverse the whole table of his values. He watched his family like the ghost in his own machine, though no one noticed his spectral manner and all took him to be the same flesh and blood which had left the house that morning. He was sure that he was not suffering from guilt, more from a persistent numbness, as if the dentist he had not visited had dosed him too generously with a narcotic. His teeth were all right, but the rest of him had dropped out.

Would Angela ever want to see him again? At the mechanical level, at least, there had been no fiasco. He had not, on the other hand, proved the greatest lover in the world. The conditions were unpropitious; the absence of all assumed affection meant that he blundered blindly (in the light) to find what might shorten her breath or excite her urgency. She proved to be more intense than he had expected; she did not want to smile or talk. Her body did not inspire him, though it was strange to kiss a stomach lacking stretch marks, however many men had been stretched upon it or foetuses extracted from it. He thought more about her now that he was back in his own house than he had when he was with her. He found he was watching Ellen as if she were a stranger, though a stranger whose every move could be predicted. He saw her now as something accidental, a totally arbitrary person who, for reasons that now seemed vague and even casual, had become attached to him. She seemed now positively to have slighted him in having been so uncritical, so undemanding. He knew that he was unfair to be anything but grateful to Ellen for her abiding love, but he could no longer abide it. He had once sworn to be a Janus whose two faces would be the same; he now felt himself to be coming unglued. Ellen moved around him that evening like a victim for whom he could feel both tenderness and contempt. She had not changed, he knew that. It was all totally unfair, he knew that. He knew that when he looked at her – ah that sweet habitual moment when she slipped her nightie over her head and wriggled it sheer! – he would see that she was, stretch marks or no, twenty times better made than blanched and stringy Angela. There was nothing about her familiar body that displeased him, save its familiarity. He was dismayed to find just how much even her flesh seemed altered in his eyes; the butcher's callous glance followed her as she slipped in beside him. Her trust seemed fatuous. Cow-eyed *who* was it in Homer? Artemis? Hera!

Did he love them both and want them both? Did he love one and want the other? Did he love or want either of them? The mathematics of the triangle posed versatile problems. She turned towards him, hesitating over her bed-time novel: should she read, what did he feel like? He felt like nothing at all. She should. Sweat broke out on his face, quite as if he were the plump novelist under Angela's caustic lash. He shrivelled from his wife. It occurred to him that he might have brought home some unspeakable disease; Angela did not lead a discreet life. She had even been to bed with black men: a *trio*! (Tenor sax, bass and drums.) He wished that he had never had anything to do with her. He wanted so badly to put her out of his mind that he could think of nothing else.

'Not to worry,' Ellen said, 'I've always got my book.'

'Still on a tale of two sisters?' Colin said. 'Short weight was never heavier.' He kissed her shoulder and squeezed her arm. He was touched by his own duplicity. Every move he made, however ordinary, was transmuted into something outrageous and rakish. He might wish that everything was as it always had been; he was thrilled that it never could be.

He began to understand the cult of the spy. Deception was a way of life; it spiced every moment. Anxious to turn idle experience to industrious effect, he considered a novel about a double agent who works with genuinely equal diligence for two incompatible masters, who loves with sedulous infidelity both his loyal ladies and whose twin lives are delicious to him precisely because he is getting double rations. Such a man could be at once the ardent director of counter-espionage and the tireless master spy whom his department is seeking to ensnare. Given that no ideology can wholly satisfy an intelligent man, that no system, once perfected, can fail to be imperfect, what better way of impersonating the paradoxical dandy that every stylish human being would love to be than to seem to conform, prim and proper, dour and dowdy, with two incompatible roles? How good he had been, the good boy Colin, at listening to Mrs Cramp's mortal symptoms (the old girl still lived at the top of West Hill) and how often he had protested sincere interest in Major Hutchinson's three-fingered career as a signals officer in Rangoon! And how cheerfully he could have pulled the plugs on either! What better training than a suburban youth for developing the ruthless duplicity of one's feelings? A made-over Mrs Cramp was known to readers of his Sunday column as Longevity Lil, the grand old granny of Granada-land, while the Major's War Memoirs were now said to be the *donnée* for a new rock opera. Viva suburbia! Only Angela had seen that Bragg was the querulous truth that gave all this geniality the lie, while Ellen continued to be gulled – because it suited her, because she was as nice as he pretended to be (oh for whatever worthy reason!) – into believing that he wrote his amusing and admired little pieces because, basically, he was an amusing and admirable little man. She did not want him to get away from her. He had to get away from her.

'I can't,' he said, slumped in one of the Bernstein's spoon-backed

Regency chairs, with the braid coming loose. There were tacks underneath, going rusty.

'You can,' Angela said. 'You must.'

'What right have I got to do it to them? How *can* I?'

'You'll hate them for it in the end if you don't. You can't expect them to make you leave; some things you have to do for yourself.' Angela was typing as she spoke. She was a marvel: she could scratch the eyes out of a right-wing director with two pecking fingers while at the same time sharpening the horns of his dilemma. 'You're afraid of feeling guilty, I presume?'

'No great presumption. I don't want to hurt Ellen, I don't want to hurt the children.'

'Hurt them,' Angela said.

'The gospel according to Bragg. I don't *want* to,' Colin said.

'I love liars,' she said.

'Snake!' he said, kissing the hot mouth and cribbing the accurate malice sticking its tongue out of her little Olivetti.

'Are you going to let them grow up imagining that the world is what it can never be? You're defrauding them, those innocent kids of yours, the nice little wife —'

'Angela, I told you —'

'They *know*, so why conceal it from them? Why make them guilty with a happiness they must realize sooner or later can't endure? Broken homes are the best kind. They're a public service. Happiness perpetuates the old reactionary nonsense, keeps society in the state of bogus harmony it's our duty to destroy.'

'You *do* admire the Bolsh.'

'No wonder you're planning some pissy book about security! But you *know* how fraudulent society is about itself. You *know*. I want you to write a book that blows the lid off. Why else do you suppose I've been bothering?'

'I wish I knew.'

'You think I'm some nymphomaniac junkie who can't distinguish between one prick and the next? You think your prick's what interests me? I can't do without them? No, it's talent I care about. People who can blow the whole thing sky high.'

'It's never going to be as simple as that.'

'Of course it isn't — that's why people like you are necessary.

Crucial. And yet you hesitate. You think about people's feelings. That's all a screen, Colin. Feelings come later, feelings are a luxury. What matters here and now is basics: the social armature. We've got to bust its ribs. Were you in Paris in '68? The Sorbonne?'

'Couldn't get a flight,' Colin said.

'It's almost too late, Colin. You think you've done something revolutionary by screwing some scrawny up-market bird? Horse-shit. I didn't get you into this so you could have a belated run as over-age balding playboy of the month, but because – fuck it – I'm a critic and I *care*; you're a talent and you'd better do something about it. You can't get away with home and beauty any longer: I'll blow the whistle on you if you chicken out. I'll blast your blasted books, for a start. From *outré* to out-tray. You'll see.'

'So that's the song the sirens sing,' Colin said.

'We've got to get the hell out of this benighted country,' Angela said. 'We've got to find Archimedes' platform and then lever the whole damned place out of its rut. We've got to fly, Colin, before we lose the use of our wings.'

'You see,' he said to Ellen, 'I feel myself blocked. It's nothing you've done. It's what I've done. The compromises I've made. I've written a lot of stuff and I've been quite pleased with some of it. I'm not ashamed of what I've done, but I haven't done what I should have. I haven't been hard enough with myself. I haven't gone to the limit.'

'Who is she, Colin?' Ellen said.

'I'm trying to get you to *understand* something,' Colin said.

'And I'm showing you I've understood. Angela Lane presumably?'

'Yes,' Colin said.

'How could you?'

'I know,' Colin said. 'I know how it must seem to you and I suppose you expect me to be absolutely abject and apologetic and everything else that begins with a. Well, quite honestly, I don't see why I should be. It's not as if I'm walking out without saying a word.'

'That way you might at least have left the oasis without poisoning the well.'

'I'm still going to look after you,' he said.

'You never looked after me. I looked after you.'

'Yes, well, there we are,' Colin said. 'I'm talking about money, if we ... Why do you think I wrote all that rubbish?'

'Have you been to bed with her?'

'Of course. Well, you shouldn't have asked, should you?'

'I'm going,' she said.

'What does that mean?'

'I'll race you,' she said.

'Don't be ridiculous.'

'I'll leave a note for the children,' she said, 'and the milkman; and then I'll be off. Or perhaps I'll write to them. I don't think there's anything else, is there? How many pints do you want?'

'Ellen, come back here.'

'No thanks.'

'This is impossible, this is – we've been together for twenty years. You can't –'

''Bye,' Ellen said.

'You're upset,' Colin wrestled her on to the sofa. 'You're upset and –'

'No, I'm not,' she said. 'I'll tell you something, shall I? I'm a Lesbian.'

'Have you been drinking?'

'Yes,' she said. 'I'm a drinking Lesbian. Want to see my closet? It's bulging. I started with sloe gin and recently I've speeded up.'

'Ellen.'

'Hortensia,' she said. 'I'm going to change my name. I'll keep the Smith because it's so original. Hortensia Smith. I'm going to open a restaurant with Imogen.'

'Imogen who?'

'We're going to run it as a Lesbian co-operative.'

'Who is this bloody Imogen?'

'Who is this bloody Angela?'

'I don't *love* her, Ellen. If you'd just let me *explain*.'

'No need,' she said. 'I'm off. Explain to the wall.'

'I'm not letting you out of this room.'

'I'll dive through the window. If you don't let go, I shall bite you.'

'Sit *down*.'

'You know the silliest thing I ever saw?'

'Presumably it's still Camilla Davies at the R.A. dinner.'

'Balls. I shall be more than happy never to see any more of the things.'

'You're not a Lesbian,' Colin said. 'You know you're not.'

'You can bring her out here to live, if you want to, and she can be a mother to your children.'

'They'll never wear it,' Colin said. 'You're *not* a Lesbian. There isn't anyone called Imogen. This is appalling; this is utterly appalling. I don't know what we think we're doing. Ellen, 'I love you. I've always loved you. I'm totally unable to believe any of this. It's grotesque. Think of the children. I don't *mind* if you're a Lesbian, but you're not, are you? You've been reading about them in the *Methodist Gazette*.'

'Yes, I am,' she said.

'I'm sorry, but I happen to know you're not. There aren't any *really*. You know you can't walk out on the children. They worship you. You could never do it.'

'I'm doing it.'

'Not Imogen O'Leary? You're having me on. You *are* having me on, aren't you?'

'If you really think you can be the salvation of the world, you'd better go and get started,' Ellen said. 'And leave the children to get on with it. They probably *can* get on with it. You remember those peasants we met camping at that mosquito farm outside Amalfi? They'd grown up together without a mother or a father and they seemed amazingly self-sufficient.'

'Timothy and Giles are not peasants. Nor are Lucy and Justine. Justine's only *six*, Ellen, you're not seriously –'

'No, I'm flippantly, I'm facetiously; and I'm enjoying it, aren't you? You're not *serious* about being the saviour of civilization, are you? You're walking out on your wife and children because Angela Lane managed to twinkle twinkle on the box for ten minutes and you were so pleased to have met her you had to go and – where did you do it?'

'I don't think knowing that's going to help.'

'The Strand Palace?'

'One can't park. The Wellington Towers, if you must know.'

'How was it?'

'It was fine. The hotel, I mean, of course. Excellent. Three stars.'

'They have curtains, don't they, you can operate from the bed?'

'How the hell did you know that?'

'Imogen told me.'

'I wouldn't mind opening a restaurant,' Colin said. 'I think it might be rather fun.'

'You'll be too busy proving that your whole life until now has been a domesticated mockery. Well, if you haven't got any other unselfish surprises to spring on me, I shall go and get a few things together.'

'All right,' Colin said, 'you win.'

'No, I don't,' she said. 'I've knocked the board over. I'm sick of the whole silly game. You pick up the pieces, if you want to. I want to do something else.'

'Presumably you never loved me in the first place.'

'Yes, I did,' she said. 'I really did. What a fool, wasn't I? Write about that.'

'If you knew how little she means to me,' Colin said. 'I feel as if I've been bewitched, I really do. I can't think how I got into this. Ellen, whatever you may think of me, shouldn't we really be thinking about the children? I mean, we've had our – our little difficulties before – whatever other people think – we know we have – but we've never wanted to hurt the children. Is this really the time to start?'

'The children are as tough as boots,' Ellen said. 'And they've got it all in front of them. Don't pull the children on me. I've had them for fifteen years.'

'I'm not going anywhere,' Colin said.

'Fine. In that case you'll have the run of the place.'

'And nor are you. Ellen, you're my *wife*. It *isn't* Imogen O'Leary, is it?'

'Isn't it?' Ellen said.

'Ellen, could we possibly begin this conversation again, as it were from the beginning?'

'I don't really want to, Colin, very much, if you don't mind.'

He rubbed his forehead, as if there was something on it that wouldn't come out. 'I realize very well that you probably now hate and despise me.'

'No, I don't,' she said.

'Yes, well . . . that's . . . but however you feel, and I do understand that you feel it, there is a genuine crisis here. I may be selfish, but I refuse to make that too much of a reproach because in the last analysis we're all either selfish or self-deceiving –'

'God, you're dull sometimes,' she said.

'Dull? Am I? Well, perhaps that's what I'm talking about. Isn't there any way that I can make you appreciate that, make you see that if you really love me . . . ?'

'No,' she said. 'So don't worry.'

'Are you being deliberately cruel?' Colin said.

'I should think so, wouldn't you?'

'Good, because that's rather a comfort.'

'You know they've all walked out on her, don't you?'

'Who have?'

'Her men.'

'Angela's? Have they? Where does your information come from, if I may ask?'

'It's common knowledge.'

'We must move in different communities.'

'She's this week's free offer,' Ellen said. 'You don't have to be very well informed, it seems, to be better informed than you.'

'Well, I don't care if the whole Brigade of Guards walked out on her; she's got brains, Ellen; she knows – she knows – what is it people know from a hand-saw? *She* knows. I've got to break out, Ellen –'

'Oh really? A moment ago, you were breaking in again. Do make up your mind.'

'She believes in me, Ellen. You read her review.'

'You seem to be perfectly suited for each other.'

'Ellen, tell me, please, because I don't think I can tell myself, how is this going to end? You seem to be the bright one in this house at the moment, momentarily at least –'

'Thank you.'

'You tell me. Please. I mean it.'

'You're going to persuade me duty obliges me to stay with the children and keep the home together while you go off and allow your genius full rein. You're going to cry, just a little, and you're going to tell me that this isn't anything permanent, that it will all work out eventually – just give you time – and that when it does, you'll be eternally grateful to me for having been good and staunch – staunch, that's one of your words, isn't it? – and you'll tell me that, absurd though it is, you hope I'll not turn the children against you or bring my lovers into the house. You'll nag me into admitting that I haven't *really* been having an affair with Imogen O'Leary and that I'm not really a Lesbian and that I really do still love you, despite everything, and that I do realize, because I'm a wise and sensible woman, that this is probably just an age thing and something to do with the hairs that keep blocking the basin after you've had a shampoo, but that as far as you're concerned you have to believe that there's something more behind it than *anno domini*, and that you really do have something vital to say and you must say it before it's too late. Finally, you'll ask me to help you pack the things you need and I shall prove how wonderful I am by remembering where your shaver is, oh and the pills for the asthma, in case that ever comes back again. So off you'll go, like a woebegone little schoolboy, at least until you turn the corner, slightly hurt if I don't wave to you from the bay window as you toddle down the drive. And then shall I tell you what'll happen?'

'Oh Ellen,' Colin said.

'I'll tell you what'll happen: you'll go to Angela's and you'll feel wonderful. You'll be free. You won't have to do anything you don't want to. You'll eat in restaurants and you'll leave the washing up to the out-of-work actor who does the domestic in his or her spare time. After a few days you'll creep back here for a few papers and your notebooks, in case you want to use a couple of long-lost jokes again and you'll ask if everything is all right and I shall say it is, because I shall know that this is something we have to see through, won't I? Oh yes, do take that any way you please! I wouldn't be surprised if you went off to Turkey. "Colin Smith is on holiday", it'll say for the burglars in the paper. Or Egypt, why not Egypt? Alexandria! You'll be ever so amusing and informative about Cavafy. And she'll have a collection of pieces to get into shape and some travel articles to write –'

'How the hell did you know that?'

'And you'll find an apartment, rather old-fashioned and needing fans because there isn't any air-conditioning, and it has to be big because all *her* fans like Tony and George and Mike and Rick and Freddie and maybe even *Noam* will all be coming through to see you both and discuss serious things late into the oriental night with all its amazing colours, all of them unfortunately better described before, and during the day, if you ever manage to get up, you'll sit down to this real book you're writing, or planning to write, or blocking out or researching for or ... And when Turkey and Egypt and Bali and Haiti and Waikiki haven't quite worked out, you'll try New York and Benares and Lima, Peru and Patagonia and maybe Punta del Este (or is it Eshté?), which won't work out either, until finally you end up in ... I know: California. Good old California! Not Hollywood, of course, but – how about Big Sur? Big Sur meets smaller Sir and Tiny Madam. That's exactly where you'll go and practise primal screams with really bright and liberated people and that way you'll discover that books are a cop out and that all you really have to do is transcendentally meditate once a day and all the rest shall be added unto you. Upon which you'll come home, cured and together and probably bearded as well, by which time Madam will have concluded that you're burned out and that in any case Simon Porter is the love of her life and it's her duty to wean him away from the sterile environment of the Hamptons and liberate his true potential. Colin Smith will be no longer on holiday and probably no longer Colin Smith either. And you know what I'd really like to do now? I'd like to trample on your glasses.'

'Go ahead,' Colin said. 'I'm exhausted. I really am. You're amazing, but I'm absolutely knackered.'

'Don't think you're not going,' she said. 'After all that, you'd better bloody well go. As far as I'm concerned, you've *gone*.'

'Ellen ...'

The telephone rang.

'That's probably her,' Ellen said. 'They don't like to be kept waiting. How long did you schedule our little scene?'

'She wouldn't phone here. Please answer it, Ellen.'

'Why? It's always for you.'

'Ellen, *please*. I'm not here. I've gone, haven't I?'

She made thin lips against a smile and grabbed the receiver. 'Yes? Yes, it is. When? Where? I see. Where is she now? I understand. I'll be there in ... twenty minutes. Where do I go?

Casualty. Right. No, no, I quite understand. I'll be there as soon as I can.'

'What is it? Ellen, what is it?'

'Lucy's fallen off her horse. She's got a broken leg. Otherwise . . .'

'Thank God.'

'Yes, rather,' Ellen said, going out into the hall for the car keys. 'Isn't it a bit of luck?'

'You know what I meant,' Colin said, daring his double to smile in the mirror above the dead hearth.

The next week, the readers of the Sunday paper were shocked to read of the death of Professor Bragg, the well-known expatriate beard and controversialist. He had thrown himself into an otter sanctuary on the Pacific Ocean, Colin Smith reported, after an inter-disciplinary total frankness encounter group at the Mescalin Institute, Big Sur, California. It was, wrote Smith, too soon, and just possibly too late to assess the nature of what had been lost, though two otters were certainly on the list.

The Smiths went down to Newbury at the end of May. Lucy was on crutches but she was also on the mend. Colin worked steadily at his novel, *Lock, Stock and Barrel*, which was about security. It went very well and when it was published, a Literate Club Alternative Choice, it was dedicated to 'Ellen, as ever the Muse'.

Welcome Aboard

'We finally did it,' Gabe said, as they turned left into First Class, 'we finally got someplace ahead of time. We finally didn't have to rush. This represents some kind of a breakthrough and I should like to congratulate us.'

'Hullo, sir, madam, did you enjoy your holiday?'

'How do you like that? If it isn't the smiling Mr Mountain!'

'Hi there, Mr Mountain,' Cheryl said. 'Do you think you could find somewhere for these? I'm even more loaded up than I was on the flight coming out.'

'I let her out alone just one morning in Paris and now I'm going to have to work right over the Labor Day week-end to pay for the damage. Not that I regret one red cent of it. Not one red cent – just the rest, that's all! Kidding, baby. May I introduce my brother- and sister-in-law, Mr and Mrs Bookman? This is Mr Mountain, Wes, took such good care of us on the flight out. Mr and Mrs Bookman have been on a honeymoon in Venice. Same time we were on our money-moon in Paris, isn't that right, Cheryl? Boy, is that one expensive city today!'

'Why not go the whole way?' Cheryl said. 'Why not show him your cheque stubs?'

'I'm not actually his brother, as a matter of fact,' Wes Bookman was saying. 'My wife is Mrs Shapira's sister, but Mr Shapira and I are not really related. We should have two in non-smoking and two in the smoking section.'

'Think he really wants the family tree?' Marsha said.

'How are we going to start out?' Cheryl said. 'The boys over there and the girls over here or what?'

'We can switch around, can't we?' Gabe said. 'It's an eleven-hour flight, minimum. We're bucking the Gulf Stream all the way, isn't that right, Mr Mountain? I just hope we get away on time. One thing I hate, it's sitting on the ground listening to people apologize.'

'Mr Mountain, do you have such a thing as a glass of water?'

'Didn't you take your drammy yet?' Cheryl said. 'I took mine at the hotel. You should take these things ahead of time.'

'I didn't take my second one and now I feel like maybe I'm going to need it.'

'Not too bumpy so far, Marsha.'

'Gabe, you leave Marsha alone. I have to endure your sarcasm; she doesn't. Soon as he gets near an airplane!'

'You two girls sit, nurse your hair-do's, relax; Wesley and I'll go and smoke a cigar, what do you say?'

'Go and smoke your cigar. Put an airplane ticket in his hand and right away nobody can say anything without he starts being sarcastic. I hope you're not like that with Marsha, Wesley, when you've been married as long as Gabe and me.'

'Gabe and I,' Gabe said.

'You see what I mean? Now tell me I'm making it up. This is the last long trip I take with you, Gabriel Shapira, so help me.'

'Would you ladies care for something to drink before take-off?'

'No, thank you. I'll take my drammy and then I think I'll just –'

'You close your eyes, Marsha *mia*,' Wes said. 'It won't be long now.'

'Eleven hours,' Cheryl said. 'What's the movie? I bet we saw it already. *And* didn't like it.'

'I hope this was a good idea,' Gabe said, 'us all travelling home together. Cheryl gets like this before a flight. I thought travelling British might calm her down; those long 'a's are kinda relaxing. So Venice was O.K., right?'

'Venice was unbelievable,' Wes said.

'I can believe it,' Gabe said. 'We stayed one time on the Lido, which was nice, but kind of a drag when Cheryl wanted to go to the glass-works and stuff. Back and forth in the motor-boat all the time. Did you go to the glass-works? Fabulous. She didn't like it. Finally we moved to the Gritti, but the damage was done, you know what I'm trying to say?'

'We didn't leave the hotel too much,' Wes Bookman said. 'A little shopping, that was about it. We took in the square, nothing too demanding.'

'Got your exercise in the hotel, right?' Gabe said. 'I always

163

knew that Roxana was a mistake. I knew it at the wedding. We gave you the vermeil forks, remember? Did you get those or did she?'

'I let her have all the domestic stuff. I didn't want to figure I was eating off a fork she'd used, even if it had been in the machine.'

'What kind of a name is Roxana, anyway, a Jewish girl from Sherman Oaks? I know exactly how you feel: take the forks and go. Shouldn't they be getting ready to close those doors pretty soon now?'

'Won't be long now, sir. Can I get you gentlemen something to drink?'

'I'll have a bloody Mary,' Gabe said, 'no ice. Same for Mr Bookman. It seems to be kind of full back there.'

'Full all the time now, sir, with the stand-by passengers.'

'Used to be you could stretch out, more space than in First Class. Now it's Disneyland back there, like one of the "E" rides, you know what I mean? Will you look at those two women, Wesley. I swear to God I don't know which of them is more beautiful. Ten years between 'em, who'd guess it with their clothes on? You shoulda seen Cheryl last night putting her hair-do to bed. She never moved all night. To look at her, neither did Marsha.'

'I like a woman keeps herself neat,' Wes said.

'One night you had to look but not touch, right? Well, one night won't hurt you. I'll bet she's something. I knew her when she was a little girl, but she still looked at you like she was making a promise you wouldn't be sorry if she kept. Am I right?'

'Marsha is a very warm girl,' Wes Bookman said.

'And a nice temperament. I'm not saying anything against Cheryl, because Cheryl and I've been married eight years and they've been eight good years, but Cheryl is someone gets very tense; she has a highly strung nature, she can snap sometimes. Ping! I guess that's what I love about her: this element of danger. Of course she's a few years older than Marsha; Marsha could grow to be more that way herself. People do that, they get older.'

'Just look at them, aren't they something? Could be twins. I wouldn't be surprised they slept halfway to L.A. I hope they do. I want them fresh as paint at that airport, because we're going to have Max, we're going to have May and Bernard, we're going to have the whole *schmeer*. I could do without that, as a matter of fact, after eleven hours, but what can you do? Family! How's Leslie these days?'

'He's with his mother. I don't see him a lot. She's created a lot of hostility. He has kind of a weight problem, but he's O.K., he's fine.'

'Ladies and gentlemen –'

'It had to come, didn't it?' Gabe said. 'It just had to come.'

'Captain speaking. We have a small problem that's just come up. We're hoping it won't keep us long, maybe ten minutes, maybe a little longer, but of course we'll keep you informed. Meanwhile please relax, we're doing everything we can.'

'Sounds like two hours, minimum,' Gabe said. 'I know those ten minuteses.'

'Bloody Mary?'

'What's the story really, Mr Mountain, on this?'

'One of the baggage hoists is on the blink, sir, is all it is, I believe. We shouldn't be too long. Nuts?'

'Huh? Oh. Please. Always happens when I get here early. *Now* what the hell's going on?'

A young man in a polo-necked white sweater, knitted skull-cap and jeans was at the door of the plane which led on to the ramp. He was dark-complexioned and had curly black hair. He was insisting that he had to leave: he had forgotten something. The steward said that it would be very inconvenient if he disembarked now: the flight would have to be held up while they found his baggage. With the second hoist not functioning properly, that could mean a long delay. The young man said that he had just realized that he had left a vital book behind somewhere. He could not leave without it.

'How can a *book* be vital?' Gabe said.

The young man said that he was travelling only with a light bag (he held it up), so there was no need for any search. He just had to leave the plane, because this book was very important.

'He left his Koran in the hotel,' Gabe said. 'Can you believe this guy? I'll bet he's some kind of a P.L.O. fanatic just left his nerve in the toilet. Look at those eyes. A book already!'

165

'He wants to get off, let him get off,' Wes said. 'He has a right and furthermore who needs him? He wants to read, let him go to the library.'

'What is it, Gabriel? What's happening?'

'We're losing an Arab,' Gabe said. 'Don't worry about it, baby. Go on back to sleep.'

Unfortunately, the steward explained, even though the young man had no luggage in the hold, the fact that he had boarded the aircraft and then left it again meant that they would have to make a search of where he had been sitting and anywhere he might have gone in case he had planted something in the meanwhile. There would, the Captain regretfully confirmed, have to be a further delay while the security staff did their checks. He hoped that the passengers would bear with him.

'If I ever see that kid reading anywhere near Marina del Rey, I'll kill him,' Gabe said. 'That's the most inconsiderate thing I ever heard of.'

'All you had to do was offer to replace the book for him when we got to L.A.,' Cheryl said.

'Damn,' Gabe said. 'Why didn't I think of that?'

'I thought of it,' Cheryl said, 'and I've had two drammies.'

'The guy wanted off,' Gabe said. 'Why keep a gunman on the flight if he wants to get off? You want to spend the next week on the tarmac with Colonel Gadaffi? I don't. What's the story now, Mr Mountain?'

'They're just checking the toilets, sir, and we're hoping it won't be too long.'

'Because my wife is beginning – I can tell – she's beginning to get a little tense.'

'Would you like another cushion there, Mrs Shapira?'

'No, my hair ... I'm just going to close my eyes. I have this tendency to migraine. I hope this doesn't precipitate something.'

'Did Cheryl ever figure it could be diet, her migraine problem? I know a corporate lawyer in Palm Springs, cured himself of terminal cancer with a diet exclusively of squash, Hank Dancy, do you know him?'

'Cheryl gets tension headaches. This has been going on for years. Ever since she had her nose taken care of on account of her sinuses. I don't think squash is going to help her any. Hank Dancy? I don't know any Hank Dancy. Hank Alpert.'

'Dancy. He advises some bright people. He advises Murphy, he advises Sheldon Franks. Hank Alpert is a shyster, someone was telling me. Do they really have to take the plane to pieces every time some crazy kid forgets his library book? Hank Dancy's a *fancy* shyster, which is something else. I never heard of this on T.W.A.'

'The British are ultra-cautious,' Gabe said. 'I guess they're right. Better a few more minutes on the ground than a guest appearance as a hole in the ground in *Airport '80*.'

The Captain was speaking again. He sincerely hoped that they would be on their way within half an hour or forty minutes at the outside. 'I bet that means an hour,' Cheryl said. 'I bet that means an hour minimum. This plane is going to take off two hours late, if we're *lucky*. I knew we should have flown T.W.A. We should've flown T.W.A.'

'Relax,' Gabe said.

'You hear how he talks to me?'

'You want a magazine, Cheryl? You want *Cosmopolitan*? They have it.'

'You've been married eight years, he'll probably talk to you like that. Don't *ever* tell me to relax like that again.'

'Shall we try a little massage? Marsha, suppose you go sit with Wesley and I'll give Cheryl a little massage.'

'All you'll do is spoil my hair.'

'I won't even touch your hair. I'll stand behind your seat if you like. That way –'

'The back's too high. You've been smoking a cigar. You know what cigar smoke does to my sinuses.'

'I thought after that operation you weren't going to have any more sinuses.'

'Medically, you are so ignorant: I didn't have sinuses, I couldn't function oto-rhinally at all. Medically you're illiterate, Gabriel, you know that?'

'Maybe I should go get a book on the subject. Maybe that Arab could lend me one he isn't using.'

'I told you before about your sarcasm. As soon as I'm under stress, you can't resist it, can you?'

'All I wanted to do was give you maybe a little massage. How sarcastic is that?'

'I'm sorry, Gabriel, but I don't think I can stay on this airplane.'

'It won't be long now, madam.'

'I do not think I can stay on this airplane. I can't breathe.'

'Sure you can. Try some deepies. They look great in that pink angora.'

'You diminish me, Gabriel,' Cheryl said. 'Did I ever tell you that? You really and truly diminish me.'

'Cheryl, believe me, there's plenty left. I think you're the most beautiful woman for your age in the world. Now will you please relax, close your eyes and tell yourself –'

'Another couple of days in London would've done me a lot of good,' Cheryl said. 'Why did we have to fly home with Wesley and Marsha? They don't need us. Is there somebody you've fixed to see? I'll just bet there's somebody you've fixed to see. "For my age", what does that mean? Who is she, Gabriel?'

'She? She's a guy called Wallace Bergonzi, coming in from Albuquerque Friday. Coming in to see me about a property in Anaheim. They're just trying to take care of us, sweetheart, is all they're doing. She!'

'I feel terrible. I can't tell you how terrible I feel.'

'Cheryl feels terrible,' Marsha said.

'I know,' Wes Bookman said, 'I know. I think maybe you should go back and sit with her.'

'Gabriel can sit with her,' Marsha said. 'What's the matter? Don't you want me to sit with you?'

'I was thinking of Cheryl,' Wes said.

'Think of me,' Marsha said. 'I'm your wife, remember? As a matter of fact, I'm feeling a little jumpy myself. Those drammies, they settle you and they upset you all at the same time.'

'How about a little canapé?'

'I ate a canapé, I'd throw up.'

'It was squash, wasn't it, Hank Dancy took when the doctors had given him up?'

'Will you please not talk about food right now, Wesley?'

The Captain felt that he had to warn them, much as he

regretted the situation, that there was going to be a further hope-fully small delay because one of the warning lights was on the blink. They were sure that it was nothing, but they would have to get the engineers to run through the standard procedures.

'How long this time, for Christ's sake?'

'I don't suppose it'll be very long, sir. Would Madam like any-thing?'

'I'd like to get off this plane and on to T.W.A.,' Cheryl said, 'if you really want to know.'

'I'm afraid they've already taken off,' the steward said.

'That's exactly what I mean,' Cheryl said.

'Would you care for a magazine?'

'I already broached that,' Gabe said.

'As soon as there's any news, Madam, I'll come and let you know.'

'I doubt that'll be soon enough,' Marsha said, 'the way Cheryl looks.'

'Gabriel,' Cheryl said, 'I want you to be very understanding. I need all your understanding right now, because I have to get off this plane.'

'Cher, you heard what the guy said.'

'Which is precisely why I have to get off this plane, Gabriel. Now please don't treat me like a child –'

'You're behaving like a child.'

'I ask for your understanding and . . . Did you hear yourself?'

'We've been sitting here for one hour and forty minutes, Cheryl, why crack now? We'll be away in a few minutes.'

'I don't get off this plane in about ninety seconds from now, I'm liable to pass clean out, Gabriel. Now please tell the steward to get that door open.'

'Cheryl's flipped,' Wes Bookman said. 'It was always coming. It's come.'

'We have to get her off the plane,' Marsha said. 'Believe me, I know that sister of mine. Better get the things together.'

'Come on, Marsha,' Wes said. 'Gabe can handle this, surely.'

'Are you serious?'

'We only agreed we'd fly home together at the last minute. We –'

'This is my sister you're talking about, Wesley.'

'Mr Mountain, I'm sorry, but my wife wants to leave the aircraft.'

'Mrs Shapira, is there anything I can do to reassure you? This is being done for your safety, believe me, and I'm sure it won't be long now.'

'I just want to get off this plane.'

'We're going to need our packages,' Marsha said.

'Come on, Cheryl, give it a few minutes, what do you say?'

'The Captain would like to have a word with you, Mrs Shapira, Mr Shapira, if you could just –'

'I'll bet we're all set,' Wes Bookman said. 'I'll bet we're on our way.'

'We were all set,' Marsha said, 'he'd have started his engines. Why do you always have to try and snow people?'

'I'm so sorry about this,' the Captain came through to say, 'but I do hope you understand. It's been a concatenation of trivialities today and I sincerely believe that there's light at the end of the tunnel. It shouldn't be long now.'

'I want to be in a tunnel, I'll take a train,' Cheryl said. 'Now will you please ask them to open that door? I have a right to leave this plane if I want to, and I want to. Now *please*.'

'May I just explain something? If you leave the aircraft now – which you have a perfect right to do, no one's disputing that – but if you leave the aircraft now, we shall have to get your luggage out of the hold, because if you leave the flight, we can't – according to international regulations – proceed with your bags on board. Given that we have this small problem with the luggage hoist, which I was prepared to leave as it is, since it won't affect us in the least operationally, your disembarking will mean a further delay of probably up to two hours for the rest of the passengers. So I wonder – with my most sincere apologies – whether you could see your way to resuming your seats to avoid that having to happen? In a few minutes, we could very well be on our way.'

'I wasn't trying to snow anybody, Marsha. See?'

'Will you please open that door, Captain, before I have an attack? Gabe –'

'She starts screaming, she won't stop. Believe me, I'm in a

position to know. Mr Mountain, will you please open that door before I hold the airline personally liable?'

'It means unloading all the luggage, Cheryl,' Wesley Bookman said. 'We'll be a couple of hours –'

'Wesley, do you want me to pass out? Gabe can wait for the luggage.'

'Is that all our packages?' Marsha said. 'Do I have my *pâtisserie?*'

'I know!' Wesley Bookman said. 'How about if I stay on board with the luggage and see you all in L.A.? It'll save –'

'Wesley, do I hear you right? I can't believe my ears. We haven't been married a month yet, not one month have we been married yet! You stay with the luggage, my friend, and you stay with it for the rest of your *life.*'

'I'm trying to help, Marsha.'

'You stay on this plane and you never see me again as long as you live.'

'I'm thinking of Cheryl.'

'Well, think of *me.*'

'If you'd just leave Gabe to take care of her, there'd be no hassle.'

'She's my sister. You think I can do a thing like that? She's your sister-in-law.'

'She's a grown woman. She's been married three times. She's free, white and at least twenty-one . . .'

'I don't care how many times she's been married. When I've been married three times, I still hope she'll want to look after me. And what kind of a crack . . . ?'

'Fine,' Wes Bookman said, 'fine. Lead the way. I'm sorry, folks. Y'all have a good flight now.'

'Traitor,' Marsha said. 'It's not our fault they let some P.L.O. freak on the plane in the first place. We were here before anybody. Everybody was like us, we'd be practically in L.A. already.'

'I'm very sorry about this, Mr and Mrs Shapira,' the steward said.

'The British just can't cut it any more, Mr Mountain, that's the truth of it. They just can't cut it any more.'

When the door was unsealed, the young man in the polo-necked sweater, the knitted skull-cap and the jeans was waiting outside. He was holding a large volume bound in red cloth boards. Close to, Gabe could see that he had a star of David on a gold chain around his throat.

'It was on the bus,' the young man said to the steward, 'wasn't that lucky?'

'Lucky!' Gabe said. '*Lucky?* You've wrecked our whole goddam trip. You've fouled up our whole European experience. You've probably destroyed these people's marriage and you talk about luck!'

'All I was trying to do,' Wes said, 'was make things easy.'

'Wesley, please, I just don't want to talk about it.'

By the time they reached the main building and looked back, the plane was already moving away from the stand. 'Holy Christ,' Gabe said, 'they're leaving with our bags. They're leaving with our bags.'

'Evidently we don't look like P.L.O.,' Wes Bookman said. 'The Captain decided to risk it. Well, thanks to us, the kid caught his plane. One man's sister-in-law is another man's *mazel*.'

'Terrorist,' Gabe yelled through the glass. 'Hijacker!'

The Best of Friends

'Lucy Stayman!' he said. 'What're you doing here?'

'I'm supposed to be meeting a Japanese publisher,' she said, 'but I don't think he's going to show.'

'I'm sorry I'm not a Japanese publisher,' Peter Rudolf said. 'I only wish I was your English one. You've had a tremendous success.'

'I've had a small success,' she said.

'And I think it's tremendous,' he said. 'If *Baby Talk* was only a small success, I wish you'd bite some of my authors, is all I can say. Are you writing another one? I trust you are.'

'Researching for one,' she said.

'What about this time?'

'Children.'

'*Again?*'

'I've only done the one,' she said.

'Hence again,' Peter said. 'I didn't mean to imply any criticism.'

'Did you not?' she said.

Peter did his grin. 'Still the same old Lucy! Still the same *young* Lucy, by the look of you. How do you manage it? *Baby Talk* was really very impressive. Cass was full of admiration. I nearly wrote to you.'

'Oh, nearly thank you.'

'One never really believes people need it, does one? What aspects are you dealing with this time?'

'So-called psychological problems,' she said.

'So-called, eh? That sounds aggressive.'

'Inquiring,' Lucy said.

'Inquiries are aggressive. How's Michael?'

'Michael?' she said.

'Your husband.'

173

'Oh *Michael*. He's terribly well, or at least he was the last time I saw him. He's in Florence at some seminar.'

'The trivial round, the common task! It must be all of ten years,' Peter said. 'And the children? They must be practically writing books of their own at this point.'

'Adrian's a punk; Penny writes poetry and David's on a kibbutz. Good for him, we thought.'

'Very,' Peter said, 'if you like grapefruit – and Jews, of course. We were still living in Phillimore Gardens, for God's sake, weren't we, when . . . ? The night of the famous dinner party.'

'I don't think my gentleman's going to come,' she said.

'Promises, promises!' Peter said. 'I was actually quite piqued, you know, that you didn't give Gabriel and me the chance to publish your book. I presume Michael warned you off.'

'To be honest, I never thought of you.'

'Then must you be honest?'

'As the sort of publisher who could possibly want it. It wasn't exactly highbrow.'

'Nor is lunch,' Peter said, 'but what are you doing for it? There's obviously been some failure of communications between yourself and the Rising Sun.'

'I could always phone Martin, I suppose.'

'Why phone Martin Farmer when you've got me?'

'To find out what's happened.'

'Ten past one? If he's a publisher at all *comme les autres*, you'll get nothing at this hour apart from a switchboard girl with a mouth full of sandwich. Highbrow! I'm still not averse from making money from time to time, you know. I suppose the next book's already spoken for, the one you're researching?'

'Murmured for,' she said.

'Murmured for! What's it going to be called? Do you like fish?'

'I love fish. It's called *Kid's Stuff*. It's only a working title.'

'Oh well, work on it,' Peter said. 'It *is* ten years, you know, fully. Ten years last May. May '68! What's this Japanese man's name? We could leave word for him, if you're worried. He could join us. They like fish.'

The Rudolfs had still been living in the old maisonette in Phillimore Gardens. Peter was setting out peanuts and gherkins, ready for the dinner party, while on T.V. black and white students pelted the riot police in the Boul' Mich. He and Cass had sat under those wrecked trees to drink existential coffee and eat yellow, elastic croissants Chez Dupont, where all was *bon*. Peter winced at the tear gas as it clouded his romantic memories. For the first time, he realized that he was no longer on the side of the young. The freedom of others appalled him. Though in public he would still proclaim his enthusiasm for their cause (had not old Sartre leaped the barricade of age to side with the *jeunes*?), a secret voice whispered for the old order. He and Gabriel Page had just got their business started. He was keen on books on the new liberties, but he was less keen to see them taken. As the students rallied behind a dead bus, the doorbell rang. He fed himself a mouthful of nuts, extinguished the revolution and went towards the front door.

'Peter, someone's here,' Cassandra called from the kitchen.

'I'm on my way,' he said. 'Something smells good. Is it what we're eating or what you've put behind your ears?'

'Both,' Cass said. 'I always put Madeira sauce behind my ears.' She was wearing sexy glasses and an aquamarine and viridian kaftan, half off one shoulder. Steam had poached the glasses; bright eyes looked at him through misty lenses.

'Vivian!' Peter said, with both hands.

'Hullo, Peter, is George here?'

'Not yet,' Peter said, 'but —'

'Has he called?'

'Not while I've been here. And I *have* been here . . .'

'He said if he wasn't home by seven, he'd see me here at eight.'

'Well, it's only just gone eight. Come on through and have a drink.'

'Have you been on the phone yourself?'

'No, I've been watching the goings on in Paris and wondering whether they should be filed under comedy or tragedy. What do you think?'

'Hi, Vivian,' Cass called, as they passed the delicious kitchen door. 'Be there in a minute. Where's George?'

'Good question,' Vivian said.

'Now!' Peter said. 'Sherry? Scotch? Vodka? The sherry's nice and cold.'

'All right,' Vivian said, 'sherry.'

'I'm so glad you could make it tonight. We've got Michael Stayman coming, and his wife. He lectures on Eastern Europe at L.S.E., but you've probably seen him on the box. How did the play go down in Brighton?'

'Brighton's rarely a problem,' Vivian said. 'One always gets strong backing from the buggers' union. London's another matter.' He was at the window, looking down through the spring trees. 'The little shit!'

'What's the matter?'

'The little *sod*. Look here, do you mind if I go down? He's just driven up in some bloody Triumph sports car and we'd better sort it out before your best Minton becomes involved.'

'We're not using it,' Peter said.

Vivian started for the door, but met Cassandra on her way in. 'Vivian, my dear sweet plump admirer, I'm so sorry, but I had a crisis with the kasha. Peter, do I get a drink?'

'Cassie my sweet, I love that thing you're almost wearing!' Vivian kissed his hostess, but the doorbell was his cue. 'I'll get that, if I may.'

George was there, but he was not there soon enough to placate Vivian. Vivian said that he could at least have phoned and left a message. Peter winced closer to Cass as George replied that he had tried, but that the number had been engaged.

'That's a lie,' Vivian said, 'and I can prove it. Who drove you here?'

'Do you remember Crispin le Coq?'

Cass goggled at Peter. 'I don't believe Crispin le Coq.'

'You're a little tart basically, aren't you?' Vivian said.

'Well, it wasn't him,' George said.

'It *wasn't* Crispin le Coq.' Cass stood close against her husband as the two men quarrelled. The kaftan was too long, but Peter jabbed a practical promise against the striped silk and Cass's eyes glittered behind the spectacles.

'Actually,' George said, 'if you're that interested, it was Caroline Montagu and she said to give you a big kiss, not that I shall bother.'

'Oh, she's got a new car, has she? Because –'

'She's got a new car and a new left tit and call her if you don't believe me.'

Cass's tongue tasted of Madeira sauce between Peter's lips. They broke apart hospitably, husband and wife, as an armed armistice brought George and Vivian at last into the room. George was short and muscular, with Mediterranean eyes and fair hair. He wore a leather jacket and brown check trousers with a built-in belt, gold buckle shoes. 'Mother's been in Brighton all week, hasn't he?' he said. 'Result she's got a guilty conscience and a nasty temper to go with it. You wouldn't think I'd been taking snaps all day, would you? Cassandra, my duck, I'm not really too late, am I?'

'You're never too late for me, George,' Cass said.

'I'm sure that's meant kindly,' George said. 'These are for you actually, mother, and I rather wish I hadn't bothered now.' He held out a once-used manilla envelope towards Vivian.

'Oh *George*!' Cass said. 'Are they yours? I want to see.'

'Look over mother's shoulder,' George said, 'if you can see past the chip. Vodka on the rocks would do me beautifully, Peter.'

'George,' Peter said, 'I wanted to ask you something, and that was: what do you know about Corsica?'

'It's an island in the Mediterranean,' Vivian called over. 'In case you didn't know. He's pig-ignorant from Cardiff on that sort of thing.'

'*George*,' Cassandra said, 'they're absolutely horrible, these photographs. They're *vile*.'

'Well, mother *was* dying at the time,' George said.

'I never knew you were that sick, Vivian,' Peter said. '*Dying*, were you really?'

'We were only on a diet of extreme unction for three whole days,' George said. 'Administered by drip. Tell me more about Corsica.'

'Well, I've got a manuscript in by a rather good writer, about vendettas – chap by the name of Lesley Armitage, who actually turns out to be a woman, rather surprisingly –'

'It *is* rather surprising when people do that, isn't it? Not to say embarrassing.'

'*George*,' Cass said. 'Don't think I don't have ears. I do.'

'– and seriously, it absolutely cries out for photographs. Hence I thought of you. What I want is some typical faces, i.e. untypical ones. That grainy actuality touch you're so good at. What's so fascinating about vendettas according to this book is how long they last, how they lie fallow and then erupt again, like volcanoes, with absolutely unstoppable force.'

'This is the one I've chosen for the back of my Collected Works, Peter, when you finally decide to publish them.' Vivian held up one of George's photographs for a face. 'The author. Dead or alive!'

Peter smiled and nodded and managed to look down at the watch he had casually shaken free of his sleeve. 'I hope they're coming,' Cass said. 'Or might they have a hotter ticket?'

'I doubt it,' Peter said. 'Michael isn't like that, and anyway what could be hotter than the present company, not to mention the cook?'

'Presumably you were friends together at Oxford,' Vivian said. 'You and Master Stayman.'

'We were friend*ly*,' Peter said.

'There was a certain amount of tension,' Cass said, 'because one of them secretly feared he admired the other more than the other one admired him.'

'And which was which?' George said.

'That was what the tension was about,' Cass said.

'It wasn't, in fact, quite like that darling, really. Michael always wanted to be an academic. Fellow of All Souls or bust. I was never quite in that league, though I genuinely believe that my Fulbright year in the States was worth a quinquennium of sharpening epigrams at High Table.'

'Have some sour grapes, Vivian? We've got *loads*.'

'I also managed to meet you, darling.'

'You weren't at Oxford, Cassandra?' George said.

'I was at Columbia,' Cass said. 'I trailed Peter back to Oxford but I was never strictly speaking "up". I'm sorry, my angel, but I really and truly don't believe they're coming.'

'They do tend to have problems with baby-sitters,' Peter said, 'if you remember. The last one they had robbed a bank, just before they were due at the Royal Academy dinner. Seventeen-year-old girl apparently and she robbed a bank. The Midland, I think it was, in Cricklewood Broadway. I can't imagine why they were asked. Michael has no visual sense whatever. He always thought Domenichino was the Italian for Sunday.'

'Some guy she met at a sculpture class,' Cassandra said. 'She got pregnant and they decided to work this heist, which didn't work at all. I thought it was the National Provincial, Peter.'

'Typical of Michael's luck really. Even his baby-sitter got his name in the papers. Do you think I should give them a ring? I don't know about you, but I'm getting hungry.'

'I think you should give them a diary,' Cass said. 'Are you sure you said to come tonight?'

'I *know* I did. I gave Michael the date; I also said Wednesday.'

'Only I have a feeling that the moment is rapidly approaching when I shall have to start telling George and Vivian how lovely it is to be just the four of us for a change.'

Finally, Peter was obliged to telephone the Staymans in front of the others. They had no extension in those days. The phone rang and rang and Peter had concluded that they must have left, when it was picked up. 'Hullo,' he said, 'who is this? *Lucy*! Lucy dear, this is Peter Rudolf. Yes, hullo to you. Lucy, um, look – not to put too fine a point on it, we were expecting you to dinner tonight. Well, I did tell Michael specifically. Perhaps I could have a word with him, if ... He's *what*? What to see? Good heavens, what on earth for? Because it's absolutely the bottom, that's why.' Peter covered the receiver. 'He's gone to see *Amok*, if you please.'

'*Amok*? What's *Amok*?' George wanted to know.

'It's what Peter shows every sign of running,' Vivian said.

'Lucy dear,' Peter said, 'the thing rather is that we've got some people here whom we've asked specially to meet him – and you. I'm sorry, Lucy, but I honestly do find it somewhat incredible. Of course I *believe* you. Clearly it isn't your fault. Why didn't you go to *Amok* too? No baby-sitter. I see. Well, look, when Michael comes in perhaps you'd do me the service of mentioning to him that Cassie's been cooking in his honour all afternoon and just see if the faintest flush of conscience crosses those manly cheeks. We can indeed all make mistakes. All I wish to suggest is that it's Michael who's made this particular one. It's not a question of being *angry*. However, if I am angry, it's because, quite frankly, you appear to think it's some kind of a favour to come to dinner at all. Yes, well, the damage is rather done at this point, don't you think? Should he give me a ring? Yes, I think he should, don't you? Alternatively, if he comes in during the next half-hour or so, put your skates on and ... What? Oh God, Lucy, I don't know what you do about a baby-sitter.'

'I'll go and sit on their babies for them, if you like,' George said.

'Nothing's too young,' Vivian said, '*nothing*.'

Peter had put the phone down. 'She's a child,' he said. 'She's a *child*.'

'You can't blame her,' Cass said. 'It was Michael you said you spoke to.'

'Said I spoke to? I *did* speak to him.'

'I rather recall a similar muddle with Paolo.'

'Similar? How could it be similar? Paolo speaks about two words of English, neither of which came into our conversation. So what's similar about it?'

'And what about the time when I met you at the Tate at the same time as you were meeting me at the National Gallery?'

'Is it seriously at my door that you thought the Rokeby Venus was in the Tate? I had my diary open in front of me, Cass. He thinks he's God, that's Michael's trouble.'

'Only when he isn't quite feeling himself,' Cass said.

'He'll probably come charging round here any minute,' Vivian said, 'as soon as he can change into sackcloth and ashes.'

'They form no part of his wardrobe,' Peter said. 'He might at least have ditched us for something worth seeing. But *Amok*, really!'

'Nobody's necessarily ditched anybody,' Cass said. 'People do make mistakes, you know.'

'Not Michael. A hundred per cent on every paper is slightly below average with him. He's the man who gave selfishness a bad name. We were due to play bridge together for the university. It wasn't a Blue sport or anything like that, but we had put in considerable practice, and two weeks before the match, he cried off. Pressure of work. Two weeks before the match. I had to play with Albert Brittain. Sod the man is what I say. Friends? You can't be friends with a man like that.'

'Well,' Cass said, 'it looks like it's going to be just the four of us for a change!'

Peter had not, of course, made a reservation at 'The Plaice

Around the Corner'. People were waiting and he had an unsmiling minute before Bruno found him and Lucy a table under a tank where greenish-white lobsters tried to fight with claws cuffed by rubber bands.

'There's something I've always wanted to ask you, Lucy – well, at least since you became the concerned parent's guide to the subject – and that is, when does childhood end? Indeed, *does* it end? Has yours ended? I'm not at all convinced that mine has.'

'Michael says it's when you stop liking snow.'

'That sounds like him. Tell me, when does he get back from Florence?'

'He may be here Tuesday and he may not.'

'That's true of more or less everyone, isn't it?'

'Can I have the *Sole Véronique*?'

'If anyone can, you can. And a bottle of Chablis I think, don't you? Tell me, when's Michael going to get that professorship?'

'He was offered one,' Lucy said, 'last year. Unfortunately in New Zealand.'

'Baaaa,' Peter bleated. 'Presumably he's holding out for Oxford.'

'He likes it in London,' Lucy said.

'When he's here,' Peter said. 'Is he away a lot?'

'He's away a bit.'

'He won't say no to Oxford, though, will he, when the moment comes?'

'I don't think saying no is ever going to be a problem for Michael,' Lucy said.

'Well, that's our generation for you,' Peter said. 'No to life; yes to everything else.'

Lucy took a cool hand from against the glass of the lobster tank and joined it to the other to make a prop for her neat chin. 'You had an affair with Susie Padgett, didn't you?' she said.

'Who the hell told you that?'

'She did,' Lucy said.

'It was a hell of a long time ago,' Peter said.

'That was when she told me,' Lucy said.

'Were you surprised?'

'Surprised? No, I wasn't surprised.'

'I'd like to see you surprised,' Peter said. 'As a matter of fact, *I* was surprised. I never really liked her all that much, poor Susie. She had a baby, you know. Not mine. Somebody's.'

'I know,' Lucy Stayman said.

Peter was working at home the morning after the failure of the Staymans to come for their share of the Madeira sauce. He found cause to dawdle over a manuscript, hoping and dreading that Michael would call. He wanted to be there to pick up the telephone. It was twenty to eleven when it finally rang; it was eleven before he was able to make himself heard. 'Michael ... *Michael* ... Michael, I *have* listened. I've now been listening for the best part of half an hour. That's ... Frankly, as far as I can see, the only reason you've phoned is to – I said as far as I can see. No, I'm not in the least myopic. I don't even wear glasses. Ah, well if that's how you feel, one can only say that it was the pinnacle of hypocrisy ever to pretend that we were any sort of friends at all. I am not spoiling for a row. Rubbish. When? I've never been anything but unfailingly polite to Lucy, though I recognize that it might be very convenient for you to pretend otherwise. No, what I find – what I find painful is that we're supposed to be intelligent, sophisticated people – oh come on, Michael, you know *exactly* what that means – and yet we're prepared to see the whole structure of our friendship crumble to nothing over one silly incident. Pathetic. I agree. I'm relieved to hear you say so. Good heavens, Michael, you and I ... if we can't find common ground, what hope for the Arabs and the Israelis, what? I'm sorry? Look here, can't you show enough rudimentary imagination at least to concede that the damage is unevenly divided as between the two parties?' Cass came in with a stiff fan of gladioli in glazed paper. Peter put his hand over the mouthpiece ('Not from him, are they?'), while Michael crackled at the other end of the receiver. 'Would you believe it? He really and truly thinks he's the one with the grievance!'

'From Vivian and George,' Cass said. Her presence sharpened Peter's tone when he was again able to speak. 'Look here, Michael, don't call me a second-order nit-picker and I won't call you a complacent bloody egotist with a distinctly sick-making line in academic arse-licking. If you must know, I was thinking of Hugh and I was thinking of Maurice. I'll tell you what it boils down to, mate, and that is: do you think I'm worth knowing or not? That's to say,' Peter added, glancing across the gladioli, 'Cass and I are worth knowing. Because you're behaving like a self-satisfied solipsist. Do I remember what? Well, in this case even Wittgenstein would agree that what the solipsist thinks is quite definitely *false*. Look, I'm still prepared to believe that this is something we can get over, once ... Once *what*? Is that a joke?'

'Once what?' Cass said.

Peter waved her down. 'I'm not going to apologize in any circumstances whatsoever, so let's get that straight. Whose *filet en croûte* was it anyway? Mine. Cass's. I was not in the least rude to Lucy. I said nothing of the sort. What? That isn't of the sort; it's entirely different and it also happens to be precisely and exactly the case as I see it. On the contrary, *under*stated. Well, I know I'm right too, so what can we do about it? I happen to think this is rather a sad day. No, I pity you. I pity your students. I also pity your wife. I've never heard of married men going to the cinema on their own in the first place, but that's by the way. I know I can always hang up. Because, my dear Michael, I keep hoping that some vague sense of your own ineffable smugness may yet break through the carapace of vanity in which you are more and more inclined to cloak yourself. However, after your infantile article on Berlioz last week I suppose I ought to know better. Damn. He's hung up.'

'Aren't they beautiful?' Cass said. 'He's not worth it, Peter.'

'I'm well aware you never liked him. However, he happens to be one of the few people in the world who actually *is* worth it. And then he goes and makes us look like completely second-class citizens in front of a pair of bloody pouffes like George and Vivian.'

'At least they were a pair of bloody pouffes who managed to turn up,' Cass said, '*and* sent me some flowers. Are you going to the office today?'

'I can imagine what they've been saying around town ever since. Are you trying to get me out of the house or something?'

'Don't snap. I wondered if you wanted lunch. Listen, either he forgot or you gave him the wrong date.'

'He's always been jealous of me really. When I won the *Isis* poetry competition, he went out of his way to disparage the intellectual calibre of the judges, apart from deliberately mispronouncing Kingsley's name. All part of the same pattern: he can't bear anybody else to exist at all.'

'Then you're well rid of him,' she said, 'aren't you?'

'Am I? *Am* I? Do you expect me to go through life without any sort of intellectual companionship at all?'

'Thanks, Peter,' Cass said, 'you're a pal.'

'I'm supposed to be completely indifferent, am I, to losing the friendship of probably one of the four – certainly one of the *five* – brightest men of my generation?'

'You don't love me any more, Peter, do you?' Cass said. 'Our marriage –'

'Marriage!' Peter said. 'The whole world reduced to that – and that expanded to be the whole world. No wonder the young are absolutely contemptuous of the whole business. No wonder ... I thought I had something of value in my life and I lose it and all you can say is that I don't love you. Can't you see how degrading it is to be that limited, to be that ... that ... ?'

'That dull?' she said. 'I not only see it, I feel it.'

'Darling, I'm sorry,' he said. 'I'm sorry. I'll tell you what: let's take the afternoon off and go and see *Amok*! Oh, come on, Cassie, what's happened to your sense of humour?'

'You mean why don't I laugh when you say something that isn't funny?'

'Just don't blame me,' he said. 'This time just don't bloody blame me. I've tried; you haven't. So don't blame me.'

'Peter, are you screwing Susie Padgett?'

'Am I doing *what*?'

'I thought so.'

'Susie Padgett! I'm not screwing *anyone*. You ought to know that. You're crazy.'

'I was a bright girl when you met me, Peter. I'm beginning to feel like I'm nobody whatsoever suddenly. I bore even myself. I clearly bore you.'

'Crap.'

'I'm not spending my life with somebody who despises me, Peter. I just am not.'

'No, you're certainly not,' he said, arms around her, one hand finding flesh in her badged hip pocket. 'Susie Padgett? Are you crazy?'

The evening after he had lunched with Lucy Stayman, Peter took Cass to the theatre and then to dinner at a Chinese restaurant where other people always said they had had amazing meals. An open spiral staircase took them to the smart upper floor. It had recently resumed service after a spectacular killing had closed it for redecoration: a man and a woman had been shot over adulterous Peking duck. The murderer, an ex-policeman, had not known either of his victims by name. It was a nice point whether he could be accused of murder in such casual circumstances, but his insistence that he had considered his targets to be 'guilty' was enough to convict him. When invited to speak from the dock, he deplored the absence of the death penalty and declared that society was collapsing for lack of proper discipline. The blood on the upstairs walls, though now covered with what looked like flocculent smoked salmon, had revived the restaurant's fame. A couple of hot American publishers leaned over to shake Peter's hand as he and Cass went to their narrow table.

'So how was Lucy Stayman?'

'Almost exactly the same. The little pursed mouth, the china-blue eyes, the smooth skin.'

'The pink rabbit without the ears,' Cass said. 'Jesus, that was a terrible play. And the notices were marvellous.'

'Give the critics a comedy that isn't funny and a plot that they can predict and you'll soon be the key humorist of your day and a master of surprise to boot. I'm rather hoping to persuade her to write something for us, Lucy. Martin's got her under lock and key, but I'm trying to lob a rope ladder to her casement window. She just might be tempted.'

'Might you?' Cass said.

'What? Oh. You mean ... ? No, I don't think so. It's funny really, but I don't find her in the least attractive. I mean she's perfectly nice looking, but ...'

'You didn't find Susie Padgett attractive,' Cass said. 'And we know what happened there.'

'Finally, Susie *was* attractive. Lucy isn't attractive for reasons which have very little to do with what she actually looks like. There's something about her that doesn't quite add up.'

'But the rest of her comes to ten just the same, doesn't it?'

'Whose child did Susie have, Cass, do you know?'

'Isn't that Reggie Strang over there with the Wantage woman?'

'That's been happening for ages,' Peter said. 'I suspect that what finally puts one off in an indefinable sort of way is that she's been married to Michael for all these years. She still seems so incredibly *virginal*. Marriages, children, affairs – who knows? She doesn't give a thing away. There's still something absolutely unfledged about her.'

'You sound pretty interested for someone who's finally put off in an indefinable sort of way.'

'I have this rather morbid apprehension that if one undressed her, not that that is my purpose or desire, she'd turn out to be entirely hairless. Not a trace of what so astonished Ruskin when he came upon it, so to speak. You remember he was said to have been stricken with impotence on his wedding night when he found that Effie actually had pubic hair?'

'Men do have their problems, don't they?'

'They have everybody's,' Peter said. 'There hadn't been any sign of the stuff in the paintings of the *quattrocento* and his subscription to the more recent issues of *Playboy* magazine had been unaccountably held up in the post. One of the most extraordinary men of his time was broken by something every smutty commuter can now bury his nose in at any bookstall in the land! Must the elimination of mystery automatically entail the devaluation both of art and of experience?'

'Is that my starter for ten?' Cass said.

Peter's second lunch with Lucy Stayman was better planned. His secretary booked a table in a whitewashed brick basement in which a cookbook writer put her food where her readers' mouths were. 'The proofs,' Peter said, 'are in the puddings.'

'My children tell me I'm the worst pastry-maker in the world. What do you think I should do?'

'I think you should write this *Encyclopaedia of Childhood* for us,' Peter said, 'and hire a housekeeper to roll your children's tarts. Gabriel absolutely agrees with me. You could do it as a one-off for us. No reason why it should affect your relationship with Farmer and Burstall because this isn't something you've come to us with, it's an idea we've brought to you. Try the syllabub; it sounds like the quintessential diet-breaker but it's actually not all that rich, just expensive! Michael didn't come back yet, I gather?'

'No,' Lucy said. 'Not yet.'

'What would he say if he knew we'd had lunch twice in a week, I wonder?'

'Probably that he hoped you were going to pay me a whacking advance.'

'Marriage,' Peter said, 'I wish I understood it. Do you understand it?'

'Michael says it's an invaluable arrangement whereby a man and a woman can live together without wondering whether they ought to get married.'

'I like it,' Peter said. 'You know, the first time I saw you, you were wearing a panama hat and most, if not all, of your school uniform. And here we are having a business lunch, God help us. Business! How I hate it!'

'Oh really?' she said. 'I like business.'

'Then by all means let's do some,' he said. 'Meanwhile, tell me about your daughter's poetry.'

'It's not all that special,' she said, 'but it is in French.'

'That is special,' Peter said. 'She's at the Lycée presumably?'

'Michael wanted her bilingual.'

'And he always gets what he wants, of course, doesn't he? I recall rather well trying to cause your eye to stray vaguely in my direction one long-lost afternoon in a punt on the river. Nothing! You seemed much too young to be so decided. It didn't seem right. I mean, Michael was an extraordinary person, but he wasn't exactly – what shall we say? – conventionally handsome ever, was he? I always wondered what the secret was, for your total devotion.'

'I loved him,' Lucy said.

'Now,' Peter said, a modern hand on hers as the pudding came, 'tell me whether you like that or not, because we can always have something else.'

The following week, Peter was obliged to honour one of those dates so long inscribed in his diary that it had never seemed likely to come. A chum in the British Council had rung him soon after Christmas and persuaded him ('You can't possibly be busy that far ahead, dear boy') to give a paper to a cultural conference to be held in a Balkan city recently rebuilt after an earthquake. ('Frankly, Peter, it's a question of which do you want: our

UNESCO or theirs?') He had prepared a short statement on 'The Publisher and his Responsibility', but he feared that it was nothing like dull enough. On the eve of his departure he removed facetious phrases like 'friction and the reading public' – imagine that on simultaneous translation! – while Cass was wifely about packing.

'I wish you weren't going,' she said.

'Not half as much as I do,' he said. 'However, it's less than a week and Nicky'll be at home and so will Natasha at the weekend.'

'I suppose I can always start Proust again.'

'Much smarter to *finish* him again. Alternatively, you could start life again. You probably ought to have a wild affair.'

'Meaning that you're planning to?'

'Cassie, come on . . .'

'There was Susie Padgett,' Cass said.

'And absolutely no one since. It just so happened she caught me at a particularly vulnerable time.'

'Yes,' Cass said. 'Bed-time.'

'She was unhappy. I was unhappy. It does happen to be some nine years ago since we climbed into separate cabs. I haven't seen her since. We've had Nicky since then, for God's sake. Anyway, why rehash for the umpteenth time something you've already taken some pretty thorough revenge for?'

'Paolo had nothing to do with revenge,' Cass said.

'Well, whatever the motives, you certainly selected a pretty radical way of improving your Italian.'

'When are you next seeing Lucy Stayman?' Cass said.

'That's strictly business,' Peter said. 'How many times do I have to tell you?'

'And I know what business it is,' Cass said.

'Balls. No, Cassie, balls. I'm a publisher. I've listened to women for the last x years telling me how one mustn't discriminate, how one must treat them as – as persons – you've said it yourself, as you have to admit, and when one does so, the innuendos come pouring in from all sides. Do you want us to have a chaperone? Three lunches don't exactly constitute . . .'

'Oh there've been three, have there?'

'However many there've been,' Peter said. 'My attempted seductions are without the smallest carnal intent, I assure you. The only sheets I want her between are the balance sheets. I explained to you –'

'Yes, you did,' Cass said. 'However, this time I don't intend to find out what's going on by having someone feel so sorry for me that he can't wait to call and tell me what the whole of the rest of London knows already.'

'If Vivian thinks I'm ever going to forgive him,' Peter said, 'He's got another think coming.'

'I was supposed to forgive you,' Cass said.

The flight was delayed, but it was uneventful: they took off, they landed. Thousands of packaged people, after all, made the same journey during the summer months. Nowadays the Iron Curtain was permeable after the most trivial down payment. Could Yugoslavia properly be said to be behind it? Yet Peter felt his apprehensive age as he walked out into that grey world. The unpronounceable language threatened him like a new boarding school where he would never understand the slang. The prospect of a concrete room with a narrow bed filled him with homesick misgivings.

When he entered the headquarters of the Conference on Cultural and Social Structures, the welcome board was intimidating with improbable names – Dr *Bojkt?* – and promises of chamber concerts by provincial ensembles. There was no colour in the echoing lobby, merely shades of grey and beige. The smeared windows looked new; one could guess that they had never been opened and that, once opened, they would never shut. It would surely not be long before someone somewhere started to hammer. Peter was unsurprised to learn that he was expected to double up.

'I did specifically request a single room,' he said. 'On the form.'

'I think you'll like Professor Lengyel, Dr Rudolf.'

'I have no doctorate, Miss –'

'Dr,' she said. 'Dr Taubman. I'm helping momentarily behind the desk because I happen to have some English.'

'You sound as if you've got most of it,' Peter said. 'I'm sure Professor Lengyel is a delightful man, but I haven't shared a room with another man since I left university and I very much hoped I'd never have to do so again.'

'He's a very intelligent person,' Dr Taubman said.

'It's not his intelligence that I question,' Peter said, 'it's his socks.

And his toothbrush. I'm aware that it sounds ludicrously inhibited of me, but there it is. Is there any chance of a hotel?'

'The conference has proved so popular, you see, Mr Rudolf, that ... Why don't you leave it with me for a few minutes and I'll see what I can arrange?'

'It's awfully good of you,' Peter said. 'Is there a bar or something?'

'There's a bar and everything,' Dr Taubman said.

A bearded man was drinking fruit juice and checking a typescript. He watched Peter over his spectacles as he paused to analyse, briefly, the fortunes of two chess players in brown suits who were sitting at a trestle table near a picture window just too high to allow anyone to see out of it. Peter despaired of them making another move and glanced at the bearded man, who was wearing a check shirt with a three-buttoned cuff and a denim suit, the jacket pronged on a single upright of his chair-back.

'Good Christ,' Peter said.

The bearded man did not look up. 'What the hell are you doing here?' he said.

'I don't believe it,' Peter said. 'I simply don't believe it.'

'By no means entailing that it isn't so,' Michael Stayman said.

Peter stood by the table on which, he observed, Michael was working in a language with a paucity of vowels. 'How are you, Michael?'

'Am I a physician?' Michael said. 'Of all the people I never expected to see!'

'I never expected to see you, come to that.'

'I was given to understand that this was strictly for grandmasters and above.'

'They want me to share with a man called Lengyel. Do you ... ?'

'Rudi? You'll have to sleep with your trousers on.'

'I suppose you've got the presidential suite,' Peter said.

'*And* the presidential sweetie. Actually, I'm staying with some friends who've got a villa.'

'How do you manage to have friends in a place like this? Let alone with a villa.'

'I am a Balkans man, you know. This is my patch.'

'This really is a hell of a coincidence. Did Lucy tell you that we bumped into each other?'

'I've been in Thessaloniki looking at some files.'

'This really is extraordinary! Ten years and then I come across you both at opposite ends of Europe within less than a month! Do you feel like a drink?'

'Fruit juice,' Michael said, his pen fierce in the margin for a moment. 'Pineapple preferably.'

'A few minutes ago I was feeling so depressed I was rather hoping for abrupt news of some domestic crisis so that I could do an honourable scuttle and now ... What's the Serbo-Croat for pineapple juice?'

'Try pineapple juice,' Michael said. 'Boris there has more languages than a Neapolitan pimp. What's your paper going to be about?'

'Oh – the publisher as patron and, well, pimp, roughly. Cant and commerce. How does one keep one's list to port, as you might say. What about you?'

'The basic spiel on translation. Is it a help or a hindrance to mutual cultural masturbation? Preliminary remarks; remarks; concluding remarks; any questions; any answers. And I'm sure we're extremely grateful to Dr Stayman.'

Peter brought the fruit juice back to the table. There was no danger of slopping the meagre contents of the large glasses. 'Well, such as I have, I give unto thee. Here's to you, *traduttore traditore*, and to a full resumption of diplomatic and personal relations. God knows, it's about time.'

'I say, you didn't pay for these, did you?'

'Well, obviously.'

'Are you not on the diplomatic list? Poor old Peter, still the eternal victim!'

'By the way, Michael,' Peter said, sipping maltreated apple, 'I very much enjoyed that stuff you did about "Nietzsche and his Consequences". It's been said before, of course, but you did say it again.'

'That's my Peter,' Michael said, with sugared lips, 'I'm relieved to see that you haven't let a few disappointments corrode your capacity for topical malice.'

'Disappointments?' Peter said. 'I must have missed something!'

'I've rather got the impression over the years, from one or two things that've been said in various quarters ...'

'Gabriel and I have built up a bloody successful small publishing house from a joint original investment of roughly two pounds ten and a packet of Lyons tea. I don't find that disappointing in the least, though of course those who've never left the cloister might well think it easy to cut the extra-mural mustard until they try, which they're not now likely to do.'

'My goodness me,' Michael said, 'haven't we turned elaborate?'

'Only in academic company,' Peter said. 'One's always afraid that simple language may prove unintelligible in polysyllabic circumstances.'

Michael turned the empty glass in his fingers. 'I wasn't thinking about business,' he said.

'Some aspects of it are extremely enjoyable,' Peter said. 'For instance, I'm fishing for Lucy at the moment.'

'All I can say is, I hope the compleat angler's going to give her a fat advance.'

'Precisely what we imagined you'd hope,' Peter said.

Dr Taubman came into the bar, her bun bursting into trails of fine brown hair which she threw three times over her shoulder like lucky salt. 'Ah, Mr Rudolf, I think I've managed to do something for you. Oh, you've met Dr Stayman.'

'Yes, and not for the first time.'

'We're old friends,' Michael said. 'What's your name again?'

'That is so nice,' Dr Taubman said, 'so long as you don't form a click. This time we are not going to have any clicks, Michali. Remember Ioannina?'

'Cliques!' Peter got it.

'Now, Mr Rudolf, I hope I find you a very small room – perhaps a little hot – but all to yourself.'

'As long as Professor Lengyel doesn't take it personally. I should hate –'

'I look after Professor Lengyel. I see you later Michali, is all right? I have to go have a quick word with Saki. He has some very terrible trouble with the Bulgarians in the annexe. Then we go to the villa.'

'Do you know her well?' Peter said.

'Quite well. She works out of the University of Leipzig. She's had rather a tangled history.'

'Amazing English.'

'Amazing most things. She translates from three languages and speaks about eight. She can lecture in five.'

'Fuck her,' Peter said.

'That's a matter for private negotiation,' Michael said. 'She was born in Cairo during the war – Greek mother –'

'Ah so you've got Greek in common!'

'And Roumanian actually, though mine's purely conversational. Her father was a German refugee, worked in Allied intelligence, if one can ever quite believe in corporate intelligence. Anyway, he went back to Germany in '45 and got himself shot by Stalin a purge or two later.'

'Well, at least we don't do *that* to each other,' Peter said.

'He was rehabilitated after the Twentieth Congress and he's actually recently been awarded a Lenin Medal. There's some talk of reissuing his texts on Nationalism. You'll find his name's already back in the footnotes to Lukacs in the latest edition. There's also talk of collecting his correspondence –'

'For a dead man he seems to be having rather a lively career. Why did they shoot him?'

'Basically, I think, to establish his credibility.'

'Discuss and explain, would you, please, Michael? I don't quite –'

'Oh surely! He'd been rather successful in recruiting agents for the Russians in the vodka belt of the American and British diplomatic baggage. If they'd greeted him on his return with flags and bands, all his chums would've been immediately suspect. When the Russians put him up against a wall, it meant that all his contacts were rendered above suspicion. He'd been a double agent, obviously, and the Americans actually believed until quite recently that he'd been one of theirs. It may even have been his idea, Rita thinks, having himself shot. Rather like –' Michael waved a hand towards the bent-backed chess players under the high window, '– one of those supremely satisfying sacrifices when you abandon your queen for the higher glory of check-mating your opponent a couple of moves later. It needs nerve.'

'It needs fanaticism. A man who goes home knowing he's going to die and still gets on to the plane? Are people like that really of the same stuff as you and me?'

'And you and I,' Michael said, 'are we really of the same stuff?'

'Of course we are,' Peter said. 'Of *course* we are. Basically. *Aren't* we?'

'If you say so, my friend.'

'Well, whatever happens we're not going to shoot each other. Behaviour like that – killing people on your own side – killing people at all – I find it so deeply repulsive, I don't know whether to laugh or cry, do you?'

'Oh, one does both, Peter, one does both!'

The amiable use of his first name, tucked intimately between the two legs of the repetition, gave Peter a sentimental thrill.

When Rita Taubman returned, with a squishing noise as her crêpe rubber soles worked on the newly swabbed tiles, she seemed to Peter to have developed a more interesting personality in the few minutes of her absence. The grey eyes were now bruised with knowledge and endurance; her previously shapeless body was fragrant with the scent of tragedy. When she put her rather square hand on Michael's chequered sleeve, Peter read intriguing sensual maturity into the casual, confident gesture. 'Bulgarians all sorted out?' he said.

'Sorted out? Bulgarians? Never! But I did have an idea. You are a friend of my Michali's, I tell you what I'm going to do, I'm going to find you a bed at the villa –'

'Oh that'd be marvellous,' Peter said.

'I want you to have a nice experience,' she said.

The 'villa' was a small, new stucco house with large tubular-steel gates painted the colour of fermented raspberries. The gates creaked on to a narrow garden sown with gravel. They walked between margins of grey concrete to a front door pierced by a wired porthole. The wood of the floral furniture looked as brilliant and brittle as treacle-toffee. 'I hope you didn't expect anything more sumptuous,' Michael said.

'I expected nothing whatsoever.' Peter tested the varnish for stickiness before leaning his briefcase against it. 'I must say though, I never realized that virtually the whole place was going to be brand new.'

'You heard about the earthquake, surely?'

'Yes, but one never quite believes in earthquakes, does one? You can't help wondering why people hang on in places that threaten at any moment to open up and swallow them for dinner.'

'We can't all live in Putney, can we?'

'We can try,' Peter said. 'I wonder if the Persephone myth origin-
ated in an earthquake incident. Rather naive aetiology, but –'

'I'm not awfully hot on Greek mythology,' Michael said, 'I'm
afraid.'

'That's roughly why I thought I'd bring it up,' Peter said.

'I don't start seriously until 1750.' Michael was fingering a crack
in the new wall above the fireplace. 'I stayed in the old Hotel
Macedonia just three months before it collapsed. Have you ever
been in a tight corner?'

'All my corners have been rather loose-fitting, I'm glad – and
slightly ashamed – to say.'

Rita Taubman brought in a tray with a large striated pot and
unmatching cups and put it down next to some plastic anemones.
'Camomile,' she said. 'I hope you like it.'

'I hope I do,' Peter said. 'Have you, Michael, been in one?'

'Not really. Though we did once cross a rather hairy border
in a bit of a hurry, didn't we, Rita?'

He might have reminded her of some amorous exploit; Dr
Taubman flushed and looked at Peter with flattering complicity.
'With Michael,' she said, 'things are always likely to be a little
hairy, I think.' She clamped his beard for a moment between
thumb and forefinger. 'Now, I must get back to the conference
centre because Professor Lovsky appears to have mislaid his notes.
"Linguistics Now!" I see you both later.'

'Yes, indeed,' Peter said, 'and thank you so much, Dr Taubman.'
Peter poured pale tea, while Michael unzipped his continental
briefcase. 'You know,' Peter said, holding out a courteous cup,
'I've always thought it was really foolish of us not to stay friends.'

'I'm not sure I'm all that good at friendship,' Michael said, nose
over the tea.

'You're bloody awful at it, judging from experience!'

'I'm not sure that I even know what it's supposed to be.'

'What's anything supposed to be?' Peter said. 'Friendship, love . . .
I suppose it's all part of having lived this rather cushy life:
we've never really been down to the wire, as they say, over
anything vital. I think we've probably missed something, don't

you? Though there's something faintly suspect in envying people their cruel experiences. We've never needed to be really loyal to each other and we've never had the satisfaction of knowing we have been. Result: a sort of systematic flippancy. One wants to care; one doesn't dare. One wants to be available; one isn't sure that one's wanted. One wants to give, but one doesn't want to be taken! We fashion great grievances out of trivial occasions and the only diet that really suits us is a large bite from the hand that feeds us.'

'You know you gave me one date and then expected us to turn up on another, don't you?'

'Oh good heavens,' Peter said. 'Good *heavens*, I wasn't talking about *that*. After ten years, what *does* it matter?'

'Hence my decision to raise it,' Michael said.

'We shall never really know, shall we? This tea's rather nice; tasteless but nice. You remember the old Wittgensteinian example of the man who turns over a card and then shuffles it back into the pack, claiming that it was the nine of diamonds? He can neither be proved right nor proved wrong. There is absolutely no evidence and, from want of some eternal video tape, no chance of there ever being any. The rare instance of the empirical metaphysical, wasn't that what we used to call it? There certainly was a card, but we can never know which. It was or it wasn't the nine of diamonds! You did or didn't fail to come on the right day!'

'I rather think your wife was inclined to the view that the mistake was yours.'

'Wives often are, aren't they? Her name's still Cass by the way. We must be two of the longest running shows in town, when you come to think about it, you and Lucy, Cass and me. Oh I daresay we've had our ... but ... Lucy told me your definition of marriage, by the way. Very Michael, I thought.'

'What were we going to eat that night?' Michael said. 'If we'd come?'

'I think it was *filet en croûte*, wasn't it? Feel like coming after all? *Amok*! Michael, really!' They sipped the tea. Sitting in the gimcrack parlour of the villa, as if in the provincial waiting-room of a doctor who was never going to see them, Michael began to flip backwards through some flimsies covered with cyrillic typing, when Peter pulled out a journal of penology and went through the motions of checking something in the index. He was pleased when

Michael looked up to see what he was reading. He displayed the back of the journal. 'Do you do good works at all?'

'I leave that to successful publishers,' Michael said.

'I visit prisons.'

'And how good is that?'

'Hard to say. However, I do. I visit rather an interesting man in Wandsworth who tried to kill his wife.'

'What stopped him?'

'Ran out of steam, presumably; he did break her arm though *and* rearranged her nose. Charles Savage.'

'Trying to live up to his name, I assume. They can be a terrible burden.'

'Yes, imagine being the *other* Michael Stayman. *Not* the famous one. You'd never think he'd hurt anybody, this chap, actually. The odd thing was, he'd already left her. A few months later he heard she was having it away with somebody and he went and half beat her to death. Even though he swears he was the one who'd walked out in the first place. He had another woman and everything. Rather dishy. I went to see her.'

'Talked about it freely, did he?'

'Eventually he did. When we'd finished talking about the ultimate nature of the real and other tea-time topics. One day he said, "You're probably wondering how I come to do it. Well, the truth is, it's the only time I ever really enjoyed being with her. I really enjoyed it, Peter," he said. "It's just what I always wanted to do, give her a walloping." '

'And what moral posture did you strike when he came out with that?'

'I'm not called upon to strike moral postures,' Peter said. 'I just stay the forty minutes.'

'One never knows for certain when one's pleased a woman, but you can be fairly certain when you've broken her nose.'

'You think that's the attraction?'

'After the long diplomacy of marriage, the fist at least has no sullen ambiguities. Why have you been seeing Lucy?'

'Oh, simple: I'm busy seducing her, aren't I? Martin Farmer's got her and I want her. Martin's bright, but he's lazy. Lucy deserves proper marketing and real attention. I can give her both. Do you mind?'

'I hope you'll both be very happy,' Michael said. 'I wonder if it's ever occurred to you that you weren't actually entirely sorry when we had that muddle about dates?'

'I should like to endorse your subtlety, Michael,' Peter said, 'but you're quite wrong. Cass and I had rather a row about it, afterwards, well, arising from it and . . . well, enough said. Everything's fine now, of course. We had another child eventually, Nicky, but for a while . . . did you ever meet Paolo Benvenuti?'

'Paolo Benvenuti?' Michael said. 'Sounds like a Florentine painter.'

'Nearly right. He's a Florentine prick. Frankly, as far as you personally were concerned, I felt humiliated and – why not let's admit it? – rather deprived, if you must know.'

'It occurred to me that perhaps it rather suited you to saddle me with some exemplary social lapse, something that would put me under some sort of penitent obligation. Unless, perhaps, you were looking for an excuse to abuse me to Lucy –'

'For what possible purpose?'

'There's always the sheer fun of it,' Michael said. 'Or to get closer to her maybe.'

'Why would I have wanted to do that? She didn't write books in those days. I never abused you to Lucy in any way whatsoever. I remain honestly convinced that you were the one who made the deliberate mistake.'

'You may be convinced,' Michael said, 'but I'm not persuaded you're honest.'

'Look here, Michael, the last thing I want to do after all these years is re-open old wounds.'

'After all these years,' Michael said, 'what else do you want to do?'

The conference proved more enjoyable than Peter had thought likely. His paper was quite a success; the remaining jests, even in translation, went down rather well. That evening, they went to a little restaurant in the town, one of the few buildings to escape the earthquake, an all-wooden structure of asymmetrical charm, where Rita ordered *blintzes* and red cabbage, followed by a lot of fiery aquavit. They reeled home, Rita between the two men who were singing 'There's a tavern in the town', as they had in the first-year streets of Oxford, in unsubtle celebration of their recent release from National Service. As they reached the villa, the air was full, in Peter's stimulated imagination, of warm possibilites. Rita put her arms around his neck and kissed him on the mouth. 'Peter dear, I'm so glad you are a friend of Michael's. Otherwise we might never have done this!'

'Pity the evening has to end,' Peter said.

He lay in bed and listened for the creak of surreptitious feet along the landing. Or could it be that Rita, with passionate directness – after all she had been through, why not? – would actually come knocking at his door? How would it feel, that soft, naked warmth against him, the untrammelled bun? She and Michael had known each other for years; surely nothing had stopped them from becoming lovers. He could even imagine – one could imagine anything! – how they might both come into his room, bright from preliminary satisfaction. How rarely, when he thought about it, both of his parents had come in to say good night to him at the same time!

No one came to his door, nor did he overhear any amorous expedition. He woke to a wet day. There was a 'plenary session' in the morning, during which the highest hopes were expressed for the cultural and moral mission of literature in a changing world; no platitude was too trite not to be refurbished and applauded. In the afternoon there was to have been an excursion to some Roman ruins, but steady rain deterred them. 'Besides,' Michael said, 'I've had more uplift than even the most decadent tit could well endure. Do you still play bridge at all?' A couple of American academics were anxious for a game. Michael informed Peter that Schenck and Liebermann were an extremely logical pair: they played every hand strictly according to the odds. They were likely to be difficult but predictable opponents. Could English agility match Teutonic earnestness?

It took a high proportion of the aces and kings to turn the final trick, but Michael and Peter, after a five-hour session, emerged the winners by some forty-three points. At fifty cents a hundred, it enabled them to bring several bottles of suspect champagne back to the villa for the last supper. The other guests were Professor Lovsky and his wife, Dora (who knitted), and Stelio and Eirene Kyriakoulis, who had met Michael in Thessaloniki. Peter was told that he had been researching in the papers of the Sephardic community deported by the Nazis. Michael had a side interest in Ladino.

Professor Lovsky was determined to have a fun evening. After the stuffed pork and most of the sweet champagne, he told the story about the American, the Englishman and the Pole. 'They want to get into the Olympic Games, only they don't have a ticket, you know it? O.K., so they decide they'll have to bluff their way through the competitors' entrance. The American puts on the tracksuit and the running shoes and he gets hold of a long pole, you know, and he goes up to the man at the gate and he says, "Homer Sneyd, United States, Pole Vault." The guy looks at him and says. "O.K., in you go." So up steps the Britisher and he's wearing the blazer and the white flannels and the nautical cap and he says, "Oliver Truslove-Smythe, Great Britain, Yachting." The guy checks him out, "O.K., in you go." Up steps the Pole. Wrapped from head to toe in barbed wire, little slit for the eyes, little slit for the mouth, that's it: the rest is barbed wire. "Jerzy Kowalski," he says, "Poland, Fencing." '

'The Greeks frowned. Michael smiled. Rita looked at Professor Lovsky's wife with a gentle and affectionate tilt of the head. Peter roared with laughter. 'You've heard it before, Dr Stayman.' Josef Lovsky said.

'And I'll almost certainly hear it again,' Michael said. 'It's a goodie, Joe.'

'Tell me, Professor Lovsky,' Peter said, kneading broken bread, 'as a matter of interest, would you have told it if you hadn't been Polish?'

'I haven't been Polish for years,' Lovsky said. 'A joke's a joke; if it's funny, it's funny. Dr Stayman doesn't agree.'

'I never argue with a tautology, Professor Lovsky, especially when it's older than I am.'

'Michali, you're being naughty. He can be very naughty when he tries.'

'If I stepped out of line,' Lovsky said, 'in any way . . .'

'Not at all,' Michael said. 'It's just that my name was Lovsky before I changed it.'

'Boy,' Lovsky said, 'that British sense of humour! That straight face! You're not an easy man to read, Dr Stayman.'

'Even though he's available in several languages,' Peter said.

'*Kirie Kyriakoulis, katalaveinete olo afto?*' Michael was asking.

'Not all of it,' the Greek replied. 'I get the words, I don't get the joke!'

'We should all talk Greek for a while, I think,' Rita Taubman said.

'All talk Greek!' Peter said. 'That's a *Greek* joke, I presume.'

'A Greek joke, dear Peter, is a Turk with a broken leg.'

'Yes,' Michael said, 'and two Greek jokes is a urk with two broken legs. The melancholy truth is, given half a chance, we all hate each other like poison. No? Think of your man in prison, Peter, who never really enjoyed his wife until he beat her up. Look at Mrs Lovsky, for that matter: how she'd love to drive one of her needles up to the hilt in my ribs, wouldn't you, darling? Do we really want international co-operation and the unlimited exchange of chamber orchestras? Are we really fascinated by new bearings in the Serbo-Croat theatre and the South Slav contribution to meta-linguistics? War is the only sincere human activity and the polemic is the only heart-felt form of inter-cultural endeavour. The rest is nothing but careerism and caramel custard.'

'I disagree entirely, Michali, entirely.'

'That's because you know something about war, Dr Taubman,' Peter said, 'and suffering. Whereas the nearest Michael or I have been to it is doubling across the square at Mons with a bull-throated bugger shouting one-two, one-two. I don't agree with you either, Michael, actually –'

'And aren't you glad you don't? It's the first time you've looked positively alive since we sat down tonight.'

'Rubbish. Roast pork is one of my best things.'

'Peter, why the laborious *bonhomie*? You're the practical proof of what I was saying: you've been consumed with hatred for me for the last ten years –'

'This is something we didn't know,' Rita said.

'It's not something that can be known,' Peter said, 'because it happens not to be true.'

'You're smiling, Peter, but deep down inside the ramparts you're busy hustling ammunition to the guns. Neat adrenalin is being served in the officers' mess. Alarm bells are ringing. Action stations! Erk-erk, erk-erk . . .'

'He's so naughty,' Rita said, leaning against Peter. 'You mustn't let him bait you.'

'You're a Greek and I'm a Turk,' Michael said, 'and why deny it? You can't wait for me to break a leg. What about this afternoon when I went down in that three no trumps doubled? You could have killed me.'

'All you had to do was duck the first spade.'

'And the way you ranted on about that piece I wrote on Berlioz . . .'

'Well, well,' Peter said, 'you certainly can remember things when you want to! Who's the Greek and who's the Turk around here? It was a profoundly silly piece, as I'm sure you now recognize after a lapse of ten years.'

'That's as may be,' Michael said, 'but I'm concerned with what you said about it, not with what it said. Your animosity was practically pathological.'

'You mean I didn't like it. The fact is, I would never have said a word about it if you hadn't stood us up over a dinner party and then lacked the rudimentary grace to apologize –'

'Peter, you know what you are? You're a spoilt child.'

'*Ceteris paribus*, you'd have done exactly the same thing. In *spades.*'

'In *spades*?' said Mr Kyriakoulis. 'Barbed wire? Fencing? I don't . . .'

'One day, Michael, someone's really going to let you have it,' Peter said.

'If you two Britishers are going to have a serious set to,' Mrs Lovsky said, counting stitches, 'maybe we should clear some dishes –'

'If you two Poles want to clear some dishes,' Michael said, 'clear some dishes, you two Poles.'

'Now wait a minute, young man – I come from Baltimore, Maryland, and my great-grandparents were from Paisley, Scotland.'

'Which is where you get your knitting patterns from, I presume.'

'Michael has an exceptional sense of humour,' Rita said.

'Yes, and next time he's going to make a big effort to bring it with him,' Peter said.

'You see?' Michael said. 'You *see*? You can't wait to draw blood.'

'I *was* smiling,' Peter smiled.

'Oh was that a smile? I thought you were trying to get the mince out from between your back teeth. Ten years, and he's still got his stiletto tucked into his sock for easy access –'

'Michael, must we really unpack the-mouldering past all over Rita's delicious dinner?'

'Why so mealy-mouthed all of a sudden? These people don't mean anything to you. You'll never see them again in your life. After that embarrassingly lightweight paper you read, I can't see them exactly paying your fare to Tokyo for the next international festival of cliché and platitude. So why not let's unzip and flash truth for once in our diplomatic lives?'

'Was that diplomatic or dipsomaniac?'

'You've been deploring my absence from your intimate counsels for the last decade. Well, here I am. Unmistakably available. Have at me, sir, have at me while you've still got the cut-price chance.'

'Just because we may not see people again,' Peter said, 'doesn't give us an automatic warrant to bore them silly, or to insult them. My friend didn't mean any offence, Mrs Lovsky.'

'The dummy speaks for the ventriloquist! The second oldest plot in the world!'

'You two!' Rita said. 'Really, boys!'

'Are you drunk, Michael?'

'On Bulgarian pop? I'm honest, Peter, which is probably why I seem unfamiliar to you. You talk about the need for honesty, but as soon as I take you up on the idea, you go as red as a school-girl who's off for the first time.'

'Rita's been good enough to find me a room,' Peter said. 'I'm damned if I mean to repay her by making a shambles of her farewell dinner.'

'I'll handle Rita,' Michael said, 'if she's lucky.'

'The truth is, you resent my having been given a bed here in the first place. You'd much sooner I was shacked up at the Macedonia with Rudi Lengyel or whatever his name is.'

'Rudi Lengyel!' Mrs Kyriakoulis was radiant with understanding. 'Such a darling sweet person!'

'Joe, suppose you bring out some dishes?' Mrs Lovsky said. 'This is a Communist country, you know; no law against helping here.'

Professor Lovsky picked up the used pork. 'You sure know how to throw an evening to the piranha fish, Dr Stayman.'

'Michael, really,' Peter said, 'what is the matter with you?'

'Fancying our chances with Rita, are we?'

'You must be mad.'

'Come on, of course you do. No great shame in it. She's a very hospitably shaped lady.'

'Do I gather you have prior claims?'

'You fancied her like mad the other night. I wouldn't say prior. Simultaneous, if you like. And you do like, don't you?'

'Do you make a habit of this kind of thing? What is it about dinner parties that brings out the shit in you exactly? Or is it something to do with me personally?'

'Peter, you really are paranoid. No wonder Cassie ...'

'Christ, Michael, I'd advise you to –'

'No wonder Cassie *what?*' Michael said. 'I mean, come on, let's have a small *New Statesman* competition for the best ending to that particular sentence. No wonder Cassie ...? All I was actually going to say was, "No wonder Cassie is widely regarded as the best-natured wife south of the river." Or is she widely regarded as something else as well and I've not been informed? I am out of the country a lot.'

'You're a real stirrer, aren't you? You're a real stirrer.'

'Is this a joke?' Mr Kyriakoulis said.

'More than like,' Michael said. 'I think we're just about getting to the punch line.'

'Aren't you the quintessential arrogant bastard? And to think that I honestly thought we were grown up! Ten years, I honestly thought we could behave like a couple of grown ups at last. Instead of which, you're clearly as fond of snowballs now as you were then. Always assuming you can wrap yours around a rock before you throw it.'

Professor Lovsky's unsmiling face appeared around the door. 'Rita would like to know who wants yoghurt? It's in the kitchen if you do. Dora and I are going to take a little walk, so ...'

'Don't photograph any secrets while you're out,' Michael said, 'or you'll only have Peter coming to visit you in gaol.'

'You really are a baby, aren't you? Here we are, over forty years old, with all the equipment we're ever going to have to enable us to behave like mature human beings and you're still an infant in the tertiary stages of megalomania. I offer you – I offer you –'

'What do you offer me? The chance to do a pre-publication puff for your next major study of the Balkans by some half-pay journalist who once almost knew his way around Bucharest? A shared holiday cottage in the Pyrenees with a six-mile hairpin drive to the nearest bar? A slice of re-heated *filet en croûte*? What?'

'Sod you, Michael Stayman, don't you ever hit anywhere except below the belt?'

'Well, that is where the fun is, isn't it? Peter, your problem is, you think I'm basically a nice man. Like you. Well, I'm not: I'm a stranger from another race. I have the morals and the temperament of an intellectual commercial traveller. I'm not the very-decent-when-you-get-to-know-him old College chum you're so determined to make me. How are things between you and Cassandra?'

'I don't answer questions like that from strangers from other races.'

'Like that, eh?'

'You're really pleased with your performance here tonight, aren't you? Frankly, I think you've made a total gorilla of yourself. If I was Rita, I'd be bloody furious –'

'If you were Rita, you'd be putting a touch of scent between your legs.'

'That's the basis of your whole idiotic vanity, I suppose? You have a wife like Lucy and you spend your time shagging shady ladies behind the Iron Curtain. I thought you were a serious person, a true scholar, a man of integrity, someone I could truly admire. Even during all those years we weren't talking, I – I – I –'

'Presumably you know your real trouble, don't you, Peter? You're in love with me.'

'Ha! Don't flatter yourself. Love? I find you pathetic. And if by "in love" you mean to suggest that I find you anything but physically grotesque –'

'Oh I'm not suggesting you desire my body, though you wouldn't, for whatever weird reasons, be the first. I mean you love me. I'm what you'd like to be. What I think is what you wish you thought. What I do, you wish you did. Including Rita.'

'You're actually proud of that, are you?'

'What's pride got to do with it?'

'What about Lucy?'

'Does your indignant tone imply that you think that I should lead a life of exclusively connubial bliss? Frankly, I find bliss a fairly rare commodity; I snatch as much of it as I can. I rather hope she does the same. Oh Peter, Peter, Peter ... what a grizzled old hypocrite you are!'

'Hypocrisy's had rather a bad press lately,' Peter said. 'Personally, I think it's due for a comeback. As for the idea that I'm in love with you –'

'Ah, you'd like to get back to that, would you?'

'I'd certainly like to knock that stupid, conceited look off your face.'

'Yes, well, that's all part of it, isn't it? Good heavens, I'm not *blaming* you, Peter – I quite appreciate it's not something you've consciously *decided*. Love isn't like that, is it? One doesn't feature it in one's Spring List; it simply crops up. How often have you actually been in love in your life?'

'Will you kindly stop interviewing me, Michael? When I saw you were here, I decided to make the best of it –'

'You were tickled pink. It made your trip.'

'I hoped we'd be able to start again from scratch –'

'Well, here we are scratching. What more do you want?'

'I'm not so eaten out with self-esteem that I can't recognize intelligence when I see it. I'm not determined to claw down anyone who seems remotely capable of being a rival. If I may be personal for a moment – and I don't see why I should be the only one who isn't – it makes me a little sick to think of someone like you married to Lucy and then –'

'And then?'

'If I had a wife like Lucy ...'

'I gather you want to talk about your marriage?'

'By Christ, Michael –'

'Dear God,' Professor Lovsky said, 'they're still at it.'

'Good night, Professor,' Michael called.

'He's the rudest man I ever met in my whole life,' said Mrs Lovsky, tucking a skein of wool under her chin as she went upstairs.

'I think perhaps we should ...' Peter looked at his watch. 'We've got the closing session in the morning. What is it? "Culture and Post-Culture: the Psychoanalytic Paradigm?'' I wouldn't want to oversleep and miss a thing like that.'

'You wish you were free,' Michael said. 'Is that it?'

'Free?' Peter said. 'What's free? Freedom is the recognition of a certain kind of necessity, that's what the fashionable parrots used to say, isn't it?'

'Don't give me psittacosis and I won't give it to you! You know what intellectuals most resent about the Soviet Union, about the whole Communist mirage? About these people here? It's not the Gulags really; not the domestic vulgarity or the diplomatic cynicism. It's that they've let us find out about them, let us take package tours to their dismal cities and shake hands with their porky potentates and sip their tepid tea. The Iron Curtain's turned rusty on us. They've deprived us of our wettest dreams. They've robbed treachery of its charm. We've got nothing to be lusciously unfaithful to. We thought they had the key to the millennium and it turns out all they can really do is rig the Olympic Games and introduce cheating to chess.'

'Pretty speech,' Peter said, 'but what's it all about?'

'Sorry, have I run ahead of you? I'll pop back. We're cornered, Peter, is what I'm saying. We've only got sex left, the only unsleeping idea in our brainy little heads. They've let us down, the bloody reds, by being so unattractive that not even a happily married man could really fancy them. Oh if only they'd kept Socialism a little prettier, if only they'd let us deceive ourselves as to her virtue, how willing we would have been! If only Eastern promises didn't have such blindingly bad breath, how quick we would have been to paddle across the Rubicon and throw in our shifty lot with them! We wouldn't mind them being cruel, at least to others, if only they'd stayed faintly glamorous and intellectually adroit. Oh I saw you when you walked into that conference centre, you were all excited: you thought you'd entered the headquarters of hell. Mephistopheles will see you now! You tucked your virtue tight between your legs and you were determined never to surrender. Intellectual hatches battened down! Poor Peter, nobody really wants you or your virtue. No Jesuitic comrade is going to argue you into a compromising position; the Damascus road is closed and blinding lights are out. Life's a library book too many people have read before. You hoped it would all be Dostoevsky plus; instead of which, it's Graham Greene minus. And that doesn't leave a lot. I had a girl in Odessa for a packet of chewing gum last year.'

'Please cease offering me your confessions, Michael. I shan't publish them, so don't bother.'

'Of course, I flatter myself she wouldn't have done it for just *anybody's* chewing gum.'

'Liked your flavour, did she?'

'Poor Peter, you want a world that doesn't exist, full of moral fineness and deep issues. Oh so do I, but the difference between us is that I know I can't have it. Hence you're capable of loving and I – I really don't think I am, except in the most abstract sense, which is why, despite the evident futility of it, I persist in being a scholar. You have all the romantic passion which ought to make you a seeker after truth – but romantic passion today means that you're always looking in the wrong place for the wrong thing. You talk about friendship – I'm touched –'

'You hide it well,' Peter said.

'I had a friend in Poland,' Michael said. 'A brilliant man. Byzantinologist. Long talks into the night and finally elaborate plans for getting him out, and his wife.'

'Across a hairy border, I presume?'

'Eventually we bring it off. Terrifically emotional scenes in some God-awful frontier town. The wraps are off. We can all be ourselves at last! They come to live in Earl's Court. Chipped china, broken English. They bore me stiff. I never see them any more.'

'Was it your child Susie Padgett had?' Peter said.

'Why, want to share the school fees? I'm a one-man band, Peter. I'm not particularly proud of it, but there it is. I'll play my own organ, thanks all the same. I know myself; I don't claim to know anybody else. I'm not all that sure I want to.'

'And you really think I want to be you? Like hell I do!'

'Mark the ambiguity! Oh, you wouldn't want my anal cyst, I know that. Don't worry: I had it out last year. Nothing matters, Peter. Face that and then be happy.'

Peter bunched crumbs into cemented greyness. The table was clear but the cloth was mapped with stains of various colours and ridged from absent dishes. 'Things do matter, Michael, and you know they do.'

Michael turned his clouded glass against the light. 'You're a better man than you know, Peter, and a rarer. You're like too many people in the West, all longing to turn their backs on what's worth having because you can't bear to think that that's all there is to have. You think you're being honourably non-materialistic, you're really being greedy. Accept the fallibility of things, accept the passing of the years, enjoy the golden bowl even though it's cracked and above all, don't spend your time trying to put people right. Undemanding selfishness is an economy we need more than any other. And please don't bother to burn with indignation about me and Lucy. Lucy's tougher than you think. And don't think you've got anything over me either, with Rita, I mean. Lucy and I have no secrets.'

'Ah, that's your secret!' Peter said.

'It was a simple muddle, Peter, you know, our not coming to dinner.' Michael stood up and turned out a bright lamp, his face abruptly crepuscular. 'It's not a very exciting revelation, as revelations go, but I swear to you it was. A simple suburban muddle. Don't let it go to your head, but I'd sooner've had a meal with you and Cassandra than gone to *Amok* on my own. A classic petty *mésentente*. By all means invest it with whatever dark significance you want, but I promise you – we had every intention of coming the following week, and so our friendship might have continued and borne whatever waxy fruit such things bring forth in their season. A weekly session of mutual "Mastermind"? A month in the country with emotionally charged games of croquet on a bumpy lawn? Civilized but adulterous excursions to the bushes? Who knows? Who finally cares?'

'We shall never know whether it was a simple muddle or not. You simplify; I complicate. You're cynical; I'm sentimental. You despise; I care. You're bored; I'm interested. You're cold; I'm hot. You win; I lose. Who's right? Who's wrong?'

'Dear Peter, dear poor sweet Peter ... I love you sometimes, I really do!' Michael put his hands on the other's shoulders and bent and kissed him on the lips. Peter was hunched under the weight of the kiss for a moment, before he reared back and hit

Michael with the flat of his hand, across the beard. Michael laughed and nodded, as if he had sweetly proved his case. Rita came in and saw his red smile and Peter's straight face. 'Ah, an *English* joke, I assume?' she said.

Peter said, 'Good night, Rita, thanks for the dinner, and everything. Good night, Michael. I shan't forget this.' He walked out and listened for a cruel cackle of laughter. No sound came from the room he had quit. Now he could imagine Michael and Rita kissing, open-mouthed; he could, and it was his sweet curse, imagine anything he pleased. Equally, he could analyse Michael's kiss in a dozen ways without ever knowing its purpose.

When he returned to London (Michael went off to Vienna, to do some checking), he telephoned Lucy. There was a little tavern next to the Savoy, if that suited her. It did; they faced each other on barrel-backed chairs.

'You saw Michael,' she said.

'I saw Michael.'

'And how did you find him? Different?'

'He's always different,' Peter said. 'We had a full and frank exchange of views. We beat some Yanks at bridge (we did have all the cards). And he gave a very good paper, I must say.'

'He said he liked yours.'

'Did he really?'

'He said he did.'

'Have you thought about our project at all?'

'Quite a bit actually,' she said.

'And? Or is it "but"?'

'I'm rather coming round to it.'

'I hoped you would. I've thought a lot about you. I'm really glad I saw Michael. It's cleared a lot of things up in my mind. He and I –'

'What?'

'We're somehow too alike, I've decided. We're like two positively charged particles. We can't get really close without springing apart. If we had less in common, we'd have more. Before I saw him again, it bothered me that you were married to him. I couldn't make out –' Peter made a little gesture. 'I couldn't make out how you could stand him, frankly, and –'

'And now you can?'

'I'll be honest. I couldn't bear to think of him physically, and hence, somehow, no more could I of you. Am I making sense?'

'You're making something,' she said.

'Since Skopje, I feel somehow, well, liberated, as they say.'

'They do, don't they?' Lucy Stayman said.

'I realize that what really hurt me that night wasn't Michael so much –'

'What night?'

'Positively the last time we talk about it, but that night when you didn't come to dinner. What hurt me was the fact that my attempts to charm *you* didn't make you in the least bit willing to – well –'

'Betray Michael?'

'You could say.'

'And am I now?'

'That's for you to say, and for me to hope, of course.'

'Yes,' she said. 'This *Encyclopaedia of Childhood*, when do you want it exactly?'

For Joannie

So far she has only been a model, *the* model: her face on every fashionable plate. The world leans towards her with its most amiable smile. Beauty could be some sort of handicap, everyone is so kind. Her pettiest achievement is coddled with applause; her prettiest hesitation prompts helping hands. Yet when she hears that the great director wants her in his next film, she is less complacent than incredulous: 'But I can't act,' she says.

Her agent twirls his *kir royal* between browned fingers and looks into those expensive eyes. 'Angel,' he says, 'modelling is acting. Maybe the most demanding kind of acting there is. No script, right? You don't do anything, you just are. And that's exactly what a movie star does: she just *is*. You've been acting all your sweet life, and now here's your chance to work with the king. This is your time, angel. The bells are ringing. Are you seriously not going to answer them?'

She sips her blackcurrant champagne, and puckers her short, never snub, nose. 'It's not just any old stand-there part, Jonathan. I have *lines*. Scads of them. Did you see the script?'

'Did I see it? I weighed it.' He presses the cool Scorpio from his necklet to the centre of his forehead and drops it against his Fiorucci chest. 'Angel, you're not a girl who has to winch her way to the top. I'm aiming to ease you down right there on the summit. Everest-time, sweetheart. Don't be afraid of it: the guy's a genius.'

'Everest and a genius and all at the same time! Did you ever hear of vertigo?'

'Let's not talk about old movies. Angel, you're the most beautiful woman in the world. Would you be five hundred an hour if you weren't? He'll be lucky to have you. And remember: they came to us. Nobody's snowing anybody. I never told them you studied with

Strasberg. This is a director who could get an award-winning performance out of my aunt Sophie.'

'You mean the one that studied with Strasberg?'

'At least meet with him, angel. At least take the meeting. Your first picture and I'm going in there to talk about seven figures.'

'You won't get them,' she says.

'But I'm sure as hell going in there to talk about them. You're worth it, kid. Believe me, you're more than a pretty face.'

'So are you, Jonathan.'

'Well, I work out, don't I? Let me tell you something else: I'm talking to them about Joannie for the Countess. I wasn't going to tell you, but I am. I'm already actively into that.'

'Are you really?'

'No, not really. But I will be. I know she's on their wanted list because Howard Roth told me she was. You know Howie.'

'I know Joannie and she's a hell of an actress. With her along, it'd give me terrific reassurance.'

'You and I are sharing the same space on this one, angel. She'd be a plus in her own right for the picture and she'd be terrifically supportive for you personally.'

'Can we make it a condition of sale?'

'Sure we can,' Jonathan says, 'sure we can, unless it turns out we can't.'

The director lives at the beach. His wife thinks Beverly Hills is 'tacky'. They rarely come into town; they never go to the parties. He works at home. His house is equipped with its own cutting and projection rooms, but then so is everybody's. In addition, however, he has the very latest electronic gadgetry: he can scan a dozen different versions of a sequence within just a few minutes. He can entertain entertaining possibilites beyond the means, and the patience, of less technological men. He never hurries and he always worries. He looks for flaws even in perfection. He can be like some perverse alchemist, tireless in pursuit of a formula for turning gold into lead. All of his films are odd-balls and all of them have bounced clear the way to the top.

He says he will arrange a car to bring her out to Malibu. She dresses and dresses again, undresses and re-dresses, until she is satisfied. ('Joannie, promise me he'll really think I didn't have time to change.') When the car comes, he is driving it himself for chrissake, a guy like that! ('Joannie, are you *sure?*') It is a ranch-wagon, with defective trim and rusty gouges out of the side. When he first sees her coming, he pushes open the buckled door and leans over and greets her with his sallow face almost down on the passenger seat: 'Hey, kid, you want to be in the movies?' She gives a comic shrug, a young girl robbed of both composure and nervousness at one neat stroke. The back of the car is choked with electronic junk he introduces to her as his new chess opponent, Basil.

That night she tells Joannie what a terrific day they had. 'I was really impressed, I mean *really*. He has the whole movie in his head already, but at the same time he's flexible. Like *he* was asking *me* what I thought.'

'And what's she like?'

'She's a superb cook. We had these *blintzes* . . . Personally? Very secure. Strong. A wise woman. She's kind of small and dumpy, but *attractive*, you know. I'll tell you something you may not believe: we talked about you more than we did about me. He's truly thrilled about you playing the Countess. He's some admirer of Joannie Hanson, this guy, believe me. You're going to love him.'

'Don't wait for me,' Joannie says. 'You go right ahead.'

'Don't worry: he knows all about us. No hassle. Anyway, I told you: he has this wife.'

'One for you, one for me.'

'She doesn't only cook, by the way. She's also an astounding water-colourist. Gifted? God! You should see her things.'

'So you're going to do it, right?'

'All I have to do is stand there.'

His attentiveness does not slacken, even when the deals are finally inked. He stops by the house to take her personally to fittings and make-up sessions. When she wants Joannie along, he positively values her advice and experience. Pretty soon they are having family barbecues on the sanitized sand below the beach house with the kids from his first marriage. By the time shooting is due, the girls are in total agreement: he is something else. And what about those water-colours of hers?

When the limousine comes up the driveway past the mailbox

to their stilted little house above Benedict Canyon at six o'clock on the first day of principal photography, she is almost surprised (and a little disappointed) not to see him at the wheel. He is on a high rostrum when they walk across the Spanish set, nodding their good mornings to the chippies who can always chisel and check out chicks at the same time. He looks down when they look up, but he is plotting a stand-in's position through his view-finder. The stand-in reads a yachting magazine in a two-foot wig and Bermuda shorts. A third-assistant comes up to Joannie with just a few changes for the scene they were going through in the car. They hope to be ready for the star right after lunch. Meanwhile would she like to check out her caravan while Miss Hanson goes to make-up? She finds a gift on the counter: a perfect little pot of rhinestone caviare. 'Don't eat it all at once,' the card says, signed 'the ogre'. ('The great thing about being regarded as an ogre,' he told them one day at the beach, 'is you don't get too many callers at the house. So occasionally you have to eat a kid. So?')

Joannie is almost unrecognizable when she next sees her. She has on the wig and the crinoline and her face is a beauty-spotted mask. She seems very calm. Only the pinch and flare of the powdered nostrils indicate how she is having to control herself.

They walk through a rehearsal. The Countess has to step from the cut-out of a carriage and walk across the patio of Don Juan's house to where Robert (two million dollars and ten per cent of the gross) is giving orders to his servant, referred to by the crew as 'scare-a-mouse'. The Countess has to argue with him for a rewritten moment and then pull out a pistol and fire it at Juan's breast. The rehearsal is complicated by a proposed swallow-dive from the camera on the big crane, a bitch of a shot for a first morning, which is why the director has scheduled it. ('My pool,' he once told them, 'only has a deep end.')

They reach the noon break without having even tried for a shot. The director stays on the set. He has not spoken to the actors. They eat in their costumes, over which a bumbling wardrobe lady arranges muslin bibs. Joannie can hardly move and never speaks.

After lunch, things are at last ready for a trial take. 'Action!' Joannie climbs from the cut-out barouche and walks flawlessly across the floor. The second camera pans as planned and is right there, on cue, as Juan, with a flick of gloved fingers, dusts gun-powder and spent dialogue from his doublet, while the Countess sinks to his uncreased knees. 'And cut.'

The director comes down from the rostrum in his stained denims and goes first to the cut-out and then slowly across the patio, making knight's moves, his sneakers avoiding the lines. He looks at Robert and then at Joannie. He might be seeing her for the first time in his life. 'Is that it?' he says.

'Did I do something wrong?'

'You're the actress,' he says.

'Jonathan!' The agent and his beautiful client are standing at the corner of the set, behind one of the brutes. 'Why is he *doing* this? Why is he trying to destroy Joannie?'

'Nobody's being destroyed, angel. This is the movies. Joannie can handle it.'

They do the scene sixteen more times. They never reach the next set-up at all that day. Joannie is totally exhausted when they finally get into the homing limousine. Even without her make-up, she looks different: distant and drained. Yet she resumes the next morning with no sign of apprehension. Can she be unaware of how she was humiliated? He *is* an ogre. 'Jonathan, why is he *doing* this? Is he going to treat me this way.'

'Angel, relax.'

Relax? By the time they line up her first shot, she has forgotten all the generous weeks of preparation, the homey huddles and hamburgers over the script, the video-taped improvisations, the electronic evenings with Basil. She has a long walk and then a short line, direct to camera. Can she ever do it? 'Action.' She does it. Has she said the six words in the right order? 'Cut.' He comes down from the camera car and walks up to her and stares at her for a long, unsmiling moment. Then he leans forward and kisses her on the lips. 'Ace,' he says. 'Next set-up.'

He drops her off at Benedict Canyon himself that night. She walks on up to the shaded sun-deck where Joannie, who has not been scheduled this week, is watching her arrival. 'I bet he was just giving me an easy ball,' she says over her chilled Chablis. 'What odds that shot isn't even in the final cut? He'll probably come down like the wolf on the fold pretty soon now.'

'And don't I know which fold?' Joannie says. 'You know he wants me off the picture, don't you?'

'Come on. He said to say hullo. He said specially. *Joannie*. Come back here.'

Jonathan has to give her the news when they are down in Mexico, shooting the bull-fight. There have been big little hold-ups over insurance, because Bobby insists on doing all his veronicas himself and even a shaved horn can make a big hole in two million dollars, and the gross. 'Angel, it's really very simple. It's nobody's fault but we're six weeks behind already and I have Joannie contracted for a play she really wants to do in New York, goes into rehearsal in a month and a half. They were going to shoot her scenes finishing last week and instead . . .'

'Did he plan this, Jonathan? If he planned this . . .'

'Who plans this kind of a thing?'

'Because I told you before: Joannie goes, I go.'

'Suppose you talk to Joannie about this. Because she has a lot of respect for you, angel, and you quit now, how much of it is going to be left? Joannie is a disciplined professional. You talk to her about it.'

'He postponed shooting on her three times to my knowledge. He planned this.'

'Angel, I give you my word of honour . . .'

'I never heard of a Scorpio with one of those before,' she says. 'Or two of *them*, if it comes to that.'

'*Angel*.'

Joannie says of course she has to stay. They will be together again when the picture's in the can. It is too true that she has this play to do. She is not in the least resentful and she absolutely does not feel betrayed or let down. 'Baby, you have this week's greatest director in the world in love with you, you're giving a performance, he has people waiting in line to see the rushes, so for my sake, never mind yours, don't blow it, O.K.? We may need the bread.'

'In love with me? I'll give him in love with me.'

'You do that. For Joannie, O.K.?'

Joannie flies out, alone, with flowers. Soon there comes an invitation to have dinner with the great man in the penthouse.

His wife has a one-woman show opening in San Francisco, otherwise she would have loved to be there. He gives her a *tequila* and speaks sincerely about Joannie. 'Two into one just wouldn't go,' he says, squatting on a mirror-studded cushion by her feet and toying with the golden chain that graces her ankle. 'She was giving a very professional performance, she really was.' He raises tired, almost pleading eyes to hers and is amazed by the sudden, swallow-diving kiss, full on his salty lips. 'Oh,' he says, 'I don't remember that in the script.'

'You haven't seen the changes then, have you?'

'I loved you when I only knew you in two dimensions,' he says. 'And now ... I'm eighteen again.'

'Listen, I'll play the eighteen-year-olds around here, O.K.?' she says. 'I knew we were going places the minute I saw that ratty-looking car of yours. Just my style!'

'I had those panels beaten in specially for you, didn't I?'

'Yes? And how about Joannie? You had her beaten in too, didn't you?'

'You're wrong there.'

'All's fair, right?'

'That's unfair. I recognize Joannie's quality. I also recognize you and she ... and I can understand that. Now it's time to graduate. Baby's gotta walk! After all, you said you wanted to play eighteen.'

'Be nice to me,' she says. 'Because I'm crossing the line here, you know that, don't you? This is strictly a first for me, no kidding.'

He is nice. He is gentle and confident and, in tactfully due course, as nice as he can be. She moans and she says 'Oh' and '*Oh*' and she does things she has never done before as if she has already done them all. At last he judges the moment right for the right moment: at the climactic brink, sure that she is tumbling with him, he flings himself, with a last spurt, irrevocably over. 'I love you,' he says. 'I love you. Oh, how I love you!'

She is looking down at him and there is unmelted ice in those by-the-hour eyes. '*Well*,' she says, 'is that it?'

Oxbridge Blues

No one ever accused the Geary brothers of being alike. It was true that both had blue eyes, but then Victor was dark and Philip was fair. Victor was always said to be going places; Pip to be doing quite well considering. Their parents, sensitive to the strain on Pip's psyche, sent him to a less demanding school than his brother. He scraped into Selwyn, while Victor was a scholar at King's. If Pip had any consolation, it was that he was both bigger and stronger than his older brother. Yet it was typical that Pip should just miss his Blue (an American Olympic oarsman came into the reckoning at the last minute), whereas Victor had been President of Shooting and, without raising a sweat, was elected to the Hawks' Club, thus becoming eligible for an enviable tie. Pip smiled at the news; Victor frowned. 'These things don't matter any more,' he said. Good luck weighed more heavily on Victor than bad on his junior.

Good old Pip drank a lot of beer with the boys and was always free for a frame of snooker. Victor preferred wine, if it was worth drinking, and was usually at the library. Pip reckoned he did bloody well to get a Third in Geography, two summers after Victor had walked away with a starred First in Economics. Pip's sporting connections secured him a job with a travel agency, after a score of sorry interviews for more promising prospects. Victor had already passed top into the Treasury. He was soon walking to lunch at the Reform, often parading across the park in the company of an assistant-secretary. They swung their umbrellas in unison, bowlers tilted slightly forward, like civilized Guards' officers. Pip commuted daily to Bishopsgate from Hatfield Peverel, where he lived with his parents.

Victor was not only cleverer than his brother (and than most people), he was also better looking. Wine put on less weight than beer, but he had a fineness of feature – high cheekbones, white skin, keen brows – and an accurately hawkish air: he never had to pounce more than once. Philip had a broad nose, as if he had fought for some boxing title, and lost; his jaw had the beefiness to be seen in thick Roman copies of Greek originals. Victor's brilliance was made flesh in the intensity of his gaze and the elegance of his long, white hands. He frightened a lot of women, but usually they contrived to be frightened in his direction. It was no great surprise when he acquired Wendy de Souza, or she him. Each took the other as a kind of prize to which no one else could possibly be entitled.

Wendy was the star of her Oxford year. She acted famously for O.U.D.S. and a gushing reviewer said that she was the only girl in Oxford who managed to be naked with all her clothes on: she had one of those mouths and two of those eyes. Her poetry appeared in *Poetry* and some of it was in French. She knew words like *couillons*. An Earl (admittedly Irish) at Brasenose was reputed to have offered her acres for a single kiss. ('Where exactly?' said a jealous theatrical. 'The kiss or the acres?' said another.) Someone wanted to know if it was true that she had been born in Alexandria. 'Someone has to be,' she said, in that Fortnum's accent of hers, and quoted Cavafy, the bitch.

Her worst enemies admired her. She was expected to go straight into starring roles in the West End. (Her décolleté reading of Goneril had brought producers down from London.) Instead, after a single meeting in the rooms of a pear-shaped, matchmaking Head of House, she decided that she would marry Victor Geary. 'He is the man of my life,' she declared. 'That pale face is my fortune, and don't bother to point out the misquotation.'

What did it matter that she failed, surprisingly, to get a First? Victor had enough academic distinctions for both of them; her beauty made nonsense of mundane rankings. The wedding was reported in all the papers as the smartest of the year. It took place in the chapel of the college where they had met. All the foreseeable Cabinet Ministers, Heads of Legation, Judges, Nobel Prizemen and Regius Professors from the two great universities were among the congregation. How could some sub-editor fail to put the caption 'Oxbridge Blues' under the photograph of the smiling couple? (Actually Victor was frowning, but no one looked at him when Wendy was on his arm.)

Nothing distinct was said in the society magazines about either set of parents. Victor's father was, in fact, the Essex branch manager of an insurance company; Wendy's was a wholesaler of oriental and Middle Eastern food. Neither was anything to be ashamed about, but in any event beauty and brains provided their own pedigree.

They went to live in a narrow terrace house in Canonbury. (Doors were only just beginning to turn primrose yellow in the borough.) Mr de Souza helped with the deposit. Victor's Treasury position was impressive but his stipend was not. He supplemented it with articles for journals with very long paragraphs, either anonymously or under a pseudonym. (Though he never smiled about it, he was often in the amusing position of annotating his own cuttings, sometimes cuttingly, before passing them to the mandarins.) Wendy was soon preparing a series of broadcasts of European poetry; she read a number of the selections herself in that husky voice of hers. She and Victor continued to see their Oxbridge friends, most of whom had married each other. The first pregnancies were reported, and the first separations.

Pip was still travelling up and down from Essex, the bachelor. He seemed happy to plan world-wide itineraries for bankers and Caribbean holidays for the classier sort of share-pusher. He learned tactfully to distinguish between what a man was prepared to spend on the firm and what was available for the wife and kids. As time went on, he grew fluently cosmopolitan: he seemed to have been everywhere. 'How did you find the Carlyle, sir?' he would ask, and, 'Was I right about the *pistes* at Méribel?' Who would guess that he had never left England except to play club soccer in Knokke-le-Zoute? He got a discount for Victor and Wendy when they went to Turkey, but they both contracted enteritis in Ismir, while looking for Seferis's birthplace, and their thanks were shaded. Pip took holidays with his parents in the Lake District, which his mother remembered from her childhood. Victor and Wendy could not imagine how he could endure the life he led. All he did was to read cheap thrillers and play soccer with this team of clerks and workers from a local jam factory, watch dreadful television (he would quote the commercials) and dig his parents' garden. Presumably there were girls, but it all seemed hopelessly provincial. How could he be so happy? Victor frowned when he thought about Pip, but then he frowned when he thought about most things.

Wendy was always asking him what was wrong. 'Nothing,' he told her.

One day, soon after his twenty-ninth birthday, Pip rang Victor to announce that he was engaged to be married. 'Anyone I know?' asked his brother, who was waiting for a call from the Chief Secretary, to whom he had forwarded a rather sly minute.

'Most improbable,' said Pip. 'She's a girl called Maxine. I call her Max.'

'Wait a minute,' Victor said, 'I just want to be sure that there isn't anybody on the line. Did you hear a sort of click just now?'

'I thought it was you, mate, disapproving.'

'Don't be silly. What is there to disapprove of? Marriage is an honourable estate.'

'She's scared stiff of you,' Pip said. 'You will be nice to her, won't you?'

'I'm nice to everybody,' Victor said. 'Where did you meet?'

'At a local hop,' Pip said. 'The Rotary have an annual do in Chelmsford. I don't know if you remember the Dimmages, used to live along the Maldon Road?'

'It is rather a long time ago,' Victor said.

'Oh I know, there've been fifty budgets since then, haven't there?'

'What sort of girl is she?'

'She didn't go to university, if that's what you mean,' Pip said.

'That isn't what I meant at all. Millions of people didn't go to university.'

'Yes, but you don't know many of them, do you? She helps a vet at the moment. She's the Dimmages' niece. She's only twenty-two. I think she's rather bright. I know what you're thinking, what would I know about bright?'

'She sounds like just the girl we need,' Victor said. 'Frenchie's developed a bit of a lump in one of her tits. Do you think she'd take a look at it?'

'At the usual rates, I'm sure she'd be delighted, old son.'

'You'd better bring her to dinner. I'll have a word to Wendy and see when's the best day.'

'Preferably one when you haven't got eight professors and the man who's made the big breakthrough in astrophysics, if it's all the same to you.'

'We know very few astrophysicists,' Victor said. 'Would you rather it was just the four of us?'

'Max isn't a fool or anything, Vic —'

'*Please* don't call me Vic; I hate being confused with a cough cure.'

'Aye there's the rub!' Pip said. 'It's simply that she's never been exposed to the full Oxbridge artillery. Any day next week, except Thursday. Thursday we're going to see her parents, in Mitcham. Tell me, how are things with you at the moment? I gather they're a bit sticky.'

'You have the advantage of me,' Victor said.

'I only wish I could serve an ace, then! I meant this credit squeeze and the balance of payments. If you make the travel allowance much smaller, I shall have to go out and work for a living. I wouldn't like to have your job at this stage.'

'No, well, you're not likely to get it, are you?'

'Any day except Thursday,' said Pip.

Victor frowned and replaced the receiver. He lived in a state of agonized complacency. He had nothing to worry about, and it worried him. He was well thought of by his superiors and he was too firmly on the ladder ever to have to bother about the snakes. His wife was not only enviably beautiful, she was also loyal and good-natured. How could he complain if, having married a girl from whom he might have expected a life of testing anguish, he found himself with a grocer's daughter who was always there with a smile and a hot meal when he got home from Whitehall? He could hardly reproach her for wanting to give up an arid job at Broadcasting House in order to look after the house or for her adorable hints that she longed to have a child. Why was he secretly so appalled by the peace of mind to which he was treated? When the first of their friends broke up, or divorced, he wondered what curious immaturity rendered Wendy so banal. He had married Goneril and here was Cordelia. She had even turned down a chance to do Baudelaire in the *Critical Studies Series*. She bought women's magazines. She said she liked the pictures of babies.

Maxine would have to turn out to be pregnant, of course. Her puffy complexion showed it more than her body: motherhood had struck her a blow across the face. Her hair had been elaborately done, in metallic ringlets, as if to distract the eye from the rounding parcel in her lap, but the colour was so brazen that one looked instantly downwards. Victor and Wendy were used to discussing sex in recently liberated terms with their Oxbridge friends, but Maxine's condition, and her rural provenance, put an embargo on Canonbury frankness. Even Frenchie's lump (benign, nothing to worry about, honest) proved more an embarrassment than a source of conversation. It was left to Pip to mention the forthcoming baby, after a spoon-clicking soup course, and so deliver the evening from silence. He seemed more loudly contented than ever. He told City jokes and made Wendy laugh her candid, ringing laugh. Maxine's eyes rolled anxiously in her head, as she observed her host's thin humour. When she had wiped her lips ('Ever such good chicken'), she asked earnestly about Wendy's work; she only wished she had the qualifications for doing something brilliant.

'I only do it for the money,' Wendy said, 'don't I, darling?'

'Of course not,' Victor said, opening the reserve bottle of plonk. Pip could certainly put it away.

'This is ever such a nice house,' Maxine said.

'We got it when it was young,' Victor said. 'Where are you thinking of living yourselves?'

'There's a cottage just down the road from Mum and Dad,' Pip said. 'Where the Red Indians used to live, if you remember.'

'Red Indians?' Wendy covered her mouth. She could see from Victor's frown that she had better not laugh. 'Whatever do you mean, Pip, Red Indians?'

'People called Wigg,' Pip said. 'Hence wigwam, hence Navajo, hence Red Indian. We used to go and wah-wah-wah until they came out. Remember, Vic?'

'Not really. You're seriously going to go on commuting? You must be mad.'

'I'm not too serious about it,' Pip said. 'I've got chums on the train who bag me a beer. I do my neighbour's quick crossword over one shoulder and I cop a quick read of the juicier bits of *Woman's Own* over the other, not to mention a spot of crafty legmanship with the pick of the typing pool across the aisle. The time passes.'

'What about your writing, Pip? You haven't mentioned that.'

'Not in this house,' Pip said.

'*Writing?*'

'It's not what *you'd* call writing,' Pip said, 'but yes. Only to amuse myself, you know. I used to read a lot of these trashy thrillers, but now they've got tables in the trains, some of them, so I thought I'd try my hand.'

'I'd like to see one of them,' Wendy said.

'Oh come on, Wendy, wait till I start writing them in French, then perhaps ...'

'Have you shown them to a publisher or anyone?'

'Of course not. It's just to pass the time.'

'What're they about?' Wendy said.

'Sort of down-market James Bond,' Pip said. 'Nothing you could possibly be interested in.'

'I've never understood James Bond,' Victor said.

'He does use some long words, doesn't he?' Maxine said.

The wedding took place in Hatfield Peverel. The company was not glittering. The soccer club was there, and relatives whom Victor had forgotten. A couple of beery chums of Pip's from the Goldie boat of 1958 were the only university representatives. Victor apologized to Wendy for dragging her to so dismal an affair – 'Oh, I enjoyed it,' she said. 'Didn't you think Pip made a good speech?'

'Just the sort of thing to turn the wheels of the Rotary Club,' Victor said.

'Did you know that Maxine did A-level French and History? She got B's in both. And an A in Art.'

'Very impressive,' Victor said.

'I do envy her the baby,' Wendy said.

'We can't afford it,' Victor said. 'We really can't.'

'Why can they?'

'It was an accident,' he said.

'I wish I could have one of those,' she said.

There was a mini-budget that November and a maxi-budget in the spring followed by another mini-mini-budget in the summer, when the pound came under renewed pressure, and Victor with it. He tired but he never flagged. The birth of Sandra Jane was quickly followed by Maxine's next pregnancy: Dominic. The name struck Victor as pretentious, though he sent floral congratulations which proved more expensive than he had expected. Damned inflation! Wendy's desire for a child seemed more and more bloody-minded. Victor asked whether she would like him to resign from the Treasury and take a job in commerce. 'Can you get one?' she said. It was Maxine who telephoned with the news of the last straw. 'You'll never guess what, Victor. I had to tell you. Pip's had his book accepted.'

'*Book?*'

'One of his thrillers. It's been accepted. It's going to be published.'

'A common consequence of acceptance,' Victor said.

'Sorry?'

'There's no need to apologize. Who's doing it?'

'It's going straight into paperback,' Maxine said. 'They're rushing it out apparently.'

'That's very nice news. What's it called?'

'I don't think you'll like the title very much. It's called *A Bit of Spare.*'

'Sounds just my sort of thing,' Victor said.

'Pip wanted to call it *Randy Rides Again.*'

'Presumably that was rather too up-market,' Victor said.

'He's invented this character called Randy O'Toole. Do you think he ought to change it?'

'He isn't publishing this thing under his own name, is he?' Victor said.

'Why not? It's not as if he's got a reputation to lose or anything, is it?' she said.

'I wasn't thinking of him,' Victor said. 'When is this volume due to appear?'

'Any day. They want to get the second one on the stalls by Christmas.'

'The second one? How many are there?'

'Oh hundreds,' Maxine said. 'Pip reckons he's got at least fifteen ready to be typed and he says he can do them at the rate of about one every ten days. I expect he'll have to use a few whatdoyoucall-'ems, don't you, so's not to saturate the market?'

'Pseudonyms,' Victor said. 'I must say one hopes so.'

'I just thought you'd like to know. Give my love to Wendy, won't you? I listened to her on Friday, talking about that Greek poet. It was ever so interesting, tell her.'

'I'm sure she'll be delighted,' Victor said.

A Bit of Spare was not reviewed in *The Times Literary Supplement.* It was not reviewed anywhere. It did not need to be. The first printing was 30,000 and it was soon supplemented. Victor bought a copy at St James's Park station, thrusting it hotly into his briefcase as he saw one of his principals approaching. He read it on a bench in the park during his lunch interval. It was quite as horrifying as he feared. Randy O'Toole made James Bond seem like a character in Henry James. The globe-trotting narrative was littered with spreadeagled corpses and flimsy French underwear. Breasts thrust, nipples stiffened and thighs flashed. Hoarse cries burst forth and moans of rapture escaped. Hardware crackled and knuckle sandwiches wiped the grins off swarthy faces. Gore spurted and limbs snapped like tinder. Randy was a lean package of irresistible virility. Legs parted before him like the Red Sea. At the climax of the book, he managed to get the villain smack between the eyes with a .38 just as he was provoking a screech of rapture from a previously frigid albino Venus, firing simultaneously from both barrels. Victor Geary closed the book with disgust and an intolerable awareness in his, what was the phrase? – mounting manhood – that his brother was not only a cheap disgrace, but the stuff of which best sellers were made.

Randy on the Job followed soon afterwards. Pip's travel agency, of which he was now a partner, promoted a tie-up with the publishers. Tours were arranged to 'Randy Rendezvous'. Victor was so humiliated that he considered applying for a transfer to the Foreign Office, with a view to some distant posting. The randy jests of his colleagues failed to entertain him. He walked past the Smith's at St James's Park – 'The New Philip Geary Is Here!' – with averted eyes. He tried to believe that the nightmare would pass. It persisted. Pip's imagination was evidently as boundless as it was crude. A female agent called 'Darling' made her unsubtle appearance. When Pip revealed that he had bought a Rolls-Royce Silver Cloud, Victor minuted that the tax levels on the upper income brackets ought perhaps to be looked at again. Wendy wanted to know when she could go for a ride in the new car.

'You can't be serious,' Victor said.

'Not all the time, no,' Wendy said. 'Hence ...'

'I don't in the least grudge Pip the money,' Victor said, 'but I do think he might have contrived a way to get rich without quite such a consummate display of totally farmyard mentality. One would never think he'd been to Cambridge.'

'It doesn't do anybody any harm,' Wendy said, 'when you come to think about it.'

'When you come to think about it,' Victor said, 'you'll realize the utter *scandal* of an intelligent person uttering that sort of shallow nonsense. I don't say that Pip's books ought to be banned, but no one, surely, could argue that they shouldn't be burned. That kind of muck acts on the body politic like – oh like a spoonful of sugar in a diabetic's coffee. God almighty, Wendy, why go to university if you can't show some sense of discrimination. He's welcome to the money, but *really* –'

'They want us to go with them to the Aegean in June,' Wendy said. 'Maxine called. They're hiring a yacht and they want us to go with them.'

'I can't afford that sort of thing,' Victor said.

'Pip's treat. They insist.'

'I can't afford the time,' Victor said. 'It looks as if there may be a policy U-turn with a view to a spring election and I shall have to be in London. Don't tell anyone, of course.'

'Everyone's guessed already,' Wendy said. 'A holiday wouldn't hurt us, for once.'

'If you really want to swan around the Aegean in a yacht on the proceeds of Pip's disgusting rubbish, we'd better do it, I suppose.'

'That's settled then,' Wendy said.

'Presumably Dominic and Sandra and the new one, what's it called –'

'Justin.'

'Presumably you're prepared to endure their endless row, for the pleasure of water-skiing in front of coachloads of gawking Germans.'

'Any day,' Wendy said.

The yacht was bigger than even Victor had expected. The children had their own quarters and their new Norland nanny. Also on board was a film producer called 'Curly' Bonaventura, who had bought the six-figure rights to *Randy Rides Again* (of course the title was too good not to be used in the end) and he had options on the rest of the series. He was also 'actively planning' a film of *Darling Does It*, if he could find the right girl. Bonaventura seemed the very type of the bone-headed Hollywood producer and his wife was a bottle-fed blonde. He called Pip a genius and said that he would do anything for him. Victor had to qualify his contempt when he discovered that 'Curly' had won the top prize for Latin verse composition in Italy in 1938 and was a certified marine engineer. As for Carlotta, she had studied the cello under Casals and played so beautifully one evening when they were anchored off Santorini that it brought tears to the eyes, dammit.

The weather was perfect; the *meltemmi* held off, the sea was calm. There was just enough breeze for them to be able to sail without the engine. The cook was excellent, the captain accommodating. They put in at the small islands like Folegandros and Anafi. Pip was enraptured. He went looking at houses. What could be more delightful than to own a little beach and a shack nearby? They were giving them away, if you had the money. Victor frowned at a Greek newspaper. Only the long words made sense to him and Wendy was too busy having a good time to help him with the short ones. 'Curly' was always available to take her water-skiing. She was over thirty, but no one would have thought so. Maxine was quite the matron by comparison. She came and leaned on the railing next to where Victor was looking pessimistic about trends, a paper clip in his mouth. 'You ought to try it,' she said, 'water-skiing. You've got the figure. Pippy's much too thick around the middle, but you've kept your figure brilliantly.'

'All that sitting around I do,' he said.

'You do make me laugh,' she said. 'What about this sun?'

'Yes indeed,' Victor said, as the breeze rattled the flimsies.

'You're quite right,' she said, 'it's all a bit of an outrage really, living like the idle rich, lazing about like this, all these meals and things prepared for us.'

'It is the business of the wealthy man/To give employment to the artisan,' Victor said.

'Who is that?' Maxine said. 'It's not Chesterton, is it?'

'Belloc,' Victor said. 'You were close.'

'I wish I'd been educated properly,' Maxine said. 'The thing I really envy about you, Vic, is, you've got inner resources. I wish I had inner resources.'

'I don't imagine you're ever likely to need them, are you, Max, now?'

'Don't be too sure,' she said. 'Haven't you ever read Greek tragedy?'

'In my day,' he said, 'I was known to. Why?'

'Because people do have falls, don't they? I've been catching up in a Penguin. You can have too much and then suddenly you don't have anything at all. It can happen, can't it?'

'Not if you have Curly's accountant. Though of course it may entail living in the Bahamas or somewhere penitential like that. I trust Pip doesn't have to be on the train from Hatfield Peverel every day in order to maintain his inspiration, because that could become a bit prohibitive at current rates.'

'He's got these two electric typewriters,' Maxine said. 'One for Randy and one for Darling. We may have to go to Hollywood soon actually, because Curly wants him out there for the casting and stuff. Pip wants to take a house on the beach.'

'That sounds rather exciting,' Victor said.

'If that's the sort of thing that excites you,' Maxine said.

'I was thinking of you. You're looking very California at the moment, I must say.'

'Mothers of three shouldn't wear bikinis, in other words!' Maxine said. 'Wendy's really beautiful, isn't she? Curly can't take his eyes off her. I must say I fancy a swim, don't you, before the next dose of vine leaves and things? Coming?'

She waited while Victor locked his papers in the cabin. Randy O'Toole had made him security-conscious. They passed Curly and Wendy on the gangway. Wendy's body was almost black with the sun; her teeth gleamed at a joke that Bonaventura was telling, in Italian. Victor's holiday had interrupted a crash course in the language (*anticipando* the Common Market), but he failed to appreciate the punch line which the producer signalled by putting an arm round Wendy's shoulders and squeezing her to him. 'Ciao, Victor.'

They swam to a small beach, from which they could just see the others having drinks on the after-deck of the yacht, under the laced awning. 'I say,' Maxine said, 'I'm going to take my things off, do you mind?'

'I don't mind a bit,' Victor said. 'After all, nakedness began in Greece.'

'I'd never have done it once,' she said, 'but I think it's the money. I don't care what I do any more. It's ever so much nicer, I find. Why don't you do the same?'

'I might well,' he said, 'but you go on.'

'You didn't think much of me, Vic, did you, when you first saw me?'

'I reserved my position,' he said.

'You are a scream sometimes, honestly,' she said. 'Reserved my position! That's one way of describing it, I suppose.'

'Describing what?'

'You keep such a straight face,' she said, 'I can't help laughing.'

'I wish I knew something about music,' Victor said, kicking off his trunks.

'That's better,' she said, 'isn't it? Just as long as Nanny doesn't see us.'

'Do you think she'd send us to bed without any supper?' Victor said.

'I imagine that would be the last place,' Maxine said. 'Why don't you take a course? In music. It's never too late.'

'I don't think I could endure to be a beginner,' he said.

'You only live once,' Maxine said.

'It is a comfort, isn't it?' Victor said.

They could hear Maxine's laugh even on the boat, where Wendy was sipping a daiquiri, legs stretched to the last of the red-faced sun as she listened to Curly's account of a snowball party he had given in Beverly Hills with the temperature in the high seventies. Carlotta watched as Curly showed Wendy how he had inserted a snowball in the front of a stuffy starlet's dress. Pip saw what people meant about that mouth and those eyes.

Maxine and Victor swam slowly back to the boat. The murmur of their voices promised that they had found something serious to talk about. When they had hauled themselves aboard, they stood dripping, at the far end of the deck, and finished their long sentences. That same evening, Maxine declared that, if Pip didn't mind, she wanted to go to Oxford, not California. They could afford it, couldn't they? 'We can afford anything,' Pip said, as Carlotta tuned her cello.

'Your idea presumably,' Wendy said later in the stateroom.

'She envies you,' Victor said.

'I hope you disillusioned her,' Wendy said.

'Of course,' Victor said. 'I disillusion everybody, don't I?'

'Oh Victor,' she said. 'I feel as if I've done you a mischief.'

'Why,' he said, 'what are you planning?'

'Planning?' she said. 'You've got the wrong idea about me. You think I'm a person of serious purposes and educated taste. I'm really much more flippant than you like to think; I'm basically a creature of impulse.'

'Are you really?' he said. 'And whither are you basically impelled at the moment?'

'Curly wants me to come to Hollywood,' she said.

'In what position? I think I can imagine the costume.'

'He thinks I could be in the films,' she said. 'Not that I believe him.'

'Maxine believes him,' Victor said. 'She reckons you're quite the potential star.'

'He needs a personal assistant really,' Wendy said. 'A girl Friday.'

'You'd have the rest of the week to yourself, I presume.'

'Should you mind terribly? The climate sounds so attractive.'

'Midsummer snowballs, I'm told. What do you mean, should I mind? I'm not going, am I?'

'If you forbid me,' she said, 'I won't either, will I?'

'I don't believe in forbidding people,' Victor said. 'If you haven't got the discrimination to decide these things for yourself, I can scarcely imagine that it would do any good forbidding you. Is he going to pay you for your services or are you giving yourself away?'

'Somewhere or other, Victor, there's a whiff of squalor about you, isn't there?'

'I thought I was behaving with remarkable nobility in the circumstances.'

'I realize that you want me to hurt you,' she said. 'I'm not sure why. But the only way you can express it is by suggesting that I'm not capable of anything except a sort of cheap opportunism.'

'Perhaps that's why you married me,' he said.

'I married you, believe it or not, because I thought you were the most beautiful thing I'd ever seen. I think you find even that rather reprehensible, don't you?'

'You thought I was going to be a success,' he said.

'And aren't you?'

'The world no longer believes that success consists in being underpaid for most of one's life and having a K. and a pension to show for it at the end. The world may well be right, but there isn't much I can do about it now, since I don't possess the means of attracting the attention of Mr Bonaventura. No one buys the film rights of articles in *The Economist* exactly, do they?'

'He thinks you're brilliant, but you do rather intimidate him.'

'He's probably just as clever as I am and he's certainly richer and presumably more attractive.'

'No,' Wendy said, 'just more alive.'

'He's a joke,' Victor said.

'Perhaps I was in need of one. And all I'm taking is a job.'

'And a screen test, I hope. Maxine thinks *I'm* rather droll, as it happens.'

'Maxine! Does she really?'

'Look here, you know what his sort of job implies, don't you, when it comes to bed-time? Just because he's the image of your father, doesn't mean that all he's after is a hand with the groceries, you know.'

'Is that what discrimination means,' Wendy said. 'Sir Victor?'

Maxine went up to Oxford in the following October. The children and their Nanny went with Pip to California. Wendy and the Bonaventuras had gone earlier. They had to find a house for Pip, with the pool and the tennis court. Victor told his friends that his wife was researching for a comparative study of Fitzgerald and Faulkner. If he was lonely, he did not show it. If he was melancholy, he neither moaned nor drank. He went home every evening, with a briefcase full of papers. His work, rather than showing signs of domestic stress, was even more thoroughly argued than before.

When, after her first year's studies, Maxine received a First in Mods, she gave Victor a call. 'You're the only one it means anything to.' She came up to town and they went to the theatre. The play was kindergarten kitsch and they left at the interval. Maxine was slimmer and seemed younger. The maternal puffiness of her face had been refined by careful food (she could afford it) and by the studious régime she had imposed on herself. Her chance had come late and she was determined not to fluff it. Thanks to Pip's generosity, she had lived very comfortably and very quietly. The 'boys' were too young for her. She had a large allowance and she was dressed in an Israeli leather suit and Ferragamo shoes. Her hair had been done by a man in South Molton Street. But what particularly enchanted Victor was her inexhaustible appetite for unparagraphed talk. They went to a restaurant club (Pip's account) and leaned together, discussing Ezra Pound, the Pisan phase, until they were the last people among the candles. She had taken a room at the Dorchester, where she proposed that they continue their analysis of the relationship between intellectual style and social content, unless he had better things to do. What could be better? He was seduced less by the smart clothes and the markedly smarter accent than by her ravenous interest in his opinions, but the smart clothes were not displeasing and the accent was happier for the Oxford varnish. What was more, she was really rather clever: she listened, brilliantly.

It must have been three or four in the morning before anything personal was said, and then it was said quite impersonally: 'I married the wrong woman, you know. I thought that Wendy and I would have conversations like this all our lives, but she never wanted to. All she ever wanted to talk about in the bedroom was bed.'

'I should never have said anything if you hadn't,' Maxine said, 'but of course I *knew* the minute I met her, that night at your house when I was supposed to play the kennel maid. She's lovely, but she's not for you.'

'I had no idea that you had a mind at all at that point,' Victor said. 'I suppose I was a terrible prig, and I still am, I daresay, except that you're not the same person as you were then, are you?'

'Now I'm a prig too,' she said. 'Thanks to Pip. We shouldn't ever forget that.'

'The difficulty,' he said, 'is indeed to know how we ever shall. In spite of everything, I don't relish putting him down yet again, but I suppose we shall have to tell him.'

'Well, in view of what he and Wendy are up to,' Maxine said, 'I don't really see why we should hang back, do you?'

'I'm sorry?'

'Oh Victor,' she said, 'surely you realized?'

'I had the impression that it was the diminutive wop who'd taken Wendy's passing fancy. You're not telling me it was Pip all the time?'

'Oh Victor, I feel terrible. I thought you knew. I should have known better. Do you mind terribly?'

'Whatever can she see in him?'

'That's not very nice. You are talking about my husband.'

'I'm not under contract to say nice things. You know very well you couldn't ever abide to live with him again. He wouldn't understand a word you were saying. And think of those manuscripts of his, all those bums and titties, you'd never be able to stomach it.'

'Oh Victor,' she said, 'Pip was very decent to me, you know, when I was just a little nobody. And he's always looked up to you. He's always wanted to be something you could be proud of.'

'Look here,' Victor said, 'I've greatly enjoyed our searching analysis of the modern sensibility, but it's no use pretending that there wasn't a sub-text, any more than you took your clothes off in Greece just because the great god Pan happened not to be dead after all, if you had the money. There's obviously been a long-standing case of crossed wires in the Geary family and it's high time it was put right.'

'This is a moment I honestly never dared to hope would come.'

'You should have indicated sooner,' Victor said. 'I suppose the truth is I never really *trusted* Wendy from the moment she turned out not really to be first class. She was beautiful and she was agreeable, but she never began to be the same sort of stuff you are, and I am. When you come to think about it, Pip and she were made for each other.'

'Just like you and I,' Maxine said, pulling the cover off the bed. 'And just think how convenient it is, we shall none of us have to so much as change our names, shall we?'

'Of course,' he said, undoing his belt, 'this is all strictly conditional on you getting a First in your Schools.'

Forgetting It

They returned to the island while the spring flowers were still moist. (Summer would see them dry.) The cottage was a ruin; the weeds on the breached roof a calendar of neglect. A long-lashed donkey looked out from where the door had been, eyes spectacular with flies. 'No one lives here any more,' she said.

'Oh,' he said, 'it could probably be cleaned out in no time.'

'No,' she decided.

They walked back along the rocky path towards the harbour. The unmortared walls prevented them going side by side. Two men were painting the stained concrete of the shuttered hotel with round brushes fixed to broom-handles. The painters had made paper caps of yesterday's headlines.

They sat at the café under the arcade on the quayside. A sign on the cracked window said: 'We catch, we cook, we serve.' They looked out at the white church (named for peace) with its twin racks of silent bells, glistening on a shelf above the shuffling water. One could sense coming heat; it was held off by a last screen of spring mist. He moved his chair, as if preliminary to broaching a subject which lay, like that heat, just the far side of declaration. Did he hope that she would start? He strained for a cue, eyes loaded with pleading reproach. 'You're just as beautiful as ever,' he said. Was this the unpopular subject?

He sighed and raised his cup. The boiling coffee bit his tongue. He swallowed pain like a pill. 'Drink some water,' she said.

He inspected her hand, quite as if it had been left there on the table and he wanted to see whose it was. While he looked at it, she was looking at him. 'You think we shouldn't have come,' he said. 'You think we've done the wrong thing.'

'Do I?' she said. 'I don't think I do.'

The calf of one leg was fattened by the knee it rested on. Its whiteness dismayed him; he might have brought an invalid with

236

him. He wanted her strong, so that he need no longer be, so that he might cry out, might be more like her. But first she had to be like herself and this she refused. She resembled that sullen heat couched behind the spring mist, ardent with denial.

'We can always catch the next steamer,' he said, 'if this was a bad idea. There are other islands, lots of them. Shall we go or shall we stay?'

'I don't mind,' she said.

He said her name several times.

There was no steamer for another four days; they might as well see if there was a house they liked. Summer residents left their keys with a Roumanian caretaker in the village; there was quite a choice. Things had changed since the year they rented the cottage from a peasant who had never seen a typewriter. (Niko was rich now, from the summer tourists, and spent winters in the capital; his daughter was learning to be a stenographer.) They chose a modern place, a whitewashed tower with a flagged terrace from which the owner, in a blazer, could judge the seamanship of summer yachtsmen as they made anchor below the church.

He smiled, as they agreed the inventory, to see the luxuries they had come to do without. But how could one complain at the wide Dunlopillo mattress? It was better than Niko's straw. (Once, going into the cottage's tree-beamed bedroom, she had yelped at a pyjama-striped stranger humped in their narrow bed. He called her crow for a while, because she had been scared, his fair wife.) 'There we are then,' he said, as the gas popped and glimmered blue, 'everything seems to work.'

Each day he took, as he had taken, a fresh lease of patience. He was on a kind of emotional diet; he lived slim. Rage whispered in him, wary infidel in a cathedral. He could not blame her, and blamed her for it. And she? Dutiful regularity was promptly installed: meals appeared, tasty as ever, but his compliments did not warm her. She ate a standard portion, playing the patient taster for his sake. (The seconds were all for him.) Her consideration denied him mourning.

They slept apart on the comfortable mattress, under the gathered mosquito net they had no need to use.

On the third day, the sun lanced the caul of mist. Shadows sprang on the hillsides, detail stippling the rocks. The village houses stood forward, black-eyed. They walked up, past bolted cafés stencilled with vacant summer invitations and smiled at the flat-footed peasants, if not at each other. The donkeys' hooves scuttered on the shallow steps and the peasants grabbed their tails.

The beach beyond the village was a hooped moon of sand, eaten into eclipse by the working sea. Knobs of pumice bobbed grey against the winter jetsam. They sat in the new sun and he spread oil on to her whiteness. She would wear her swimsuit, despite the solitude. Did she not know that the beach was notorious, in the season, for its nudity? And now who could see them? 'I'm all right,' she said.

He could not be naked with her covered. He sat in his jeans, head forward over dry sand he heaped and heaped between his knees. He got up at last and walked down to the sea, showing a passing interest in shells. The water scalded his foot, it was so cold. He undid his belt and finally stood naked at the hem of the water and looked back at her. She had turned on her face, hands latched under her forehead, white soles exposed. He punched his shins into the water, left, right, left, and thrust himself down into the icy punishment.

When he came back, she turned on one elbow and rumpled her forehead, freckled with sand. He bent and kissed dry lips. 'How was it?' she said.

'Cold. But very beautiful.'

She stretched her neck.

'Or did you mean the water?' he said. He crouched to put his mouth to her shoulder and pressed it there, like a brand. 'There are lots of fishes,' he said, at last. 'You'd think you could catch them with your hand, as many as you wanted, but of course you can't. Are we ever going to be able to talk?'

She was busy doing little things, flicking sand from her body, seeing what the time was. 'Of course,' she said, 'whenever you want to. What shall we talk about?'

'It wasn't either of our faults,' he said, 'was it? Was it my fault?'

'Of course not.'

'Well, I certainly don't think it was yours.'

'That's probably enough for one day,' she said. 'Sun, I mean.'

He stood up, dizzy, robbed of blood. The mountain in front of him was capped by a nipple of white, where an old monastery caught the sun. A green valley ran back from the beach and a peasant nudged his donkey between flower-pink bushes, coming at once towards them and away, threading a secret eye through the line of the already dry river. He had a little boy up behind him, whose brown legs drummed the animal's flank, feet flashing. The child waved and shouted something, greeting or abuse.

'It's not too late,' he said. 'Why is it too late?'

He touched her that night across the cool bed. She rolled towards him, but made no warmer move. She dared him, his wife, and he could not bring himself to her. Her meekness maimed him. He sat forward, bowed between his legs, and shook his head. When at last he looked over at her, she was asleep, legs apart, head averse. He got out of the bed and went on to the terrace. There was a light under the arcade; the café owner's wife was working at a fish with a knife. The ship's hooter fetched him round and he saw the cut of its bows in the oily water. Were there not other islands and other women?

They brought the American up to the house the next morning, the caretaker and a toothless, mocking man in a flat cap, carrying a whittled stick like an unhorsed jockey, a flannel vest buttoned to his creased throat. The stranger was not too tall and pale and shy. The three foreigners were being put together, all of them seemed to realize, as a kind of jest: they were of a class. When at last the caretaker and the mocking man went away, the three of them had to start again, as if they had not yet spoken at all.

'I'm real sorry busting in on you. They insisted —'

'It's always the same, don't worry about it. They can't believe one doesn't want company. And they tend to think that everyone who isn't one of them is, well, one of us, you might say.'

'Sure seems that way. Listen, I don't want to take up any more of your time. Thing is, I was here before and I wanted to see what it was like when nobody was around.'

'Nobody ever is.'

'Right,' the stranger said. 'My name's Russell, by the way, Russell Miller, if that's of any importance. To me it's like a tag. Are you a writer?'

'Our name's Moxon,' Charles said. 'I'm Charles and this is Kat. Katharine. No, I'm not a writer, I'm an actor. Why? So is Kat.'

'An actress,' Kat said. 'Or was.'

'Kat,' Russell said. 'That's nice. I figured being here on your own like this ... I'm a writer. At least I'm a poet. I guess it isn't quite the same thing.'

'Do you want some coffee?' Kat said.

'I came here to be alone, you know,' Russell said. 'I certainly don't want to intrude on you people.'

'You're welcome,' Charles said. 'Miller eh? No relation of Henry, I suppose?'

'Well, I've heard of him, of course, but we're not related. There are a hell of a lot of Millers in the world.'

'And Henrys,' Kat said, from inside.

'I was thinking of that time he met an old enemy of his on some railway platform in Poland, I don't know if you ever read that bit, and they fell into each other's arms, they were so happy to see someone they knew and spoke their language. What was an old enmity at a time like that?'

'Only we're not enemies,' Russell said. 'Do you work in the movies at all? I might have seen your face.'

'I work mainly on the stage, and in television, London mostly.' He might have been auditioning, Charles, his voice catching American rhythms. 'Were you ever in London yet?'

'My wife died last Christmas,' Russell Miller said. 'We were planning to go.'

He wore cut-off jeans and a yellow T-shirt. His arms and legs were covered with blonde hairs. He carried a nylon backpack. There was a curious polish on his high cheekbones, like rubbed marble. He had offered them smiles when he was introducing himself, but now as he drank Kat's coffee, his face fell into deeper lines. She stood over him with milk in a punctured can. Charles said: 'I'll have a little more of that, darling, if I may.'

'You're a poet,' Kat said. 'What sort of poetry?'

'I have some with me as a matter of fact.'

'You make a living by writing poetry?'

'I'm a motor mechanic,' Russell said. 'I work in a bodyshop.'

'A motor mechanic, are you really?' Charles said.

'No, really, I'm a poet. I pretend to be a motor mechanic.'

Kat said, 'Do you want to have lunch with us?'

'Do you think poems should be read or spoken?' Charles said.

'If they're spoken right, they should be spoken, I guess. But

I'm not too good at reading my own work. I guess I lack the confidence. And ...'

'What?' Kat said.

'My wife died last Christmas,' Russell Miller said. 'And I write a lot about her.'

'That's terrible,' Charles said.

'Yes,' Russell said. 'She was very beautiful.' He showed them pictures of a rather plain girl. 'So I don't find it very easy right now.'

'Beautiful,' Charles said. 'You have children?'

'No,' the boy said. 'We never did. That's somebody else's there in the picture. My sister's.'

'Are you staying long?' Charles said.

'What – ?' Kat had begun to speak at the same time..

'I'm sorry,' Charles said. 'Darling ...'

'I just wondered what your wife's name was.'

'Miriam,' the poet said. 'Her name was Miriam. I guess I'll stay a month maybe. I want to see if I can work. We came here, you see. Last summer. We had a great time. Were you ever here in the summer? It's great. Great music, great people; we met some amazing people. Now ... I want to see if I can get something together for Miriam, if you know what I mean. You see, I stayed here and she went to Athens, to see the doctor. And that's when ... I hope I won't be in your space or anything.'

'Don't worry about us,' Charles said. 'We don't have any exclusive rights.'

'Leave us some of your poems,' Kat said. 'If you feel like it.'

'Be happy to, ma'am,' Russell Miller said. 'I guess I'll go sleep down on the beach. I left my bedroll over at Flora's place. I don't imagine anyone will object, will they?'

'I can't imagine it,' Charles said.

'Only Miriam and I slept on the beach before and the police came down and there was kind of a heavy scene out there for a while. I heard they killed a guy here last summer, an Australian, got drunk, they beat his head in. Well, see you later. Thanks for the coffee, ma'am.'

Charles read the poems and passed them to his wife. She read others and passed them to him. 'He's not much of a poet,' Kat said, 'is he?' He laughed when she said that and shook his head.

'These are terrible, aren't they?' Kat said. 'They're embarrassing.'

'He'd better be one hell of a mechanic,' Charles said.

She went abruptly into the house (as if he had disagreed with her) and he could see her combing her hair. She had caught the sun; her legs gleamed under the denim skirt. It hung unevenly as she worked her raised arm. She had a body again.

'Let's have another one, Kat,' he said. 'Please.'

She took the poems with her when she went to the shops the next morning. He offered to go with her but he was sketching, wasn't he? He had brought a block with him, but this was the first time that he had opened it. He had a scalpel and some charcoal pencils and he sat on the wall of the terrace sharpening them. They broke easily; one had to be subtle. He watched her walk along the quay and over the little bridge towards the harbour beach. Russell was standing in the water up to his knees, combing his long fair hair. Charles felt the flesh quicken in his jeans as his wife went towards the boy. He put the scalpel and the charcoal pencil on the wall of the terrace and shaped his face with his hands.

She stood at the water's edge. The boy turned towards her but did not come out of the yellow water. They talked like that. The two painters, in their newsprint caps, were at the near end of the beach, on tiptoe with their broom-handles under the eaves of the whitening hotel. A boy rode past them on a donkey, jabbing a cruel little stick into its rump.

'Oh Charles,' she said later, 'it's so awful. I wish I wasn't me.'

'And I wish you were,' he said. 'Why didn't he come to supper?'

'He went up to the village,' she said.

'You had a long talk,' he said, 'didn't you?'

'He's very young,' she said.

'Come to bed,' Charles said. 'Blast you.'

They had been together too long for him not to know when she was resisting him, even when she was not. If they had not been married, whatever that meant, he might have won her. But since she was his, he could not take her. Some silly donkey called out its longing in the night.

'What did he have to say for himself? You haven't really said.'

'She was killed in an accident,' Kat said. 'She was twenty years old. She was pregnant, five months.'

'So that's why they were coming to London,' Charles said. 'Did you tell him?'

'He didn't ask,' she said. 'He gave me some more of his poems. He's very prolific.'

'If you hate me,' Charles said, 'hate me. But hate me in the open. Where we can make something of it. Hate me to some purpose, do you think you could? Hate me or leave me, or both. You're killing me with this; you're making me into what you always said I was, and I wasn't, something without any qualities of my own, something that can only – what? – reflect, isn't that what you said?'

She took her basket the next morning and went shopping, hair in a kerchief; the wind was coming. When she got back, she made lunch of tuna fish and pasta. He watched her fret the black pepper between her fingers before she brought the dish to the table.

'You've come to life,' he said. 'Did you see our friend?'

'Have I? Yes, I did, as a matter of fact.'

'Has he written you another poem?'

'He didn't see me,' she said. 'He was taking the sun.' She tilted her own head at an angle to the heat and closed her eyes, the actress again. When she opened them, she was smiling, and so was he, but not at the same thing; that was why they were smiling. 'Sitting against the hotel.'

'I'll bet he did see you,' Charles said.

They walked up to the post office after the shadows had begun to lengthen. There might be a telegram; one never knew when there would be work. There was nothing for them. ('There wouldn't be anything for me,' Kat said.) Some impulse, after her remark, made him say, 'Anything for Miller?'

The old postman looked over the tops of his spectacles, the foreign bundle still in his hand. There were letters which had never been collected and sounded as brittle as old blue leaves. He sorted through them and swivelled an envelope towards them: Russell Miller.

'We'd better tell him,' Charles said.

'I know him,' Kat said. 'I'll take it down to him.'

She turned the letter over. There was a panel for the sender's address. It came from Miriam Rapke, in Athens. It was dated the previous August.

'I don't think we should wish that on him,' Charles said.

'You give him?' the postman said.

'I give him,' Kat said.

'Kat,' Charles said, when they were outside, 'you can't give him that letter. You have no business –'

'I never said I was going to give it to him,' she said. 'And no, I have no business.'

'You said it a minute ago.'

'Oh to him,' she said.

'I think you should take it back in there,' he said. 'I really do.'

'Oh do you really?' she said.

'You can't give it to him, you can't not give it to him. You're forked, Kat.'

'We're all forked,' she said.

'This is immoral, Kat, it really is.'

'*Immoral?*' she said. 'You ass. You royal ass, you really are.'

'And cruel. What're you going to do with that letter, Kat? I think you should give it to me.'

'Is it addressed to you? What does it have to do with you?'

'You're asking me to be an accomplice,' he said. 'You're involving us both in – in something . . .'

'Immoral?' She arched her back, hair tawny in the reddening light. 'Cruel? Well?'

'Kat, give me that letter, will you please?'

'Go in and tell him you disassociate yourself from all responsibility, why don't you? Have me arrested! They can beat me up. One old letter, what does he care?'

'I want to know what you propose to do with the damned thing.'

'I know you do,' she said.

The letter lay on the table while they had their supper. He pushed his plate away. 'You'd better go take it to him,' he said. 'You've started this, you'd better go through with it.'

'You've caught the sun,' she said. 'Your face is all red. Have you got a temperature? You look red-hot.'

She seemed to him to be almost plump, her darkening skin packed with flesh, not fat, but alive and powerful.

'Give me the letter,' he said, 'and I'll go and give it to him.'

'Don't be ridiculous,' she said.

'Ridiculous?' he said. '*Ridiculous?*'

'Of course,' she said. 'Why would he want you to give it to him?'

'It's his letter, goddammit,' he said. 'It's his and I'd be giving it to him.'

'Goddammit!' she said. 'Must you do imitations?'

'Kat, I want that letter. Do I have to take it from you?'

'Yes,' she said.

'I'm not afraid of you,' he said.

'I don't care what you are,' she said, the letter against her breast.

'Giving him that letter would be an act of cruelty I wouldn't normally believe you capable of.'

'You don't know what I'm capable of,' she said.

'Hurt me,' he said, 'if you're going to hurt anyone. If you're going to hurt anyone, hurt me.'

She walked out of the house and he stared after her; she might have quit the stage before her cue. By the time he had accepted that she was not coming back, she was already on the way to the harbour. She was gone into the purple of the evening. He could have caught her but he stayed there on the terrace. There was some element in her which was beyond him and always had been and that difference had now coloured her completely, as night had purpled the island. He went into the house and found the packet of new poems which Russell had offered in exchange for the ones she returned. He took the hot lamp from the table and carried it on to the terrace and from there he acted the poet's lines into the darkness. He shouted their faults.

She went along the beach to where the bedroll showed darker than the darkness. As she walked she unbuttoned the many-buttoned cardigan she had put on. Standing above him, she shivered; her body burned with the cold, like a glow-worm. She bent down, the shine of her flesh folding a shadow in its centre like a child, and crinkled the letter. He swam up out of his dream towards her. He was hot with it. 'Miriam?' he said. 'Miriam?'

'Yes,' she said, 'yes, my darling; yes, my baby.'

From over the bay the shouting ceased. There came now only the sound of a donkey bellowing into the night.

Suppositions

'You're looking very smart,' he said. 'Have I seen that before?'

'I've had it for ages,' she said. 'You were with me when I bought it. You remember: for the Russian trade delegation. You said the pockets would come in useful for stealing caviare.'

'I was young and witty then,' he said. 'It looks very *sophist.*, as Josephine would say, unless there's been a change of jargon recently. You're coming up to town, I presume?'

'You should have been a detective,' she said.

'Thank you,' he said.

'Is the egg all right?'

'The egg's perfect,' he said. 'A well-nigh impeccable egg.'

'I want to get some shopping done,' she said. 'And Josie's asked me to buy her some new stockings from this shop in Sackville Street. *Junk*, is it, or *Swank*? Something ending in k. The in-crowd isn't wearing tights any more apparently. They're all going back to stockings.'

'Tights supply a sort of supplementary virginity, really, don't they, when you come to think about it? Hardly the thing for in-crowds.'

'Josie says they're hot and sticky.'

'In-crowds often are,' he said. 'Do you want to have lunch?'

'Oh,' she said, 'isn't it your day for Barraclough?'

'Oh Barraclough! I can always shift Barraclough.'

'Truth to tell, darling, I'm supposed to be having lunch with someone already. I thought I'd told you.'

'Meaning that you're supposed by some people to be having lunch with someone, but actually aren't? That you're having lunch with someone only because you're supposed to, as a matter of duty? Or that you're having lunch with someone that you might not be supposed to, but suppose you will all the same?'

'You have it precisely,' she said. 'No wonder the Secretary of

246

State thinks the world of you. You really can be a terrible Wyke-hamist sometimes, can't you?'

'With the change of government,' he said, 'it's no longer forbidden. Who is it? A man?'

'Yes,' she said, 'as you ask. It's Toby Kingston.'

'Toby Kingston,' he said, 'are you really? That's rather up-market of you. How did you happen to meet friend Toby?'

'He was at that beastly cocktail party the Ridleys gave and you were supposed to meet me at, but didn't, for reasons of state, or so you stated.'

'The temporary typist's spelling actually. His wife's in the bin, you know. Where are you lunching?'

'At the House of Commons,' she said.

'Oh well,' he said, 'take your sandwiches.'

'I'm rather excited about it. I've never been and he's going to show me the ropes.'

'His reputation *is* somewhat ropey.'

'We're only having lunch, you know.'

'You're only *supposed* to be having lunch,' he said. 'Do you want to drop into the Ministry afterwards and we can come home together, or what?'

'I can't bear that commissionaire,' she said, 'the gimpy one. I'll see you back here. I shan't be late, I don't suppose.'

'Toby Kingston?'

'Giles, you're being ridiculous. I hope you know you are, because you are. And if you do know you are, I wish you'd stop. We've been married eighteen years –'

'And you've never been to the House of Commons. I quite agree: it's high time you went.'

'You're trying to make something out of this. I can't imagine why.'

'Can you not?' he said.

It was unusual, in the morning, to have her there in the Volvo, considering herself in the vanity mirror. They spied together on the image they saw up there and he agreed when she touched the dove-grey brush to its right eye before snapping the make-up into the little bag in her pleated lap. She smiled at him – silly! – and looked away. He smiled, and did not.

He kissed her, have a good time, as she parted from him at

Waterloo – Bakerloo for her, Northern Line for him – and was refreshed by the puzzlement in her new eyes. He imagined, as he marched past Smith's with its promising, promiscuous parade, how the word would filter back to him, with an apologetic 'I assume you know' that his wife had been seen with Toby Kingston.

The prospect was not wholly painful to him. They had been married for a long time. The age of frankness had come too late to spice their intimate conversation. They discussed things more boldly with their co-educated children, who were free with the modern vocabulary, than ever they did with each other. Their only four-letter word was love. There were things they had never done or said, at least to each other. Would he at last have the chance, in the unsleeping hours, to blurt out, in uncontrolled reproach, all the things he had always wanted to do, and would do now, by God, better than Toby Kingston, thanks to Toby Kingston? She would be surprised – her smart perfume going deliciously salty as they said unforgivable things, and forgave them – by the passion of his invective, by its knowing coarseness, its savage precision. He would introduce himself to her again, anew, after all these decorous years. He would show her a thing or two, with the lights on.

The Assistant-Permanent-Under-Secretary was markedly perky during the morning conference. Two of his rather insolent ideas were gratefully appended to the Minister's margin (they later armed tart replies in the House, during question-time). Who could have guessed that he was imagining his wife in the echoing lobby, under the marble eyes of long ennobled Prime Ministers, saying 'Hullo' to that rumpled rummy Kingston? What was the betting she'd be wearing new stockings?

Would the house be empty when he reached home and came round, one hand on the warm bonnet of the Volvo, to the pass door that took him into the modernized kitchen? Would he be able to savour, in the unlit evening, the cold comforts of the cuckold? 'Oh sorry, darling,' she would burst in to say at last (could it really be nine o'clock?), 'but someone fell on the line at Baker Street and we had to wait for ever in the tunnel. I don't know how they stand it every night, those poor wretched commuters: the smell! I hope you haven't been worried?' He would smile and use language to her. Later, he would demand once more the inventory of Kingston's tricks, and kicks. He would say violent, not wholly disagreeable things and it would finish, perhaps, with her face against the Formica, shoes still on.

'Hullo, darling,' she called, as he came in from the garage. 'I was beginning to worry about you.' A shiny cheek (hands in oven gloves) was offered to him. 'How was your day?'

'Moderate,' he said. 'And you?'

'Don't ask,' she said.

'Oh but I want to,' he said.

'He was horrible. *He* should be in the bin, not her. You should have told me what he was like.'

'I thought it was obvious,' he said, 'and I thought perhaps the obvious was what you were after.'

'You're supposed to know me better than that,' she said.

'Yes,' he said, 'I suppose I am.'

You Don't Remember Me

'I know your face, of course,' Martin said. 'We weren't in Rep together, were we, by any chance? Worthing? Could it have been Worthing? I was there in '57.'

'No, I was never an actor, I'm afraid. Considerably less glamorous than that. It was the old Gloucester Club. We used to play sixpenny bridge together.'

'Good *heavens*, of course: the old Gloucester! Dear old Mrs Mac! Wait a minute, you're not Opie, are you?'

'Very close. Impressively close. I'm Opie's partner. Or I was. Opie's dead, you know. I'm Victor Milsom.'

'Victor Milsom, of course you are! *Dead*?'

'I'm afraid so. He died in Juan-les-Pins; well, in Cannes actually. We were playing in the Congress. Peritonitis.'

'What a dreadful thing! You played the Forcing Two, didn't you? With Ace Responses. Ruptured appendix presumably?'

'And Blackwood for kings. He thought it was food poisoning. We'd had some snails. We were lying second at the time. Do you still play at all? We get quite a decent game up at the golf club here, you know, especially at the week-end.'

'Golf! Now you're talking,' Martin said. 'I get a good bit of that in, when I can. Poor old Opie.'

'Ten years ago now. It's quite a decent little course; I play a fair amount myself, none too brilliantly, but . . .'

'It looks very pretty from the road,' Martin said. 'Is it very difficult to get in? Long waiting list?'

'I don't think a famous actor would have too much of a problem. Are you living around here now then, may I ask?'

'We've just acquired a place, as a matter of fact,' Martin said.

'Wait a minute,' Milsom said. 'You're not the Metcalfe who's bought Yardley Hall, by any chance, are you?'

'Guilty as charged,' Martin said.

250

'I was the estate agent,' Milsom said. 'We handled the place for Colonel Partington's widow.'

'Well, damn your eyes is all I can say! You kept very quiet about the dry rot in the tithe barn, didn't you?'

'*Caveat emptor*,' Victor Milsom said. 'Or hadn't you heard?'

'I have now,' Martin said, 'but it's a bit late in the day, isn't it? No, as a matter of fact we're over the moon with the place. I daresay we paid slightly over the odds, but today's extravagance is tomorrow's bargain, isn't it? And it had better be, hadn't it? We're thinking of doing up the barn and selling it separately. You could handle it for us, if you like.'

'Be a pleasure and a privilege. Are you planning to settle down in the country now then, after all your success?'

'*After*? Are you implying it's all over or something? Do you know something I don't?'

'Very little, I imagine. My wife watches you all the time, particularly that Film Quiz you do.'

'Meaning that she doesn't watch me when I'm Chief Inspector 'Arry 'Awkes?'

'You really should have been a policeman,' Milsom said, 'you're so quick at drawing the wrong conclusion.'

'Ah, a liberal! Do you live down this way yourself? Or ...?'

'Yes, it's just a modest little local business,' Victor Milsom said. 'I've been here for the best part of twenty-five years.'

'The best part of twenty-five years is nearly always the first five in my experience.'

'You've recently got married, haven't you?' Milsom said.

'We have regularized our union,' Martin said. 'The missus and I. Yes ...'

'Sheila Armitage, isn't it?'

'Sheila Armitage it *was*; Sheila Metcalfe it is and evermore shall be. No, you're quite right. The last girl I saw you with wore granny glasses and home-made sandals and had one of the biggest shelves I'd ever seen. Out here, she was. What was her name? Mona?'

'Monica,' Milsom said.

'Yes, I wonder what happened to her.'

'I married her,' Milsom said.

'Did you really? I expect you were absolutely right. Well, look here, this is marvellous, bumping into you. We don't know a soul in the district, we just saw the picture of Yardley Hall in the paper and down we came and ... the rest you know. Really nice to see you again, Victor. What does one do about the golf? I mean, can I just turn up there and have a round? Are there any formalities?'

'It's open to the public during the week, on payment of the usual green fee –'

'Well, I daresay I could spring to that,' Martin said.

'But I'll have a word with the secretary, if you like. That is, if you're thinking of becoming a member. We can always do with a few famous faces –'

'I'll try and rally some of the clan then,' Martin said. 'No, seriously –'

'We have got a bit of a waiting list, but I am on the committee.'

'Are you indeed? Trust me to have friends in the right place! I'm not sure how often I shall be able to play, but obviously I'm most likely to be around at the week-end – we've got Sheila's old flat in town during the week – and it'd be rather a drag if one couldn't get a game on a Saturday or Sunday.'

'You can always play as my guest in the interim.'

'As soon as we're straight,' Martin said, 'you must come round and have a drink. The roses are still absolutely marvellous; especially those orange ones in the walled garden. Knock-out. And do give my regards to your wife. I'd've taken her off you, you know, in the old days, if I could, but you were obviously giving her the treatment she wanted. Poor old Opie, though, what a ghastly thing to have happen!'

'Yes, well, I must be on my way. Welcome to East Anglia!'

'Soon as we're straight,' Martin said, 'I'll give you a buzz.'

Sheila was arranging furniture with the two men who had brought the stuff down from London. She was wearing hand-painted sneakers and a pair of yellow dungarees, with her hair hidden under a green silk scarf. The men had the overweight agility common to their trade and their insolent patter was calculated to amuse but not annoy. There were tips to come. They greeted Martin with looks of flattering envy. Sheila had clearly been doing her sexy stuff.

Yardley Hall was a big, double-gabled yellow farmhouse with Georgian windows and stone floors. It was too big for them really, but each had children from earlier disasters and they were not cottagey types. They could afford a certain grandeur, though they were determined not to be grand with it. The removal men treated them with an impressed familiarity to which, as actors, they were accustomed: everyone always felt that they knew them personally and fed them lines appropriate to the characters they commonly played on the box. (Sheila was always being addressed as 'dear Gwendolen', because of her Harrodsy part in 'Can I Call You Back?') The men quizzed them about the other people in their shows as they manoeuvred the baby grand into the long drawing room: what about that jungle bunny Barry Coleman, Martin's Detective Sergeant in 'The Patch'? Was he really a Brummy or was that acting?

When the heavy stuff was all parked, Martin brought in beer and cheese and a jar of pickles, and they sat on the big hearth and had a picnic, quite as if the four of them were mates working for the absent owners. 'It's a bit of a giggle really, us buying this socking great place,' Shelia said.

'Nonsense,' Martin said. 'One should make a point of living in the style to which one is not accustomed. As a matter of fact, it's amazing how quickly you get accustomed to it.'

'Dead right, squire,' one of the men said. 'And good luck to you.'

'You see? I've come into my title already,' Martin said. The men accepted the spare bottles of beer and some of the five-pound notes Martin had been getting from the bank when he met Victor Milsom, and they all shook hands.

'Best of luck with it then, squire. See you on the telly, dear Gwendolen.'

Sheila waved them off down the drive and came back into the house, shaking her blonde hair free. 'Well, if it isn't the lady of the manor!' Martin said.

'And if it isn't, it soon will be,' she said.

He kissed those delicious lips. 'Welcome to East Anglia,' he said.

Monica was now a substantial matron, though she still wore sandals; she had had three children and the oldest was just twenty-one, studying engineering at Manchester, Ralph. She and Sheila spent the early evening going round the garden. Monica turned out to be an expert on pruning and layering and dividing. Sheila took large-lettered notes, with a big red and blue double-ended pencil. Victor and Martin practised chipping old golf balls up towards the gazebo at the bottom of the front lawn, under the monkey-puzzle tree. Sheila had cooked one of her quiches and they ate it with a bottle of Sancerre, followed by strawberries.

'We really should have asked you to supper first,' Monica said. 'I told Victor. This is all wrong really.'

'Not at all,' Martin said. 'We're the ones trying to clamber our way into local society and it's only right that we should make the first servile move.'

'Local society,' Monica said, 'I don't imagine you'll be wanting too much of that!'

'It's not as bad as all that, Monica,' Victor said. 'I'm secretary of the local Rotary, you know, and we've had some quite impressive speakers. I don't suppose –'

'*Victor*!' Monica said. 'He promised he wouldn't ask you till you came over to see us.'

'Oh don't worry,' Sheila said. 'Martin'll do anything for a round of applause.'

'Not to mention a round of drinks,' Martin said.

'You must get terribly bored with boring people asking you to do things,' Monica said. 'Or do you like being known as Chief Inspector?'

'Well, I was once dragged in to stop a race riot in Notting Hill by a black lady who absolutely insisted that I was the only policeman they trusted. I could've done without that, I must say.'

'And did it work?'

'It did actually. It wasn't really a riot, of course. Just a bunch of kids exchanging beer bottles at rather a rapid rate.'

'Chief Inspector 'Arry 'Awkes was hequal to the occasion, was he?'

'That particular one, yes. He was trembling in his oversize boots, but no one seemed to notice. They all came clamouring round for autographs.'

'I should think it'll lower the crime rate, just having you move into the district,' Victor said. 'Do you play bridge, Mrs Metcalfe?'

'Sheila,' Sheila said. 'No, I don't play anything, I'm afraid.'

'I'm going to teach her to play golf,' Martin said. 'It's good for the waist-line, darling.'

'If you did feel like coming along to Rotary one day, I know it'd be hugely appreciated,' Victor said. 'We meet at the Dorothy in the High Street, not far from the bank. I'm afraid we don't pay. It's just the honour and the lunch.'

'The honour's less likely to upset you,' Monica said.

When the Maxi had gone off down the drive, Sheila and Martin took a walk around the dark garden. The tobacco plants scented the quiet air. 'I rather like her,' Sheila said.

'Funny folk in the sticks! I'm not at all sure she always knows what she's saying, you know.'

'And I'm quite sure she does. He's funny too. "Does it offend you if I smoke my pipe?" People don't say those things any more. And yet he's got quite a twinkle in his eye. You get the feeling that they're going home to more than a cup of cocoa, don't you?'

'God, isn't it super down here?' he said. 'I don't think we should ever leave.'

'Why, are you planning to?' she said.

'Well, we'll wait until we've flogged the barn, shall we?'

'You go. I'm staying. It's such a relief, after London, living among real people! What she doesn't know about gardens! I can see myself being really happy, darling, you know that, here? Truly.'

Victor rang and invited him to play golf the following week. The course was much better than he had expected. It was not up to Sunningdale or Royal Wimbledon, where the Green Room Golfing Society played, but the turf was in good trim and the lack of challenging contours was prettily offset by narrow fairways and gouged bunkers. The little lake cost Martin a ball at the fifth and challenged his spoon play at the seventeenth, where Major Harper, the Secretary, clapped as he holed his chip for a birdie after he had only just avoided bombing the fishes for the second time. Playing level, he beat Victor two and one but he suspected that the estate agent had been discreetly hospitable. 'I really enjoyed that,' he said.

'Victor tells me that you're thinking of joining us,' Major Harper said.

'If I can find anyone to put me up,' Martin said, 'I should like that very much.'

'You should introduce him to the Chief Constable,' the Major said. 'I'm sure he'd be happy to second you. After all, you're both in the same line of business, more or less, aren't you?'

They went into the club house and Martin played the sporting gentleman to the secretary's satisfaction over drinks at the bar. Molly, the barmaid, recognized him at once, though she refused to allow him to pay for the gin and ginger. 'Members only,' she said. 'Sorry, Chief Inspector, but you wouldn't want me to bend the rules, would you?'

'You keep your nose clean, lass,' he said.

Yardley Hall soon became the only place Sheila wanted to call home. Was this overalled gardening fanatic the same hard-drinking lady with the huge bill at Browns which had exasperated her ex-husband even more than her scarcely discreet affair with Martin? When the Chairman of the Parish Council came round to pay his first respects, she had him on his hands and knees in the greenhouse, trying to see what was wrong with the old hand pump in there. ('Nothing like well water, is there, councillor, for seedlings?') She was happy to reassure him that, of course, they could use the Hall grounds for the Fête next year as usual. The Rector came and congratulated her on her (actually Mrs Parker's) scones. ('What the *hell* did you talk about?' Martin said. 'Morals,' she said.)

Sheila even began to hope that dear Gwendolen might be killed off sometime during the next series, so that she could stay at the Hall right through the week. 'Christ, darling,' Martin said, 'you can't do that, we shall go bust.'

'You make plenty for two,' she said.

'I daresay,' he said, 'but I've got four, haven't I?' (Thelma and their son Christopher were living in Shepherd's Bush.)

'I can always grow things,' Sheila said. 'There's tons of money in asparagus, Mrs Parker was telling me.'

'There's a hell of a sight more in dear Gwendolen,' Martin said. 'You couldn't possibly do without London, you know you couldn't.'

'I know,' she said. 'I'll have it down for the week-end. While you're playing golf.'

He did the Rotary lunch (the second Wednesday of the month) and amused the guests with a few brass-type tacks from Chief Inspector 'Awkes, followed by some modest words from the actor who played him. Hawkes's fictional patch was an 'inner city'; his

Detective Sergeant, 'Paddy' Laverne, was played by this black actor Barry Coleman, with whom Hawkes had a rather gritty relationship. 'How do you really get on with "Paddy"?' asked one of the Rotarians.

'We've both got a job to do,' Martin said, in 'Awky's gruff accent. 'We talk the same language on the job, we just don't 'appen to 'ave the same social life. Well, they're 'appier with their own, aren't they, if you're honest?'

'But how many people are?' said a voice from the back. 'Honest? What do you really think about the way they're taking over the big cities? Is the same thing going to happen out here, do you think?' Some heads turned, but most of the members recognized Bob Bailey and did not need to look.

'Oh come on, Alderman,' someone said. 'No politics!'

'It's a fair question to ask, I should have thought,' Bailey said. 'Unless you object to answering it.'

'If you do object,' Victor Milsom said, 'we shall quite understand.'

'No objection at all,' Martin said. 'If you want a straight answer, I should much prefer to be having lunch with Barry Coleman than with the gentleman who asked the question. In fact, I think I'll go and give him a ring as soon as I get out of here and see when he's free.'

Martin was sufficiently angry to be surprised when his answer was greeted with applause. Members were relieved to have a chance to rebuff Bob Bailey without actually having to say anything against him. When Victor proposed his vote of thanks to the speaker, he apologized to Martin for the 'embarrassment' he had been caused.

'I don't embarrass easy, lad,' Martin said.

'I hope that you'll bring Mr Coleman to have lunch with us one day,' Victor said, to some applause, 'because I know he'd be very welcome.'

'You didn't need to say that,' Martin said, as they took their cigars out into the early closed High Street, 'but I take my hat off to you for saying it.'

'I despise that man,' Victor said, as they watched the Alderman get into his Austin Princess. Bailey was a local builder; the red-brick shopping precinct opposite the Dorothy had been constructed by his firm. 'Unfortunately . . .'

'Don't take offence on my behalf, Victor,' Martin said. 'That sort of man's always going to be around, and he's always going to be in a minority, so let's not bother about him.'

'He's a very good actor, isn't he, Barry Coleman?' Victor said.

'He's a damned sight better golfer.'

'Really?'

'He nearly turned pro, but he decided to be an actor instead. Easier life. Well, it is for some.'

'I've had a word with the Chief Constable, by the way. He'd be happy to second your membership application.'

The Alderman's Princess was parked at the club when Martin next went to play. Bailey himself was perfectly civil (why should Martin have been offended?) and nodded across to the celebrity from the bridge table. Victor was puffing at his metal-stemmed pipe, frowning at the dummy like a man for ever condemned to make the best of a bad job. Martin shook his head when there was a call of 'table up' after Victor had surprisingly, and skilfully, landed his contract.

'I don't know what took you so long, Milsom,' Bailey said.

'I wanted to make it seem difficult, Alderman,' Victor said, digging for dottle.

Martin liked him.

When they started taping the new series of *The Patch*, he mentioned to Barry Coleman that he had joined a new club down where he was now living. 'Oh man,' Barry said, 'I know Yardley. Nice! I used to go past there on my way to Harwich. I've got this bird in Felixstowe I go to see. Very nice! I drive right past there.'

'Come down and play next week,' Martin said.

'Why should a player of my class waste his time playing with someone like you, bwana, that's what I want to know?'

'Get stuffed, Coleman. Do you really have to go to Felixstowe for it?'

'You're not looking for some sick leave, bwana, by any chance?'

Martin grinned and thumped Barry on the shoulder. 'What about Thursday?'

The afternoon was grey and it soon began to drizzle. Barry went round in sixty-nine, never straining, always giving the impression that he was merely practising, which he probably was. There were not many people in the club house when they came in, glistening

with the well-being that comes of having done something con-
spicuously uncomfortable for no good reason. Major Harper was
chatting with Molly as she lifted the grille in front of the bar. He
shook hands with Barry, when Martin introduced him, and agreed
to join them for a drink, now that Martin was qualified to pay!

'I really enjoyed that,' Barry said. 'Lovely little course.'

'Do you live near here?' the Major said.

'Not yet,' Barry said, 'but I'm thinking about it.'

'He's going to get the Alderman to build him a bungalow,' Martin
said.

Martin took Barry back to Yardley Hall for supper. Sheila was
wearing cherry velvet pants and a 'tarty top', black slippers. She
had been bottling fruit all afternoon; Mrs Parker and she had
sterilized fifty Kilner jars, and filled them. 'My God, Sheila,' Barry
said, 'you'll be doing home hints before you're done.'

'Before I'm done?' Sheila said. 'It's too late for that, I'm afraid.'

'Barry's so impressed with the weather, he's going to buy a
cottage in the village,' Martin said.

'Seriously, Barry?'

'We saw that old thatched place just across the aerodrome,'
Martin said. 'They've been paying him in coloured beads till now
but, with this new deal, he's got so much of the stuff, he doesn't
know where to put it. Well, you must admit it'd be convenient,
Coleman. You could give me a stroke a hole in the afternoon and
still be in Felixstowe at night in time to stroke a hole or two there.'

'Cheeky bastard.'

Barry came back a week later and decided to buy 'Constable
Cottage' (it was believed in the village that the painter, or at least
his brother, had once stayed there). He met no obvious hostility;
after all, he too was a celebrity. The excellence of his golf also earned
him respect, though he was perhaps a little too good; such effortless-
ness smacked of contempt for those who could not so easily explode
out of the steep bunkers and whose approach shots did not nibble
the green and trickle to within a yard and a half of the pin. However,
Martin was in little doubt that the club was proud to have the
Chief Inspector as a member; why should it not be equally honoured
to have his Detective Sergeant?

'You shouldn't force him on people,' Sheila said. 'It's not fair
on them and it's not fair on him.'

'With a skin Barry's colour, nothing's going to be exactly fair, is it?'

'Don't you like it down here?' Sheila said.

'Sheila, for God's sake! What're you turning into? If Victor's prepared to second him, I don't see what there is to worry about.'

Victor telephoned to say there was a minor procedural problem.

'Like they don't want a black member?' Martin said.

'No. But I'm sorry to say that there's an unwritten rule that no one can propose anybody until he himself has been a member for a full calendar year.'

'Unwritten, eh?' Martin said. 'Oh well, if that's the case –'

'I'll propose him myself,' Victor Milsom said. 'No problem.'

'Oh Victor, will you really? That's most awfully nice of you.'

'What are friends for?' Victor said.

Barry's name had to be posted on the bulletin board, next to those of other candidates, so that members might add their signatures, if they wished, to those of his proposer and seconder. Since most of the candidates were local men, with business or family connections, it was not necessarily an ominous sign that Barry failed to attract many other sponsors, though Victor's reputation was enough to secure a few. The main decision would be taken in committee. There the prospects were favourable. A plan was afoot to extend the club house and build an indoor swimming pool; to finance it, extra money was needed and there was general agreement that the entrance fee should be raised and the membership extended. The waiting list which Martin had been privileged to by-pass would be more or less abolished, though clearly not every hacker in the county could be admitted to the course. Such considerations hardly applied to a scratch player like Barry Coleman.

Martin was rehearsing a new episode of *The Patch* when Victor telephoned from Yardley. 'Bad news, I'm afraid, Martin.'

'Not Sheila?'

'No, no, no, but I'm sorry to say they've turned down Barry Coleman.'

'Oh for Christ's sake,' Martin said.

'They didn't stipulate on whose account,' Victor said, 'but I rather think it's Bob Bailey's. It seems that he's divvied up for the extension to the club house and he's put in a generously low tender for the swimming pool as well.'

'The dirty bastard,' Martin said.

'Yes, well, it went to a vote and ... I couldn't take part myself, of course, since it was my candidate. It is a private club. The committee ... I don't think there was anything personal in it –'

'No, well, that's not really all that encouraging, is it?'

'I'm not sure that I'm with you,' Victor Milsom said.

'If it wasn't personal, what was it? I could understand it if Barry had chewed holes in the greens or taken his shoes off and wiggled his toes in the bar, but as far as I could see, he behaved himself as if he were a white man, more or less, don't you agree?'

'It's all very unfortunate,' Victor Milsom said.

'I'm sorry?'

'There's a hell of a wind blowing up here,' Victor said. 'I said it was all very unfortunate.'

'Look, Victor, I have to go and arrest someone on the roof and it needs a bit of rehearsing. I'll buzz over and see you on Saturday morning, if I may, when I get down to Yardley again. Does Barry know?'

'I don't have his ... I thought you'd probably ...'

'Yes, I probably should. I'll see him tomorrow; he wasn't called today. Well, well ... few are chosen, are they not?'

'I'm just as upset as you are,' Victor Milsom said.

'I'm not upset, Victor. A bunch of people like that, what the hell do they matter to me or anyone else? I shall have to resign, of course. I'm not going on playing there in circumstances like this.'

'Mr Metcalfe. They're ready for you, sir.'

'I'll see you at the week-end,' Martin said.

Barry laughed and laughed when Martin broke the news to him. 'Man, what does it *matter*? I don't have to look for places to play.'

'I know that, Coleface, but it's the kind of thing that makes me boil.'

'If I boiled at things like that, I'd have steam coming permanently out of my ears. Forget it.'

Martin drove down to Yardley on Friday night, very late; they had not finished in the studio until right on ten, and then there were drinks in the bar, the usual cocktail of euphoria and anti-climax. What was television? You did it and people recognized you in the street for as long as the series lasted and that was it. Yardley was a good hour and a half's drive, even if you played private eyes on the dual carriageway and let the Bristol have its big head. It was a sort of madness, rushing up and down like this, with the wind beating in at the windows to keep the alcohol from over-working. Was it really worth it?

Sheila, bless her heart, still had the light on in the bedroom window. She was reading a book on plant propagation which Monica Milsom had lent her. It was the perfect restorative: Sheila with her breasts above the turned down sheet and the technique of grafting open on her raised knees. The wind thumped and rattled the old house and Martin knew that third time he really had struck lucky. It was certainly worth it. Yardley Golf Club? Who needed it?

Victor Milsom was sitting over some papers in his little study, overlooking the willows. The Milsoms' house was an old mill; willows grew thickly along the stream. Men came and cut them to make cricket bats, when the wood was ready. Victor lit his pipe ('You don't mind if I smoke this, do you?') and looked at Martin with glinting eyes. 'I've considered the whole matter,' he said.

'In all its aspects?' Martin said.

'And I've come to the conclusion that you're absolutely right. We have no course but to resign.'

'Oh nonsense, Victor. Why should *you* resign? It's my business if *I* do; Barry's my chum and it's my fault that he's been humiliated like this. As a matter of fact, he thinks it's all a huge joke. He's not in the least bothered. Come on, man, you've been a member of the club for twenty years. You'll probably be Captain next year; I heard them talking about it in the bar.'

'It's a matter of principle,' Victor said. 'I was the proposer.'

'Only because I couldn't be.'

'That's scarcely the point. I was the proposer and my candidate has been black-balled.'

'From birth, old boy, from birth. It's not worth making a fuss about. This is your patch, Victor. You've made your life here.'

'It's a matter of honour.'

'Oh bullshit, man. It was only a bit of fun for me, proposing Barry.'

'Seconding him. I'm sorry, Martin, but my mind's made up.'

'If you're doing this for me, I warn you: I'm not the grateful type. Not only will you soil your own doorstep, giving me a bad conscience'll probably put an end to our friendship as well.'

'I've made my decision. What you feel about it honestly isn't relevant.'

'Think of Mona. *Monica*. She'll never forgive us. Besides, you know damned well you'd love to be Captain of that pissy little club.'

'That's no longer the point,' Victor said, tapping his pipe against the stone sill.

'Sleep on it,' Martin said. 'Don't do anything rash. And above all don't imagine that I shall think any the less of you. I probably won't give it another thought. I promise you Barry won't. Wait till the wind drops. No man can make a sane decision with this kind of stuff going on.'

As he drove off, he realized why Victor Milsom's eyes had glinted so strangely. He had been crying.

When Martin turned the corner into Hall Lane, he saw a dark cloud blowing over the hedge that guarded the house. He sneezed three times at the dust as he hooked the white gates back among the laurels. Just as he was getting back into the Bristol, he saw Sheila running towards him up the drive, legs splayed with the effort to speed along the gravel. She was crying and shouting, hysterical with the ghastly news he instantly guessed. 'The barn –' she said. 'The barn . . .'

'I know,' he said. 'It's fallen down.'

'The whole thing,' she said, 'like a pack of cards. Martin, it's flat. It's completely flat.'

'*Caveat emptor*,' Martin said. 'Blast the man.'

'It just folded up and – there was nothing left of it. It happened right in front of my eyes.'

'Pompous little provincial poop. You know what Opie died of, don't you? Boredom.'

'Who was Opie?' Sheila said.

'Oh I forget now,' Martin said.

Private Views

Marsden sees her first in a Chelsea basement at a party given to celebrate the yellow-jacketed publication of Ferdy Plant's whodunnit. Its plot, according to a Sunday pseudonym, concerns a man whose wife is murdered, whereupon her secret life is disclosed. The husband who loved her comes to hate her with such intensity that he contrives, through patient ingenuity, to be found guilty of her murder. This post-meditated crime is declared 'unsubtly schematic' by the reviewer, who awards Ferdy only beta query plus, though deeming him 'newcomer of the week'.

The girl is with a married man who himself is later found murdered. His killers leave no clue and his wife remarries, happily. He is supposed to have been shot in error: two men of the same name live in his block, Harry Groves. As a result of the shooting, the other Groves's life is investigated and he is sent to prison for offences which might have remained undetected, had it not been for his namesake's misfortune.

When the girl goes over to join the uncritical circle round a stammering, eloquent critic, the married man drinks whisky, no water, side by side with the hired barman whom he knows from another time. The girl looks new – she can only be eighteen or nineteen – but there is something decided, and decisive, in her youthfulness. Though she is still at art school, there is no trace of paint on her fingers. Her beauty makes so little claim – since it assumes so much – that Charles Marsden need not hesitate to look at her. She is a goddess whose nakedness one will never surprise. She wears a long and susurrant dress of purplish, pleated wool, with a strict belt. As she listens to the wit, she holds a waisted *copita* of sherry, freckled with light like her own ferrous eyes. She never smiles.

Her unquestioning silence provokes clever answers; the critic fumbles for keys to unlock her humour. Her departure leaves him criticized. He has to pin the tail of his remarks on a donkey of a woman, who fails to get the point. The critic, whose name is Household, is one of those toadies so eager to please that he does not dare to say a good word about anybody.

'Well, who is she?' Marsden asks.

'Charlie, really, do you not know Katya Lowell?'

'I've been in Ireland, haven't I?'

He has recently come down from Oxford, with a mediocre degree. ('Frankly, I never expected to do quite that well,' he tells his mother.) He elected to read Medieval French only a month before his final examinations. Such flippancy suggests shallowness, but Marsden is more bored than foolish. His disdain for academic honours announces private means. He exemplifies that obsolete Oxford strain whose finest affectation is to delay allegiance until it can find a cause sufficiently lost to deserve support. Charlie sets his watch (an uncle's) with a relish for punctilious anachronism. Katya Lowell, first observed in a world of unfinished things (the pillared wallpaper is half posted in the flat), strikes him as uniquely complete, as if she had already come into her title. He watches her like a paraded *objet de vertu* as she goes over to the corner where her Harry Groves is agreeing with the barman. Unsmiling eyes make an appointment, for which they leave.

Marsden is not much up on women. He has enough friends – and friends of friends – for London to present no lonely problem. The party takes place in a spacious past when it is still possible to park in the West End. Marsden drives a Sunbeam Talbot, with a recognizable open roof. He has rooms in Vicarage Gate (Mrs Jump). There is no shortage of local company. Ferdy's brother, Theo, shares a flat with Marcus Hicks just along the way. Jim Farber and Pip Lethbridge are up Campden Hill. Women do not come into their domestic lives, except to dust. If Marsden needs someone on his arm, he takes his sister, Camilla. As for bed, he prefers breakfast.

Marsden has not yet acquired his title or the Irish acres. He has some money from a bachelor uncle who spent most of his life, but not much else, in the East. He can afford to enjoy himself, and a happy few others. Marsden had difficulty only in filling his mornings, so he started to go to auctions. Marcus was working in Bond Street; they would meet for a fishy lunch. Marsden bought little and sold less. If the art market entertained him, he disdained to play it, except playfully. He specialized in English interiors and compiled a monograph which he refused to a publisher, though he did have it printed privately. He liked hidden things.

Theo Plant presages the end of a certain London period by electing to marry this Peruvian cellist of his. Marcus Hicks picks at early gulls' eggs one day before announcing that he is interested in a widow, a Countess as it happens. When Marsden congratulates him, Marcus scans his face for surlier reactions. ('Are you sure you're not upset?') Charlie replies that he is thinking of going to Tangier for a bit. A chum of his Singapore uncle has a house in the casbah; among the blues and whites and pinks there are windowless rooms, cushioned and carpeted, where one can arrange unknown visitors. Marcus Hicks is as sallow and narrow-faced as a knave in a black suit. He has long fingers, articulate bones in skinny gloves. The boss on his wrist is hairless as a button.

'Shall you mind her, do you think?'

'Theo's done it, after all, why should you be embargoed? She sounds to be quite a catch.'

'They are rather catching, you know, once you get used to them, the sex.'

'So I'm promised,' Charlie says.

'How's your father these days?'

'In health and in Ireland. Long may he remain in both.'

'Are you and Camilla coming to Potts at the week-end?'

'That was the plan,' Charlie says.

'Because you can meet her in that case. We're going down Friday.'

Potts is the small country house owned by Marcus's stepmother, near Leatherhead. Camilla and Charlie get lost as usual and have to put the pleated roof up over the Sunbeam; spring hail rattles like spilled pearls. Brother and sister are said to be alike. 'She has my nose,' Charlie once observed, 'but I'm lucky: I've got her eyes.' Rumours do circulate about them, but they alone know the secret: none of them is true. Their resemblance is so striking that even without scandal they have an intimate sense of each other. 'If we slept together, there'd be no call to wake up.'

The Countess is particularly taken by them, a dark-eyed woman, white skin, sharp nose. At dinner she wears a little black dress and a lot of diamonds and is garrulous with her hands. Her hair is new ginger and her mouth very red. 'Oh I am going to be such dear friends with both of you!' she exclaims. 'If Marcus – my very dear Marcus – allows it. Oh he likes you both so much, you know!'

'Oh, is she Polish possibly?' Camilla wonders, over the Sunday morning kedgeree.

'Oh I think she's probably rather attractive, don't you?' Charlie says.

'Oh I think she's probably *very* attractive.'

The Countess comes down late, washed face, blanched mouth, head in a bandanna. Marcus fusses around her and is short with everyone else. The couple leave for London before lunch, just as the weather is making the others look up: there seems to be a serious chance of croquet after all. The Countess is muted in her farewells. Her hands never say a word.

Charlie goes to Tangier for a week, ten days really. While wandering for presents in the old town, he meets an Arab boy who has picturesque holes in his ragged clothes and a vocabulary of husky directness. They go to a café where men are smoking hashish. Charlie tries a pipe. He has his first sensation of being old as this old child watches him. Desire is done down by the solicitude he reads in the other's eyes. 'I'm tired of boys,' he says, tenderly. The boy offers to show him the brothels: he has only to say when. Charlie tips him well but neither touches him nor makes another rendezvous. He is late for dinner. The master of the house fears that he has had an accident.

Theo Plant has opened a restaurant, 'The Gunroom', where the best cutlery consists of swords and spurs. He features three or four entrées and crinkled salads, but the specialities are summer pudding and spring boys. On his return to England, Charlie buys some unusual sporting prints (in Essex, funny county) and delivers them to Theo at 'The Gunroom'. He finds Marcus Hicks dining with Camilla. The Pole has had a misfortune. She has used some suspect shampoo and her hair has fallen out. 'Not all of it, you understand, but most.'

'Poor thing,' Charlie said. 'Is she very low?'

'She is a trifle low,' Marcus said. Camilla looked particularly stricken, though her hair was fine. 'She's turned rather reclusive.'

'I've told him it'll grow out,' Camilla said.

'Look here,' Marcus said, 'are you going to join us or what?'

'I'm dining unfortunately,' Charlie said.

'Will you be home later?'

'I do hope to be home later.'

Charlie is drinking tea with Mrs Jump at soon after midnight when the bell rings. It is Marcus, and Camilla. 'Not to put too fine a point on it, my dear Charlie, Camilla and I propose to get married. I hope you're not going to be upset.'

'Why,' Charlie says, 'have you got plans for me?'

'It's rather sudden, though it doesn't feel so.'

'What about the Countess?'

'There is certainly that,' Marcus says, 'which is partly why we've come round.'

'I'm to be uncle Charlie, am I?'

'She likes you awfully,' Marcus says, taking a sudden demotion to the fifth form. 'And I wondered ...'

'You really want to marry him?' Charlie says.

'Well, he asked me, didn't he?' Camilla says. 'And I've always liked his hands.' Her eyes allude to that bare boss on Marcus's hairy wrist and Charlie observes a strange gleam above his sister's mouth, a glaze of desire like a ghostly moustache. Now that she is beyond him, he rather wishes they had done all the things rumour proposed.

He goes the next morning to see the Countess. He buys some magazines to cheer her up. In one of them he finds a picture of Katya Lowell, unsmilingly enjoying a joke. The critic is wincing behind her, in a velvet smoking jacket; smoke gets in his eyes. The Countess seems scarcely to remember Charlie. She still wears a bandanna tight around her head and her face is bland of make-up. At first she is disposed to believe that Charlie has engineered the engagement between his sister and Marcus. They sit in the room overlooking the park with as little to say to each other as common patients in a waiting-room. Charlie has his magazines in front of him. He is tactful to begin with and then, when the Countess's reproachful eyes sweep him for the eight or ninth time, he loses patience. 'I didn't pull your bloody hair out, you know.'

'Oh he was so kind to me,' she says. 'That is how I knew.'

'Knew what?'

'That he was going to leave me.'

'You wouldn't have been happy,' Charlie says. 'You've had an escape really, you know. Marcus would have led you an awful dance.'

'Oh I know,' she says. 'Do you think I don't know? I know.'

'Rather what you wanted, I presume.'

'What do you know about it?' she says, but nicely.

'I'll bet you it doesn't matter a damn,' Charlie says, quickened.

'What is that?'

'Your hair. Show me.'

'I have none. *None.* I have none. Not a blade.'

'A blade! Show me. I'll bet you it doesn't detract in the least.'

She looks at him with widely awakened eyes and goes and locks the drawing-room door. She stands in front of him and unlatches the bandanna. Her head is small and white, like a peeled vegetable. The ears are delicious. Her eyes accuse Charlie, not of what has happened, but of what he wants. He kisses the chalky lips until they redden. 'I think we have a future,' he says. 'Why don't you dispense with the rest?'

Her breasts are blue cheese to Charlie's uninitiated eyes, but they ripen to loveliness when she discloses, abruptly, the hair she still possesses, in abundance. 'There,' she says. 'That is a woman. Now you know what a woman is.'

Marsden leaves her the magazines, except for the one with Katya Lowell in it. That he takes back to Mrs Jump's. All the Countess's hair has grown again by the time that Camilla and Marcus are married, but Charlie likes her to hide it, so she still binds it under a bandanna. His desire is aroused, when they are alone, by unwinding the turban and allowing her hair to fall over the white ears. Charlie resists the temptation to move in with her, though he visits her roughly every day.

Jim Farber has decided to open a small gallery. One of the first artists to whom he gives a show is Katya Lowell. Charlie has put a pound or two into the place and goes to the *vernissage*. She seems unchanged, though it is several years since Chelsea. (The married man is dead.) She is wearing a belted green dress, scooped out at the neck, but chaste with a drawstring. Her strapped feet are bare and brown in Florentine sandals. She accepts congratulations with an unsmiling nod, as if she were acknowledging a joke she has heard before. Charlie does not speak to her and soon leaves to go and see Anya.

However, he returns the next day. Several of the pictures have been sold. Red stars confirm their desirability, as wedding rings can that of certain women. Her paintings are English interiors. Some bear the names of people: David, Iris, Wendy and Gavin, Miles, Harry. But there are no people in them. Another sequence is anonymous. The paintings are entitled merely 'His Place', 'The Flat', 'Punishment' and 'Scene of the Crime'. Charlie stands for some time in front of 'Punishment'. Jim Farber has been busy on the telephone, to Brussels, but comes, bearded, to stand beside him. 'I like her paint,' Charlie says at last. Jim Farber is slightly older than Charlie. They were at school together and Jim punished his junior two or three times.

The room was clean, the paint without impasto. A round, gate-legged table (one leaf autumnal) was laid for breakfast under a window looking deep into a garden pricked with daffodils. The garden was no larger than half a postcard; the daffodils, pin-high, were depicted in subtle counterperspective. In the foreground was a Windsor chair, a dress laid across it. Charlie recognized the purplish wool, a date from an old diary. The belt was over the back. There was a red star in the corner of the canvas.

'I realize it's not normally done,' Charlie says, 'but could I possibly know who bought it?'

That evening he gave notice to Mrs Jump. He was awfully sorry but he had to find a place of his own. He rejected several flats which the agent, personally recommended by Theo, proposed to him. He had finally to take the young man to the Farber gallery, to show him exactly what he wanted. 'And I do mean exactly.'

'It's going to have to be rather large in that case, isn't it, sir?'

'Oh yes, it is.'

'Are you getting married, sir, may I ask?'

'Of course,' Charlie said.

It was his culminating act of dandyism, the flat. He told himself, and no one else, that his decision to decorate it according to the prescriptions posted in the Farber Gallery was a capping caprice. After this, he would lead a normal life. He even proposed to take a job. Most of his friends now worked; there was practically no one to see in the mornings, if one was not to go on going to Bond Street. Pip Lethbridge (who had met a ballerina, just as she was hanging up her shoes) introduced him to these people in the City.

The prospect of being employed by Norwegians amused him rather, so he went along.

Before he begins at the bank, however, he makes an important new acquaintance. The purchaser of 'Punishment' turned out to be a man called Jarvis Green, one of the new names in finance. He has spent his youth in Canada and has returned to old England with young money. He is scarcely older than Charlie but already has a large house, 'The Retreat', in Ewell unfortunately, and a reputation for agile enterprise. A poker game takes place at his house every Friday night. He is hospitable but withdrawn. He has a pale face, modern spectacles and receding hair. He looks as worried as an honest man. When Charlie approaches him, about buying 'Punishment', he seems already to know who he is, although he has not yet come into his title. Perhaps Jim Farber has said something. 'Who?' Green says.

The financier (as the newspapers call him) is disinclined to sell the picture, although he has had to go and check that he is indeed the owner. He invites Charlie to the house, however, and acts as though he owes him some debt of gratitude. Charlie asks his advice about joining the Norwegians. 'I think you should, Charlie,' Jarvis says.

Jarvis Green's house is built in glazed brick and has a green-tile roof. A lot of money has been spent on it; it resembles a road-house of the thirties. The bathrooms are identically appointed, though in different shades. The paintings all carry hooded lights. At Christmas, Jarvis Green selects one of them to reproduce and insists, in smallish type, that it comes 'From the collection of Mr and Mrs Jarvis Green'. Charlie is touched by the mild look of puzzlement behind Jarvis's week-end spectacles. Is his fear that the money will never run out and that it will always put upon him this tax of thinking what to do with it? Charlie's connoisseurship is precious to his host and, without profitable motive, they profit from each other's company. While the breakfast room is being finished at the flat (it takes time to match the gate-legged table exactly), Charlie even comes to stay and travels up to town in Jarvis's other Rolls. Alas, one can no longer park in the West End.

Jarvis is married to an actress whose early parts called on her to unbutton her shirt or to get it wet. Shona is dark, not to say dirty, and her career has lost its way, despite the fact that Jarvis once invested a Swiss sum in a vehicle intended to carry her to the stars. Jarvis accepted the loss with good humour but it was not the kind of joke he cared to hear twice. Shona now wears her hair low on her forehead and collects bottles. There is a child, who lacks friends.

Charlie is a success at the bank. He plays Royal Tennis with one of the partners. On the day after Charlie's father dies, the bank is due to give a three-wine lunch for Jarvis Green. Rumour promises that he and the bank are coming to an arrangement. Fred Kirby, the Norwegians' favourite mouthpiece among City Editors, is one of the guests.

Charlie wears a funereal tie, but he goes to the lunch. He has a few drinks first with Pip Lethbridge, in London Wall, and when he looks through the peep-hole of the partners' dining room, he sees that Jarvis is already there. He pushes open the door on its leathern hinges (a silent house tradition) and misses the low step into the room. He stamps out one loud syllable which raises a dozen faces in his direction. 'Good Lordship, it's Charlesworth,' Jarvis Green says.

Fred Kirby makes space for Charlie to sit beside him. Fred has long been Jarvis's loud supporter against the City establishment. Fred's paper is the people's friend and he has encouraged its C 3 readers to back Green's 'big deal for the small man'. Kirby has a good war record (though not in a good regiment) and shrapnel in the right leg. He likes rich company and rich food, but there is some steel in him, and always will be. He has promoted Jarvis not least because he is not a gentleman. It amuses him (and his Canadian proprietor) to see the City yield ground without breaking ranks.

'By the way, Charlie,' Jarvis says, 'I'm most awfully sorry about your father. Presumably all your friends are going to have to start calling you "My Lord" from now on.'

'Not all of them, sir,' Charlie says. 'Just you, Jarvis.'

'Well,' says the Chairman at last, 'I rather think it's time I proposed a small toast.'

Just how close is the relationship to be between the bank and the Jarvis Green Organization? Fred Kirby notices that the new Lord Marsden drinks without enthusiasm to the liaison. 'I thought you and Jarvis were rather good friends?'

'We are,' Charlie says, 'and here's to him and to my brave employers and their, I hope, long spoons.'

'Spoken like a true friend, old boy, spoken like a true friend.'

'He cheats at cards, you know,' Charlie says, 'not that I blame him.'

'I beg your pardon?'

'Jarvis.'

The Chairman is too far away, and too earnest with enthusiasm, to catch what Charlie is suggesting, but he suspects a curdling in the smooth afternoon and looks sourly at Charlie. Before the party breaks up in time for after hours trading, Fred Kirby is awarded a green folder of facts and figures. He is already fashioning his piece: 'Jarvis Green – that no-nonsense, new-school-tied young man who knows what's what and be damned to who's who – told me that his new fund will give everyone a chance to participate in the exciting industrial and technological prospects. Special situations are Jarvis's speciality. Few people will want to miss being aboard when his gravy train pulls out on Monday morning ...' Yet before Kirby limps back to his limousine (as City Editor he has city perks), he makes a date for lunch with Charlie Marsden.

They go to a chophouse, good grills, no women.

'Come on, old boy, what've you got on him?'

'Jarvis? Nothing.'

'You're looking for something to do, I gather.'

'Am I? I've got these acres, you know,' Charlie says.

'What happened at the bank exactly?'

'I left it,' Charlie says. 'Working for people's a pill.'

'You said he cheated at cards.'

'It's rather endearing, don't you think? It's a skill, not a necessity. He doesn't mind losing. He's a very generous chap. However, yes, he does. He wants to see what he can get away with, even though he hasn't got any use for what he gets.'

'So you think he's a wrong 'un, old boy, do you?'

'He's the sort of man your readers want him to be,' Charlie said. 'You should know. After all, you made him up.'

Fred Kirby looked at the old wine through new glasses. ''47's all finished, maestro?'

'You had the last bottle, Mr Kirby.'

'On to the '52s then. There isn't much more to make of him really now, is there? What goes up must come down, old boy. Rule of the road. What's your grudge?'

'I don't have a grudge. I rather like the bastard.'

'There must be some dirt,' Kirby says, 'because there always is, isn't there?'

'Well, man is a dirty beast,' Charlie says.

'So what do you feel about doing this little job for us?'

'I'm not gunning for him, you know, Jarvis.'

'We'll pay by the bushel,' Fred Kirby said. 'I wouldn't curse you with a contract or anything. A gentleman's agreement, what do you say?'

'Who's the other gentleman?' Charlie said, but he shook hands.

The success of 'The Gunroom' encouraged Theo Plant to open two more restaurants: 'The Golden Bowl' and 'The Silver Ditto'. The latter was in Battersea, but Theo's clientèle followed him across the river and 'The Silver Ditto' soon acquired that louche reputation respectable people required for parking in unlikely postal districts. Charlie took the Countess there occasionally. One evening he saw Katya Lowell dining in a red-benched booth with Jarvis Green.

The Countess proved a practised and practising lover. She had her own money and her own place. When tact was required, she knew not to touch. Without expecting constancy, she was constantly available. She educated Charlie to respond to her love, but she never imagined that he would love her. They pretended to a solemnity which was evidence of their facetiousness. They were refined in their foreplay, which always took place after the event. Charlie's appetite for that white, dark-whiskered body was maintained by the subtlety of her service. They were lovers without being in love and passionate without passion. For Charlie, during the months of their affair, there was the chance to elaborate, in private, a style nowhere current in public. They revived a small era, for two. They never discussed marriage; they were too polite.

Charlie had brimmed with desire when he was twenty, but had always spilled it before it could overflow. He had never supposed that sex and love went together. He had never exclusively desired boys; they had been available and he had availed himself. The Countess bore him the particular affection a woman feels for a man whom she has weaned away from his own sex, but the diligence she showed was actually less than Charlie required. The basic equipment was not so very different: meat and fish, 'The Silver Ditto' proved, can take much the same sauce. Even so, the spontaneity with which he fell in love with Katya Lowell that night in S.W.12 did rather surprise him. He had seen her before more than ten years earlier, and she had looked much the same. He had remarked her then and he had continued casually to remark her ever since, but as one might a monument which, to one's mild astonishment, moves from one part of town to another. The Countess observed his new interest. 'Who is she?' she says.

'Don't you know Katya Lowell?'

He discovered that Jarvis Green's Canadian activities had been probably no more unscrupulous than those of any other operator. However, he did gain some unexpectedly choice information about his acquisition of some grain elevators near Montreal. An angry man with a memory and bruises knew his cousin, a lady-in-waiting. Charlie began to compile a dossier on Jarvis, less from animosity than from that curious determination not to be beaten which had led him, in the Bond Street past, to continue bidding for a lot he did not greatly want. He went through old balance sheets and provincial newspapers quite as if he were composing a pointless and punctilious monograph. The secrecy of his labours lent them glamour. The Countess called him naughty for concealing things from her and fondled him for it. She suspected a new boy.

Falling in love with Katya Lowell is something he could have done without. He is eager to see her again not least because he hopes that it will prove to have been a mirage, this sudden embarrassing flower. He rationalizes his excitement by arguing to himself that it must be her connection with Jarvis Green which has excited him. Since Jarvis has no notion that anyone is hunting out his past, Charlie has no difficulty in resuming visits to 'The Retreat', where he enjoys the challenge of detecting the marked cards. A certain affection revives for Jarvis whose grand good fortune has not yet cured him of his hobby. One Friday night Charlie mentions Katya Lowell's name (Shona has retired to count her bottles). How well does Jarvis know her? There is something older about Jarvis now. His hair is thicker, a new shade of luxuriant auburn. He has adopted contact lenses, which darken his eyes. His face still has no lines (people would only read between them) but he has never before shaved so noticeable a beard.

'Katya Lowell?' Jarvis says. 'I like her work. You know that.'

'Do you know her personally at all? What's she like?'

'She's very beautiful. You must have seen her.'

'I'm told she never smiles,' Charlie says. 'Why is that?'

'She smiles,' Jarvis says.

Jarvis was always dangerous, but before he was dangerous with ignorance, which thought things simple. Now he appears more sinister, as if he knew what things were like, and still thought them simple. Is he involved in drugs? Does he buy or does he sell? Shona wears a tiny silver spoon beneath her dry shirt. Cards are now merely sociable. Jarvis goes out in the middle of the game to say 'Yes' to people who have called. He has a butler who bulges. Yet in public he continues to play the benefactor. His stock is high. He is building a home for handicapped children. His own child has lacked friends and is now at a school which has classes of one.

Charlie's dossier grows fat. Is his fascination with Jarvis maintained because Jarvis is a line, however charged, which may lead to Katya Lowell? He is not the only hope. Camilla keeps a busy table. She entertains a lot of foreigners and people; Marcus's firm has taken over a failing French sale room and gallery. *Ça remonte maintenant*. It is easy for the Hickses to invite Katya Lowell, among interesting others.

As soon as Charlie heard that she was coming, he announced to the Countess that their liaison was at an end.

'Oh you are in love,' she said.

'It wouldn't be honourable to continue, Anya. It would be pleasant; it wouldn't be honourable.'

'Is it a woman?'

'It is a woman.'

She kissed him for his fidelity. 'Is she yours?'

'Is she mine?'

'Is she yet yours?'

'I haven't actually spoken to her yet,' Charlie said.

'You *are* in love, my darling. You *are* in love.' The Countess looked out in reproach at the printennial park, as if it had been slyly installed behind her back. She broke open a diamond bracelet on her wrist and held it in her hand, a transplanted peasant weighing produce. 'So ... this is not a little premature? What will you do if – things do not happen?'

'I love her,' Charlie said.

'I understand. But this is nice in some ways. We can stay friends?'

'That's exactly it,' Charlie said. 'If we didn't do this now, we never could. I should have to be cruel.'

'And you are not cruel, dear Charles, are you?'

He kissed her hand. She had been his foreign cruise. He had learned much and he was happy to be home. His love was serious; he prepared for it as if for a vocation. He did not desire Katya Lowell; he wanted her. Conquest would not be enough. He intended marriage. He was prepared to be patient and courtly. He would conceal from her only what style deplored. Because he was in no hurry (though he thought of nothing else), he felt neither embarrassment nor timidity when he sat across from her at the Hickses' dinner. He rehearsed no jokes, deployed no winsome solemnities. He watched her talking prompter's French – a single word reviving her neighbour's garrulous *analyse* – with the complaisance of that married man who had slipped whisky, no water, when she went, challenging and submissive, to listen to the now transatlantic critic. Now that he was in love, he was able to look, almost dispassionately, at the object of his passion, quite as if she were already his long possession. The first time was an anniversary. The curvature of her nose, its minute and delicious deviation from the true in both the vertical and the horizontal axis lent unnerving asymmetry to those amontillado eyes; their perfection was subtly compromised and hence perfected. The lips were full, not loose. She never pouted; she was never prim. If she smiled, which Jarvis said she did, her smile had left no powdered trace. In the candlelight the butterfly shadows under her cheek-bones were velvet bruises. It was exquisite to love without speech or introduction. As a boy, he had never imagined love but now, recreating a spurious childhood of romantic reverie, he would improvise a long and longing love. She seemed to honour his invention by the paucity of her own speech. She says only enough to keep the chatter brilliant among her neighbours. Her first look at Charlie notices that he notices; the directness of her glance, intensely feminine, yet sexless in its intensity, stuns him. There is nothing he would not do; nothing he can. He is defenceless to the knife that lodges in him; he feels everything, he feels nothing. Each stage of his love seems so complete that nothing can be added to it, yet here he is more helpless, more exalted than ever. How will he get up from the table? He rises without difficulty. How will he come down? He comes down beside her on Camilla's fawn leather sofa.

'We have a mutual friend, it seems,' he says.

'You play cards,' she says.

'Yes,' he says, 'what do you do?'

'I paint,' she says.

'With Jarvis.'

'I see him,' she says. 'When I want to.'

'And you want to?'

'You know Jarvis,' she says.

'I know Jarvis,' Charlie says, refusing the brandy, but not the pause the butler brought, 'and I love you.'

'Really?'

'Surely you knew? You are the great and only love of my life.'

'Thank you,' she says.

'I expected you to know. From dinner.'

'I've seen you before,' she says.

'I should like to marry you. This isn't a casual thing. It isn't a modern thing. It's eternal. I love you and I always shall. I realize this may upset your immediate social arrangements and I don't expect an immediate response, but ideally I should like to marry you tomorrow. Or tonight. I should like to catch a steamer and marry you when we reach the open seas. I believe one can still do that.'

'I'm so sorry,' she says, as if he were mortally ill.

'No, no,' he says, 'no, no. Don't look away. This isn't something I shall brandish like a writ. My offer of marriage is now assumed between us, and for ever. I mean it, totally. My love is quite unconditional. I shan't restate it, except on invitation, but a love like mine won't be repeated. It's unique. You are the only woman I shall ever love. Thank you for not smiling.' He makes this speech with a sort of casual humour, as if offering a cigarette, or a city, to someone he suspects does not smoke, or travel. A proposal which might have capped a long courtship becomes its prelude. There is nothing concealed between them, no threat, no trap; he has disclosed his hand by offering it. When he looks at the flat, steel ring on her finger it is as if his glance can make it golden; if she says 'Yes,' it will.

She proves more accessible than Camilla forecast. Charlie ceases to confide in his sister as he and Katya Lowell begin to meet more frequently. Camilla might almost be a rival, lacking the Countess's cosmopolitan code. Charlie is polite; he is unusually polite – 'Look at Charlie's flowers!' – but he is preparing to remove himself from the world of the Hickses. He and Katya will probably live abroad, though he does not fail to notice her attachment to London; the ticking taxis she likes to have waiting at restaurant doors, the underground into which, with a girlish wave, she dives like a brave or drunken guest into an unheated pool. She carries an aura of luxury, but she luxuriates in the mundane. She will wear a model coat one day – and hand-made shoes – and the next she will be in a duffle and scuffed boots. She has a character independent of fashionable consistency. Charlie loves her for the care which she encourages him, without overt encouragement, to lavish on her. She bicycles over to take a hire car to new places he has scouted. They never go to any of Theo Plant's restaurants. Charlie makes an unspoken case against all that they have known before, though he never spoils things with sarcasm or jealousy. When she is not free, he shows no sign of disappointment. He is chaste, even when he is alone; he is waiting for her, even when they are together. Does she suspect that sometime after this meal or that excursion he will try the typical touch: the hand, the kiss, the breast? He remains passionately correct; cadged compensations mean nothing to him. 'You must have had a lot of women,' she says.

'I've had one,' he answers, truth clowning a tactful lie.

And what of Katya Lowell? It is of no moment to Charlie if she is a virgin or a whore. He loves her. The intensity of his feelings does not interrupt his investigations into Jarvis Green. Any man, he comes to realize, as the spoil heap grows, sufficiently researched will yield a criminal, a lunatic or a fool. The more he studies Jarvis the less specific he seems. The dossier fattens but the man grows thinner, until he might be anybody, this wartime refugee from Birmingham parents, the Canadian schoolboy, the teenage victim of a stadium proprietor with carnal designs. The more he discovers the less printable use it seems to Fred Kirby, for if every dull and terrible truth were to be told, everyone would be condemned, which is why such truths are never printed. There is something wonderful in the detail available, if one searches, in a life lacking in all charm or distinction. Jarvis Green is a cheap fiction, a *collage* of incidents from commonplace sources. The history of Jarvis Green is so in tune with the times that one cannot shout it above the hum of the chorusing crowd. Fred Kirby seems to be doling out money for copy bound to go on the spike. Then, one night, Charlie meets Katya Lowell and knows she has been hurt.

She pins his unboxed, leopard-spotted orchid on her lapel and its greenhouse bruises seem allusions to her own.

'How did it happen? It wasn't an accident.'

She smiles. She smiles! 'No,' she says, 'it wasn't. I would have said to anyone else that it was, but not to you, not any more, dear Charles. I want to marry you.'

He gives the waiter the impression that he is anxious to order. The climax of his hopes compels him to give no vulgar sign of it. He has always meant to marry her (his love spreads backward now to give purpose to the moment of his birth, since he was born for this) and now she has come to him. He will neither grab nor exult. He is a lord. Is it unfashionable? Then it pleases him to honour what others find outmoded. In a world where nothing noble is allowed, all nobility becomes the dandy's choice. His lordship takes her lean hand and kisses it. From his pocket he produces a jeweller's box, amateur magician with a single trick. 'I love you,' he says. 'Do I know your parents?'

'I have no parents,' she says. 'I have no one.'

'You have me.'

'This is very beautiful.'

'I had it made. I approve of patronage, don't you?'

'Decidedly,' she says, 'since I approve of you, dear Charles.'

'Shall I kill him for you?'

'I want to marry you,' she says. 'Forget the rest.'

'Both can be managed. I'm perfectly serious.'

'I know that, good Charlie; that's why I am. You mustn't kill anybody.'

'Whoever it is,' he says, 'it can be managed. I can always take my time.'

'Do you love me less because of it?' She holds his hand and forbids it to be a fist.

'Love you less? I told you: my love is infinite; it can never be less, or more. Did they die, your parents?'

'Yes, of course. They'd be alive otherwise, wouldn't they? Don't imagine me an angel, will you?'

'Have no fear. I don't *imagine* you at all. To me you are the only reality. I accept you totally, which is something quite different from imagination. Is it a man?'

'Naturally,' she says. 'But please ... I promise you, it's immaterial.'

'Venice, India, Granada, Borneo, where?'

'Venice,' she says, 'but not yet – when it's cold and out of season and we can hear the wind blowing old stories in off the lagoon.'

'And I can finish my Armenian dictionary,' Charlie says.

Jarvis Green keeps a flat, Charlie hears, in Pimlico. Mr Aplin, a private detective, watches it for Charlie, account to the City Editor. His next badly typed log reveals that a woman arrived recently (date appended) and left, after dark, in sunglasses. Charlie has been making some inquiries about steamers. He hopes to be married aboard, without fuss or guests, and to spend at least some months away from England. He speaks once of not returning at all, but Katya nods and kisses him at this and he knows that she does not wish it. The plans for their departure are confirmed. They book on a Greek ship whose Captain can perform the necessary rites. Katya and Charlie buy luggage, then she leaves him, in a cab, for the last time, perhaps. The report of the private detective discloses that a woman goes that night to Westmoreland Street and that she is wearing a model coat, scuffed boots. When Katya and Charlie meet again he looks at her, not with suspicion or fear or jealousy, but with attention. They are not yet lovers; he has never touched her body or even seen it. They do not swim or bathe together. She is always dressed.

He neither hates nor despises her. The information of Mr Aplin counts against Jarvis; it has nothing to do with her.

They sail on the *Elene* from Tilbury. The gods give them rain and a taxi and a Greek primed to carry the luggage up the ridged plank under a snappy awning. The dossier is ready for Fred Kirby. A more cunning man than Charlie might have made dispositions to secure a fortune when the first articles appear and the City bears start to bait their prey. Can anything save Jarvis once the lawyers sign the warrant: publish and he's damned? Fred's proprietor, however, does not want to give the green light too fast; he prefers to flash an unobtrusive amber to warn some at least of the paper's readers. To this end, sly emphasis is given in the gossip columns to Jarvis's private life, his absences on sunny islands when decisions are taken: up to his neck in the Caribbean, how cool can a a tycoon be? The chart of Jarvis Green Securities dips; a reverse head and shoulders makes its downward prognosis. Pip Lethbridge asks Charlie what he knows. Charlie says that he cannot say that he knows anything. 'In that case, one's safe obviously to stay in,' says Pip, and gets out.

Charlie cares only for the moment when he and Katya Lowell will be together in front of the Captain. Yet, like a dreamer who tells the truth even though he recognizes the court is made of playing cards, honour requires him to ask Kirby to withhold publication until his return from Venice. (It smacks of cowardice to cut a man down *in absentia*.)

Captain Panselinos affects surprise, first at the request and then at the money, but Katya becomes Lady Marsden in the Bay of Biscay. Steel turns to gold. Not until they return to their cabin does Charlie see his wife's nakedness, and the marks upon it. She studies his face for contempt or horror. She sees neither. Marriage does not alter the rhythm of his tact. It is no crude green signal for him. He lends it a meaning beyond possession or permission, beyond all present devaluations. What is laughable to others does not make him smile; because others laugh, he does not. 'I want to kill him,' he says. 'I'll tell them not to publish; I'll kill him instead.'

'Charles, please, do neither,' she says.

Though Katya has been to his flat several times, she has never remarked the coincidence between its décor and the paintings in her show at the Farber Gallery. She walks through her own creation without recognizing it; her art is beautiful but her beauty does not respond to it. All right, he will love her for her indifference to his compliment. There can be no question of their living in the flat (since it is a joke she does not choose to see), so he commissions the young estate agent (now on his own, Peter Bent, in Clarges

282

Street) to sell it for him during his absence. 'Are you not getting married, my lord, after all?'

'Of course,' Charlie said.

They go ashore at Venice under veils of rain, as if fugitives from some scandal so divine that they can be lent the weather to dress their incognito. The lagoon is thin of colour; Katya might have mixed its washiness from the cleaning spirit in a blue glass. Most of the tourist shops are closed. They seek deserted places, distant *fondamenta*. They find a boatman, mantled in a glistening cowl, whose French polished cabin can be theirs for the month. He is surly and Charlie disdains to tip him in advance to procure his geniality. Only on the last day, out in the staked lagoon, does Charlie give him what might have made him sing. He shows no gratitude. He is a man of character. They like him better for his unsold expression and that evening, lying in a broad and canopied bed, under plaster rosettes, they are willing to believe that here and there they will find more such alien beings to furnish and not intrude upon their seclusion. Charlie has what he wants; dream and reality march in step. But Venice is at once perfect and imperfect; Katya is loyal and loving, but she cannot lie and Charlie loves her too much to connive at pretty pretence. She reminds him of that letter from Albertine in which the girl agrees to accompany Proust's narrator to Venice, a letter which comes when she is already dead. 'I've always known,' she says. 'I always knew that I would meet someone that deserved my love and to whom I would want to give it and it would be too late.'

'It's not too late,' he says.

'Oh Charlie, my lord, my lord!'

'Nothing can prevent me giving you what you want. I love you too much.'

'That's it,' she says. They are on the Giudecca; the paling sea jostles over the settled granite of the jetty, transparent as lace on a Flemish wrist. A bridge takes a high step over the narrow canal and they stand up there, isolated captains on a stone ship, as the waves cuff and spread along the quay. She turns to him with tears running uneven along the uneven nose. He kisses salt. 'You love me,' she says, 'and that is why ... it's no good.' She shrugs and turns her face upwards so that rain dilutes the tears; particular and elemental blend. 'I must go back to England,' she says.

'We'll go anywhere you want to go,' he says. 'You doubt love's range; I don't.'

'Charlie,' she says, 'I love you. Don't weaken now. I love you. Nothing that happens in the world can ever affect that. People might say that I recognize in you only what reflects my own self. It's not true. I recognize your love, and that's not the same at all. Don't doubt my love, but I've been what I am for as long as I've been alive, just as you say you loved me before you even met me. I was what I am from before I knew it, let alone you. I never met anyone whose love I trusted and believed before. I saw it in you like a gift that no one could refuse, a kind of talent. I honour it, Charlie. Oh and by the way, I've always dreamed of titles, of election, of a special world. You and I and our boatman . . . !' She smiled lovely pain.

'Who began it? That man at the party, the one who was killed?'

'Harry? I can't make him the scapegoat. I wanted it, Charlie. I escaped and I couldn't endure it. My parents died and I escaped, how could I go unscathed? Unpunished?'

'You have me,' he said. 'I haven't escaped.'

'And then I began to sell,' she said.

The clouds shuffled the scenery above their heads, parting to show ragged blue wounds that closed again, stitched with the warm rain. A black-cloaked woman in another story went along a wall with a canvas-capped basket. 'Perhaps I killed him,' Charlie said, 'Groves. I'll certainly kill the others.'

'Which would only make me deserve it more,' she says. 'You're too intelligent not to know that. We can't run and we can't destroy what pursues us. Hurt him, you destroy us. Don't let them print what you've written.'

'It's almost out of my hands.'

'Burn it, Charlie. Unless you're willing to play his part.'

'The only thing in the world I can't do is not love you,' he says. 'Be cold.'

'Ah, there we are then, aren't we? I'd die with you, Charlie. We can take the ship back and at night there's always the rail and the sea . . .'

'Blasphemy. I married beauty and beauty must live,' Charlie says. 'And I want to live with it.'

She turns and kisses him, the rain gushing over their gargoyle faces. They hold the kiss as if some cruel director refused to cry 'cut'. They go back at last to the ferry stage bludgeoned with water that swells their coats. They are lumbered like the wood of a dishonest woodman who sells it wet, by weight. They steam in the warm lobby of the palazzo and accept amazed attention. ('What were you *doing*, Contessa?') At dinner they mourn, delicious together under the candelabra, and the waiters bless them with happiness. That night Charlie is pierced by her coarse cry and cries himself, knowing that she is artist enough even to manage a perfect fake. 'No,' he says. 'I'll have them burn the stuff. I haven't had the money and besides, the best parts are at my bank. Perhaps I always knew.'

'Oh Charles, you'll hate me in the end.'

'No,' he says. 'I shall never hate you and I can never take his place because of it. Perhaps it will pass one day and we shall be alone again.' As they spoke, they were placed by the cruel director in sight of the corner of the Doge's palace, where Adam and Eve are rubbed by the chemical wind.

They return to London. Charlie calls Jarvis Green and arranges, in return for the destruction of the dossier, that his wife will see her cruel lover whenever she wants to or whenever he summons her, which is the same thing. Charlie dines on those occasions with Marcus and Camilla and company. It is generally agreed that he and his wife are ideally happy. Jarvis Green's shares recover. He and the Norwegians are successfully married. This year his Christmas card reproduces 'Punishment', by Katya Lowell.

MORE ABOUT PENGUINS, PELICANS
AND PUFFINS

For further information about books available from Penguins please write to Dept EP, Penguin Books Ltd, Harmondsworth, Middlesex UB7 0DA.

In the U.S.A.: For a complete list of books available from Penguins in the United States write to Dept DG, Penguin Books, 299 Murray Hill Parkway, East Rutherford, New Jersey 07073.

In Canada: For a complete list of books available from Penguins in Canada write to Penguin Books Canada Ltd, 2801 John Street, Markham, Ontario L3R 1B4.

In Australia: For a complete list of books available from Penguins in Australia write to the Marketing Department, Penguin Books Australia Ltd, P.O. Box 257, Ringwood, Victoria 3134.

In New Zealand: For a complete list of books available from Penguins in New Zealand write to the Marketing Department, Penguin Books (N.Z.) Ltd, P.O. Box 4019, Auckland 10.

In India: For a complete list of books available from Penguins in India write to Penguin Overseas Ltd, 706 Eros Apartments, 56 Nehru Place, New Delhi 110019.